# Billion
## Dollar Girl

# Billion
# Dollar Girl

## megan shull

RAZORBILL

# RAZORBILL

An imprint of Penguin Random House LLC, New York

First published in the United States of America by Razorbill,
an imprint of Penguin Random House LLC, 2022

Visit us online at penguinrandomhouse.com.

Library of Congress Cataloging-in-Publication Data
Names: Shull, Megan, author.
Title: Billion dollar girl / Megan Shull.
Description: New York : Razorbill, [2022] | Audience: Ages 10–14 years |
Summary: After thirteen-year-old River Ryland is discovered
to live mostly alone and a visit from Social Services goes horribly wrong,
River runs away and a case of mistaken identity gives her
the chance to live a life she never imagined.
Identifiers: LCCN 2022019025 | ISBN 9780593524572 (hardcover) |
ISBN 9780593524596 (trade paperback) | ISBN 9780593524589 (ebook)
Subjects: CYAC: Runaways—Fiction. | Mistaken identity—Fiction. | LCGFT: Novels.
Classification: LCC PZ7.S559428 Bi 2022 | DDC [Fic]—dc23
LC record available at https://lccn.loc.gov/2022019025

Printed in the United States of America

1st Printing

LSCH

Design by Tony Sahara
Text set in Minion Pro
Cover art © 2022 by Dana Sanmar
Cover design by Kaitlin Yang

I have been in Sorrow's kitchen and licked out all the pots. Then I have stood on the peaky mountain wrapped in rainbows, with a harp and a sword in my hands.

—Zora Neale Hurston

You probably already heard, right? I'm sure you did. It's cool. Some people only want the short version. The after. The don't-tell-me-everything-only-what-I-want-to-know. But for me to tell this story, for you to get it, I have to start a while ago. Before, before. Before everything. And then you'll know. And anyway, it's my story. I get to tell it. It happened to me.

# 1

Look, I think we can agree: the chair right outside your principal's office is *not* where you want to be sitting the second-to-last day of seventh grade. No.

But here I am.

Waiting.

Worse? I was called here over the loudspeaker, as in: "River Ryland, please report to the main office. River Ryland."

Yeah. Thanks a lot.

Also, the secretary with the crazy frosted hair—you know, the lady who sits right at the door when you walk in the main office? She keeps looking at me.

I'm not nervous, okay?

I'm more, just, annoyed. I mean, I was in the middle of grabbing lunch with everyone, planning our end-of-the-year Six Flags Magic Mountain day (tomorrow), talking about shrieking on the Viper (the best ride ever), and now I'm sitting wedged next to the copy machine, head down, staring at my chipped turquoise toenail polish and the dirty gray carpet.

I look up when Ms. Martinez's door swings open and she pops her head out. "River?" she says, signaling for me to come in. If this was one of those Disney movies and *not* my very unexciting thirteen-year-old life, Ms. Martinez would have the starring role as Middle School Principal. She is wearing a green sweater with short sleeves and a skirt, and her long, dark hair is twisted up in a bun. She has brownish eyes and those tortoiseshell reading glasses people keep on the very tip of their nose.

Ms. Martinez's office is windowless and cramped and there's a slight smell of tuna fish sandwich. It's kind of stuffy. There's just something about this room that makes you want to hold your breath. I sit down in the chair farthest away from hers.

Ms. Martinez closes the door, which is *never* a good sign.

I take a long, hard look at her as she moves behind her big, cluttered desk and sits. She doesn't scare me. Whatever. I've handled *much* worse.

I don't settle back into the chair. Basically, I don't plan on staying in here long. I keep my spine stiff and the bones of my butt balancing on the edge of the seat. There is about one minute of intense silence. I quickly glance at her, then stare at the pile of cream-colored files and papers stacked on her desk.

I don't fidget.

I keep very still.

Honestly? Half of surviving stupid meetings like this is waiting it out.

Ms. Martinez reaches for a huge black binder, sets it flat in front of her, opens it, and shuffles through some papers—licking her finger before turning each page—finally stopping to examine whatever it is she was searching for.

She glances up, lifts an eyebrow, and says, "Do you have any idea why you're here?" She waits.

I shake my head *no*.

Ms. Martinez leans back in her swivel chair and takes her glasses off. "River," she says slowly. "You are a very smart young lady. Very determined. Your aptitude test scores are off the charts. Yet you just barely squeaked by this marking period, and your grades show it.

Can you please help me understand why you have missed twenty-two days of the school year with chronic, unexplained absences?" As she speaks, she does not take her eyes off mine. "Well?" she asks, waiting for me to answer.

I say nothing.

Ms. Martinez sighs. "River, every single student at this school matters to me. I don't stop thinking about your well-being simply because it's summer vacation. Do you understand that?"

"I guess—yeah," I say with a small laugh.

Ms. Martinez looks at me carefully. "Why are you laughing?"

I shrug a little.

"This *isn't* funny," she warns.

I cross my arms. I do not speak. If you are ever going to get out of a situation like this, you have to be ready to keep your mouth shut.

Ms. Martinez watches me.

I stare back.

"River, you need to be honest with me right now. This is serious," she says, sounding stern. "When you don't show up for school, that raises a lot of red flags." She pauses. "Legally, your mom is responsible for getting you here. My sense is—and I could be wrong—that there is something going on. Is everything okay at home?"

"Yeah, totally," I lie.

She puts her glasses back on, picks up a piece of paper, looks at it and then back at me. "I see you've moved quite a bit. Is that right?"

"Uh-huh."

"You are currently living with your mom on Pitts Hill?"

I nod back at her. I shift in my seat.

"And your father?"

*I don't have one* is never the answer I give. "Oh, um . . . yeah. He's like—he's living in California," I blurt out. "He's a lawyer. I'm staying with him this summer. He has a pool!" *A pool. Nice touch*, I think as I force the corners of my lips into the tiniest smile. I am an excellent liar. I've done it a thousand times. I really know my lines.

Only—

Ms. Martinez is looking across her desk at me like she doesn't believe a word I'm saying. Now it's suddenly very quiet. Besides a faint conversation on the other side of the door, the room is uncomfortably silent.

"River, I'm going to ask you this just once." Ms. Martinez pauses and locks eyes with mine. "There is an extremely troubling rumor going around that you are living without a reliable adult at home. Is this true?"

"What? No!" I say quickly, and I add a light laugh as if it's the craziest thing that I've ever heard and not totally the truth. "I live with my mom, and she just, like, whatever—she works a lot."

She nods. "Okay, so if I go to your house tonight at seven—because I'm going to do it—what am I going to see?"

"Nothing." I shrug, like it's no big deal. I'm really good at pretending things are normal when they're not.

Ms. Martinez raises her eyebrows. "Good! That's a great time for me to swing by then."

"Wait, no!" I suddenly sit up straight. "I mean, uh, you can't come by tonight because, um—my mom, she's working late," I say, lying again.

Ms. Martinez does not miss a beat. "Then I'll give her a call and she can make sure to join us."

I feel my heart begin to pound.

More silence.

"You look very tired," Ms. Martinez says, studying my face. "River, I'm going to ask you a question and I want the honest truth." She waits. "Is your mom taking care of you and—"

"Everything is *fine*, Ms. Martinez," I cut her off. I work to make my voice sound light and convincing and try very hard to look at her like everything *is fine*. Even though everything isn't. "Really," I add, with a big fake smile. "It's all good."

"Well, great!" Ms. Martinez says. "Then it should all go smoothly when I stop by. And listen, I'm going to tell you the truth and I know it's hard to hear it. If I see signs of neglect, I am mandated by law to report it. A social worker from Child and Family Services will be with me when I visit."

"Wait, what? No, no, no, really, Ms. Martinez, we're good. We're fine," I repeat. "Really. Look, it's just—I'm on top of it. I mean, my mom, she—she works late and, like, we don't have a lot of money and . . ." My voice trails off.

Ms. Martinez has gotten up and is standing in the now-open doorway to her office. "I'll see you at seven o'clock—and I *will* be there," she says firmly.

I stand.

I exhale loudly and I'm pretty sure I roll my eyes. I'm not trying to be rude and I'm sorry if it seems that way. I'm just, God. I'm so pissed! With everything going on right now, I have to deal with *this*? I mean, like—*Why is she doing this to me! I can take care of myself.*

I am halfway through the door when Ms. Martinez begins to turn away, but then she stops. "River," she calls out.

I freeze.

We look at each other.

Ms. Martinez's eyes brighten. "I want to see you happy and safe," she tells me.

My throat feels like closing, but I don't let myself show it. Instead I smile back and say, "I'm fine, Ms. Martinez. Really."

"Well, you deserve to be cared for, River, and that's part of my job to make sure you are." She pauses. "It may not feel like it right now, but"—her face softens as she looks right into my eyes—"you can trust me. You don't have to handle this alone." Her eyes suddenly go wide, like she has an idea. "You know what?" she tells me. "Hold on one sec."

I wait by the door while Ms. Martinez hurries back to her desk and returns a second later, handing me a small business card with a phone number written in blue ink below her name.

"That's my cell. It goes directly to me."

"Thanks," I say. "I'm fine, though," I lie, and shove the card into my pocket.

"River, it's okay to ask for help," she says.

I say nothing. I don't even blink.

"If you're in trouble—"

"I'm not. I'm fine," I repeat, and my throat tightens.

"Okay," Ms. Martinez says. "Well, listen, if you ever are *not* fine, please call me, okay?" She pauses and gives me the slightest smile. "I promise. No matter how bad it is, we can figure things out together."

# 2

The second I step out of the main office, I walk as quickly as possible to the girls' bathroom at the end of the hall, bend over the sink, and splash cold water on my face. Only, I can't wash away anything I feel right now, and when I examine my face in the bathroom mirror, I'm still thinking what I was thinking five minutes ago, which is, *Well, my life is basically over.*

I lean in, close my eyelids, then open them.

Still there. Still me.

I have dark circles under my eyes. I bend over the sink again and cup my hands. This time I use soap and try to scrub the tiredness off.

In case you're wondering?

This really doesn't help.

And my hair. Oh man. I haven't had a shower in five days. It's greasy and tangled, and there's a big kink in it from where the rubber band has been. I use my fingers to comb it out, but I can't work them through past my ear because my long, dirty-blond hair is so knotty and gross. There's no taming it. I stare at myself—my pale skin, my thick, bushy eyebrows—take a deep breath, push the wispy pieces of sweaty hair out of my eyes, and force a faint smile. You know that saying, *Fake it till you make it*? That's me, right now.

I hesitate before I walk back through the heavy yellow doors to lunch. I glance down at my jeans and smooth out Emi's faded green Clarksville soccer hoodie she "loaned" me last year.

I stand up straighter. I take a breath.

Then—

I lean in and push.

I'm sure you have seen your share of seventh-grade girls sitting together in a noisy, really loud middle school cafeteria, right? I hang out with this group of like, six girls. All my friends are obsessed with fashion. Our table looks like a *Teen Vogue* cover shoot for the special summer edition: *Four Fashion Essentials You Can't Live Without!*

- ✓ ripped jean shorts
- ✓ cropped white T-shirt
- ✓ white Birkenstock sandals
- ✓ gold necklace with a heart pendant

Me? Spoiler alert: these are all must-have items that I *want* but do not have. There's definitely jealousy, I'm not gonna lie. It's just a feeling of *wishing* that's hard to describe . . . But yeah, it's not possible, so I have to get by with what I can. None of my friends even know, but I am usually head-to-toe dressed in thrift-store finds. My style is more *make it work, fit in, do not stand out.* You'd be surprised what people give away. It totally looks like I bought everything, just because I guess I kind of know how to put it together. I also know how to flash a big, fake, *everything is totally great!* smile, which is exactly what I do when my whole group of friends looks up at me walking back into the cafeteria toward them.

"Oh my gosh, you *never* get in trouble. What happened?" is the first thing Bella says when I slip back into my seat at our round table.

"What did you do?" asks Harper, sounding almost excited.

"Oh my God!" Addison chimes in. "Ms. Martinez is so scary!"

Izzy nods, eyes widening. "I know, right?"

My best friend, Emi, pulls her chair in closer and hands me her half-eaten bag of chips. "What was that about? Are you okay?"

For a second, all eyes are on me, and I immediately feel my body tense. There's a whole side of my life that people don't know, but it's getting harder to hide. There's the me everybody sees at school, and then there's the real me. *No. I'm not okay*, I think. But that's not what I say.

No. What I do is laugh. And what I say is, "Oh"—and I flash a smile—"it was no big deal."

"No big deal?" asks Emi.

"Yeah, no big deal," I say, and shrug it off with my most believable grin and dig into the bag of chips. "Who's down for the Viper tomorrow?" I ask, quickly changing the subject.

"The most epic ride ever!" says Addi.

"That ride looks *insane*," says Harper.

"Oh my gosh, I cannot *wait*!" Izzy's whole face lights up. "We are going to have *so* much fun! And I want to do that swing ride that we can all fit on! And when we get really hot, we can do the water slide. It goes, like, straight up, then drops literally *straight* down! It's *so* scary!"

Harper leans in. "Don't freak out, but I'm pretty sure I heard that Kyler Sutton and most of the lacrosse boys are going too."

"*Ooooh*, Riverrrrrr," Addison sings. "Kyler Sutton!"

Everyone turns to me and immediately breaks into hilarious laughter. "What?" I say, quickly feeling my face flush. For just this once, I play along. Honestly, I've never talked to Kyler Sutton or really any other eighth-grade boy. I've never even dated in my whole life! I hear things that boys say about me, and I'm like, *That's not true.*

The truth is, I am awkward and shy. I don't really know what to say around people, because I feel different. I *am* different.

"Kyler Sutton is totally in love with you, River!" Izzy blurts out. "He's like, so completely adorable the way he looks at you in the hall."

"I know, right!" Emi elbows me and giggles. "You two would be the *cutest!*"

Bella covers her face with her hands. "God!" She peeks through her fingers at us. "He's *so* hot!"

"Total relationship goals!" declares Addison. She turns to me. "*Everyone* has a crush on you, River. You are just an amazing-looking human, and it's literally not fair!"

I shake my head and feel my cheeks heat up.

A second later, just as Izzy is saying, "You guys, trust me, River and Kyler are going to be officially a *thing!*" the bell rings, and all at once, everyone from our table stands and scatters to fifth period.

# 3

I have social studies and Emi has English, and the rooms are right next to each other, so we walk down the yellow hallway and go to the left up the stairway and then we take another left down the hall to our classes.

Emi is in the midst of describing to me her worst possible nightmare. "Oh my gosh, my mom is so annoying!" she tells me. "She took my phone away last night. Can you believe that! God. Seriously. Ugh!"

I look at her freckles and the little neon-yellow rubber bands on her braces and try to smile. I do my best not to be a jerk about it, but—it's just kind of like . . . how do I explain it? It just seems silly. A phone?! I *wish* that was all I was worried about. Having a phone or having those things that are so normal to Emi are not even a possibility in my life. I don't waste my time thinking about things that aren't gonna happen.

I change the subject. "I love your top! Where did you get it?" I say, flashing a smile and trying not to sound envious.

"Oh, this, yeah, I saw it at the mall and I was like, 'I *have* to get that!'" Emi giggles a little. "My mom gave me her credit card," she says with a shrug. "Oh my gosh, also, I got the cutest blue romper, and this awesome crop top. It's like, white and it's flowy and amazing!" As she's talking, she keeps reaching up and running her fingers through her hair, which is long, golden blond, and straight, straight, straight. Emi stops just outside both our classrooms. I notice her perfectly done fingernails. They're bright, shimmery bubblegum pink with glitter. Her mom takes her for a mani-pedi every Monday night.

I turn toward her. "I'll see you after school, right?"

"Oh, um . . ." There's a pause. Emi's face looks suddenly worried.

I wait. "I mean—we're going to your house, right?"

"Um, yeah. I can't." She blurts this out as she spins away from me into her class.

My mouth opens. "I thought we—" I start, but then I stop. Emi's already gone and the door to her classroom shuts loudly, leaving me standing alone with this blank look on my face.

"River," I hear, and turn toward my classroom.

My social studies teacher, Ms. Howard, is standing in the doorway. She has a stack of papers tucked under her arm. She looks irritated. "What are you doing?" she asks.

For a split second I don't move, and me and Ms. Howard just stand in the hallway and silently exchange looks. Then the bell rings.

Her eyebrows go up. "Let's go!"

And I follow Ms. Howard through the door into class. I have that pit-in-your-stomach kind of feeling. *Everything is going downhill, fast.*

**4**

Outside, by the buses, I look all around before I spot Emi waiting for me like she usually does by the side parking lot carpool line, where her mom picks her up.

"Hey," I say. I look at her and smile.

"Hey," she says. She tosses her glossy, long blond hair behind her shoulder and gives me this nervous look. She's acting weird.

We are in the middle of the sidewalk on the second-to-last day before summer vacation. It's crazy-hot and the sun is bright. Almost every kid in the school is out here waiting for buses and rides.

I hoist my backpack and throw it over my right shoulder. I look at Emi and ask, "Can your mom give me a ride today?"

"Oh—um . . ." Emi glances away, then turns back to me, and the look on her face right now makes my throat tighten.

"What?" I say quickly.

I'm staring at Emi.

She shifts her eyes. She can't really look at me. "I'm so sorry," she finally says. "It's just, um . . . My mom. She like . . . she says you can't come in the car with us."

"Oh, it's okay," I say, and shrug it off. "I can take the bus."

Emi shakes her head and glances at me. "No, I mean *tomorrow*."

I look at her, confused. "Tomorrow?"

"Magic Mountain," she says.

"Wait, what? I thought we were going together. We've been talking about it for like, since—"

"I know," she says. "It's my mom, she . . . she changed her mind and—" Emi suddenly stops, and almost on cue, her mom pulls up in their brand-new shiny-white Range Rover.

I glance over Emi's shoulder at her mom, who is now smiling at us through the open passenger-side window. Her bright yellow-blond hair is the exact same color as Emi's, and she's wearing big, oversized dark sunglasses. She raises her hand and waves to me.

I wave back, then look again at Emi. "Wait, what do you mean she changed her mind?"

Emi glances toward the parking area, then back to me, takes a deep breath, and says, "It's kind of just—um—" She stops and smiles a nervous smile.

"Just say it."

"Um. My mom . . . she—" Emi's smile goes away. "My mom doesn't really want me hanging out with you anymore because she thinks you're a bad influence."

I'm like, "What?" *Seriously? Emi gets into way more trouble than I do.* "What do you mean? What did I do?" I look right at Emi. "You can tell me," I say.

Emi takes another big breath. "It's not, like, *you*. It's—" She stops again.

I go, "What? What is it?"

And Emi says, "It's your *mom*."

My heart drops.

Emi looks everywhere but me as she explains, "My mom, she doesn't want me to hang out with you anymore. She says your neighborhood isn't, like, that safe. We can't even go outside, and there's no adults in your house and there's never any food, there's never *anything* to eat and—"

I cut her off. "But why can't I go with you guys tomorrow?"

Emi shrugs a little. "Our car is full," she says, shifting her eyes again. "There's no more seats."

I try to smile. "But I can squish in," I say, sounding pathetic.

"It's not just that," Emi adds quickly. "My mom doesn't want us to get stuck paying for everything like—"

I go, "Wait. What?"

Now she looks right at me. "I mean, we *always* end up paying for you, River. You *always* need rides. You *never* have any money."

I am trying my hardest to make it look like I'm not about to cry. I'm so angry inside. I bite down on my lip.

Emi runs her fingers through her hair again and laughs a nervous laugh. "I'm sorry," she says. She tries to smile.

Right at this moment Emi's mom hollers out the window, "Emi!"

Emi nods toward her mom's car and very softly says, "I gotta go."

"Emi, wait—"

Emi takes a step back. She's still facing me and she says, "You should totally do Camp Pinecliffe! We're all going: me, Bella, Izzy, Addi, Harper. We can hang out there! It's *so* fun! It's right on the lake and we can go tubing and swimming and there's, like, this ginormous slide right into the water!" Her face lights up. "No, really. Think about it!"

I shake my head. "Emi. My mom can't pay for camp."

"Oh," she says. We exchange painful glances. Then her eyes suddenly flash again and she goes, "Maybe you could, like, get a scholarship or something!" and she takes another step back.

I look at her, like, *Are you serious?*

"I mean, you never know!" she says, sounding all bright and

cheerful, like a scholarship is just totally going to happen when we
both know that it is totally *not*.

"Oh, uh . . . there's one more thing," Emi says, cringing.

I go, "What?"

She pushes her hair behind her ears and looks right at me. "My
mom wants me to get my hoodie back."

I say, "Like, now?"

Her face turns serious. "Sorry," she says.

So. Right there with a zillion kids bumping by us and summer
whirling around, I whip the hoodie over my head and hand it to her.

Then we stand there—me in the T-shirt that I had on underneath
and my jeans with holes in the knees, and Emi, clutching the hoodie
that I was just wearing to her chest—and we just, like, look at each
other for a few more terribly long seconds.

I tell myself, *Don't say anything*, but . . . "Emi, my mom is *not*
a bad person," I blurt out. "We just—we just don't have any money
and—" I stop.

Emi takes another step away from me. As she does, she glances
behind her at her mom and their big, white, fancy car, then looks
back at me. "Sorry," she mouths quietly, and tries to smile.

I'm staring at her.

I don't cry.

I don't even show it.

"Totally, I get it. Whatever," I say, and shrug. I stay planted right
there on the sidewalk and watch Emi turn and run to her mom's
stupid white bazillion-dollar Range Rover, open the door, hoist herself up, and slide into the leather seat, safe inside. I don't move. I

stand watching as the white Range Rover pulls away, then turns left out of the parking lot, and I keep watching until I can't see it anymore. And I'm literally standing there thinking, *Could my day possibly get any worse?*

**5**

I miss my bus.

And I don't run after it, waving my hands and screaming, "Stop!" I turn from watching Emi's car drive away, only to see the whole line of buses moving forward. I'm like, *Seriously?* I don't even move. I stare at the line of buses—including the one I'm supposed to ride—passing me by, in my jeans and my sweaty T-shirt and my falling-apart back-pack weighing down my shoulder. Kids are wildly waving their hands at me out the open windows. "River!" they shriek and shout at me, with big it's-almost-the-last-day-of-school grins. "River!!!!" I barely smile back. I don't even wave. I wasn't expecting that at all—Emi's mom. That's messed up. What did I do to her? She's such a snob. Her stupid fancy car and her stupid sunglasses . . . I mean, *whatever*. She thinks she's so much better than us. Everything would be better if I just had money. I was *so* excited to go to Magic Mountain, and now that's not even happening.

Screw that.

I don't need her.

I don't need any of them. I'm honestly so mad right now I feel like punching someone—

Instead, I take a step and just start walking.

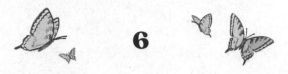

# 6

If I miss the bus to or from school, I have to walk.

Four miles. I'm used to it. I pretty much walk everywhere I need to go. I wake myself up and get myself ready for school. Sign my own permission slips. Get my own food. Sunny doesn't have a car, and I don't think she'd be down for dropping me off or picking me up even if she did. It's like, I'm supposed to be the kid and she's supposed to be the mom, but it's more the other way around. I'm seriously more responsible than she is. The only person I can rely on is myself.

The first half of my walk is closer to the school, past blocks and blocks of houses that are just so cute and friendly, each one painted a really fun bright color—like blues and greens and even yellow. Most have big front porches and yards with flowers. My favorite house even has a little birdbath and a swing hanging from a tree. Every time I walk by, I picture what it would be like to live in a house like that—with one of those very normal families where the mom and dad are home for dinner. Emi lives in Summit Hills, *the* most expensive neighborhood in Clarksville. It's pretty much all humongous stone mansions. Emi has a hot tub, a trampoline, a puppy, and her own room with a big double bed. She has a mom and a dad who both help her and have important jobs. Emi's mom's a real estate agent and her dad's a lawyer. They have a nanny, who sets out a tray of fancy snacks! Dinners are made every night, and as a family they like, sit around and talk about how her gymnastics practice went, and school and what homework is due. I remember the first time I went there after school, it was like a freakin' TV show! I didn't think this really happened in real life. It just blew my mind.

Everyone's like, "Oh, you have a young, cool mom. You're so lucky." But it's not like that. Sunny works as a waitress at a bar until three a.m. Sometimes she works the overnight shift. She's not home very much. It's not a big deal. *Whatever.* I'm used to it. It's just how she is. She just does what she does. On the weekends she goes out with her friends and comes home at four in the morning and sleeps all day—she has no idea what classes I'm even in. And since you're probably really wondering but too afraid to ask, let me just tell you now, okay? My dad was never in the picture. I don't even know his name. Sunny has never even told me anything about her own family. I've never even met them.

It's just me and Sunny.

She's it.

After about an hour of walking, all those cute houses with the porches and the grassy green lawns with flowers disappear. And I begin walking on a busier road: bus exhaust, trucks, potholes. In case you're planning on dropping by (and I *don't* recommend it), this is how you know you're getting closer to where I live: after Dunkin' Donuts, and the Chinese Buffet and the gas station on the corner with the metal bars over its windows, the sidewalk changes, and you begin walking over cracked, crumbling cement and past boarded-up brick buildings, and rows of abandoned houses with broken windows that just sit there because nobody lives in them anymore and nobody cares. Pitts Hill is pretty much past all that. Oh, you'll smell it, and if you don't (but you will), just look for the big hazy clouds of exhaust from the bus garage. If you're driving, you should probably hit the locks. People might come up and talk to you. I'm just giving you the heads-up: *Don't.* After the bus garage, take a right at the chain-link fence with the BEWARE OF DOGS sign tied to it, and head up the dirt street. Do you see it? Or can you at least picture where I live? There's not a WELCOME TO PITTS HILL TRAILER PARK sign or even a light. It's not one of those places with double-wide mobile homes and daffodils and HAPPY EASTER flags. There aren't any kids playing, because there are no other kids. It's just a bunch of beat-up-looking rusted trailers with lime-green siding sitting on a gravel lot. My neighborhood isn't that safe. And it's scary. And by scary, I mean you might get this feeling in your gut like, *Whoa. This is sketchy.* People hang out outside their trailers drinking and smoking cigarettes, randomly break into fights and yell at all hours of the night, have loud parties all the time, keep their huge dogs chained up outside all day, blare their television 24/7, and almost always give me suspicious sideways looks and have something to say when I walk by. So when I do walk by, I keep my head forward. I don't look around. I *always* have my guard up. I don't even open my mouth. There's a disgusting sewer smell leaking from the trailer three away from ours, and so about twenty feet before that, right where the dirt road turns to gravel, I start holding my breath until finally—*I made it!* I walk up the slumping, rotted-wood front steps.

# 7

When I see it, when my eyes actually zero in on the letters and my lips move silently to the words, "You've got to be *@&#%! kidding me," is what actually falls out of my mouth. The sign is bright orange and taped on with a wide strip of silver duct tape right on the door, and I stand there on the steps with my jaw dropped open and read it twice:

## NOTICE
## OF EVICTION

<u>LOCKOUT</u>

COURT CASE NO. **7.3109**

FAILURE TO PAY RENT

## CLARKSVILLE
## SHERIFF'S OFFICE

I reach out and rip the stupid sign off the door, tear it up, shove the pieces into my backpack, and fish around for my key. Only when I go to try the key in the door—

"No. No, no, *nooooooo*," I plead. "This cannot be happening to me right now." *They changed the lock.* I'm locked out and Ms. Martinez is coming at seven! I need to figure out a way to get inside. I need to break into my own house, and I don't waste time.

In the back, behind the pile of trash that stinks because it hasn't been hauled away, I find what I need: a window I can open. It's the bathroom. The window is small and high, taller than I am. Do I even think twice? No. Screw that. It's like, *when I set my mind to something, get out of my way.* A stupid lock on the door is not gonna stop me.

I drop my bag on the ground, step through the overgrown knee-high weeds, and jump, grabbing onto the windowsill with one hand. With my other arm, I reach up until with the very tips of my fingers I push the window open wider. Once I get it open enough, I grab my bag, stand on my tippy-toes, and toss my backpack through. I hear it crash down on the other side. Then I jump up again, grabbing onto the windowsill with both my hands and pulling, then pushing myself up and over and in—my head and chest go through the open window first. "Jeez," I say under my breath as I worm and wiggle in with the rest of my body, lowering myself, headfirst, arms out like I'm doing a handstand, right into the bathtub. I'm a lot stronger than I look.

I sit up in the tub and I almost laugh a little. I mean, I'm in the bathtub and it's really the first time I've even sat in it for a month. We haven't had electricity or running water since Sunny didn't pay the bills and they got turned off. And it's gross in here. I look up and scrunch up my face. The ceiling above me is half caving in and almost completely covered with black mold from a leak in the roof.

Also—

I'm bleeding.

"Crap," I say out loud. I scraped up my arm pretty good. I get out of the tub and stand in front of the sink that doesn't work and take the bottom of my T-shirt and wipe off the blood as best I can. We're not a first-aid-kit kind of family. I have stuff to do.

Did I mention our whole house smells like a giant damp ashtray of stale cigarettes? It hits me as soon as I step into the dark wood-paneled hallway, and I automatically cringe and try not to breathe.

I pull my T-shirt up over my mouth and nose. Sunny's a smoker. Smoking is disgusting. She's promised me she's going to quit, but yeah—she's promised me a lot of things. Sunny is not someone who cares about cleaning. There are piles of her dirty laundry everywhere, dishes stacked up in the sink, ashtrays filled, empty bottles lying around, week-old plates and bowls with food stuck on. Like I said, Sunny's not big on cleaning up. It's embarrassing to tell you this. But there's no time to sit around feeling sorry for myself. I have no idea what time it is. I have no idea if Sunny is even going to get here before Ms. Martinez does. I have no family around. There's nobody who's going to step up to help. And even if there was, I mean, *whatever*. I'm too ashamed to say anything to anyone. I'll fix this like I always do: by myself.

A minute later I am throwing everything—plates, glasses, cups, Sunny's clothes that are lying around, dirty towels, *everything*—into a garbage bag and stashing it all in the closet. I try and tidy up as best I can. I try and make it look like it isn't a total and complete wreck.

When I'm done, I stand in the middle of the trailer and look around. It's still a dump, cluttered with Sunny's stuff, but I did a pretty decent job. I walk over to the fridge, open it, stare in, and laugh a little. It's empty, and the tiny light that goes on when you open it is out. No power. I don't know what I was thinking even opening it. I mean, it's not like there's suddenly going to be food in there. I go to the one drawer where I hide snacks for when I'm really, really starving. Everything in the drawer is something Emi smuggled for me from her house. She's the only one of my friends who has been here before. I open it and look down—

I stare into the empty drawer and shake my head. "Thanks,

Sunny," I mutter. My Reese's Pieces are gone. So are my bag of pretzels and Snickers bar. All that's left is one package of ramen noodle soup.

Except, yeah—

No water.

Would you be grossed out if I tell you I rip open the package of dry ramen noodles? I do. You'd be surprised at what I can trick myself into eating when I'm really, really hungry.

I sit on the floor, crunching on dry noodles in the dark, and just stare off into space in a daze. I try and not be here, even though I am. I am here, even if I don't want to be, and so I try and picture Sunny and where she might be . . . Probably work, but potentially *not*. Sunny loves to be spontaneous. She doesn't like people telling her what to do. I wonder if Ms. Martinez even reached her on the phone. Sunny has a phone. I do not. I breathe out loudly. God. *Sunny. Come on.* I try talking to her, hoping that somehow, she'll have telepathy and hear me . . . I'm really not kidding. I pull my knees up against my chest and rest my forehead on top of them—

"Sunny, *where are you?*" I whisper into the floor. "Sunny! *Please* come home."

**8**

Sunny's real name is Laurel Ryland, but *no one* calls her that. And unless you'd like to get a seriously fierce stare-down, I recommend not calling her Laurel either. Ever since forever people have called her Sunny. It fits her. She just has this energy about her. When she's feeling good, she's almost magnetic. People are just, like, drawn to her. There's something about her that's hard to put into words. She's kind of like a hurricane. When she walks into a room, you know it. Heads turn. She is impossible to miss. People are always commenting on her looks. It's almost always the first thing everyone says when they meet her.

They stare.

Usually their mouth kind of drops open, then they turn to me and say, "Oh my gosh, your mom is *so* pretty!"

Sunny doesn't look like any of my friends' moms: her tattoos on her arms, her hair (dyed goldish blond, thick, and really long), which almost always has this slept-in wavy rock-star look. But what makes her Sunny . . . it's more something that's impossible to describe—it's this toughness that she has inside. The way she stares directly at you and never looks away first—it's like this crazy confidence. Nobody gets in her way. Nobody tells her what to do. Ever. Sunny does what she wants. When she wants. Always.

And she goes out a lot.

She comes home at three o'clock in the morning, and if she's made a lot of money, sometimes she wakes me up and we go to Denny's. I tell her, *No, I have school, I have to sleep,* but . . . that's just Sunny. She had me when she was really young. She never finished high school. She's really not a grown-up.

My life has pretty much been chaos from day one.

The thing about Sunny is, you never know how she's gonna be. She has good days, where she's home and everything seems great, and days where she stays in bed for, like, a week, barely saying a word. I'll go to school and come home and she'll still be in bed. Other times she'll just like, work really late and not come home until a few days later. The worst part is there's no way to predict how she'll be or when I'll see her. Just when I think she's never coming home, she shows up. She isn't the type of person to apologize for anything. That's just a fact.

But there are upsides too.

Like, Sunny lets me do *anything*. Anything I want! I don't really have any rules. I can see any movie I want to see. I can stay up as late as I want, I can sleep in as late as I want, skip school and do what I want all day long. And if Sunny doesn't feel like getting up, she sleeps in too. Like I said, sometimes she'll stay for days locked in her room. She'll live in her bed. I usually put Pop-Tarts on a paper towel and slide it under her door. Or I'll fix her something. I'll make sure she eats. I take care of her. I clean the house. I remind her to pay the bills. I listen to her problems. Nobody else knows that side of her. That's sort of how it's always been.

Sunny doesn't make the best choices when it comes to men. She dates a lot. In fifth grade, when I would walk up to the trailer after school, I started to recognize the different cars that Sunny's boyfriends drove. Chad (pickup truck), Omar (red Jeep), Travis (a motorcycle, and he dropped me off at school a few times; that was actually pretty cool). Sometimes I'm like, *oh God, Chad's here*, he's annoying and he drinks a lot. Sunny gets *so* fake when any of them are around, and it drives me *nuts*, and I'll walk in and she'll be like, "Oh, hey, honey, did you have a good day?" I'll just be like, *Honey? Really?* I'll just, like, shake my head and leave my own stupid house. There is this one guy, Brett. Whenever he comes over, he and Sunny will just disappear for a long amount of time. She won't even tell me where she's going. Now maybe you get it—what I mean when I say: I consider myself the parent, and Sunny's the kid.

I am Sunny's best friend.

She tells me *everything*.

She depends on me.

And I need to be ready if she needs me. Like, if she doesn't want to be alone, she talks me into staying home from school, and I'll do nothing but hang out with her. Sometimes, if she's made a lot the night before in tips, we'll go to Walmart and buy, like, ice cream for dinner and lie around all day and binge-watch an entire season of *Planet Earth*. Sunny does *not* like to share me. She doesn't really like me hanging out with my friends. She wants me to hang out with *her*. Most of the time I end up missing out. I see my friends at school, but . . . I miss out a lot on stuff like birthday sleepovers, being on a team, just being a normal kid. I just feel really, really guilty leaving Sunny when she needs me. I think about this, like, every day, pretty much. I worry about her. I keep telling myself that this is just the way things are right now, that maybe something good will happen soon . . . What else am I going to do? I've had to grow up kinda fast.

It has to be getting close to seven.

I scooch over so my back is directly against the front door, and

I sit there and hug my knees and stare out into the darkening room. I hear the voice in my head telling me what I already know but don't want to say, *Sunny is still not here.* I just keep staring into space. I feel the anger inside me moving through my body. I hug my knees tighter. I try to swallow. I try to just shut down. I try not to feel. If I let myself feel how I really feel . . .

It's not going to be good.

I am so angry right now. I don't know what I was thinking. She never chooses me, and she's not going to change.

*Sunny's not coming.*

*I can't believe I ever thought she would.*

# 9

**W**hen I hear them, I am still sitting on the floor, my back up against the front door, hugging my knees. Hiding. I hear their voices get closer and closer, then feel the floor underneath me shake as they climb the busted-up steps to the trailer. I am honestly more scared than I have ever been.

I feel myself tighten.

There's a loud thump on the door. Then, "Helloooo?" It's Ms. Martinez. "River?" she calls. "Laurel?"

She's not alone. "Try again," I hear another lady's voice.

My heart is beating so fast right now.

I don't make a sound. I barely breathe. I just bite my lip and sit here, completely still. If I stand up and open the door for them, they're just going to see the truth . . . *that Sunny isn't here. The way we live.*

The other lady coughs loudly. "By the look of this place," she says, "I think we should have gotten involved a long time ago."

"Absolutely," Ms. Martinez agrees. "I met with River. What a great kid, tough as nails. She's a real fighter . . . strong. Brave. Right now, it's her against the world, you know? Mom's a train wreck. This young lady is basically raising herself. You can tell she just has so much potential . . . very smart, self-motivated . . . head and shoulders above her peers in terms of maturity."

The other lady sighs. "Let's try one more time."

They knock louder. I feel the vibration of the door on my back. "Hello? River? It's Ms. Martinez," she calls out. "Anyone home?"

*Knock, knock, knock.*

More silence.

"What do you want to do?" asks the lady.

"Make the call," says Ms. Martinez.

"I think you're right," the lady agrees.

I hear silence for a long minute, then—

"Hi, this is Katie Federman, with social services. I'm with Principal Martinez at Pitts Hill. Yes. The trailer park on—yes, I can hold." There's a pause. "Okay, yeah, great. We're at—"

"Unit six, Pitts Hill," Ms. Martinez offers.

"Unit six, Pitts Hill," the lady repeats into the phone. "Yes, that's correct, it's the trailer park," the lady goes on. "We are here to support a young lady by the name of River Ryland. Yes. River Ryland, Ryland, R-Y-L-A-N-D. Yes, that's correct. Ms. Martinez met with the young lady today to inform her that she and I would be stopping by and we needed to see her and her mother. Ms. Martinez reached out to the mom, Laurel Ryland, via several phone messages. Now that neither the mother nor River are here, we need to involve you. It's becoming a real safety issue. Ms. Martinez is very concerned. Frankly, so am I. Yes. Thank you. Great. We'll see you in a few then."

There's a second where I can tell she hung up from the call. I hear the lady's voice again and it sounds different. "Okay, great," she says to Ms. Martinez. "The police are going to meet us downtown and we'll figure out an emergency plan."

I hear Ms. Martinez say, "I should never have let her leave my office today. God. My heart goes out to this kid."

"Well, now it's a bigger issue, yes," says the other lady.

I feel the floor shake as their feet clomp down the wooden steps. Then, silence.

I don't move.

I can't. I just sit here huddled on the floor right behind the door that I didn't open and I am trying so hard not to cry, but big, silent tears leak out of my eyes and roll down my cheeks. *I'm so ashamed of everything—of living like this, of constantly hiding the truth from everyone.* I'm so alone. I can't even describe how it feels. Everything hurts inside. I'm just so done feeling like this. Just really so tired of it. *I wish I had money. I wish I had a normal life. I wish Sunny wasn't so messed up.* When you can't have what you want most, you have to just try and swallow it. Push it away. I don't need anybody, for anything. I can't rely on other people. I can't depend on anyone but myself. People are gonna let you down. Not going to be there for you. Not going to help you out.

I know what I have to do.

I don't really think. I get up on my feet and I just start moving.

# 10

The blinds in the front of the trailer are broken and permanently down. I stand in front of them and peek out a sliver of a crack and watch Ms. Martinez and the other lady get into a car and drive away until I can see the taillights vanish down the hill.

I look around the trailer.

I don't want anything from here. I'd burn it if I could. I push open the door to Sunny's room, step over piles of clothes crumpled all over the floor, open her disaster-area closet, and pull down the brown shoebox from the top shelf. We've moved probably twenty times in my life, but wherever we go, this is the one thing Sunny makes sure to bring along. I set it on top of her unmade bed—a mattress on the floor—open the box, take out a small stack of letters, and flip through them until I find what I'm looking for. I take a deep breath in and memorize the address that I need.

Then I go to the kitchen, climb up onto the counter, reach up to the highest cupboard above the sink, and grab the box of Lucky Charms. I jump down, landing on my feet, and dump the crumpled dollar bills and change that I've been saving since forever onto the counter. It's everything I have. I was saving to buy a phone. I count up my money: "Five, ten, twenty, thirty, forty, fifty, sixty-five," then I sort through the mostly quarters and dimes and add them up too. My total bank: seventy dollars and fifty-five cents.

I jam it all into the front pocket of my jeans.

I don't even take my school backpack.

I glance around one more time. I'm not bringing anything from here. I'm leaving it all.

The last thing I do is rip a piece of cardboard off the empty box of Lucky Charms, rifle through the top drawer of Sunny's dresser, find a thick black marker, and scribble three words. I tuck the note under her pillow. I love Sunny, and I mean, I don't want her to get in trouble. I don't want her to worry. It's just—I feel so trapped. I wipe the tears from my eyes. There's nothing here for me. I know she needs me, but—

I need to get out of here, *fast*.

## 11

The front door has a bolt on it.

So, five minutes later, I'm vaulting myself out the open bathroom window headfirst. Wriggling the rest of my body like a worm, I balance myself upside down until I can grab onto the tall prickly weeds and lower my body, holding myself up with my arms, my hair hanging all over my face. I walk my hands forward until my feet hit the dirt, then I get up, brush myself off, and go.

It's not pitch-black. It never is around here, too many glaring lights from the Costco parking lot at the bottom of the hill. But it's shadowy enough, and I'd be lying if I told you that I didn't have that pit-in-my-stomach kind of feeling. I'm just so mad. I don't even care.

I start off walking, but about three steps in, I break into a run, sprinting past the dark line of trailers and the barking chained-up dogs, my flip-flops crunching into the gravel: short, quick strides until I look back over my shoulder and see I have left Pitts Hill far behind.

After a few blocks, I know I'm almost there. It's impossible to miss the strong smell of dirty air. I hold my breath walking through the thick clouds of exhaust from the long line of idling buses out front. I hate that smell.

Inside the bus station is grimy and crowded with a whole lot of strangers who don't really look at each other. Everyone looks tired, avoiding eye contact, staring straight ahead. The only seats in the entire place are metal, welded together at the arms. There is a streak of, like, pizza sauce or something red and gross smeared across the whole row.

I don't sit. I stay on my feet and stare at the wall of vending machines. I am eyeing a package of Skittles, until I do the math and realize I don't have enough money to buy just anything that I want.

I wait in line behind a mom carrying a sleeping little girl. Her head is resting against her mom's shoulder, and I just pretty much stare at her curly hair and matching cotton-candy-colored barrettes, until I hear a voice come through the ticket booth speaker that says, "Next."

The lady behind the thick bulletproof glass chews on her gum and looks me over, and not in a *big-smile-how-can-I-help-you-honey* kind of way. No. More like, *What do you want?*

I act pretty calm, but inside I'm freaking out. I'm tall. Five feet nine and a half. I look older than most girls my age, people are always telling me that, but what if she asks to see ID? What if the ticket is more money than my life savings, currently shoved into the front pocket of my jeans?

I move up to the counter.

I smile all big and fake, as if I'm not thirteen years old.

I clear my throat. "Hi," I say to the lady. My voice is much more cheerful and confident than I feel right now. Like I said, I can lie pretty good.

Now the lady hardly looks at me. "Destination?" she asks.

I pull my shoulders back. "Georgian Bay," I answer.

She's staring at her computer screen. "One way?" she asks.

I nod. "Yes, please."

"Georgian Bay," she repeats. She blows a tiny pink bubble with her gum. It snaps and pops. "That's an overnight bus. There's a driver change in Fort Smith."

I shrug. "That's fine."

She glances up. "Sixty-three dollars," she says.

"Sixty-three dollars," I repeat, and my voice is a little shaky as I dig my wad of bills out of my pocket and with my fingers count and smooth out the dollars, then clumsily slide them through the slot in the window. I take a deep breath. I only have seven dollars and fifty-five cents left.

Finally, after a long pause, the lady—still chomping on her gum—slides the ticket across the counter through the mouse-size hole.

The ticket is small. It's blue. I pick it up.

"Next," the lady calls through the glass.

And just like that, I'm out of here.

And I'm never coming back.

# 12

The bus is nearly full. There are only a few empty seats left. I have a very uneasy feeling as I scan my choices.

Empty Seat #1: I do not want to sit next to the very large man with his legs spread out, taking up as much space as humanly possible, practically both seats—who suddenly looks up from his phone and glances at me.

Yeah—no.

Behind that guy is Empty Seat #2: a guy slumped down with his eyes shut, already looking sound asleep, and the bus hasn't even moved. His long legs and big black boots are spilling out into the aisle. Just, no. *No, no, no. Not him*, I think, and—

"*Yes.*" I actually say this very quietly out loud as my eyes settle on an older lady with wavy silver hair. She's wearing a bumpy cardigan sweater. I immediately walk down the aisle toward her, and before I even ask if I can sit there, she looks up and her eyes brighten. Without either of us exchanging any words, the lady in the sweater makes room for me. She moves her legs toward the aisle and I carefully, silently scooch by her and drop into the empty window seat beside her.

After about a minute of silence, the lady turns to me and says, "Hello there," and she's smiling this really kind smile, her eyes looking right into mine.

"Hi," I answer softly. My eyes scan her face. There's something that's really calming about her. She looks like, you know, a *safe* person. She looks so sweet and kind, like someone's grandma, I guess. I mean, I don't have a grandmother, but—whatever, for some reason she looks like the kind I'd imagine if I did. She's neatly dressed. She has a coat folded up across her lap that looks like the same coat she's had for forty years. She smells good. I smelled it when I moved past her and sat down. It's like this clean, warm scent. I settle back against the hard bus seat and try to relax. The bus hasn't even moved yet. I take a few deep breaths. The lady glances down at the fresh jagged, pinkish scrape traveling up my arm, from breaking into my own stupid house.

"Ouch, that looks like it hurts," she says, sounding concerned.

"A little," I say, almost too tired to lie about anything right now.

She opens her bag and digs around. "I think I have some first-aid wipes in here someplace."

"It's okay," I say, but it's too late. The lady hands me a wipe in a single wrapped package, a small square, which I take and gratefully tear open, and begin to carefully wipe the dried blood off my arm. It stings.

"Better?" she asks.

"Yeah, thanks." I turn and glance at her. It feels good that she noticed, I guess. Right then, the bus lurches forward and makes the sharp turn onto the road. My arm and the lady's arm slightly touch on the armrest between us. She flashes me a quiet smile. I take another deep breath and settle back into the seat. The overhead lights above us turn off and the bus goes dark except for the dim glow of Clarksville streaking through the windows. I press my forehead against the glass and watch this stupid town, lit up by streetlights, and the huge Walmart parking lot slowly disappear before my eyes. *See ya never, Clarksville*, I think to myself.

## 13

**O**nce we get onto the highway, the bus is silent and dark and my teeth are kind of chattering because the air-conditioning is blasting out the little vent between me and the window. It is so freezing! The road is bumpy. I feel a little sick. I breathe in and out and tell myself, *I can do this. I've done harder things. This isn't as scary as it seems.* I turn and glance at the lady. Her eyes are closed. She looks so peaceful. Honestly, it's reassuring having her sitting next to me. Like a protection. I make myself as small as possible, pulling my legs up and wrapping my arms around my knees, and try to, like, snuggle into the side of the bus. It's not a big deal. I'm used to sleeping cramped and curled up on the scratchy green love seat in the trailer. I've slept in worse places than this. I stare out the window into the darkness and listen to the sound of silence and the bus hurtling through the night. I've never *not* had to take care of Sunny before. It's a weird feeling. It's just me now.

## 14

Who knows how long later, I wake up sitting with my shoulder crammed against the side of the bus and my head resting against the window. The last thing I remember is the darkness and the silence on the bus, and how tired and freezing I felt. I open my eyes a crack and squint into the sunshine streaming in through the bus windows. I am clutching the lady's coat, which is somehow draped over me and covering me like a blanket.

I turn and glance at the lady beside me.

She's still right where I last saw her, sitting peacefully in her chunky cable cardigan sweater. She's reading a book, and as I watch her, I think about how much better my whole body would feel if I could just shift in my seat, curl up against her, and rest my head on her shoulder . . . but yeah. I don't. Obviously. But as I'm picturing how comfy that would be, the lady suddenly looks up, catching my eye.

"Well, good morning," she says. "You really conked out!"

"Yeah." I nod.

"We've had a lot of adventures while you slept," she tells me. "We drove through a torrential rain—it was just pouring. The bus driver had to pull over at one point. Then we got stuck in traffic for hours. Then"—she pauses and laughs softly—"they switched drivers in Fort Smith. You slept straight through it all. Lucky you!"

I crack a smile. What I'm thinking is, *"Lucky," now that's a word I've never thought about myself.* I immediately sit up straighter, shake out her coat. "Thank you so much," I say, holding it out to return to her.

"Oh, you just looked so cold," the lady says. "You were shivering. Keep it for now," she says. "I asked the driver if he could turn the air-conditioning down. It's freezing cold on this bus. Please keep it."

"Oh, um—"

She looks right into my eyes. "I'm just a mom. I can't help it."

"Okay, thanks," I say, relieved to snuggle back up with her warm coat. It really *is* freezing on this bus. Cold air is blasting out of the narrow vent. I spread the coat back out so it's covering my chest and arms, pull it right up to my chin, and get cozy underneath, my knees pulled up, my bare feet folded under me on the seat. The smooth silk lining on the inside of the coat feels good against my skin. The sleeves are soft and frayed. The buttons up the front aren't plastic, they're wood.

The lady turns back to her book and I watch her silently reading. I don't even know this lady, but there's such a comfort in her sitting here next to me.

I gaze out the window, rub my eyes, and squint into the sun. The view is much different from anything I've ever seen around Clarksville. There's very little traffic on the road, or buildings, or people, really. Streaks of grassy green meadows flow past my eyes, a blur of yellow farmland, the occasional red barn or lone old white house sitting in a field all by itself. I even spot horses in the far-off distance. I shift in my seat.

"Hey, I'm hungry," I hear the lady say, and I turn to look. "How about you?" she asks me as she sifts around in a brown paper bag in her lap. She takes out a sandwich neatly wrapped in wax paper and opens it up.

"For you," she says, passing me half her sandwich. "It's too much for me to eat." She smiles at me. "It's cheddar cheese."

I am starving. "Thank you," I say, holding the sandwich carefully so I don't get crumbs all over her coat. I raise it to my mouth and take a big bite.

After I polish off the sandwich, the lady offers me a container full of bright red strawberries. "I just picked them this morning. Would you like some?"

"Thanks," I say. I pick a single strawberry and pop it into my mouth.

"And for dessert, we have salty caramel chocolate. I love that salty sweet, it's my favorite." I watch as she breaks the bar in two and hands half of it to me.

I take a bite.

She does too.

After a few minutes, the lady turns to me and raises her eyebrows. "Well, now," she says. "That's a lot better!"

"Yeah," I agree. I look at her and catch a smile.

She turns toward the window and looks out. I do too. The roads are getting more winding and narrow as we make our way toward the ocean. Everything is wet. The sun is bright. The fields are just, like, glistening in the daylight.

"Silver lining from all that rain," says the lady, and she lets out a deep sigh. "It's a fresh start. Everything is all washed clean."

"Yeah," I say, almost in a whisper, my face to the window. "I know what you mean."

## 15

**W**e're here.

The bus turns into a rocky parking lot.

"Georgian Bay," announces the driver. A half dozen people immediately stand, reaching for their bags, crowding the aisle.

I don't reach for a bag or put on a jacket.

I have no stuff.

It's just me in my jeans, T-shirt, and flip-flops. I straighten up in the seat and look into the parking lot at the people gathered just outside the windows, waiting to greet the people on the bus. There are three little girls with bright red balloons, a few mom-looking types, a tall man in a jacket and tie holding a large bouquet of flowers and wearing a big smile, two old men, and a kid sitting on a skateboard.

Part of me is so excited to get off this bus, but a little part of me kind of wishes the lady sitting next to me would come with me too, or that I could somehow stay with her.

Instead, I kind of whisper, "Well, this is me," then stand and shake out the lady's coat, fold it up neatly, and hand it back.

The lady swings her legs over so that I can carefully pass by her and step into the aisle. I don't really know how to say thanks so I just, like, look down at her in her seat and give her my best smile. There's a small silence when our eyes connect. Neither of us says anything, but somehow even that feels good.

She takes a breath.

I do too.

"It was fun to share this journey with you," she says, smiling back. Then I watch as she reaches out and slips something into my hand. I glance down and see that it's a piece of lined notebook paper folded origami-style into an envelope. "This is for when you need a little lift," she tells me, her eyes bright and connected to mine. She waits a moment, and for just a second she puts her hand over mine. It's soft and warm. And she gives my hand a squeeze. "I can see that you're a strong young lady," she tells me. Her voice is so sure and calm, and she is looking at me very intensely with the kindest eyes.

I pause for just a second, standing in the aisle, smiling back at her and trying to find the right words, when I hear a loud male voice behind me say—

"Move!"

It startles me. I turn my head. The voice belongs to a very large man, who is glaring at me. "Let's go. C'mon!" he demands. He looks angry.

I kind of freeze.

And then: I panic.

I turn and start walking very quickly—fumbling, fast, down the aisle. My heart is suddenly pounding. I don't look back over my shoulder at the lady. I don't say thank you in the way I wish I had, I don't open the folded-up origami envelope to see what's inside—I just grip it tightly in my hand, slide it into my back pocket, and hurry toward the front of the bus. I give the driver a quiet thanks and take off down the three steep steps, squinting into the bright morning light, breathing in fresh warm air that smells like summer.

The second my flip-flops land on the rocky ground, I walk over to the side of the bus and look up, my eyes scanning for the spot I was just sitting. I try to see the lady through the tall dark windows, try to catch one more glance. I raise my hand into a wave, but—

It's too late.

The bus pulls away.

# 16

In case you think I know what I'm doing, now might be a good time to tell you: I don't. Nobody is waiting to meet me with balloons or flowers. I smell. I haven't changed in forty-eight hours. I am suddenly utterly and completely alone. As in, by myself in a way I haven't ever felt.

I'm pretty used to being by myself in Clarksville, but it is different being by yourself in a place you haven't been, a place you've never seen before . . . It's a little bit exciting and a little bit—no, *a lot bit*—terrifying.

I sit down on the curb and try to think.

I look around.

There's a bunch of parked cars and a set of steps that lead down to a waterfront with docks and boats.

Okay, picture this: a girl with long, stringy dirty-blond hair, sitting on the hot cement in her jeans—ripped at the knees—in a T-shirt streaked with a break-into-your-own-house bloodstain along the bottom hem, a red scrape down the inside of her arm, flip-flops gripping against the ground, blue toenail polish almost all chipped off. There's a little snapshot of me, right here, right now. Where is here, you ask?

Good question.

That's exactly what I need to figure out, and that's why I take a big, deep breath and stand.

I head just beyond the parking lot toward the waterfront harbor, and a few minutes later I'm standing in the middle of an old-fashioned boardwalk with a bunch of tourists taking group selfies.

I look around until my eyes zero in on the safest person I can spot: a mom pushing an empty stroller, holding hands with a small red-headed boy and laughing. She's wearing jeans, a peachy tank, and those white Birkenstock sandals that I really want. Her toenails are pink. Sorry for the details—I just notice these things!

I walk up to the mom and the little boy. "Excuse me," I say in my politest voice. "Can you tell me how to get to Great Bear Lodge?"

The young mom looks at me and her eyes light up. "Great Bear, gosh, I haven't been there since I was a little girl. It's *gorgeous!*" She pauses for a sec. "Getting there is kind of an adventure. It's pretty remote."

I wait. Three seagulls swoop in and land near our feet.

She glances at her little redheaded boy, who is now chasing the birds, then back at me. "Are you heading to Great Bear Lodge today?"

"Yeah," I answer. "Do you know about how far it is? I'm walking."

"Wait. Walk?" She looks confused. "You can't walk to Great Bear. You're going to have to take the ferry."

"The ferry?" I repeat, not sure what she means.

"Great Bear Lodge is on Great Bear *Island*," she tells me.

I'm quiet. I still don't get it.

The lady squats down and lifts her little boy up, cradling him against her hip. He's so cute. He has wild curly hair and freckles and he is smiling at me. They both are. She takes a step closer. "The only way to Great Bear Island is by boat . . . unless you have a helicopter or floatplane. You can only get there by air or water. You can buy a ticket to the ferry over there." She turns toward the long wooden dock and the busy harbor and points to the pier. "See that light green wooden shack at the very end of the dock?"

I hold up my hand to shield my eyes from the glare of the sun.

"See it?" she says, stepping closer to me. "Right over there, way down at the end?"

I look toward the boats of all sizes, men standing on the decks in matching bright yellow fishing gear, and the blue, blue water in the distance. "Oh, okay." I nod. "Yeah. I see it."

"That's where you can buy a ticket and where you catch the ferry." She turns back to me and she suddenly looks a little bit concerned. "Hey, is everything okay? Do you need any cash?" the young mom asks me. "Is there someone you want to call?" She balances the little boy against her hip with one arm, and with the other she fishes into a large orange diaper bag and pulls out her phone, offering it to me.

I shake my head and take a step back. "Oh, no. Thanks. I'm good," I lie.

She looks at me carefully. "Okay, are you sure?"

I nod and flash a smile, trying to look convincing and trying to convince myself. I take another step backward, toward the pier. The mom gives me a really big smile. She has perfectly straight white teeth. She glances at the little boy. "Say bye," she tells him, holding up her hand and waving.

"Bye!" the little boy yells in his tiny voice. He swings his hand back and forth above his head. "Bye! Bye!" he shouts to me, giggling as if this is the funniest thing ever.

I smile at the two of them. The mom is still waving and the little boy is still laughing and now blowing me kisses.

I raise my hand, wave, and blow a kiss back.

Then I spin around and head toward the light green wooden shack.

## 17

I walk down the long pier, past the tourists, past an entire elementary school class eating ice-cream cones, then farther: past a whole lot of colorful fishing boats and the men in those yellow waterproof overalls and tall rubber boots. I walk past all that, until if I walk any farther, I'd walk right off the dock into the water. And there it is: the light green wooden shack.

I push open the old screen door, take a step in, and look around, and *What am I getting myself into?* is definitely running through my mind. Inside, the shack smells like a mixture of fuel and fish. The floor creaks. There is an old guy with buzz-cut white hair and the bluest eyes sitting behind a tall wooden counter.

He looks at me.

He waits.

He says nothing.

"Uh . . ." I start. "How much does it cost to buy a ticket to Great Bear?"

The man barely raises his eyebrows. No smile. No nothing. He lifts his hand and points to the sign on the wall above his head.

### FERRY RATES
**Otter Bay, Deer Isle, Juniper Ridge, North Point, Great Bear**

**ADULTS**
**One Way: $20**
**Round Trip: $40**

**STUDENTS**

One Way:  $10

Round Trip:  $20

TICKET BOOK (20 tkts.):  $360

*Ten dollars.* My heart drops. I don't have enough.

I dig into my pocket and pull out everything I have left. I count it out one bill at a time. Laying each out on the counter, including a handful of quarters, nickels, and dimes. Seven dollars and fifty-five cents.

It's all I have.

I don't look right at him. I look at the wrinkly bags of skin below his blue eyes and push the money across the counter with my fingers. "Here you go," I say, and try to sound like I totally am paying the right amount.

Without a word, I watch as the man counts the money. First the bills, one by one, then he slides the coins one at a time off the counter and into his hand.

Silence.

I feel my heart pound. "Um, it's just—" I start, then stop. I mean, what's the use in even hoping? I'm so mad at myself for thinking this could ever work. Thinking I could start over. Thinking I could change things.

Then—

The man punches something into a hundred-year-old-looking cash register, slowly places the money into the tray, closes it, turns back toward me, and hands me a ticket.

 **18**

And that's it! Five minutes later, I'm waiting for the ferry on a bench just outside the light green shack. There's a little girl in a flowery dress standing a few feet away from me, drinking a huge red Slurpee. I'm *so* thirsty, but I literally don't have even one penny left. Little beads of sweat are on my forehead. There are these teensy little bugs buzzing all around me in a swarm. I swat them away. I tilt my head back, fold my arms, and close my eyes. The sun feels so good on my face. And believe me when I tell you that I could not make this up if I tried. At first I think it's a big raindrop falling from the sky, but then . . . yeah . . .

It's not rain.

I reach up to see if it's what I think it is. I glance at my hand. It's covered in . . . yeah. *That.* By the look of the white goop on my fingers, it's as if someone dropped a scoop of melting vanilla ice cream out of a plane, it picked up speed along the way and landed bull's-eye on my head. "Are you kidding me right now?" I say into the air. I lift my T-shirt to my face and clean my forehead the best I can, then wipe the white seagull glop off my fingers. I try and pick it out of my hair but end up smearing it in more. "This is so gross," I whisper to myself. And guess what? *Ta-da!* This is the very same moment the ferry pulls up!

Of course it is.

A horn blows and the ferry, white and shiny, glides in against the dock. I watch as a guy with those bright yellow waterproof overalls and a camouflage baseball hat jumps down off the deck of the boat, throws a wooden plank onto the dock, and cups his hands. "Welcome to the *Gray Lady*," he calls out.

I get up.

I get up with globs of white bird poop smeared in my hair and down the front of my shirt and walk over and step into the single-file line behind a bunch of mostly super-rich-looking people waiting to get on the ferry: a few couples, a dog on a leash, an older guy in a business suit, a family with three little kids, a woman in sunglasses and a big floppy hat, and a mom with a baby in one of those slings, all snuggled in against her chest.

I straighten up my shoulders.

I take a few long breaths.

I glance around. I'm a world away from Clarksville and I *still* don't fit in. I don't belong. I rest my eyes on the mom with the baby, her hand gently cupping the baby's back. I feel this sudden tightness in my throat and chest. I glance over my shoulder back toward where I met the young mom and the little boy. I seriously think about turning around, somehow figuring out how to get back to stupid Clarksville, but—

No.

I'm sick of pretending everything is okay when it's not. I'm so ashamed of who I am. I just want to be somewhere safe, with water that runs and stuff to eat. I really need to get away to protect Sunny from the police. Worrying about Sunny never stops.

I want to be a kid for once.

I take a small step forward and then another until finally I am at the front of the line.

"Ticket?" asks the guy in the camo hat.

I swallow hard. I hand over my ticket. I give the guy in the camo hat a casual nod, like, *Oh, hey*, as if I've ridden a ferryboat a thousand times. My heart is pounding. I don't know if this is 100 percent the best decision ever.

I look past the ferryboat, out into the ocean. I can see all the way out until the water hits the horizon. I take a deep breath in. "Screw it," I whisper out loud. *I've gotten this far, and I'm not quitting now.* I walk across the ramp between the dock and the ferry and get on.

# 19

The ferry is white and shining under the glare of the sun. If you're picturing a giant fancy ship, well, not so much. This ferry looks more like a tugboat than a sleek yacht. I don't follow the other passengers down the steps to the rows of cushioned seats under a sun-shaded roof. I stay outside and stand on the boat's open deck. It's a little breezy, but the sky is entirely blue, and the warmth of the sun feels so good on my face.

After a few minutes, the engine rumbles to a start.

It's loud! I hear it and feel it. It makes my heart jump. I've never been on a boat before! I move closer to the railing and look down at the waves crashing and sloshing against the tall wooden beams that hold up the pier.

"Welcome aboard the *Gray Lady*," comes a loud voice over a crackly speaker. "Conditions are a little choppy, but things will smooth out as we get moving. Life jackets are tucked under the seats. Sit back, relax, and take in the spectacular coastal mountains."

I watch the Guy in the Camo Hat—the same guy who took my ticket, and who I'm pretty sure is also the captain of the boat—move to unwind the line tied up to these giant cleats holding us to the pier. He whips the line around almost like a lasso until there is no longer anything connecting us to the dock.

Another minute goes by, and the ferry lets out a loud air-horn honk. I'm not gonna lie, it scares me half to death. I reach for the railing and grab hold with both hands.

Then—

Hold up.

There's a teenage girl sprinting down the dock straight toward us, screaming, "WAIT!" and waving her arms over her head as she runs. I squint through the sun. The girl looks a little bit older than I am—maybe high school or maybe college. She has this huge backpack strapped to her shoulders and she is seriously hauling a$$. The whole thing happens so fast! The boat begins drifting away from the dock, and I watch this girl with the huge backpack, a trucker hat, and long, dark-reddish wild hair that's flying all over the place, just, like—

*Jump!*

In one fluid motion she leaps from the dock, launching herself over the water like she's some kind of Olympic hurdler, and lands on the boat's deck, on her two feet, wobbling a little, then straightening up like a gymnast who has just nailed a perfect landing. The second she lands, she does a little bow, and all the passengers on the ferry erupt in cheers, including me. "That was amazing!" falls out of my mouth.

I stare at the girl as she unstraps her arms from her pack and sets down the heavy bag with a thud. She's not too far from where I'm standing. I glance up at her black trucker hat and the ocean-blue patch that reads I'M ACTUALLY A MERMAID! I grin a little as I make out the words.

Then . . . *oh, snap.*

Something crazy happens.

This redheaded Olympic hurdler with her mermaid trucker hat and her broken-in jeans and short-sleeve tee makes her way straight for . . . *me.*

**20**

The Girl Who Is Actually a Mermaid is walking straight toward me with this huge smile. She is speaking to me. And what she says is, "Oh my gosh, Liv? It's me, Cricket!" Then she's hugging me! And it's not a *little* kind of hug. It's more like one of those tight bear hugs someone gives their favorite person on earth.

Count to three.

No, not like that. Count *slow*.

One Mississippi, two Mississippi, three Mississippi. I think you get the picture! The Girl Who Is Actually a Mermaid is hugging me and she doesn't let go! She holds on and squeezes tight. She's tall. Her hair is sort of hanging in my face. It smells like a mix of sunscreen and sweat. Finally, she lets go and steps back and just looks straight at me.

Every part of her face is smiling.

Her eyes, her mouth. "Liv!" she repeats. "Oh my gosh, it is *so* good to finally meet you in person!" Now her face is like, one foot away from mine. I'm pretty sure she's waiting for me to say something. My mind is racing, in this order of thoughts:

*1. It's obvious she thinks I'm someone else.*

*2. Did she call me Liv?*

*3. Did she say her name was Cricket?*

I just keep staring at her.

"Soooooooo?" she says. "How was your trip, girl?"

"My trip—" I fumble for words. Cricket's eyes are crazy green. She has a sprinkling of light brown freckles across her nose.

"Lady, I feel you. I'm toast! Traveling is no joke!" Cricket falls back into one of the plastic molded seats that sit in a row facing the water. She sighs and says, "I am *so* ready to get to Great Bear!"

I take a seat too.

Cricket kicks off her chunky sandals, removes her hat, and twists a handful of her hair up into a loose knot.

I try to figure out exactly what I should say or do. I can't stop staring. Cricket has a tiny ocean-blue turquoise stud in her nose.

She glances around. "Hey! Wait," she says. "Where's all your stuff?"

"Oh, um . . . I—"

"Did the airline lose your bag? So classic!"

I nod my chin.

Cricket springs up in her bare feet and hauls her huge backpack from where she left it over to me. Then she sets it down with a thud directly in front of my feet.

She drops back down into the seat right beside me. "No worries," she tells me. "What's mine is yours!" Cricket leans forward and unzips the top of her pack. "Dude," she says, "this bag has gotten me through my entire gap year. Belize, Chile, skiing in Argentina, and adventure number four, where I just was, working on a farm at a surf yoga retreat in Costa Rica!" She turns to look at me again. "Honestly, Liv! Anything you need, I got you." She waits. "Want to borrow a hoodie?"

"Oh, thanks. I'm good," I say quickly. But here's what I don't do: I do *not* tell her that I am not Liv, or whoever it is she thinks I am. Does that count as a lie? If I'm just, like, going along? Okay, wait. Don't answer that. I don't want to know.

It's just, Cricket is so *nice*!

She leans over toward me, her arm touching mine. "We are going to have *so* much fun this summer!" she tells me, or whoever she thinks I am. "I can't believe we get this opportunity! Lodge hands!" Cricket sits back, pulling her legs up in her seat and folding them under her. "Seriously, this is a super-hard gig to land, and they picked us, two seventeen-year-olds!"

"Seventeen?" I blurt out, and then immediately wish I hadn't.

For a millisecond Cricket looks at me, confused, but then she quickly breaks into a smile. "Oh! My bad. You're still sixteen, right?"

"Uh-huh," I lie, and find myself slowly nodding.

Cricket's eyes light up. "Well, we get to be roomies all summer! To warn you"—she giggles—"I do snore a little bit, but you can wake me up whenever you need to. Oh my gosh, it's going to be *epic*—we're going to have the best time ever!"

Just now I watch as Cricket glances down, noticing the sticky white goop streaked across the front of my shirt. "Oh noooo," she says. "Is that what I think it is?"

I scrunch up my nose, nodding. "It's in my hair too."

"You got it good, huh?" says Cricket. "On the bright side, that's major good luck."

"Good luck?" I repeat.

"Yeah. It's a thing!"

"A thing?" I ask. Now I'm smiling.

"One hundred percent," Cricket says. "Getting pooped on by a bird is totally auspicious! Today must be your lucky day!"

"Lucky day?" I say, and my smile gets bigger. There's just something that Cricket radiates that makes you feel good. I want to believe everything she says. I want to go along. I want to believe her. I mean, I'm sitting beside a girl I've just met, and I'm on a ferryboat heading to a small island all the way up the coast, and I have glops of white seagull poop seeping into my scalp and dribbling down the front of my shirt. So yeah. I am sure you can picture what happens next, which is: we both look at each other and just crack up laughing.

## 21

Five minutes later, Cricket is standing up, leaning over me in my seat, carefully picking through strands of my hair. "Man," she says through giggles. "What does this bird even eat?!!"

I bite down on my lower lip to keep from cracking up again and try to stay still.

"It's so goopy," Cricket laughs, but she doesn't seem bothered by the job. She combs her fingers through my sweaty, tangled hair and gently scrapes out chunks of white gooey bird poop.

Then, the last step: "Okay, close your eyes!" Cricket warns.

I tip my head back and squeeze my eyes shut. And I laugh and Cricket says, "Ready?"

"Ready," I say, bracing myself.

On the count of a giggly one, two, three, Cricket slowly pours a steady stream of water from her water bottle over my head, and within a second we burst out in laughter again.

I sit up and wipe my face on my sleeve. I glance at Cricket, now kneeling on the ferryboat deck before her bag, fishing out random pieces of clothing and offering them to me, like: "Hoodie?" and "*Ooh*, what about a fleece vest?"

"No, it's okay, I'm good," I quickly say, even though the top of my T-shirt is now soaked.

Cricket looks at me like I'm nuts. "Dude, you're going to freeze when we get farther out. The wind will pick up." She waits. When I don't answer, she says, "Liv, come on! Take something. Really. It will feel good to change."

"Okay," I finally say. "I guess I'll take the hoodie?"

"Solid choice!" Cricket tosses me her dark blue hoodie and I catch it.

"It's the warmest, coziest thing you'll ever put on," she tells me. "Just gonna warn you," she says, laughing, "it's got a little bit of a funk going on. I haven't had time to wash it in a few weeks."

I slip my right arm into the sleeve. "I don't mind," I say, pulling Cricket's hoodie over my head.

"Whoa, hold up," she says, and I freeze. "Don't you want to take that wet thing off first?" Before I even answer, Cricket begins rifling through her gear again. This time she pulls out a scarf. It's blue and square with fringe around the edges. She stands and holds it up around me like a curtain. "I'll make a blockade for you to change behind."

I look at her like, *Right here?*

She laughs from the other side of her makeshift curtain. "Just do it. No one cares."

So I do. I whip my wet, bird-poop-streaked T-shirt off. For a second I'm sitting behind Cricket's nearly see-through scarf, wearing nothing but my damp white bra and jeans. I pull the hoodie over my head.

"Done?" she asks behind the veil.

"Yep." I laugh.

Cricket lowers the scarf. "Ta-da!" she says, standing in front of me. "Hair tie?" she offers, slipping a hair band off her wrist and handing it to me.

"Thanks," I say, pushing my wet hair out of my face.

"Dude, I could pass out right here," Cricket says, tucking both her knees in toward her chest and curling up in her seat. A few minutes later I glance at Cricket and she's out cold.

I keep my eyes open.

I listen.

The quiet ocean.

The occasional squawk of a seabird soaring over us.

I comb my wet hair with my fingers and scrape it back, twisting it up into a looped pony. I settle back in my seat. I look up and all around. The ocean sparkles in the sun. I breathe in deep. I feel better than I have in a really long time. I peek over at Cricket, sound asleep in the seat next to me. Her hair is the coolest shade of red. Her arms are strong and freckled. She has golden skin. She's one of those people you just want to be around.

Look, I'm just going to bring this up again. Are you mad that I don't wake her up and tell her who I really am? Tell her that I am *not* some girl named Liv . . . that I have absolutely no idea who Liv even is?

Well, I don't.

Sorry.

Being Liv is better than being River.

I have a new best friend who's "actually a mermaid," and we still have a long ferry ride before we get to Great Bear. The view from the boat is crazy-beautiful: the ocean, the coastline, the far-off deep green mountains. The air smells so clean, and there's a perfect little windy breeze. I'm warming up in Cricket's hoodie. Every now and then I get a salty mist spray on my face. I just sit here and take it in. Loose wisps of my wavy damp hair are swirling all over the place. The sunbeams warm the top of my head and it feels so good. I sit back, all cozy in the hoodie, hugging my knees.

A little later I hear a loud yawn and look over at Cricket, now sitting up, wide-eyed, smiling at me as she stretches her arms over her head.

Then she digs through her pack and—*voilà!*—passes me snacks (fruit leather, chocolate-covered berries, popcorn). Neither of us says a word. We sit elbow to elbow, facing the water, a real-life episode of *Planet Earth* passing right before our eyes.

**22**

By hour three, I am under a spell. We are quietly passing through deep, narrow channels of water with towering walls of green mountains rising on either side. Google-image the word "fjord," and you'll see what I mean.

Go ahead, I'll wait.

It's so amazing, right?

The ferryboat moves among a scattering of small islands, first far away, then closer, and finally, we're beside them, coming into sandy dunes, with giant granite boulders and beaches with floating docks, delivering people and moving on to the next stop. The harbors and drop-offs get less busy and smaller the farther and farther away we get.

I have Cricket's hoodie up around my head, my eyes scanning the water. I've never seen anything like it! This place is blowing my mind. Cricket's already spotted a pod of whales! *Whales!* They swim right with us for a good ten minutes, their shiny black-and-white bodies bursting out of the water, then disappearing, then popping back out of the water again. Whales are so playful and funny. I see sea otters, and dolphins that swim along with us for miles. I even see an eagle dive-bombing a fish!

The ferry has stopped four times so far: at small remote beachside harbors with a few fancy resorts along the coast, bringing mail and supplies, dropping everyone off, until Cricket and I are the only passengers left. I begin to have this slightly sick-to-my-stomach feeling, and it's not seasickness.

It's *me.*

"Cricket, I'm uh—" I start to tell Cricket that I'm not who she thinks I am, but when she turns to look at me, I stop myself. I didn't plan to lie, to pretend I'm someone that I'm not, but it just feels so good to not be me. To be someone else.

"What were you gonna say?" Cricket asks, waiting.

"Oh, nothing." I shake my head and try to laugh it off.

Cricket turns toward the water. "This is about as remote as it gets. No cell reception, no screens. No roads! We are off the grid! Doesn't get much more off the beaten path than this." She breathes in deeply, then lets it out. "Mountains, forests, coastlines, ocean. This is the most magical place I've ever been." She turns to face me. "How stoked are you?"

"I'm a little bit nervous" is all I can say.

Cricket loops her arm through mine. "I feel you! The work is going to be hard, for sure, but—" She looks over at me, her eyes lit up. "We can count on each other, right? The minute I saw you, I just knew you'd be a kindred spirit. I love that, don't you?"

"Yeah," I say. *I do.*

For a long moment neither of us speaks. Then Cricket says, "It's like, right away you can just totally be yourself, and you can't help but smile because it's so exciting to meet someone who's obviously going to be your homie for life, right?"

I smile a quiet smile. Cricket just has a way about her that's very warm and very easygoing. She's always laughing and smiling. She's the kind of person who you instantly feel like you've known forever.

## 23

When the ferry first makes the turn into Great Bear Island's perfect horseshoe-shaped bay with the bluest water I've ever seen, Cricket and I are just like—

Wow. Stunned into silence.

My mouth drops open.

Straight ahead, nestled together on the glassy water's edge, are five of the most adorable little beachfront cabins built on stilts. The lodge sits tucked in behind them, perched on a cliff above the ocean cove, surrounded on three sides by the steep green mountains. To the left of the cabins is a single-drop white waterfall plunging off the cliff. I am completely mesmerized. It's just, beauty *everywhere*. "It's like something out of a fairy tale," I whisper.

"This is unreal," breathes Cricket.

I go, "Right?"

Cricket laughs and says, "Is this real life?"

Camo Hat Guy cuts the engine of the ferry, and for a few long moments there is a quietness all around: we are gliding silently into the bay and the only sound is the trickling of the water lapping against the boat. There are really no words . . . it's like, a secret hideaway emerald cove.

"Whoa," breathes Cricket.

"It's so beautiful," I whisper, and I feel my shoulders soften.

"It's like a movie or something," Cricket murmurs.

There is a long silence.

It's unbelievably peaceful.

The ferryboat bobs in the bay. The water is calm and shimmering in the sun. In the distance you can hear the waterfall cascading off the cliff and crashing onto a rocky part of the beach below. After a few more minutes of dreamy quiet, the ferry engine sputters back on and we slowly motor in toward Great Bear Island.

Cricket leans into me, and our shoulders bump. "Oh my gosh, I see them!" She points to the shoreline. "Look!"

I squint at the beach. I can just barely make out two tiny specks. Two people. My stomach gets all twisty and fluttery and I wonder if it's trying to tell me that what I'm about to do is crazy.

Then the engine is cut again and we glide closer and closer toward a single floating wooden dock jutting from the beach.

"Here we go," says Cricket.

She quickly ties her hair into a loose pony, throws her trucker hat back on, leans forward, reaches for her bag, zips it shut, threads her arm through the strap, and heaves the entire backpack up as she stands.

I get up too.

I don't have anything to carry off.

We glance at each other as the boat glides in closer and closer. Cricket raises her eyebrows. "Ready?" she says, and flashes me a smile.

"Yeah," I say, and I take a big breath.

*I have been for a really long time.*

**24**

After four hours of winding our way through a bajillion miles of deep, narrow fjords, the drop-off at Great Bear Island takes maybe three minutes, tops. Me, I have no stuff, so I jump down, leaping from the ferry's deck over the water and landing on the long wooden dock. Cricket is right behind me. With her giant pack strapped over her shoulders, she lands barefoot with a thud. Then Camo Hat Guy delivers three large wooden crates of supplies, unloading them off the ferry and onto the end of the dock, waves goodbye, and motors off.

Now it's just me and Cricket.

The two tiny specks we could barely make out from the ferry are nowhere in sight. It's so quiet, so absolutely peaceful here that it almost makes me nervous. I'm not used to it. We stay exactly where we are on the dock, standing, looking all around, dazzled. "This is wild, right?" Cricket whispers.

I nod and glance all around me in every direction.

We have stepped off the boat onto a lone wooden dock and into a completely secluded wilderness. I mean, yes, there are the most adorable waterfront cabins on stilts and the lodge perched on the cliff, but besides that, it feels like we are on the edge of the earth! The U-shaped cove with milky-turquoise water is surrounded on three sides with steep forested green mountains that hug the beach. And when I say "beach," if you're thinking tropical, scratch that. This is the Pacific Northwest. There is still snow that you can see on the peaks of the mountaintops. The ferry took us about as north as you can get. It's sunny, but it's cool and rugged and wet.

I glance at Cricket standing beside me, gripping the straps of her pack. She looks almost as shocked as I do. This place looks like we landed in a filtered Instagram picture, a dream. I feel the dock under my flip-flops. This is real. I take one last look, glancing over my shoulder at the ferry disappearing into the distance. And then we wait, standing side by side, looking around without saying a word. A minute goes by and then I feel Cricket's elbow give me a sharp nudge in the gut. She nods for me to look up toward the lodge. At the top of a set of steep stone steps built right into the cliffside, the tiny specks we saw from the boat have turned into two fully visible human people, making their way down toward us.

One, a boy about my age, is waving.

Cricket excitedly hollers out, "Hellloooo!!!" She thrusts her hand up toward the blue sky and waves back. My heart begins to pound harder the closer they get. My stomach is all twisted up in knots. My throat is suddenly tight. Ten seconds later, two people are walking down the dock straight for us and . . .

*Oh my gosh.*

My mouth just drops—

## 25

I know it the second I see her.

I am standing face-to-face with a tanner, fitter, healthier version of Sunny. Identical fiery blue-green eyes, identical intimidating don't-mess-with-me look on her face, and nearly identical long, loose hair.

Same beachy waves.

The woman in front of me is wearing a button-down denim shirt with the sleeves rolled up, jeans, and high rubber boots—the kind you'd wear if you were standing knee-deep in the water, fixing a boat, or digging for something in the mud. She's tall and her arms are very toned and bronze. I stand there and stare. I can't take my eyes off her. The only thing not exactly the same is the color of her hair—it's dark, almost black, and Sunny's is more like bleached-blond, exactly like the boy standing beside her, who—

Wait.

She's talking to me!

"Jemma," she says, introducing herself, reaching out and shaking my hand with a tight, Wonder Woman–level strong, bone-crushing grip. Jemma looks me right in the eyes. It's intense! There's a long silence.

She waits.

"I'm, um—" I swallow. "So glad to meet you!" I finally blurt out.

Jemma turns to Cricket. "I'm Jemma," she says, and they do the same Wonder Woman shake. More warm greetings are exchanged.

Oh man. I'm staring.

I'm pretty sure my mouth is still hanging open.

I glance over at the boy standing beside Jemma. Like I said, he looks about my age, maybe a little older. He has a small knife in a holster fastened to the waist of his jeans. He's in a gray T-shirt that's tight around his biceps, and he's barefoot. He's strong and wiry, with a headful of thick, corkscrew-curly hair and bright eyes.

"This is my son, Tillman," says Jemma, her whole face brightening as she looks at him.

The curly-haired boy's eyes light up. "Hey, I'm Till," he says, flashing a huge grin, revealing a gap between his two front teeth.

"I'm Cricket!" says Cricket, reaching to meet Till's hand.

Now everyone turns to me.

My whole body feels suddenly warm and tingly. I feel so guilty. In one second I have a thousand thoughts. I promise myself I will tell them all soon enough. I will. I swear. I reach out my hand. "Hi, I'm Liv," I say, trying very hard to sound like I am.

*I am Liv!*

*I am sixteen years old!*

*I am here for the summer . . . I have a job!*

I lock eyes with the boy and his crazy curls and big smile. He keeps a firm grip on my hand and looks me in the eye, holds for three slow-moving seconds, and then—we let go.

I swallow hard.

I smile quietly at him.

He smiles back. His eyes are oceany blue and he has long eyelashes. He's really tan. He's supercute . . . I imagine all my friends would have the biggest crush on him. I feel my heart pounding in my chest. I glance at his thick, sun-bleached curls and then back at his bright blue eyes. I feel all hot and suddenly *very* nervous. And it's not what you think. It's . . . it's that—

I didn't even know . . .

I have a *cousin*!

# 26

**W**ait. Can we back up a sec?

There's something I haven't told you yet. Or, wait, maybe I did. I have never met anyone from Sunny's family before, and they have never met me. So standing here on the dock, Jemma and Till have *no idea* about who I am. Honestly, I am not really sure if they know I exist. Sunny left Great Bear Island before I was born, and she hasn't been back since. They are like, in some sort of giant fight. A war.

They don't talk.

Sunny never mentions her family. *Ever.*

I only know about this place from rummaging through Sunny's shoebox, from reading old letters and basically piecing it all together. Great Bear Island is where Sunny grew up. Jemma runs Great Bear Lodge. That's pretty much all I know right now. And so, when Jemma—my aunt, Sunny's older sister—looks at me, I am careful to stand up straight and try very hard to look sixteen, and not to look afraid. I am surprised at how much I desperately want to make her instantly like me. I will do anything I have to do to stay.

Look, maybe you are thinking, if I want to stay so bad, why don't I just tell her who I am?

I get it.

You might think it's easy to just blurt everything out. Tell Jemma about Sunny. Tell her that I'm not Liv at all, that I'm actually River, her long-lost niece. Tell her about how Ms. Martinez called social services, and social services called the police . . . But, I mean, if Jemma hates Sunny so much, maybe she would hate me. Then I'd have to leave.

## 27

Till quietly steps away and starts hauling large wooden crates, one at a time. I watch as he squats down and easily hoists a heavy container right up onto his shoulder. He walks the length of the dock, across the beachfront, and up the stone steps that lead to the lodge. I'm kind of in a daze, my eyes following Till, when I hear—

"Liv?"

It's Jemma.

I quickly turn back.

"Where are your bags?" she asks.

"My bags, oh, see . . . I, I um—" I start, and I'm trying hard to sound like I'm not making up every word I say. Which is hard to do, because I am.

Jemma waits.

Cricket suddenly jumps in. "So typical," she says. "The airline lost her bag!"

"Yeah," I lie, and I'm nodding my chin.

Jemma looks at me carefully. "I'm really surprised to see you here, Liv." She pauses. "The last word I got was in the letter you sent?"

I go, "Oh, uh . . . The letter? Um—" I stall.

Jemma raises her eyebrows. "The note you wrote?"

I say nothing.

Jemma is now looking at me like I'm nuts. "That you couldn't be here for our summer season? That you were turning down the job?"

"Oh! Yeah. Umm—no!" I quickly blurt out. "I'm here!" I say, nodding.

"Good" is all Jemma says.

By now, Till has finished moving all the wooden crates and he's walking toward us down the dock. We all look up. His T-shirt is off. His jeans are hugging his hips. He walks up to the end of the dock, where we are all gathered.

"Thanks, honey," Jemma says, smiling at Till.

She glances at her watch, then back up at us. "Okay, gang," she says. "We have a lot of work to do before our first guests arrive in *fifteen* days." A second passes, and Jemma glances at me and then Cricket. "Look, ladies," she says. "I have one rule, and it's pretty simple: honesty."

*Oh God.*

"Honesty is the number one thing for me," says Jemma, and her face is really serious. "I'm always going to be honest with you, and I expect the same in return. I'm inviting you into our home, and we're going to need to trust each other. If my gut tells me you aren't a good fit, I have absolutely no problem sending you back on the next boat out." Jemma looks at me, then at Cricket. "Understood?"

"Yes, of course," says Cricket, nodding.

Jemma turns to me. "Liv?"

There is a silence.

Everyone is looking at me.

For half a second, I stand before the three of them and try to picture what would happen if I just tell the truth. But it's just so much easier to go along. I do what I'm good at: pretend to be someone I'm not.

"Oh yeah, totally!" I say, and smile right at Jemma as if I'm not already breaking her one and only rule.

# 28

Three seconds after I have flat-out lied to everyone, two huge dogs that look more like wolves come bounding down the cliffside steps. They race across the white-sand beach and head down the dock, straight for me! Just as they're about to jump up and knock me over, Jemma steps between me and the two dogs.

She's like some sort of dog whisperer or something. Without her even speaking a word, both dogs screech to a stop. They go from about to pounce on me and pin me down to immediately sitting on their butts, panting, looking up at Jemma, waiting for her next command.

I watch Jemma. Her whole face relaxes. "What good pups you are," she says, kneeling and rubbing the undersides of both dogs. She looks at me and Cricket. "Sorry about that. These two go totally insane with new people, don't you?" she says, turning back to the dogs and using both her hands now to smooth back the fur between their ears.

To be honest, it's hard to pay attention to anything right now. I can't stop staring at Jemma! It's like she's almost an identical version of Sunny. She even has the same little three birds tattooed behind her right ear. It's tiny, but I spot it when the dogs are giving her kisses. And Jemma's eyes, the way she has this intense look? It's just the same with Sunny. This is so crazy! I've never felt this feeling of being like, *related* to someone before.

I snap out of it when Till's arm brushes against me as he crouches down. Both dogs roll on their backs, and Till scratches their tummies.

Everyone is loving on the dogs. But I'm standing here on the dock, staring at Till. He's that kind of lanky-strong where you can see every muscle and every rib. Between his curls, his biceps, and his deeply tanned skin, he looks a little like a pro surfer or a kid who can easily drop down onto the dock and crank out a hundred push-ups.

Cricket has already taken off her pack and drops to her knees. "Hey, puppies!" she says as she rubs their tummies. She looks at Till. "They're beautiful. Are they huskies?"

"They're rescues," Till answers. "They're brother and sister. They were seven weeks old when we got them. Probably a little bit of husky, mostly malamute, and a little bit of Aussie cattle dog." Till grins. "Maybe some coyote and some wolf."

I go, "Wolf?" and back away a little, and as I do, the big fluffy white one suddenly flips over and stands up, then shoves her nose right in between my legs.

"Uh," I say. I try not to sound freaked out.

"It's okay," Jemma says. "She's just saying hi." She smiles. "She likes you, Liv!"

Till nods. "Yeah, that's crazy. I've never seen her do that before. There must be something familiar about you," he says matter-of-factly. "This one here is Lulu the Dragon Slayer"—Till gives the white fluffy one at my feet a scratch, then nods to the dark furry one—"and that big guy is Zeus." He nuzzles Lulu's head. "You're my best friend, aren't you," he says, and laughs as the big white dog gives him slobbery kisses.

Suddenly, Zeus's and Lulu's ears perk straight up. They both come to attention, get real still, then wheel around and take off toward the beach.

"Hey, I've got some work to do," Jemma tells us. "Tillman is going to show you around." She looks at Till. "Honey, you know the trunk up in the—"

"Got it," he says, somehow understanding what Jemma is talking about.

"You two get settled." Jemma takes a step back. "We'll talk more at dinner," she says, then turns and walks toward the beach. Zeus and Lulu immediately bound back to Jemma's side, and I watch as the three of them spring up the steps to the lodge.

Cricket, Till, and I stand together on the dock. The wind is blowing and I lift my arms and take my ponytail out. Now that my hair is free, it feels so good. I push it away from my eyes. I smile at Till, and he smiles back. I'm trying not to stare at him, but it's hard not to. I just keep scanning his face. I'm like, *Do we have the same eyes? The same nose?*

Cricket suddenly turns to Till and goes, "Dang! Your mom is one tough lady! I went full fangirl when she shook my hand! I totally froze."

"Same," I say, letting out a nervous laugh.

"Yeah," Till says, and he looks proud. "She's pretty incredible. I know she's a little bit strict but"—he gives his shoulders a shrug—"as long as you follow the rules, there's nothing to worry about."

# 29

I follow behind Till as he steps up and onto the single dock that runs along the front of the cabins. The docks are interconnected. They are all made of the same smooth, weathered wooden planks. We walk, the three of us. The seabirds soaring over the bay. The breeze. There are two small boats tied up to the dock. One is a workboat with orange-rubber sides and two big engines on the back. It looks like it goes superfast. ZODIAC is written on the side. It's rugged, secured to the dock with ropes, looped around cleats. The other boat is tied up too. It's sturdier and looks like it's a fishing boat.

Till stops and points to the smaller boat, the bright orange one with the rubber sides. "This is our Zodiac," he says. "The Zodiac is mostly a workboat for runabouts, rescues, that kind of thing. It's superlight and bouncy, twin engines in the back, superfast." He turns to the bigger boat. "This one is our fishing charter. It's thirty-five years old. We take real good care of it."

"Very cool," Cricket says.

I nod and look all around.

Everything is sparkling clean.

Orderly.

Cared for and put away, in place.

The dock is scrubbed, spotless. The ropes and lines are tightly coiled and hung on hooks, no kinks, no knots. I run my hand along the rope on a railing. It feels good against my fingers.

Yes, I am still in shock. My eyes move up toward the mountains surrounding us, then back to the beach and up to the lodge. And just to the left of the cabins: the waterfall plunging off the cliff. Every direction I look is like a photograph from a magazine. And the cabins! They're like life-size dollhouses, made of golden-yellow wood. Each one has its own small front porch facing the water.

Till stops at the first cabin. "Want a peek?" he asks, placing his hand on the wooden door and pushing it open. "They're real simple. Just one room."

He walks a few steps into the cabin. "These cabins used to be fishing shacks," he says, turning to face us. "They've been here over a hundred years." He glances around at the walls and then back at me and Cricket, standing in the doorway. "A few years back, we took them completely apart, saved what we could, and rebuilt them."

Cricket's eyes go wide. "Hold up! You *built* this?"

He nods. "We salvaged fallen trees and milled the logs into planks by hand. The pieces of wood fit together like a puzzle. No nails. Same with the lodge. It's all interlocking joints made with a mallet and a chisel."

Cricket sighs. "Whoa!"

Till smiles. "Come on in if you want."

"Are you sure?" asks Cricket, waiting at the door. "I'm pretty dirty!"

"Oh, don't worry." Till laughs. "This place is going to be mopped and scrubbed spotless by the end of the week."

Cricket slips off her pack, dropping it on the dollhouse porch. "Oh my gosh!" she says, stepping inside. "It smells like Christmas in here!"

"That's the wood," Till explains. "It's cedar and spruce."

Cricket leans forward, putting her nose to the wood-paneled

walls, and takes a big sniff. "*Mmm,*" she sighs. "Smells *so* good!"

I walk a few steps into the cabin, and right away the scent hits me. *It does smell like Christmas trees!* I scan the space. The room is kind of bare. The bed is stripped down to the mattress. But even empty . . . it just feels good in here.

Cricket drops onto the bare mattress. "That's it!" She giggles, flopping over on the bed, lying on her back. "I'm staying here forever!" she says, laughing and raising her arms in a stretch. Till laughs and I laugh too. Cricket just has this way about her, you can't help but smile.

It's silent for a few more seconds.

I sneak a glance at Till, then look away.

Cricket jumps to her feet, walks over to the big front window, and looks out at the turquoise water in the bay. Sunbeams are shining through the glass and on her face.

I look over at Till and I go, "Is this is where we're staying?"

Till's eyebrows shoot up. "Here? No." He shakes his head and the second he does, my face gets hot. "Oh yeah, duh," I quickly say, and I try to sound like I totally knew that, even though I totally *didn't* know. I have no clue.

Till is now standing just inside the open door. "The cabins are for the guests," he explains. Then his face lights up and he says, "Want to see where you guys are staying?"

"Heck yeah!" says Cricket.

Till turns to look at me. "Liv?"

I open my mouth a little, but I don't speak. I am staring at him. It's so crazy! He almost looks more like Sunny than Jemma. His hair is thick, the color of straw, and the shade of his arms and hands makes me pretty certain he spends every minute, from the second he wakes up, outside. I suddenly begin to wonder what Till's dad looks like. Or wait. Does he have a dad? Or is he like me: no dad, never had one—

"Liv?" Till repeats.

"Oh! Sorry!" I snap out of it and smile. "Yeah!" I answer. "For sure, let's go!" My answer is too loud. Awkward. Too enthusiastic. Honestly, if I'm going to pull this off, I need to start lying better and acting like I belong here and my name is Liv, and not like I just discovered that I have a family who lives in a secluded paradise!

I glance at Till again. This time I try to get into character: shoulders back, no weird long gazes! No more completely freaked out I-have-a-cousin-and-he-sort-of-looks-like-me staring! I smile at Till and he smiles at me back. He is still standing just inside the cabin's entryway. "After you," he says, extending his hand like a doorman in a fancy hotel.

I step out onto the porch with Cricket and Till.

Straight ahead, the water right off the dock shimmers in the sun, and the air is just like, cool and perfect against my face. It's so quiet and peaceful. I stand almost hypnotized by the sounds of the water rippling against the dock.

Cricket is beside me; she's already got her backpack heaved up and strapped on. She leans into me, the side of her arm touching the side of my arm, and when I turn toward her, she gives me a look, eyebrows up, like, *Can you even believe this?*

*No* is what I silently say, shaking my head back and forth in disbelief.

Meanwhile, Till is closing the door to Cabin #1, securing the latch. He glances over his shoulder at me and Cricket, and he's smiling like he has some big surprise. "You won't even believe where you guys are staying!" he tells us, spinning around and brushing past us before looking back again, eyes all shiny. "Come on!"

# 30

After we stop to check out the waterfall that spills over the top of the cliff, and after Till explains how they generate power from the falling water—"It's a Pelton wheel turbine hydropower energy system!"— and after a physics lesson that I didn't expect (the kinetic energy of the waterfall), and after Cricket fills her water bottle straight from a pipe that runs to a faucet on the dock that filters the snowmelt that rushes down the mountain—

After *all of that*—

Cricket passes me her water bottle, and I put it to my mouth and take the biggest, longest, best-tasting gulp of my life. I'm so thirsty that only half the water makes it into my mouth; the other half splashes down my chin. We stand around, passing Cricket's water bottle until it's empty, and she fills it three times. Then we set off for the place we're going to stay, which Till casually mentions is "an easy one-mile hike or so" away.

A minute later, we are walking across the beach that runs directly below the lodge. Till is a few steps ahead. I carry my flips-flops, one in each hand, and follow his footprints, sunken into the wet sand. After crossing the beach, we turn a corner and walk along the long arm of the horseshoe-shaped bay.

"We call this side of the bay the Sunshine Coast," explains Till. He is walking backward, facing us, like a tour guide. "Not all the shoreline is white sand like this. We have stretches of beach that are huge granite cliffs and giant tidal rocks." He nods over his shoulder. "Up around the point, there's a pocket of intertidal zones with these shallow pools at low tide." His eyes widen. "You can see octopi and crabs, and about a thousand other creatures. Oh, and there are some hot springs up past that too."

"Hot springs! No way!" says Cricket, walking along the beach with her huge pack strapped to her shoulders. "This place is insane!"

Just now, Zeus and Lulu appear.

We stop.

"*Ooh*, look at that face!" Cricket gives Lulu's head a scratch. "Well, hi!" she says, rubbing back her white ears.

Zeus drops a chunk of driftwood at Till's feet, and Till reaches for it, then easily hurls it far down the Sunshine Coast. Both dogs take off after it, happy as can be. While all the dog action is going on, I kind of zone out and find myself staring down the beach and taking in all these new sounds. It's like a whole different world: the water rippling onto the sand, seabirds making all sorts of squawks. It's calming. It's so different from anything or anywhere I've ever been.

"Liv," I hear Till say. "See the osprey?" He points up at the sky.

I tip my head back and look at a white bird with long, narrow, dark-brownish wings, soaring overhead. Now all three of us are paused on the beach, looking straight up at this white bird circling in the sky.

"Ospreys are really cool," Till says in a hush. "They dive right into shallow water headfirst and catch live fish right in their talons."

"Amazing!" Cricket murmurs.

"Yeah, they're raptors," Till says softly, as I follow the path of the osprey gliding over the bay. "You'll see them carrying fish," says Till, still looking up. "The females are really distinctive. They have white-breasted bellies and glowing yellow eyes."

"I've never seen an osprey up close," Cricket says, turning to me. "Have you?"

I shake my head. "Definitely no."

The three of us begin to walk again, continuing along the beach.

Till glances over at me. "Great Bear is actually a flyway for migrating birds."

I'm curious. "What's a flyway?"

Cricket laughs. "I was about to ask that too!"

"Basically, a flyway means that we're a rest stop for all the migrating birds flying over the open ocean," explains Till. "We have around a hundred and fifty species of birds. They touch down on Great Bear and refuel."

Cricket looks all around in awe. "I'm just so grateful that there are still places on earth like this."

And Till says, "Just wait," and he's got this big smile on his face. "There are a whole lot of things about this place that will surprise you."

## 31

Ten minutes in and we are a three humans, two dogs parade, walking down the narrow strip of sand called the Sunshine Coast. Zeus and Lulu are bounding just ahead of us, playing catch me if you can. We don't say much until Cricket suddenly stops. "Hey, Till," she says, "I have a question for you!"

Till goes, "Sure!"

Cricket turns and looks out into the bay. "How is the water even this color? That color blue is just totally unreal."

"It's glacial silt," answers Till, and we begin walking again. "These microscopic particles in the water that reflect the sunlight."

Cricket nods. "*Ohhh*, okay, that makes sense!" she says.

"Is it always this color?" I ask, squinting at the water.

"It changes all the time," Till goes on. "Sometimes it looks turquoise, sometimes it's like this really cool dark emerald, or even a milky green." He shrugs. "It all sort of depends on the angle of the sun."

"Wait!" Cricket says to Till. "Where do you even go to school?"

"I'm homeschooled," he answers, "but I mean, I don't have to sit in some classroom all day."

"Man!" says Cricket. "You are living the dream up here!"

Till nods up to the steep, deep green mountainside. "I'm outside every single day of the year." He grins. "One year I surfed three hundred thirty days straight, even when it was snowing or raining sideways—"

Cricket goes, "No way!"

I look over at Till and say, "Wasn't it freezing cold?"

"Oh yeah, it was on a lot of days." Till nods in the direction of the water. "It can get pretty crisp out there. But I have a wet suit." Just now Zeus appears at Till's feet, dropping the chunk of driftwood, and without missing a step, Till reaches down, grabs it, and hurls it really far. Both dogs take off racing down the Sunshine Coast. "Yeah," Till goes on, "I've paddled out in some monster waves." He pauses. "Once, when I was ten, I built a shelter on the beach right below the lodge. I slept down there for a few months."

Cricket looks over at Till. "Jemma let you do that when you were *ten*?"

"Of course," Till says, grinning. "She's the one who taught me how—climbing, surfing, exploring, building stuff . . . I can do anything I want, pretty much." Till shrugs. "I just have fun."

As we walk farther down the coast, I try to think of another question that Liv might ask, which, when you think about it, is pretty ridiculous, since I don't even know Liv! I have no idea what she'd want to know. I look over at Till and ask what I want to know. "So, what do you do for school and stuff?"

"Everything," Till answers as we walk.

I go, "Everything, like what?"

He shrugs. "Just regular stuff."

Cricket turns to Till, eyebrows up. "What *kind* of regular stuff?"

"Okay, let's see, like—" Till says, cracking a shy smile. I can tell he is not used to talking about himself. "Like, looking after the chickens and our sheep, fishing, mending, sewing, baking bread, pickling, jarring, canning, curing, cutting and hanging fish to smoke on the beach, bow-hunting and preserving meat, foraging kelp, berries, and nettles, salvaging wood from fallen logs, clearing trails, splitting and stacking firewood"—Till laughs softly—"anything, really. I guess I do whatever we need."

Cricket and I look at each other in shock. I've never in my life met a kid my age who does stuff like this.

"Wait," I say, as we ramble down the beach. "Do you just find all your food here?"

"Oh yeah! You'll *never* starve here," Till says to me. "Like, if the world is a mess and you needed a place to survive, this would be the place. There's so much you can forage and eat. It's all right here—you just have to know where to look. Fish, salmon eggs, oysters, prawns and crabs, sea urchins, barnacles, wild berries you can pick straight from the bush, stuff like that. Nature gives us everything."

"So wait," Cricket says, looking over at Till. "Is this whole island yours? Like, do you own it? Does anyone else live here?"

Till thinks for a moment as we walk. "This place doesn't really *belong* to us," he answers. "We share it."

I look over at Till. "You do?" I ask. "With who?"

Till uses his fingers and begins to count off: "Wolves, bears, wolverines, deer, eagles"—he moves to his left hand—"streams, rivers, glacial lakes, beaches, mudflats, the ocean . . . different kinds of plants"—he drops both hands—"the old-growth forest, birds, marine mammals, fish, killer whales—you know, black-and-white orcas with a big dorsal fin." Till takes a breath. "We are a habitat for so many wild species. You'll see all sorts of living creatures here."

"Dang!" says Cricket. "This is the best classroom in the world!"

But me, I just look over at Till and I go, "Wait. Did you say *bears*?!"

# 32

**Y**es. That's *my* question. *Bears?!*

I know the place is called Great *Bear* Island, but . . . honestly, until right now it didn't occur to me that there are real live BEARS here. I stop on the beach and look at Till like, *Are you serious?*

"Oh yeah. They're here," says Till, and the look on his face is *not* a joking one. "You'll see bears mostly early in the morning up in the rivers, or at dead low tides on the beach, eating the crabs under the rocks." He turns to me. "You have the tide charts that came with your packet, right?"

I'm just like, *Packet? Oh crap.* "Oh," I stall. "They were in my lost luggage," I say, lying.

Cricket glances over at me. "I've got you, Liv. We can totally share mine."

As we walk, Till nods toward the water. "The bay is mostly protected, but outside the bay along the coast, the waves will come rushing in. It happens really fast." He pauses. "You can get knocked down pretty hard. And if you get hurt here, there's nowhere to go. We're a four-hour boat ride from the nearest hospital, so just make sure you follow the rules." Till waits, then he goes, "We all look out for each other."

For the next few minutes, we walk.

No words. The ripples on the water, the seabirds, and the wind are the ones who do all the talking. I am walking along the beach carrying my flip-flops, one in each hand, thinking how good my toes feel in the sand, and how easy it feels to be with Till. To be with both of them, and then I look up and squint through the sun and—

"Whoa," I say barely out loud.

I'm looking straight ahead, and I now see where we're going! It's right on the water. Rising from the last little strip of land on the Sunshine Coast—a very tall tower made entirely of wood. As soon as my eyes pass on this breaking news to my brain, Cricket stops dead in her tracks and blurts out exactly what I'm thinking, which is—

"*This* is where we're staying?!" Only, she doesn't wait for Till to answer. She throws her arms back, slips her backpack off and lets it drop behind her right on the beach, and takes off running toward the tower, Zeus and Lulu chasing her. Her hat flies off, her hair whips up behind her. And about ten steps in, she stops and spins around. She is laughing pretty hard, probably because the dogs are now jumping up on her, putting their paws all over her jeans, barking like crazy. "Oh my gosh, Liv!!!" she says. She's beaming. "We're living in a light-house!"

## 33

The lighthouse sits at the tip of the Sunshine Coast, overlooking the entrance to the bay: set up on stilts, suspended above the water. I look straight up and I go, "How did we not see this from the ferry?"

Till laughs. "Most people don't. It's kind of hidden—the light cedar blends into the coast and the mountains and almost makes it disappear from a distance." He pauses. "That's what makes it the perfect secret lookout."

Till walks up to the huge ancient-looking barn-style door. "This is the original door. It's over a hundred years old." He leans in and places both hands on the door, then pushes, and the sliding barn door slowly rolls open, flooding the inside with sunlight.

Then—

I hear a flap, flap, flap, and within a second and a half, a flock of a gazillion shadowy birds flies out of the lighthouse and swoops right over our heads! Yeah, you are totally right if you're picturing me ducking. I mean, what's the deal with me and birds today? Cricket grabs onto my shoulder as we crouch on the ground, our arms over our heads, taking cover. Cricket looks at me and I look at her and we both crack up.

"Those are bats," Till says, stepping inside the main floor of the lighthouse. He nods up toward the massive beam across the ceiling. "They love to nest up in the rafters."

"Did you say bats?" Cricket laughs, as we step through the open doors.

"Yeah. They're cute, and really tiny," Till answers. "All sorts of creatures love it here. It's like a refuge. A few months back, there was the sweetest little barn owl hunkering down in here. We had had a long winter, fifty-something inches of rain and ice storms—it was real cold. She was soaked, and freezing, and I think she was hurt. She was super hungry. She let me walk right up to her. I brought her a mouse."

Cricket's eyes widen. "For real?"

"Yeah." Till nods. "Owls are beautiful. Their eyes are insane. And they really can turn their heads all the way around."

"Wait. Was she okay?" I ask. "Did she survive?"

"Oh yeah." Till grins. "She was just hiding out to collect herself. Then the next day I came back and she was just gone." He pauses. "I actually think I've spotted her a few other times."

I glance at Till. He's about as opposite as you can get from the boys at my school. I don't know how to describe it, but he's strong and gentle at the same time. I watch as he crouches and places the palm of his hand against the extra-wide wood boards that cover the floor. "Can you believe these are the original tongue-and-groove boards?" Till says. "My great-grandfather built this in—"

Cricket cuts him off. "Wait. Jemma's dad?"

"Jemma's grandpa," Till says. He stands. "My great-grandpa immigrated to Canada from Norway, grew up in Bella Coola, then settled on Great Bear. My great-grandma's side is Tsimshian."

"Amazing," says Cricket.

I look back at Till and Cricket, and I bite down hard on the inside of my cheek. What I'm thinking is, *I didn't know any of this.* And suddenly I feel mad, and I don't mean to be. Half of me wants to tell Till and Cricket who I am, and another part of me just wants to cry, like, *Why didn't Sunny tell me any of this?* What I do is: I don't do anything. I stand here in the middle of my family's lighthouse and shove my hands in my pockets and look away.

Cricket leans in. "You okay?" she whispers.

I lie. "Yeah, totally," I say, and try to get myself back in Liv mode again.

Till is still showing us around the ground floor of the lighthouse. "This whole structure is yellow cedar from right up in the mountains. My great-grandpa built this place first, before the lodge." Till runs his hand flat along a wooden beam. "This place is rock solid. It's a fortress." He shakes his head. "The joinery is all hand-carved, these beams are all locked into place, superstrong." He tips his head and stares up at the bare rafters. "It just blows me away to realize that one man built all this." Till looks back at us. "It really makes me stop and think." He waits. "Everything was done by hand. No machines. Cut the wood. Dried it. Milled it. He hand-cut and shaped the joints using only a chisel or maybe an axe, and it all somehow fit together perfectly—right down to the millimeter. And it's still here."

The three of us stand in the middle of the floor, and we are still. It's quiet. The path of the sun shifts and a breeze blows in through the open sliding door. I take another step in and glance around. The floor is weathered and stained but swept. The shelves are stacked and organized. The only things on the walls are colorful paper maps of the mountains pinned up.

Zeus and Lulu are now stretched out just inside the big open door, lounging beside each other, resting in the warm sunlight.

## 34

"**S**o," Till starts, and walks to the wall of shelves, "this is where we store most of our safety gear. We don't have a lot; we try to keep it simple, just what we need." He looks up. "Over here we've got climbing harnesses, carabiners, belays, pulleys. This is all rope, straps and webbing, cords, throw lines, dry suits, helmets. This stuff over here—this is like, odds and ends, a signal whistle—which is great if you're ever in trouble. This right here is an expedition medical kit, bear spray, climbing gloves, headlamps. Here's a bunch of sunglasses guests left behind. Some of them are pretty cool. Here," he says, catching my eye and handing me a pair.

I take the big purple sunglasses from his hand and put them on. They are way nicer than any sunglasses I've ever worn. I turn to Cricket. "Too much?" I joke.

"No, just right." Cricket giggles. "One hundred percent."

We all laugh, and I push the bright purple oversized sunglasses up so they're resting on my head.

"Check *this* out!" Till moves across the room and removes a cloth tarp. "This was my dad's dirt bike. It's superfast. It's not new or anything, but it's all original. I've been rebuilding it. I can't wait to get this out on the trails. It just needs a few odds and ends. It's running a two hundred fifty two-stroke, race suspension, and these super-knobby tires."

"Oh, heck yes," says Cricket. "I need this in my life!"

I nod like I care about the bike, but really, I'm studying Till's face and wondering if I'll meet his dad.

"Over here." Till takes a few more steps. "We just rebuilt these shelves. We try to keep everything clean and easy to reach so you can just grab and go: life jackets, dry bags for river trips. Oh, check this out—this is a super-nice setup." Till is looking at three long surfboards resting on wooden brackets. "My uncle carved those boards. They're super light—they're made from red cedar."

I'm like, "Wait. Uncle?" I can't help it; it just comes out.

Till reaches for the lowest board and dusts something off with his fingers. "Yeah," he goes on, "he's a master woodworker. His grandpa taught him and he's teaching me." Now Till looks up. "He can make *anything*—houses, furniture, and"—Till steps to the right of the stacked surfboards and carefully removes a tarp revealing a wooden boat, balancing on two sawhorses—"he carved this dugout canoe with an axe and traditional old hand tools. It used to be a tree."

"That's amazing!" Cricket says.

"I know, right?" Till's eyes light up. "My uncle's one of those guys who can basically do anything. Surf. Catch his own dinner. Build his own house. Fix anything . . . He knows the island better than anyone." Till pauses. "I've learned so much from him," he goes on. "How to fish, shoot a bow, handle a knife. He's pretty much taught me everything— we've been through a lot together. I look up to him a lot."

Cricket runs a single finger along the side of the carved-out wooden canoe. "It's gorgeous. Do you ever take it out?"

"Not really," answers Till. "My uncle hasn't touched it since he's been back."

"Back from where?" I ask.

"Navy," Till replies. "He got back like, a year ago." He pauses. "He was a helicopter pilot—he did a lot of secret rescue missions and whatnot."

I swallow.

Cricket says, "Wow, that's intense."

"Yeah." Till nods and walks a few feet away from the canoe.

We are all silent for a few long seconds. Then I can't help myself. "Wait, Till," I begin, and he looks back. "Is your uncle on your mom's side or your dad's?"

"My mom's," Till says.

And I go, "Your mom has a younger brother?" which is pretty dumb since he just said told me that.

Now Till kind of laughs. "Yeah." He waits, then he goes, "Why?"

"Oh! No reason," I lie. But inside, my head is heating up: *I didn't even know I had an uncle!* I look over at Till. I can't stop now. "What about your dad?"

Till's face suddenly changes, and the second I see that, I wish I could take my question back. "He died."

"Oh, Till, I'm so sorry," Cricket says softly.

"Yeah," I barely say out loud.

"It's fine," Till says, shrugging it off the way people do when they don't want you to feel bad for what you just said. I do. I do feel bad. I really wish I hadn't asked him that. And for a long, awkward minute, it's really quiet.

"Guys!" Cricket breaks the silence. "I have a *very* serious question," she begins, and there is a cheerfulness to her voice that instantly lifts the mood.

She looks all around the barnlike space, the shelves, the gear. The bare wood floor. Then turns to Till and says, "So are we sleeping down here, or is there some kind of top-secret room to be revealed?"

# 35

A second later, Till reaches up, undoes a lever rigged to a beam, and a single heavy-duty rope drops down from a secret trapdoor in the ceiling of the lighthouse's first floor. I tip my head back and look all the way up. "It's like a fireman's pole!"

"No way!" Cricket says, staring straight up. "There really is a secret room?"

"Pretty fun, right?" says Till, grinning. Then he goes, "Who wants to go first?"

Cricket laughs. "Wait, for real? Is this the only way up?"

But me? I am already tossing my flip-flops onto the floor. It's like that *American Ninja Warrior* show on TV, but in real life! I reach up and grip onto the rope and I go for it!

"Yes, Liv!" cheers Cricket.

"Nice, Liv!" Till calls up. Both of them are standing below, heads tipped back, watching me slowly work myself up the rope like an inchworm.

I reach, pull, then repeat.

I'm definitely feeling it. My arms are burning, my shoulders are smoked. I rest halfway up, gripping my feet to a knot, and the rope in both my hands. I'm ten feet above the ground. I'm breathing pretty hard, and I glance down at Cricket and Till below.

"You're crushing it!" Cricket hollers up.

"You're flyin'!" Till cheers.

I take a deep breath, and in one more big push, I reach up and pull myself up headfirst through the secret open hatch, where I sit on the edge of a worn wooden floor. My heart is pounding, and I'm out of breath. I immediately smile down at Cricket. "You got this," I call out.

"Jeez Louise, Liv," Cricket laughs. "You made it look easy!" She steps up to the rope. "Here goes!" she says, and slowly—with one loud "Holy smokes, this is hard!"—Cricket works her way up. Reaching high, gripping the rope with her thighs and feet, the same inchworm style: reach, pull, repeat.

At the top, once she's safe and sitting beside me, we bump fists. "Crushed it," I tell her, scooching over.

The two of us dangle our bare feet down the open hatch and watch Till make quick work of the rope, methodically hauling himself all the way to the top using his muscular shoulders and five big pulls. And together we all move to our feet and—

"OH MY GOSH!!!!!!"

# 36

**W**ait. It's more like:

A real slow, "*Oh—my—gooooooshhhhh!!*" Also, Cricket grabs my arm.

I'm just staring straight ahead, jaw dropped.

We are standing on an old, honey-colored wood floor in the brightest, sunniest, coziest room on the top floor of the lighthouse.

"So this is it," Till says proudly.

I look at him, his eyes shining. "Are we really staying here?" I ask.

"Yeah," he says, and grins.

"It's *so* beautiful!" Cricket gasps.

Pretty sure my mouth is still dropped open as I step forward and look all around. It is like a bird's nest suspended in a tower in the sky or a really high tree house in the tallest tree alive! The huge windows on all four sides of the room each frame a different view: the beach, the coastline, the mountains, the bay, and way out, miles and miles of ocean. And the smell of the wood! I take a big sniff. As of right this second, it's my new favorite scent! It's like, sea, air, sun, and cedar.

The upstairs of the lighthouse is one room just big enough for two single beds, one on each side. There's one tall, empty bookcase built into the wall, and in a corner of the room sits a sun-faded storage chest made out of wood. That's it. Nothing else is in here.

Cricket tips her head back and gazes up at the chunky wood beams that line the ceiling. "This place is absolutely perfect!" she says. Then she walks over to the wall of windows with the view of the bay. "There's so much light!"

"It's pretty simple," Till tells us. He has his hands in his pockets. "But it's cozy, right?"

"Totally." I nod.

"It's so zen up here!" Cricket shakes her head in disbelief.

"I know it's not exactly luxurious," Till tells us, sounding almost apologetic. He turns to look at me. "It's probably not as nice as what you're used to, but"—his eyes get wide—"you can hear the ocean waves and you can look out the windows and see the stars from your bed. And nothing can get up here—not even bears." He moves back to the open secret trapdoor entrance and closes the hatch. "Not even any people, if you pull the rope up and close the hatch."

For a second or two, we all are quiet.

Till walks over to the window that faces the bay. "Ever since I was a little kid, I've loved climbing up here and hiding out." He turns around and looks at me and Cricket. "Honestly, I was kind of surprised when my mom asked me to get the lighthouse ready for you two. This is the first time she's had *anyone* stay up here. *Ever.*" He shrugs and says, "I think it's because the lighthouse has some special sentimental value."

Cricket goes, "What do you mean?"

"Oh, uh—" Till pauses. "My mom and her sister used to stay up here summers when they were our age."

Up until this second, I have been looking out the window, staring down at the crazy-blue water in the bay, but I suddenly whip around and look directly at Till. "Wait. What?" I say, sounding panicked. Then I catch myself and try to make my voice cheerful and Liv-like. I smile at Till and casually say, "Jemma has a sister?"

"Yeah, a younger sister," Till answers very matter-of-factly. He takes a few steps and pulls the old wooden trunk from the corner of the room. Then he glances up. "This is actually her stuff."

I go, "Wait. You mean, Jemma's sister's stuff?" and as I say it, my heart begins to pound really fast.

"Yeah," he says. "I think it's mostly clothes, maybe some boots and whatnot." He nods to me. "This is what Jemma wanted me to show you. She says a lot of this stuff might fit you, so have at it."

I swallow hard. I try and push away the fact that I'm freaking out . . . I mean, *I'm looking at a wooden chest filled with Sunny's old clothes!*

Till smiles at me. "Take anything you want, Liv. Just, like—" He stops.

I look back at him like, *What?*

And Till says, "Maybe don't tell Jemma that I told you about her sister."

"Why?" I say quickly.

Till shrugs. "She doesn't like to talk about her. She hasn't even seen her in like, thirteen years."

"Thirteen years?" I repeat, and as I do, I do the math in my head. It's not that hard. Sunny must have left Great Bear the same year she had me.

"Oh," says Cricket. "That's so sad."

"Yeah," Till says, and now he looks back at Cricket, then me, and he goes, "Nobody even knows where she is."

## 37

This is blowing my mind right now, okay? Out of nowhere this panicky feeling hits me, and my head is hot and sweaty. I'm dizzy. I lean up against the wood-paneled wall and slide down all the way until my butt is on the floor.

Till rushes over. "You okay?" he asks, crouching down.

"Yeah," I lie. My stomach is all twisted up. It might be because I haven't had anything to eat, but mostly I'm pretty sure it's because everywhere I look in here, I am suddenly overwhelmed with thoughts of Sunny. I glance at the colorful quilts and sheets, neatly folded and stacked atop pillows on the two unmade beds, and wonder if those are the same sheets and quilts that Sunny used. My hands are trembling a little bit.

I bite my bottom lip.

Cricket is crouched in front of me beside Till, looking alarmed. "Whoa, Liv," she says, "are you okay? Do you need some water?" Before I can answer, she jumps up. "My water bottle is in my pack. Hold on!" she says, and then next thing I know I raise my head and look over and Cricket is carefully lowering herself down the rope. "I'll be right back!"

Now, for the first time, I'm alone with Till.

I'm still on the floor. I pull my knees to my chest.

Till sits down on the edge of the bed across from me.

We sit silently.

I don't speak.

I keep my head on my knees.

When I glance up, Till gives me a quiet smile. "Long day?"

I nod, trying to force a halfway decent Liv-like smile back.

Till goes, "A lot of travel, huh?"

"Yeah," I manage, and nod again.

Then I watch Till's eyes travel down to the scabbing cut on the inside of my arm. "Ohhh," he says, looking a little concerned. "Battle scars?"

"Something like that," I answer, and try not to think about the trailer, and how I had to break in, and everything I've done and how much I've already lied.

It's quiet. Then Till asks, "So where are you from?"

"Oh, um—" I stop. My heart begins to race. I can feel the blood rush to my face. *Get it together,* I tell myself. *Be like LIV!* I look at him and I go, "I'm not from *anywhere* like this." Then, to eliminate all future questions that I will most likely answer wrong, I lower my head and rest my forehead on my knees and I just don't speak.

It's quiet again.

Until—"I'd have a hard time being in a city," Till says. "I'd miss the openness. The ocean, the salt water on my face, the mountains."

I glance up.

"I wouldn't trade anything in the world for living here," he says. "It's tough sometimes"—he pauses, and his eyes fill with light—"but it's totally free."

I look at my cousin, who doesn't have any idea at all that he's even my cousin. He just has this quiet confidence that I'm not used to. He's so much different from any boy I've ever met. He's like, wild, he has a ruggedness, with his folding knife and insane blond curls. The only reason I'm staring at him like this is that he looks *a lot* like me. I'm not even kidding. When I look at him, it's kind of like looking at my own eyes. And yes, it's *super* weird!

Then, out of nowhere, the quiet is broken.

"A little help!" I hear Cricket yelling.

It sounds like she's in trouble.

# 38

False alarm. She needs help getting her backpack up the rope. Till lies flat on the floor and reaches down the open hatch. "Got it," he says, easily hauling up Cricket's heavy pack. Next, he gives Cricket a hand as she pushes herself up and stands. The three of us are together again. I am still sitting on the floor. The two of them are standing over me. Cricket has her hands planted on her knees. "That rope, though," she says, and laughs. I look up. Her cheeks are rosy and her black trucker hat with the blue I'M ACTUALLY A MERMAID patch is back on. Her long, dark-reddish hair is hanging down.

She smiles at me. "Dude, we are going to be jacked by the end of the summer!" Then she sits down beside me on the floor. Her back to the wall, her shoulder smooshed into my shoulder. "Here you go, lady," she says, passing me her water bottle.

"Thanks," I say, and I bring the water bottle to my mouth. I take one big swig and then another. The water from the waterfall is still cold, and it tastes really, really good. I take another sip. I smile back at Cricket because I can see her through the clear water bottle. Her eyes are beaming and the tiny little turquoise gem in her nose is sparkling. She is easily the friendliest, most down-to-earth person that I've ever met. I pass the water back to Cricket and wipe my mouth with my dirty hand.

Now Till crouches down low so we're eye to eye. "Any better?"

"Yeah, thanks," I answer. *I do feel better.*

"Good," he says, and stands back up.

Cricket and I pass the water back and forth.

Till takes a few steps, the wood-planked floor creaking under his feet. "It's bare-bones up here. There's no electricity or running water, so when it gets dark, it's all about headlamps." He looks back at me and Cricket. "You each have a headlamp, right?"

Cricket nods. "I have two." She turns her face to me. "I'll give one to you."

"Oh, I almost forgot." Till pushes the bookcase, and it rolls, revealing an open door. "We call this a 'loo with a view'!"

"Are you kidding me right now, a hideaway bathroom?!" Cricket shakes her head. "That's it," she says. "This place is legit a dream. I'm never leaving!"

Till laughs. "It's a little tight in there—but we rigged you up a bucket shower, just a pulley and rainwater collected from the roof. The water can be kind of freezing, though—sorry about that!"

"Oh, I'll be fine," I say to Till. "Trust me. A bucket shower is not a problem."

"Good," says Till, nodding. "Oh, I need to tell you guys about the—" He stops, and I can tell by his face that whatever he has to tell us, he's a little bit embarrassed.

"The what?" Cricket asks.

"The composting toilet," he finally says, and laughs. "Always sprinkle three scoops of sawdust if you go number two."

"Sawdust, got it!" says Cricket, laughing.

Till walks over to the windows that face the bay and stands in the space between the two beds. "Each one of these windows opens, so you can get a nice little cross-breeze going." He stops and hand-cranks one of the windows open; a fresh, cool breeze rushes in. "You can sleep to the sound of the ocean at night, and up here, you get the sunset *and* the sunrise."

"Love it!" says Cricket, and she stands up, and I do too. We walk over to join Till at the windows. I'm on one side of Till, Cricket's on the other. "You can see the mountains, the bay, and the lodge." Till points. "Right up there. See?"

I look out at the bay and the beach and the dollhouse cabins and the fairy-tale lodge perched on the cliff.

"The water directly below us is really deep, with a sandy bottom." Till turns to glance at me, then looks back out. "Great Bear is a sheltered cove, so it's great for swimming. Just don't swim past that big rock." He sets the tip of his finger against the glass. "See it?" he says. "That's Turtle Rock. It's a marker—don't swim past that. *Ever.*"

"Got it," says Cricket.

I nod as I look out at the enormous rock, which really does look like a gigantic sleeping turtle's back, sticking out of the see-through water.

Till glances at me. "And if you're brave, there's a spot to jump off, and it's way deep, you'll never even touch the bottom."

Cricket asks, "Jump off the lighthouse, you mean?"

"I'll let you guys find it." Till grins like he has some really fun secret. "Just something my mom and her sister rigged up when they were our age.

My throat tightens.

No one says a word.

Till nods toward the open trapdoor. "Hey, so—I better go and check on Zeus and Lulu and feed 'em." He turns and walks to the open hatch in the floor. Just as he reaches for the rope, Till looks back at me and says, "Liv, I'm *really* glad you changed your mind."

"Oh, uh—" I fumble. I'm not used to going by Liv, since it's not my name! "Me too," I tell him, and nod too much.

"Me too!" Cricket sings, and slings her arm around my shoulder and pulls me toward her.

It's quiet for a sec.

Cricket and I are standing here smiling at Till the way you do when you're trying not to crack up, when you're nervous and more tired than ever. We watch Till lower himself grip by grip down the rope until we cannot see his thick blond curls. Then, finally, we both topple onto our beds, into a fit of giggles.

# 39

It's only been a minute since Till left, and Cricket goes, "That kid has a giant crush on you, Liv!"

"What? No way!" I say, and I am shaking my head back and forth. Cricket has no idea that Till is my *cousin*! But then again, neither does Till! *Oh my gosh. What have I gotten myself into?* I honestly have no clue what's going to happen or what I'm doing.

"He totally does!" Cricket teases.

"No!" I say again, shaking my head.

"Yeah, he does," Cricket laughs.

"Noooooo," I repeat. "Just no. No way," I say pretty clearly, and laugh. I am now blushing. I flop over face-first on my bed. My bed is the one that's pushed up next to the bay-side windows, farthest from the hatch and rope. Cricket's is on the wall with the windows that look out at the mountains, the Sunshine Coast, and the beach below the lodge.

"I get it," says Cricket. "Let's have a summer of self-care!"

"That sounds good," I say, even though I'm not sure what she means. I've been taking care of myself for a long time.

"Lodge hands," Cricket says, stretching her arm out across the space between the two beds.

"Lodge hands," I repeat, reaching with my fist. Our knuckles knock.

Cricket sighs. "Just for the record, though, Till is such a sweetheart. He's so respectful and smart as heck! And those curls? Dang, he's cute!"

I laugh. "Maybe *you* have a crush on him," I tease.

"NO!" she giggles. "But he is a really good guy, right?"

"Yeah."

More quiet.

Then: "Liv?"

"Yes?" I let out a soft laugh.

"This is going to sound super random and weird," she says.

I look over at her and go, "What?"

"You and Till—"

"Stop!"

"No, not that," she laughs. "It's that—okay, this is going to sound crazy, but you really kind of look a lot alike!"

"What? No!" I blurt out.

Her eyes get wide. "You so do! For real! I was staring at you both when you were standing next to each other."

I don't say anything. I turn my head so I'm smooshed against the mattress. Then I peek out and glance over at her and try to laugh it off.

"No, really, Liv." Cricket is not giving up. "You're both blondies—the freckles, the high cheekbones, and you both have those wild blue eyes. It's true!"

I am over here, shaking my head back and forth into my mattress. But to be honest, some part of me is glad Cricket tells me this. Till and I do look alike. A lot alike. I've never felt that before with anyone besides Sunny. It's pretty cool to have a cousin and an aunt . . . to have a family, even if they don't know who I am. It feels like proof . . . that I'm from someplace real and good.

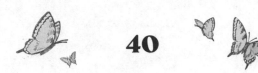

# 40

"**O**kay, I get it!" Cricket laughs, and reaches across the space between our two beds for another fist bump. "Fries over guys, right?"

I reach and bump my knuckles with hers. "Fries over guys," I repeat, laughing because I'm really not sure what *Fries over guys* even means. I'm thirteen and Cricket is seventeen—when it comes to boys, I'm pretty sure she knows a lot more than I do. Since I know pretty much exactly: *nothing*.

Cricket looks over at me. "Till is such a gentleman, just the way he carries himself, you know? You can tell he's been raised really well," she says. "I feel bad about his dad, though, don't you?"

"Yeah," I say.

Then Cricket goes, "Wait. Liv? Your parents are still together, right?"

Oh God. "Um, uh-huh." I take a guess and hope I'm right about what this girl Liv's life is even like.

Cricket rolls onto her back and looks up. "I can't imagine growing up without my mom or dad."

I say nothing.

More silence.

Then she goes, "So how old do you think Till is?"

"Fourteen or maybe fifteen?" I say, my voice cracking.

"Really? I think he's older. He's really different from most guys, right? Just like, how he handles himself."

"I guess," I say.

"Probably growing up here makes you awesome like that," Cricket says. There is silence for a while.

"Liv?"

"Yeah?" I peek over at Cricket.

She is smiling at me. "Doesn't it feel like we've known each other for a zillion years and also, random but . . . doesn't it feel like we're living in a tree house, only it's not a tree?"

"Yes, and yes," I say, and let out a soft laugh.

There's another long, quiet moment where the breeze blows through across the room and sunlight floods the entire space. Cricket stretches out on her bed. I glance over at her. She is lying on her side with one arm tucked underneath her head. She's wearing just her T-shirt and jeans, no socks. Her sandals are kicked off and on the floor. Her hat is off and her hair is tumbled all around her head. "You don't need much more than this, right?" she says softly.

"Yeah," I say.

There is another minute or two of dreamy-cool-breeze quiet. I turn over and lie on my side and face the windows that look out at the bay. I listen to the faint sounds of far-off waves. Birds chirping and calling. The sun feels so good. And slowly, all the lies I've told today, and all my worries about Sunny and the police, just sort of drop away. What is going through my mind right now is *This bed is seriously the most comfy thing that I have ever felt.* And I'm suddenly so tired. I reach up and rub my eyes. Then I flop over on my stomach and lie flat. The mattress smells musty, like nobody has slept here in a really long time. It's very soft. And it's clean. And it's a *bed*—not a scratchy stupid couch in a trailer. Yesterday I was in Clarksville, hiding behind a locked door from Ms. Martinez and the social worker. Now I'm in a lighthouse and I'm lying on a bed that's mine . . . a bed pushed up next to a wall of windows that overlook the most beautiful water I have ever seen in my life! So I'm sure you can picture me, lying here, and how my face is mashed into the mattress and how I am smiling pretty big.

Then I close my eyes.

## 41

I thought I was gonna have a really good nap!

Didn't you?

But no.

Five minutes later, Cricket's up on her feet, lifting one end of the wooden trunk and pulling it across the wood floor toward our beds.

"Do you think Till's Viking great-grandpa made this too?" Before I can answer, Cricket holds up her finger as if to say, *One sec*, and moves quickly to the bathroom. "I have to pee!"

I turn my face back into the musty mattress and laugh and listen to the secret-bookshelf passageway to our bathroom roll open, then roll shut.

Then I sit up.

I throw my feet with my dirt-crusted toes on the floor and glance at the handmade wooden trunk. *I have a great-grandpa*, I think to myself, and I smile like crazy. I've always wondered about all of this.

"Oh my gosh, Liv!" Cricket hollers from the hidden bathroom. "This toilet has an insane view!" she says, and laughs.

There is quiet for a second. Then I can hear a tinkle, then quiet again until Cricket hollers out, "No sawdust unless it's number two, right?"

"I think so," I say, laughing again.

In a minute, Cricket appears. Her hair is tied up in a messy bun. She tucks a loose wavy strand behind her ear and plops down onto her bed across from me. "Come on, girl, open it!" she giggles. Her eyes are all sparkly, and her smile is wide. "Let's see your loot!"

I lean over toward the wooden trunk, wedged in between Cricket's bed and mine. Then I reach down, flip the latch, and open it.

## 42

Ten minutes later, Sunny's old clothes are piling up on my bed.

So far, my haul:

—two bras, one light blue, one white
—undies and a bunch of socks
—a big hand-knit fuzzy sweater
—cutoff shorts
—a pair of jeans with hand-sewn patches on the knees
—three faded T-shirts

And that's not all. "Ooh, a summer wettie!" Cricket says, holding up a wet suit. "Jemma's sister was a shredder!"

I'm like, "Shredder?"

"Yeah." She hands the wet suit to me. "You know—a ripper, a wave crusher!"

I'm still, like, *Um . . . ?*

"A surfer!" says Cricket with a laugh. "I think that's going to fit you," she tells me. "Hold it up!"

I stand and hold the wet suit in front of me. It's all black and made of soft, bendy rubber that covers your arms and legs and chest, and it has hot-pink piping down each arm.

"Oh yeah!" Cricket says. "Girl, you are hooked up!"

I set Sunny's wet suit down on my bed and dig into the trunk and pull out a sun hat made of straw with a big, wide brim. I put it on my head.

"YESSS!!" Cricket laughs. "Straight chillin'!"

I keep the hat on my head, lean forward, and pull out a long-sleeved stretchy nylon shirt covered with orange and pink flowers. Now Cricket does the honors, reaching into the trunk and pulling out items one by one. "Watercolor paints, brushes, a mechanical pencil, an eraser—ooh, colored pencils!" Cricket holds up the pencils, which are bundled together by colors with rubber bands. Then she sets them down, reaches in, and fishes out a big, thick book with a hard black cover. The binding is reinforced with a strip of silver tape.

"What's that?" I ask, and as I do, I move, and sit right beside Cricket on her bed.

Cricket holds the big black book in her lap and places her hand on the cover. "I think it might be some sort of journal!" She gives me a look. "Should we open it?" she asks. "I mean . . . it might be a diary or, you know, have personal stuff in it. I feel slightly conflicted." She waits a second, then laughs. "On the other hand"—she glances at me—"we don't even know this girl, and anyway, she's not a girl anymore, right? She's a grown woman now!" Cricket looks at me as if she's waiting for me to decide.

What do you think I do?

## 43

I go, "Open it!"

I'm sitting next to Cricket on her bed. The afternoon sun is beaming into our little nest in the sky, and Cricket glances at me with a twinkle in her eyes. "Okay, here we go," she says, building the suspense, and then the cover of Sunny's journal cracks as she opens it.

We are both a little bit speechless at what we see: the first few pages are filled with illustrations, and they're *really* good: wildflowers, trees, tree bark, mushrooms, animals, birds, insects, beaches. Some in watercolor, some in colored pencils—all on the same smooth, heavyweight white paper. A few things are glued or taped right into the book: pressed flowers, actual feathers from birds, scraps of paper with bark rubbings.

"This is unbelievable," Cricket says, as she slowly turns each page. "Look at these handwritten notes in the margins. It's kind of like we unearthed a scientific journal, right? I actually did one of those in Earth Science in eighth grade." She glances over at me. "Didn't you?"

"Oh, um—yeah," I lie. *I haven't been in eighth grade yet.*

"Also, think about it." Cricket stops as if she's just realizing something. She looks up and turns to me. "Whoever this chick, Jemma's sister, is—like, when she did all this, when she made this journal, she was probably our age, right?"

I shrug. "I guess."

"I mean, there were no phones with cameras then," Cricket says, as she looks back down at Sunny's watercolor sketches. "If she had a phone, maybe we wouldn't have this. Like, it would be on

Instagram . . ." Her voice trails off, and she carefully turns to the next page. "I *love* this girl's handwriting!"

Now I let out a small laugh. I know that handwriting. It's Sunny's. There's no doubt in my mind: I've forged her signature on school forms a thousand times. I stare at the pictures and just like, shake my head. I had no idea that Sunny liked to draw or paint or had any interest in any of this stuff.

"I'm kind of relieved," Cricket says as she studies a page of butterfly illustrations.

I go, "What do you mean?"

"Oh, just that there're no deep dark secrets in here." She turns to face me. "I would have felt super guilty reading someone's diary!"

"Yeah," I lie. I would have felt *zero* percent guilty if this journal could somehow tell me why Sunny would ever want to leave Great Bear, and also what happened between her and Jemma, and why she is the way she is.

I stare down at the page.

There are no clues in here like that. Just notes in Sunny's writing that say things like, *small and furry*, with an arrow toward the yellow-orange-shaded butterfly wings. Cricket turns to the next page, labeled *Treasure Beach* in bold block letters. Underneath are notes on the changing tides and illustrations of teeny tiny critters she found.

Cricket studies the page for a long time. Then she turns to me, and her face lights up. "Oh my gosh! We have to find this beach!"

I laugh and say, "Okay, that sounds pretty fun."

We both look down at Sunny's colorful painted illustrations, labeled *anemones*, and *starfish*, and *barnacles*. There's a wrinkled ripped piece of notebook paper glued to the upper-right corner of the page. Cricket leans over, straining to figure out the smudged, hurried-looking blue script, and begins reading out loud, tracking each word with the tip of her finger. "'Today I was—'" Cricket suddenly stops. "I can't read that," she says. "Can you?"

"'South of Treasure Beach,'" I read, peering over her shoulder and easily making out Sunny's writing on the glued-in ripped strip of paper.

"South of Treasure Beach," Cricket repeats, picking right back up. *SUPER SCARY!!!!* is in all caps. Cricket stops and looks at me, like she is in suspense. It's like she's narrating a story, Sunny's story, as we sit shoulder to shoulder on a bed pushed up against windows that look out over the sea. And Cricket reads, "'Things change fast!'" She raises her eyebrows and slowly turns the page—

## 44

" 'Possible tattoo ideas,' " Cricket reads out loud, looking down at the pen-and-ink sketches—an owl, an eagle flying, a bear, a wolf, a flying fish—each with handwritten notes like, *Definitely want something like this* and *This would be cool on hip or shoulder or on the inside of wrist.*

"This is amazing," Cricket says, tapping her finger on a drawing of a lion's face. Then she says, "I wonder if she got any of these?"

I almost blurt out, *Oh, she did.* She has five tattoos: three little birds behind her ear; a lion's face and wildflowers that wrap across her shoulder; a wolf on the inside of her arm; one feather etched in black ink on her collarbone.

But I don't say any of that, obviously. What I say is, "Yeah, right? Who knows."

"Yeah," says Cricket, her eyes still fixed on the page. "I think tattoos look cool, but I don't know if they're my thing." She laughs and looks up at me. "I mean, I'm not too crazy about needles, and I'm insanely ticklish—so I'd probably be crying or laughing and wiggling around the entire time. You?"

"Me?"

"Yeah. Would you get a tattoo?"

*I think of all the times Sunny has wasted money on that kind of thing.* "Probably not," I finally say. "They're expensive."

"That's true. I never thought about that." She waits a second. Then she looks back down at Sunny's journal and turns the page. "Oh, back to nature."

Without saying another word, we flip through pages of illustrations and notes about butterfly wing patterns in neat blue ink. *Wild camouflage!* And *Cool wing eyespots.* I tilt my head sideways to read a long, neat quote Sunny wrote along the border of an entire page. I don't read it out loud, I read it in my head: *There is nothing in a caterpillar that tells you it's going to be a butterfly. —R. Buckminster Fuller.*

I don't really have the words right now to describe what it's like to sit here with Cricket pretending I don't know Sunny, pretending that I am someone else. On top of that? I am suddenly feeling kind of just—really mad. I don't even know *anything* about Sunny. I am trying to learn about my own family from sketches in a dusty old journal! It doesn't feel good. I mean, I didn't even know Sunny could draw, or paint . . . or cared one bit about butterflies—

I stare at the open book and just, like, silently shake my head. If I'm really being honest, I find myself holding my breath. Trying to keep it in . . . how mad I am right now. It doesn't even make sense to me. It's like . . . she kept so much from me.

"Oh wow!" says Cricket, stopping to admire the very last illustration before there are just a bunch of blank white pages: it's a watercolor scene of the beach and the dollhouse cabins. At the top, in Sunny's writing, is scrawled, *Work in progress.*

"So pretty," Cricket says.

I'm nodding. "Those clouds are cool," I murmur, trying not to sound mad even though my throat is tight and my right hand is clenched into a ball.

Cricket shuts the book and holds it against her chest, almost in a hug. "It's kind of wild, but . . ." She pauses and smiles. "I am so curious about Jemma's sister. I mean, this journal is amazing, right?"

I say nothing.

Cricket glances over at me and goes, "I wonder what she's doing now?"

My heart starts pounding.

Cricket goes, "I bet anything she's some kind of scientist or artist, right?"

I shrug.

"Oh! Maybe she's a botanist!" Cricket's eyes grow wider. "Or an entomologist . . . Or, like—" She stops, and now her whole face lights up. "Maybe she's a pro surfer chasing waves in the summer and a rock climber in the winter and she travels around and like, is sponsored by Patagonia or North Face and gets paid to have fun!" Now Cricket laughs. "Or," she goes on, raising an eyebrow, "maybe she's into researching climate change in the Antarctic Peninsula or something rad like that?" She looks at me. "Well," she says, "what do you think?"

"What do I think?" I say, stalling.

"Yeah, who do you think she grew up to be?"

I shrug. "Maybe she didn't become anything."

Cricket frowns. "What? No way."

"Just kidding," I say, even though I'm not. "I'm sure she turned out great," I lie. I glance across at my side of the room—the wet suit, all Sunny's old clothes—and then look up and around our adorable lighthouse hideaway. My face is hit with a cool breeze coming through the open windows, and I look over at my new best friend, who is for sure the nicest person I have ever met, and I'm thinking once again, for the zillionth time since I first saw her on the ferry, that maybe I should tell Cricket who I really am.

# 45

No. I don't tell Cricket anything about who I really am. Instead? I swallow back the very bad feeling lodged in my throat.

"Score!" Cricket says, reaching into the Viking's trunk and holding up a pair of Birks. "I have almost these exact same ones." She passes me the very same sandals I've been wanting and saving for but don't have.

"I bet Jemma's sister had them before they got so trendy and crazy expensive. I had to save up babysitting money, but it was totally worth it. They'll last forever, right?"

I nod. Sunny's old Birkenstocks have the cork footbeds and are soft brown suede with the buckled double straps. I take each one, set them down onto the floor, and slip them on. My toenails have black dirt under them. I look at Cricket. She's like, "Go ahead, try them out, walk around!"

I do, and—

"Well?" she says.

I take a few steps. "They fit!" I tell her. Inside I'm like, *This is so weird—I'm standing in Sunny's shoes.*

## 46

For the last half of Sunny's things, Cricket pulls them out and hands them to me as if it's my birthday and she's giving me gifts. She reaches into the Viking's wooden trunk and fishes Sunny's last belongings out: "And for the win, we have some big ol' rubber boots!" she says, passing them to me. "And these bad boys are the original Xtratufs! You're so dialed! These are *the* boots if you're going to be anywhere near cold water. Plus, they're kind of killer for mud boots, right?"

I take them from her hands, slip my feet out of the Birks, and pull on the tall rubber boots.

"I actually want a pair of those so bad," says Cricket, watching me as I try them on. "They're totally waterproof. They're super big in Alaska for fishing and any work by the water, on or off the boats. Do they fit?"

I stand up and wiggle my toes inside the boots and look down. They're knee-high and brown and made of flexible rubber with a yellowish cream-colored sole. I take a few steps to the far wall of windows and turn around. "They fit good."

"Duh, they're your secret mystery twin's—of course they do!" Cricket springs to her feet and walks over to me, crouching down as if she's the saleslady in a shoe store, showing me all the features. She rolls down the top of each boot until they are at my ankles.

"Primo!" she says, still kneeling, looking up at me.

I take a few more steps. "I kinda love them!" I drop back down onto Cricket's bed.

Cricket's sitting across from me on my bed. "Liv, check this out!"

Cricket holds a small folding pocketknife in her hands. She's playing with it, opening the blade and shutting it. "What a score, right? This handle looks hand-carved!" She waits. Then: "Here!" She tosses it into the air across the beds and I catch the pocketknife with both hands.

I flick it open and close the steel blade a few times. I feel it with my thumb. It's still sharp. I look up from the knife when I hear Cricket say, "WHOA. Look at this!" She is holding up a glass jar like a prize. "Sea glass galore!"

I set the knife down. We push all my new clothes over to clear a space. Then Cricket dumps the jarful of sea glass out on top of my mattress. We pick through it with this quiet awe, sorting the colors into piles:

    lavender
    light pink
    super-pretty ruby red
    turquoise
    jade
    sapphire green
    yellows
    teal

After a minute or two, Cricket says, "Whoa, look at this one." She holds a jade shard of sea glass up to the light. "Think about it. At some point, this was a bottle that someone just, like, tossed away for trash! This tiny nugget somehow made it all the way to Great Bear! Crushed by waves and sand and time. Someone threw it away, and now it's a treasure!"

I begin arranging the ocean-made sparkly glass into a winding, single train of jewels. "Maybe we can look for more!"

"YES!" Cricket says, glancing up from our pile of sea glass spread out on the mattress. "Let's find Treasure Beach!"

Five minutes later, this tired feeling hits me like a truck! Besides the sea glass, which we scoop up and put back in the glass jar, I don't bother gathering all my stuff or even pushing it out of the way. No. I just collapse straight on top of everything, facedown. One of my arms is hanging over the bed—my fingertips are skimming the worn wood floor. The emptied-out trunk is sandwiched between our two beds. My head is turned to the side so that my cheek's against the mattress, and I work to keep my eyes open as Cricket drags her heavy backpack across the floor, sits on the edge of her bed, unzips the top, and begins unpacking all her stuff. She pulls out shirts, folds them, and tucks them neatly onto the empty bookcase next to Sunny's thick, black-covered sketchbook.

Cricket is shaking out a rolled-up pair of jeans and folding them in half when she goes, "I wonder, like, do you think Jemma and her sister lived up here all summer when they were our age?" She pauses and places the jeans on the shelf. Then she looks back at me on the bed and she says, "It sounds like there's some kind of story between the two of them, right?"

"I guess," I lie, trying to sound totally casual.

Cricket laughs. "I'm just *so* curious! Aren't you? I mean, I wonder what her story is!"

Silence from me, then: "Yeah," I say softly, and feel my eyelids closing. "I do too."

I fall asleep. When I wake, my head feels super groggy. I crack open my eyes and squint up at the skylight. Sun. It takes a second for my brain to catch up to the current facts, and when I do, I tick them off in my head:

- ✓ *Lighthouse*
- ✓ *Great Bear Island*
- ✓ *Cricket* . . . who I hear clunking around in the bathroom.

I reach up and rub my eyes, then turn to the windows and look out over the water. I review the plan that I am making up as I go along: Be Liv. Get food. Rest. Try and figure out why Sunny and Jemma don't talk. Try and get to know my family.

"Yay, you're alive!" I hear, and turn to look. Cricket is standing in the open bathroom doorway with a white towel wrapped around her head and is only half-dressed in a sports bra and a clean pair of jeans with floral embroidery that looks like she stitched it herself.

"Hey, lady!" Cricket says.

"Hey," I say, stretching my arms up.

"You *totally* zonked out. You've been sleeping for like—" Cricket stops speaking for a second as she takes her towel off her head. "A solid few hours," she finally says.

"Hours!" I say, surprised. Now I sit up. "Seriously?"

"At least!" She reaches for a jar, opens it, and slathers something that smells like coconut into her wet hair, combing it through with her fingers.

"You must have been really tired! Better?"

"Yeah," I say, and sit up straighter in my bed. "How was the bucket shower?"

"Oh, it's cold!" she laughs. "But I kind of love it too."

I watch Cricket pick up her towel from the floor and drape it over a clothesline, which she has somehow strung up across our light-filled room.

She begins to tell me how to work the bucket shower. But I'm distracted by a rush of panic, all the lies I've already told and who I said I am. I realize I haven't been listening.

"Wait," I interrupt, and our eyes connect. "Sorry, what did you say?"

Cricket laughs. "The bucket-pulley thing?"

"Oh! Right."

She grins. "I was just saying the bucket-pulley is kind of a work-out. You pull on the rope to raise and lower the bucket. It's pretty clever."

"Oh." I smile. I take a deep breath.

Cricket sits down on her bed, and I suddenly notice that her bed is made. Like, extremely perfectly made, with the sheets all tucked in, and the colorful handmade quilt spread out smooth, and the pillow with the pillowcase fluffed and propped up. It looks very cozy over there. Between our beds, the big wooden trunk has been transformed into a bedside table, covered with Cricket's blue scarf—the same one she held up for me on the ferry. Sitting on top of the scarf are Cricket's water bottle, her headlamp, and a neat stack of three paperback books. I tilt my head and squint to make out the titles:

*The Catcher in the Rye*

*Harry Potter and the Philosopher's Stone*

*The Bluest Eye*

My side of the room looks like it got hit by a tornado. Sunny's wet suit is under my butt. The paints and colored pencils are scattered across the mattress, along with my new straw hat, jeans, shirts, and shorts. The rubber boots are kicked off on the floor. But then I notice Cricket has lined the windowsills above my bed with sea-glass jewels: golden yellow, reds, really pale pink. The sea glass is placed on every windowsill, adding a spotlight sparkle to each view: the bay, the beach, the coastline, the mountains.

I smile over at Cricket, standing with a hair tie in her teeth, using both her hands to tie her hair up. She takes the band from her mouth, loops it, and says, "Hey, do you have any idea what time it is?"

"Nope." I shake my head.

"Oh, wait." Cricket suddenly moves to the foot of her bed, where her empty backpack is still on the floor. "I have a watch!" She unzips a side pocket, pulls out a hot-pink rubber-banded watch, glances at it, and then looks up at me. "Holy heck," she says. "It's almost seven!" Cricket's face looks a little bit panicked. "Liv, get up! We've gotta go!"

## 49

"Just go without me," I say. I am still on my bed, though I have moved from lying flat to sitting.

"What?" Cricket looks up from fiddling with her watch. "No way, are you crazy? Let's go, girl! Get a move on!"

I laugh a little. But I don't move. Instead I crumple back onto the mattress, currently covered with all of Sunny's old stuff.

Cricket moves over to me and holds out her hand, and I take it and let her pull me to my feet. "Here, I'll pick you out an outfit," she tells me, and I laugh. We both look over Sunny's old clothes scattered all over my bed and the floor. Cricket quickly grabs cutoff shorts and a faded yellow Hang Ten T-shirt. She hands them over to me and says, "Go!" and then she claps, cheering me on, which, if you knew Cricket by now, you can totally picture because she does stuff like this and it makes you smile. She's funny.

I pick up a pair of Sunny's ancient undies and one of her bras. I carry the clothes into the bathroom and pull the bookcase door closed behind me.

Inside the "loo with a view" it's small but clean and bright, with light filtering in through the open window. And it has that sweet cedarwood scent. I sniff. *This* is my new favorite smell.

My eyes move to the composting toilet, which looks a little bit like a throne. It's not a regular toilet. It's all wood, in the shape of a tall box, and there are steps you step up. I set the pile of clothes down on the windowsill, climb the three small stairs to the composting toilet throne, and sit. And maybe you don't really want to know this detail, but . . . here it is anyway: I'm dehydrated and I haven't really had a ton to eat or drink. Hardly anything is coming out of me, but . . . I still feel like I really have to pee!

I wait.

I sit.

I run my tongue over my cracked, dry, chapped lips, then turn and look at the pile of clothes I'm about to put on and think about how weird it is that all these things once belonged to Sunny. I reach for the shorts and hold them up. There are two big sewn-on patches, hearts with red thread. I try and picture Sunny, sitting when she was my age with a needle and thread, neatly looping stitches by hand, and I feel this anger rising up. I have never, *ever* seen Sunny sew. I have no idea why this ticks me off, but it does.

"Liv?" I hear Cricket call.

"Yeah?" I say from my composting toilet throne with an ocean view.

"Are you okay in there?"

"Yeah. Totally!" I lie.

"Are you almost done? We have to hustle!"

"Yeah!" I say and—oh shoot. I don't see any . . . "Cricket?" I call out.

"Yes?"

"Is there any toilet paper in here?"

"The toilet paper is right below the—"

"Found it!" I say, spotting the single roll of toilet paper hanging from a piece of driftwood. No sawdust needed, if you follow my drift!

I stand. There's no mirror in here. No sink.

I strip down to my birthday suit. I take off *everything*:

The jeans that I've worn for a week straight.

Cricket's hoodie I borrowed on the ferry.

My underwear.

My damp, sweaty bra—I make a face when I pull that last one over my head. It smells like what you'd imagine a person would smell like if they haven't taken a shower for six days straight, *then* rode a bus and a ferry, walked up the coast, and climbed up here on a single rope.

I fold my old dirty clothes and place them in a little pile on the floor. Then I slowly step into Sunny's clothes. First the undies, then I slip on her old bra, next the jean shorts with the patches—they fit. Last, I pull her faded yellow tee over my head, pick up my old stuff from the floor, roll open the bookcase door, and quietly walk out into our bright bird's nest in the sky. I am now dressed from head to toe in Sunny's old clothes. Sun is pouring through the windows. I squint over at Cricket sitting on her bed, reading. Her hair is down, still shiny wet and falling over her shoulder in dark red waves. She is twisting it around her finger as she reads.

I'm standing at the end of her bed. I clear my throat. "I'm ready," I say.

Cricket looks up from her book. "Yay, everything fits!" She quickly sets the book down and moves to her feet. She's now fully dressed: embroidered flower-power jeans, a gray crewneck. Birks (with socks). She still smells like coconut potion, or whatever it is that she put in her hair.

We walk a few steps over to the open hatch in our floor. Cricket shoots me a look. "I'm starving," she exhales.

"Me too." I nod. "I'll go first," I say, grabbing onto the rope that hangs from the ceiling. I clamp my legs around it tight. "See you in a few seconds," I tell Cricket, relaxing my grip just enough to begin sliding down the rope. I manage to lose one sandal and then the other, but I hit the floor with a pretty soft barefoot landing, gather my shoes, and slip them on. Then I tip my head back and watch Cricket.

"Here goes nothing!" she hollers out as she lowers herself down the rope. She somehow keeps her sandals on, touching down on the wood floor and standing up straight. Then we look at each other. No words are exchanged. We don't have to even speak. It's like we just know, and the look we give each other says, *Let's gooooo!*

## 50

**W**e run the entire way down the Sunshine Coast. It's not an all-out sprint; it's more of a silent, slow jog until we turn off the coast and onto the secret cove beach, pass by the docks and the dollhouse cabins, and finally climb the steep stone steps that lead up to the lodge. Our official time: eleven minutes and thirty-seven seconds, according to Cricket's watch.

At the top of the stone steps, I stop. My hands are on my knees, and I act like I'm catching my breath. And yes, I am breathing pretty hard, but the real truth is: I am totally freaking out! I'm about to have dinner with my family and pretend that I'm someone else! Someone who I know absolutely nothing about! I mean, *can I really pull this off?* I glance sideways at Cricket. She glances sideways at me.

She's bent over too with her hands on her knees. Between heavy breaths, she says, "You're a good runner, Liv!"

"So are you," I say. *It's true.*

"Thanks, lady." Cricket grins. Then she straightens up. "Ready for this?"

"Sure," I lie. And we begin to walk, single file, on a wood-slatted path that weaves through a grassy wildflower meadow, leading us to—

"Oh wow," I murmur, looking up.

"Holy moly!" Cricket says.

Up close, the lodge is like something out of a storybook. It's not that it's big or even fancy. It's just a simple wood cabin set on the edge of a cliff overlooking the sea. The other three sides of the lodge are surrounded by bright green grassy meadows with tall purple flowers, then higher, steep green mountains that seem to touch the sky. The view is insane in every direction. It's just so pretty.

Cricket shakes her head in amazement and says, "Oh my gosh, Liv. Let's stay here forever."

I'm nodding, yes, but mostly, I'm staring up at the lodge in shock. And I'm thinking, *This is where Sunny grew up? Why would she ever leave?*

Cricket says, "Liv?"

I turn to face her. Her long hair is almost dry, and her freckles look like little specks of glitter. She raises an eyebrow. "Ready?"

"Um. Wait!" I say, and grab Cricket by the arm.

I go, "Let's peek in first."

"Okay?" Cricket says, sounding like that's a little bit of a weird idea, because it sort of is. But she goes along with it. I lead the way as we silently step off the wooden slats and onto a lime-green, cushiony carpet of moss, then creep around to the side of the lodge. Then we crouch down like spies, low enough so we are out of anyone's line of sight. On the count of three giggles, Cricket and I slowly rise, cup our hands to the glass window, and peer through.

"This place is *bonkers!*" Cricket whispers.

"Wow," I say softly, squinting through the glass.

Inside is one big, open space. Everything is made of golden wood: the walls, the ceiling, the wide-planked floor. The sun is hitting it just right. The whole room is full of light. My eyes dart around, scoping the place out: there's a guitar hanging from the wall, a bookcase full of books, a big stone fireplace surrounded by built-in furniture with furry sheepskin-covered cushions. It's simple. There's not a lot of stuff. I shift my eyes across the space to Jemma—she's sitting on a stool at the kitchen counter, reading something. Just a little past her, standing at the sink with his back to me, is a guy in a white T-shirt and dark blue jeans. He has the craziest twisty blond hair and longish, loose curls—he's basically a stronger, taller, older version of Till.

Cricket goes, "That must be the uncle, right?"

"I don't know," I whisper back.

"Holy handsome!" says Cricket. "He's a surf god!" She giggles. "Or no. He's Thor!"

"Who is Thor?" I whisper.

"The Norse God of Thunder!" she whispers back, but the thing is, Cricket is one of those people who doesn't really whisper that quietly, which makes us both laugh.

The Norse God of Thunder has tattoos up and down his arms. And as I watch him, I am thinking, *I can't believe I have an uncle,* when I hear—

"Liv?" whispers Cricket.

"Yeah?" I say back, but I keep my eyes on the Norse God of Thunder.

"You know this is going to be great, right?" she whispers.

And I mumble back, "I guess."

I glance over at Cricket, whose nose is pressed against the glass. "Just be yourself," she tells me.

And now I follow Cricket's lead. We slink, down low, crawl on our hands and knees across the moss, stand, and step up on the wooden slat path and onto the deck that overlooks the bay. A second later, we are standing in front of the lodge's tall sliding glass door. I quickly lean over and dust off some dirt on my knees. Then I surprise myself—

I don't wait for Cricket to do it.

I lift my closed fist up to the glass and knock.

# 51

After I knock, five heart-thumping seconds tick by, and then it is Till who appears on the other side of the glass. I watch him walking toward us. He's changed into fresh clothes: broken-in jeans and a well-worn baby-blue crewneck sweater with old-fashioned patches on the elbows. His hair is wet, like he just took a shower or maybe dunked himself into the turquoise water in the bay. Same big smile, same shiny blue eyes, same thick corkscrew curls.

He pulls the large sliding door open. "Hey!" he says, grinning. "You guys don't have to knock!"

I smile at Till.

He smiles at me.

Cricket is slipping off her sandals, adding them to the lineup of tall rubber boots and scuffed-up leather clogs. I take my sandals off too, parking Sunny's old Birks side by side on the end.

Then—

I quietly step across the open door, my bare feet landing on the wide-planked wood floor. As soon as I am inside, I get hit with this warm, good feeling I have never felt—it's almost impossible to describe.

"So. This is home," Till says.

Cricket walks in a few steps. "*So* beautiful," she says.

I stand just inside the entryway and look all around. The lodge is a single open space with a kitchen at one end and a stone fireplace at the other.

I glance over toward the kitchen.

Now Jemma's not there.

Neither is the God of Thunder.

I wonder, *Where did they go?* Besides this one big room, there is a single wooden ladder leading up to what looks like a sleeping loft above the kitchen area. Meanwhile, Till is giving a tour. "My great-grandpa built this lodge by hand," he tells us. "It's as simple as they come, but"—Till nods to a wall of windows with sunshine pouring through them—"he chose the very best spot."

"I'll say so!" Cricket shakes her head.

For a minute or two, the three of us gravitate over to the wall of windows opening to the deck and look out at the crazy view of the bay and the mountains on either side.

"Unreal," Cricket says.

Then it's quiet again.

Till walks over to one of the massive cedar beams supporting the roof. "All this hand-hewn wood right here"—he places his palm against the beam—"this is all my great-grandpa's work. He chiseled these by hand with an axe. See the little nicks?"

"Wow," Cricket says, reaching and running her hand along the beam.

Till walks over to the fireplace. "This right here is all soapstone from up in the mountains. There's a whole bunch of soapstone up there. It's one of my favorite spots by the river."

When Till says *river*, I get this nervous jolt. It's like my body is malfunctioning and sending a panic alarm right to my heart. I take a deep breath and try to act normal and not jittery and nervous (which I am). I slip in beside Cricket, and we stand before the fireplace, checking out the small treasures spread out along the mantel: a white feather with golden flecks, a few smooth round rocks, a small chunk of driftwood in the shape of a whale. It's like a museum: we look but don't touch. Until—

Cricket stops in front of a single framed black-and-white photo. "Aw," she says, picking it up. "Who are these cuties?"

I lean in to get a closer look: the old photo is of three kids— two girls and a boy—standing on the beach, arms around each other, smiling like best friends.

Till peers over Cricket's shoulder. "That's my mom," he says, using his pointing finger. "And that right there"—he taps the glass with his fingertip—"that little dude is my uncle."

And Cricket says, "Aw!"

Till inches his fingertip one kid over and my heart begins to pound.

I lean in and stare at Sunny. In this photo she's probably around my age, and she's dressed in a short-sleeved black wet suit. Her hair is really, really long and her face is super tan . . . She looks exactly like *me*.

## 52

"**W**ait. Who is this one?" Cricket is saying, and she taps the tip of her finger directly on Sunny's smiling thirteen-year-old face.

My head gets hot and tingly.

"That's—" Till stops.

"Oh riiiiiight, sorry," Cricket whispers. She sets the photo back on the mantel.

I turn to Till. I can't keep it in. I look right at his face and I just point-blank say, "What's her story?"

Till looks confused. "Whose story?"

And I go, "The other sister?"

"No idea," Till answers.

"Oh," I barely manage to say.

Now Cricket is looking curious. "Wait," she says to Till. "Like, have you ever even *met* her?"

Till shakes his head.

"Sorry," says Cricket.

"It's fine," Till says with a shrug. But the look on his face says the opposite of that. He puts his hands in his pockets and heads across the room to the wall of windows that face the water. It's so clear that he doesn't want to talk about Sunny. "This is cool," he tells us. "We get a huge solar gain because almost all the windows face south, so the sun keeps us warm, even in the winter."

I am only half listening now.

I'm completely distracted by the photo on the mantel and what Till just said. I mean, *do they even know I exist? That there is a River*

*Ryland . . . that I was even born?* I have a terrible feeling, and it's stuck in my throat.

I try to breathe.

I turn and look across the living room to the other side of the lodge. Jemma has returned. Now she's back at the kitchen counter, looking down at a clipboard. She's in the same outfit from when I met her on the dock: a button-down shirt with the sleeves rolled up and jeans. I'm kind of spacing out and staring at her, when I realize Jemma is speaking to me. "Hi, Liv," she says, looking up from her work. "I see you found some clothes that fit?"

I nod and take a step toward her.

"Oh, good." She looks at me for a long second, then turns back to her clipboard.

I stand right where I am.

I don't move.

My eyes travel past Jemma to the God of Thunder, who has also returned and is now at the sink with his back to me. My palms are sweating. And yes: I am staring again. A second later, when he turns to face me, and my eyes meet his, he doesn't speak. He just gives me a smile and the slightest quiet nod.

I look at him and smile back. The God of Thunder has a big, square jaw. He's lean, muscular, and tall. His face is chiseled, and his eyes are super intense. And I'm just staring across the lodge, thinking, *This is so weird. Yesterday I had no family except Sunny, and today I have a cousin, an aunt, and an uncle.*

It takes a second, but I snap out of it when I feel Cricket's hand on my shoulder. "You okay?" she asks.

"I'm starving," Till says to me. "How about you?"

"Oh—um," I start. Then right this second my stomach makes an alien-like growl, followed by a really loud gurgle. Cricket's eyes go wide. "Was that *you*?" She giggles.

Then, just as we all burst out laughing, out of the corner of my eye, I see the tall, strong guy with the chiseled jaw and the curly golden hair . . . The God of Thunder is walking straight toward ME!

## 53

The God of Thunder—who I am now almost positive is my uncle—has a white cloth apron cinched tight around his waist. "Hey, guys, sorry," he says, and smiles. "I just got in from crabbing." He lifts the bottom of his apron up, wipes off his hand, and then holds it out to me. "Nash Ryland," he says, and he looks me straight in the eyes.

"Ri—" I start to say as my hand meets his. Then by some miracle I catch myself: "Hi, I'm Liv."

"Hey, Liv, it's really nice to meet you," Nash tells me.

"Nice to meet you too," I manage to say. His eyes are two different colors, by the way. His left eye is green and his right eye is blue. I'm gazing up, still gripping his hand, when I notice more:

1. Nash Ryland's eyelashes are brownish blond and super long.

2. There is a very big scar that looks like the seam of a baseball running under his right eye, cutting across his cheekbone.

I quickly move my eyes back to his and try to pretend like I didn't notice the giant scar, but—

"You should've seen the other guy," says Nash with a wink.

"Oh yeah, I mean . . ." I fumble. "Sorry, I was just—"

"Hey, it's all good," says Nash, giving me a grin. He's got a really great smile. This is when I suddenly realize: *Oh my gosh! I am still holding his hand! I'm still gripping it hard and shaking up and down!* I'm the one who is not letting go! It's just—Nash Ryland's hand is so big and so strong. He doesn't even squeeze that hard; it's more like, his hand is thick and a little rough with calluses, like he's done a lot of chopping firewood, and, you know, fixing and building stuff. Those kind of hands. I have no idea why, but it feels good to hold a hand like that. When I do finally release my grip, I take a small step back. I am trying not to stare at the tattoo on the inside of his arm, but I fail at that too because yes, right now I'm tilting my head sideways in order to make it out. *Never quit* is inked in curvy black script along his forearm. There are more that climb up the inside of his bicep—eagle wings? A raven? Not sure—but I mean, I don't want to seem like I'm staring, which I am, so I straighten up and watch Nash reach out to Cricket and shake her hand.

"How ya doin'?" he says to Cricket with the same friendliness, and the same steady smile. "I'm Nash. Nash Ryland."

Cricket and Nash's handshake is quick and firm, but when they let go, Cricket is speechless. As in: she's just kind of standing in front of Nash, gazing up at him. There are no words coming out of her open mouth.

I grab her by the shoulder and blurt out, "This is Cricket!"

"Nice to meet you, Cricket," says Nash. His voice is soft and crackly, and when he grins, two deep-set dimples appear.

Cricket gives him a smile back. "Hi!" she finally says, blushing.

I get it. It's not just that Nash is really handsome (he is), it's more this quiet confidence. There's something about him that's just immediately kind and calm. Warm, I guess.

There is a short silence.

We are all looking at each other. Then—

"Oh wow," Cricket says, as she looks up at Nash. "You have different-colored eyes! That's so crazy!" There's a pause, then: "Wait—" Cricket laughs, and now her cheeks are turning red. "Was that totally weird to say?"

"Nah, not at all." Nash laughs too, and an easy grin breaks across his face.

Till chirps in, "This is my uncle right here." He looks up at Nash, who must be over six feet tall. "This guy charges so hard. Dude's a legend."

Nash snakes his arm around Till's shoulders. "Easy, big guy," he teases, and pulls Till into a playful headlock.

"Oh, I see how it is," Till laughs, and fights back, ducking his head right into Nash's apron. He wraps his arms around Nash's waist and attempts to throw him. But he's no match. It's like a very big, strong dog and an adoring teenage puppy. Nash is basically Galactus-level stacked. Till is quick and scrappy. Nash lets Till play around for a bit. "Easy, Tilly," he says, as he ruffles Till's thick, wavy curls and finally lets him free with a grin and a wink. Then?

With Cricket and me looking on, Nash laughs and says, "Bring it in, Tilly," and the two of them hug. Not like a bro hug with a handshake and a shoulder bump or two quick slaps on the back. They hug. A real one. A big two-armed hug. Chest to chest, where Till holds on and says, "I love you, man." Nash hugs back, lifting Till clear off the floor. "Love you too, bud," I hear him say.

For a few seconds, I almost forget about everything else that's going on. It's hard not to smile. They seem more like a kid and his big brother than uncle and nephew. I scan Nash's face, his wild different-colored eyes, his hair, even his teeth when he smiles. He is unmistakably Sunny's brother. He's definitely younger than her, though. From the photograph on the mantel, I'm guessing five or six years. He's probably in his twenties. And I'm just standing here, kind of—no, *very*—tripped out by all this, when I look sideways and see Zeus and

Lulu running toward me, and oh man—you know when you see a dog running in slow motion, in like, a pet commercial, and they start galloping and jump up and tackle you like a linebacker and knock you over?

This is what is happening right now.

What do I do?

I close my eyes. I close my eyes tight and brace myself, but—

Nothing happens.

And when I open my eyes: Nash is down on the floor between me and the dogs. "What's up, buddy?" he says, kneeling as Zeus jumps up and lands his two front paws on Nash's shoulders, then moves in close and licks his face all over. "Sloppy kisses," Nash tells Zeus. Lulu is busy nibbling on Nash's ears. "You want to play too, don't you, Lu?" he says to her, as she grins at him and wags her furry tail.

Then my rugged, super-chill uncle, who I had no idea I even had, looks up at me, cracks a quiet, mellow smile, lifts his eyebrows, and says, "Hungry?"

## 54

Ten minutes later, I sit—no, make that slide—my butt down the smooth, built-in wooden bench on two sides of the kitchen table, a massive slab of Sitka spruce, which Till tells us was split by lightning and carved out by hand by the Viking great-grandpa I didn't know I had. I run my fingers over the top of the Viking's table and touch the chiseled grooves. I can't stop thinking about how Sunny once sat right where I am sitting and how different this all is—there are no red plastic cups filled with soda, no Pop-Tarts served on paper towels. The tabletop is set family-style: covered with a mishmash of different-colored bowls, cups, plates, silverware, and neatly folded cloth napkins, a tall glass pitcher of water, and a row of lit candles.

Cricket and I are sitting on the built-in bench side, which is sort of like a corner booth at Denny's except a billion times nicer and made from a tree. The rest of the table is surrounded by chairs that the Viking chiseled out of hunks of driftwood and sculpted into seats.

Outside the kitchen windows, which face the mountains, the sunset has turned the entire sky a lavender color, filling the lodge with this unreal soft-pink light. The air smells of warm bread, melted butter, and something kind of fishy, simmering out of a tall pot that Nash is tending to at the stove.

I'm starving.

I turn toward Till and Cricket, who are both leaning in and looking carefully at the top of the table.

"Look at the grain," Till is saying. "You can see each summer and winter, the darker wood and the light growth rings—so it's kind of like a history."

Cricket examines the top of the table as if it's a giant jigsaw puzzle and she's trying to put the pieces together.

"See right here?" Till traces the line of the grain with his finger. "In the good years the old-growth rings are wide, it must have grown really well, and in the hard, dry years"—Till moves his finger a tiny bit—"like here, see that? There's very little growth."

I look up at Nash walking toward us, carrying a steaming platter, which he places on the table.

"Yum!" says Cricket.

"Oh yeah!" says Till.

"Wow!" says Jemma, who has joined us, sitting across the table from Cricket and me.

I look at the platter and try not to freak out. The platter Nash set down that everyone is *oohing* about is piled high with the weirdest-looking creatures I have ever seen! They have huge, pancake-size bodies with reddish-orange hard shells, and these crazy claws, alien-antennae eyes, and eight spidery legs!

*Oh my gosh.*

*It's not like I can ask for something else.*

I put my napkin in my lap. A second later, I glance up and see Nash reaching across the table for my hand. I'm kind of like, *Uh, what are we doing?* I look around the table. Everyone is doing it: Cricket's hand is in Till's, Till's is in Jemma's, Jemma is joined with Nash, and then there's me, unattached. Under the table I feel Cricket grab my left hand, and so with my right, I reach across the table and connect my hand with Nash.

Now we are all joined together.

The five of us.

Cricket, Till, Jemma, Nash, and me.

Linked, around a table, lit by candlelight. It's suddenly very quiet. I figure it's some kind of prayer thing, which is a total shock. Sunny is *not* the praying type. You can trust me on that.

I take a big, deep breath.

I close my eyes.

Nash moves his hand slightly. His fingers are rough and strong, and for some reason holding them doesn't feel as weird as I thought it would. I open my eyes and glance at Cricket, then Till, then Jemma, and finally, directly across from me: Nash. Nobody has their eyes closed or is like, bowing their head. Actually, everyone is really looking totally chill and relaxed. Nash closes his hand a little around mine, takes a big breath in, and then speaks in an easy, clear voice:

"Thank you for all the gifts of this day," he begins. "For rest and home, for wind, rain, and sun"—he pauses—"for the songs of the birds, from the forest to the sea, for all the living things who teach us and give us life"—he takes a breath—"for water, for sky, for earth, for fire"—he looks around the table—"and especially"—now Nash unravels a smile—"for those we love."

And in an instant, Nash lets go of my hand until—

Jemma says, "I just want to add—" and I feel Nash wrap his hand around mine again. We're just sitting here, the five of us around a table holding hands, and I feel silly saying this, but—it feels good, okay? Being together like this. Maybe someone else would think it's dumb and I don't really care. I'm here, and it feels calming.

Jemma looks across the table at me, then Cricket. "It is so good to have you two here," she says. "Liv, I'm really grateful that you changed your mind and joined us." She gives me a long, steady smile. Then she says, "Dig in!"

In an instant, it's a free-for-all: hands are reaching, shells are cracking, and little cups of melted butter are passed around the table, followed by a wooden board with a just-out-of-the-oven loaf of crusty bread, cut into thick, even slices.

"Ooh, fresh Dungeness crab!" Cricket says, picking up a giant orange-shelled crab for herself, and then, she reaches again, and this time sets one of the reddish-orange alien creatures directly on my plate. It all happens so quickly that there is no time for me to stop her.

Also? No one is talking, because everyone is hard at work taking these little wooden hammers, pounding on the shells, then ripping the crabs apart with their fingers.

"What a treat!" Cricket says as she breaks the shell open with her two hands.

I watch her, and I'm sitting here thinking, *I am not going to eat that. No way. I don't eat anything that swims, okay?*

# 55

I stare down at the creature on my plate.

WHAT DO I DO?!!

This is not raw ramen from a plastic bag!

It's not a Snickers bar I hid in a drawer.

The most different food I've ever had was Thai takeout at Emi's.

I look to Cricket for help, but she's busy grabbing one of the legs, pulling and twisting and breaking it apart.

"Oops! A little crab juice in the eye," she laughs, and half squints as she breaks a claw apart with her fingers and then scoops the piece of meat into her mouth, closes her eyes, and lets out a long, soft, "*Mm-mmm.*" Then, between bites, she says, "Holy moly, this is amazing!"

"So good!" Till says, and I look down the table at him as he flips over his crab and splits it in half with his bare hands, then uses his fingers to pick the meat out, dunk it into the butter, and pop it into his mouth.

"Ever had crab?" I hear Nash say, and I turn to look.

I shake my head, *No.*

"Hey, it's all good." Nash grins. "They taste a thousand times better than they look. It's a little bit of work."

I glance back at Nash.

"Wanna start with a claw?" he asks. "You gotta use your hands."

I nod, grab a claw with both my hands, then—and I'm pretty sure I have a grimace on my face—twist it off the body until it breaks.

I am holding the claw over my plate with both hands.

Crab juice is dripping down my wrist.

"Okay, so," Nash says, holding up a claw from his plate and giving me a demonstration, "what you want do is, hit it right about here, that's the sweet spot." He takes the wooden hammer in his hand. *Pow!* "Crack it open like this, and if you're real gentle, you can pull the meat out in one chunk." He pauses and then does exactly that.

I pick up the little wooden hammer that's sitting beside my fork. Then I whack the claw right in the spot Nash pointed out, and the shell cracks and breaks apart.

"Nice!" Nash continues, "Now, the easiest way is to break it open with your hands, then, hiding right beneath that—there you go," he says, watching me crack the shell, dig in with my fingers, and pull out the meat. "Good work, Liv!"

I look up like, *Now what?*

"Now eat it," he tells me, and smiles.

Till weighs in. "If you want the full heaven effect"—he looks across the table at me and flashes a smile—"give it a good long swim in the melted butter."

Now all eyes are suddenly on me.

Cricket, Till, Jemma, and Nash.

"Okay, here goes," I say. I take the meat with my fingers, dip it into the melted butter, pop the entire piece into my mouth, chew, and—

"Well?" Cricket says, watching me closely.

"Oh wow, that's like . . ." I pause to chew, then swallow and smile. "That's the most amazing thing I've ever tasted!"

Everyone practically cheers when they watch my reaction. A second later, I'm using my two hands to rip apart the claws and legs. I even break apart the last bit of shell with my fingers and scrape out any little chunks of meat that are left, dipping each bite in the melted butter, before popping pieces into my mouth. And in a matter of minutes, I'm very quickly splattered with the juice of the crab: my hands, my mouth, dribbling down my arms. Salty melted butter is smeared on my chin. It's not just that it tastes good, it's that . . . I don't feel that out of place. I glance up at Nash. Then I copy him: I mop up what's remaining on my plate with the crusty bread until there's not a single morsel of anything left.

**56**

Not even a minute after we have finished dinner, Till quietly moves to his feet and begins clearing the table, even though nobody asked him to. It's automatic. He just gets up, reaches to the center of the table, and lifts the bowl of discarded shells. "Are we using these for stock?" he asks, carrying the bowl to the kitchen and setting it on the counter.

"Oh yeah," Nash answers, and now he stands. "Those will cook down for a nice broth," he says, leaning over the table and picking up my empty plate with one hand and Cricket's with the other.

I immediately move to help, but—

"We got this," says Nash with a quiet smile.

I drop back down.

Now Cricket and Jemma are getting into it, having a passionate conversation that moves fast:

The forest ecosystem.

The threat of industrial logging to Great Bear.

Tide tables.

To be honest—and this is embarrassing—I have trouble keeping up. I mean, I never even stepped foot out of Clarksville until twenty-four hours ago. The safest move for me right now is to keep my mouth shut. I smile and occasionally nod, but eventually I just get this blank, unfocused feeling. I'm spacing out, looking toward the kitchen. Till and Nash, standing at the sink, washing and soaking pots and plates, drying them, and placing them back on the shelves. They are easy with each other; they make work look like fun. Across the single open space, Zeus and Lulu are passed out, stretched on the stone in front of the fireplace, which now has a crackling fire, thanks to Till, who got it going with little notice.

And now the table's been wiped clean, the kitchen is spotless. And for a few minutes, there's no more talking.

No more words.

Cricket. Jemma. Me.

We sit together. And it doesn't feel weird. Night is falling, and there is just the best feeling in here. A coziness. It's so simple, it feels so good. I sit back and relax, stare into the candles' dreamy soft light, and watch the yellow beeswax drip down the sides. This place can put you under a spell. I've never felt this peaceful and safe. I'm even sitting here thinking, *Maybe I can really pull this off. Stay. Be Liv. Have fun!* But then Jemma leans forward, folds her arms on the table, looks directly at me, and says, "There's something I need to talk to you about."

## 57

*It's over* is all I can think.

My heart begins to pound.

Jemma stands up, steps into the kitchen, grabs a folder from the counter, and returns to the table, sitting back in her seat and opening the folder in front of her. "Cricket, you are all set, but Liv—" She looks up. "Let's complete the employment forms. I know you never got the chance to when you thought you weren't coming, but now you're here, and this is important." Jemma slides a single piece of paper toward me and passes over a pen. "I just need to get your signature on the summer intern agreement."

"Oh, okay," I say, staring down at the paper. "No prob," I add, trying to sound all casual and Liv-like as I am frantically scanning the typed page, searching for Liv's last name!

"Olivia Hogan?" I read her first and last names out loud like it's a question.

"Is there something wrong?" Jemma asks.

"No!" I say quickly, and look up. "This looks great!" I say a little too loudly. I reach for the pen, pick it up in my hand. "Right here?" I point to the line.

"That's right," Jemma says. "Read it through first. Take your time." She pauses for a moment. "If it all looks good to you, I just need your signature, then we're all set."

"Okay, great," I say with this fake-cheerful voice. Then I look down at the single sheet of paper and read.

## GREAT BEAR LODGE
## SUMMER INTERN AGREEMENT

I, <u>Olivia Hogan</u>, acknowledge and agree to all the terms in this agreement, including the following: I agree to honor our core value of striving to be stewards of these lands and waters. I understand that there are objective hazards in this remote wild coastal region that pose risks, and I agree to adhere to Great Bear safety guidelines. Some, but not all, of the risks I may encounter include but are not limited to: flowing deep and/or cold water; harmful insects, predators, and large animals; falling and rolling rock; falling timber and branches; and forces of nature, including weather, which may change to extreme conditions quickly or unexpectedly. Possible injuries and illnesses that I could experience include hypothermia, sunburn, heatstroke, dehydration, insect- or animal-borne diseases, drowning, and other mild or serious conditions. I agree to work respectfully with others as a team and to be truthful at all times.

I HAVE CAREFULLY READ, AND VOLUNTARILY SIGN, THIS DOCUMENT, and I certify that the information provided is true and accurate. <u>Failure to provide true and accurate information may result in immediate termination</u>.

Signed:

_____

OLIVIA HOGAN

The longer I sit here and stare down at the paper, the more nervous I get, so finally, without looking up, I just decide to go for it! I place the pen on the paper and scribble fast.

"Ooh, nice autograph!" says Cricket as she watches me sign *Olivia Hogan* in blue ink. I wait a second, then flash a big fake smile as I push the single piece of paper back across the table. I watch as Jemma places Olivia Hogan's freshly signed, FORGED, COMPLETELY ILLEGAL form into a thin folder. "Thank you, Liv!" Jemma says. "We are so glad you changed your mind. It was a little surprising. But we really need your help." She smiles at me. "I'm so glad you came!"

"I am too," I say, and I look back at her like everything is totally normal. But the second Jemma gets up from her seat, contract in hand, to place my *forged* summer intern agreement back on the counter, I reach for my tall glass of water and bring it to my mouth and try to wash down the awful guilty feeling that I have right now.

## 58

We are still at the table.

It's almost dark outside.

With the kitchen clean and the dishes washed and put away, Nash and Till excuse themselves to chop wood out back. The candles are still flickering, the dogs are sleeping in front of the fireplace. The air coming in the open window is cool.

"Liv," Jemma says, and I look up from what I am currently doing, which is playing with the melted wax of the candle closest to me.

Jemma's eyebrows go up. "I'd really love to hear more about your essay."

*Oh no.* "My essay?" I'm pretty sure I have now lifted my hand and am pointing my finger to myself.

"We get loads of applications each summer, and both your essay and Cricket's were outstanding," says Jemma. "Liv, yours was really quite moving."

"Rock star!" says Cricket, and under the table, she knocks her knee into mine.

Jemma goes, "Really, Liv, I loved it. Can you tell us a little more?"

"More?" I repeat, and swallow. "Sure, okay, um—" I look at Jemma and smile and try to sound confident when I go, "What part do you want to know more about?"

Pretty clever, right?

No.

Jemma grins. "Honestly, I was fascinated by everything!"

"Everything," I say, stalling. "Um, let's see—" I sputter.

Now I just stop speaking.

My cheeks are heating up.

Across the table, I can feel Jemma watching me.

"You know what?" she finally says, and glances at her watch. "You must be exhausted. I think we should call it a night. Let's talk more tomorrow after a good night's sleep and breakfast." Jemma stands and pushes in her chair. "Why don't you get yourselves settled," she tells us. "The bay is beautiful in the morning. Go for a swim if you like." She glances at her watch again. "Let's meet here at the lodge tomorrow morning for a late breakfast, say, nine thirty?"

I nod. "Sounds good," I say, and stand.

"Perfect," Cricket says, scooching out so we can both move from behind the table. All three of us walk toward the door.

"Thank you so much," Cricket says.

"We feel lucky to have you both with us," Jemma says. "It's a special healing place and we—" She stops midsentence and gives me a long look. Immediately in my mind I'm like, *I must have messed up! She knows I'm not Liv!* My heart is pounding in my chest.

I don't move.

I don't say a word.

I stand right by the open door, with this cool night breeze blowing in, and Jemma breaks into the softest smile. "I'm so sorry I'm staring, Liv," she tells me without looking away. "It's just so wild—" She stops, and now her smile kind of fades. "You just really, *really* remind me of someone."

## 59

It is very, *very* dark out here—this isn't a movie, where it's all starry and bright. No. Not tonight. It is really hard to see.

No flashlights.

No headlamps (we forgot them).

Everything is pitch-black.

On the beach, Cricket and I are half giggling, half shrieking, 100 percent tripping over mounds of wet seaweed and grabbing onto each other's arms as we make our way through the darkness. And the ocean is loud! It feels like a giant animal breathing: the waves are rolling in, then whooshing out. Moving and crashing.

"Liv?" Cricket whispers loudly.

"Yes?" I squeak. I turn toward her voice, and my eyes are slowly becoming used to the dark. I can just make out the outline of shapes, and the longer I stare, the more I begin to see the different shades: the night sky, the ocean, the ring of shadowy mountain peaks around us.

"Truth or dare," Cricket says as we walk.

"Dare?" I say, and my voice kind of shakes.

Cricket stops walking and bends down.

"What are you doing?" I whisper.

"I'm rolling up the bottom of my jeans," she says. Then, without saying a word, she flicks off her sandals, whips off her socks, and just, like, sprints toward the water . . .

I don't move.

I stand on the beach and watch the shadow of Cricket running toward the bay. I'd love to tell you that I'm the type of girl who never turns down a dare, who says, *Oh yeah, let's go!* . . . but the truth is more like this: I'm not going to stand here in the dark on a deserted beach by myself, no way! I kick off Sunny's sandals and run full speed the way you do when you're afraid. And in a matter of seconds, Cricket and I are squealing and high-stepping it into the chilling-cold waves, then wading into the water until we're knee-deep in the bay—my very first time in any ocean, anywhere.

We don't go in too far.

Just a few feet, and together, we stand on the packed wet sand and let the waves come up to just below our knees, and feel the tide suck the sand away out from under our feet. Everything is dark: the water, the night. The entire scene looks like it's out of a dream. Which is why I actually think that I'm hallucinating when I see what I see. Right underneath the surface of the water are these shimmery flickers of neon-blue light. I glance up at Cricket and she glances up at me, and the best way I can describe the look on her face—and probably mine—is that emoji where the eyes are bugging out. Like: *Are you seeing what I'm seeing? OH MY GOSH!!!!!!* It's like someone sprinkled glow-in-the-dark glitter right into the ocean! I run my hand through the water. "There's hundreds of them!"

"Liv! This is insane, this is literally magical!" Cricket begins to splash around, and the two of us watch in awe as the glowing, glittering water grows even brighter and more intense the more we move our feet and the more we splash, and soon there's this flashing blue light swirling all around us!

Then, for a minute or two, we stand completely still.

Cricket stares into the neon-blue sparkles flashing just under the water's surface. "Oh my gosh, I read about this in AP Bio!" She pauses. "It's called bioluminescence, which literally means 'living light.'"

I look up at her, like, *how does she even know that?*

Cricket dips her hand in the water and scoops up a handful of shimmery blue sparkles. "They're like, these super-tiny glow-in-the-dark creatures," she says. "They're microscopic, single-celled plankton. You can't see them with your eyes." We both lean in and examine the sparkling blue light coming from her hand. "They only produce light when something disturbs them." Cricket runs the tips of her fingers through the water, dragging both her hands in a ring around her, and we watch the explosion of glowing bright blue light just below the surface.

"That's amazing!" I say.

"Right?" she sighs.

We stand together in knee-deep lit-up electric-blue water, staring down into the sea and watching the light show all around us.

And I whisper, "It's like, underwater stars!"

"Exactly!" Cricket says.

And ten minutes or so later, we finally slosh our way out of the water and walk up to the beach to retrieve our shoes. I glance back over my shoulder at the trail we've left in the sand, a path of glow-in-the-dark, sunken-in, sparkling diamonds wherever we stepped.

# 60

We gather our sandals in the dark and make our way across Secret Cove Beach, then take a right, walking down the Sunshine Coast in the shadowy night, toward the lighthouse. Cricket is explaining to me how the glow-in-the-dark tiny creatures flash with light. "It's a chemical reaction, but it's in each tiny cell," she says, her voice growing more and more excited, "and it's so amazing. They can sense us, right? I mean, they're like these microscopic particles, and they can sense us—wait, I mean, they don't know what we are, or who—but they can sense our vibration, they can feel the agitation of the water, they can feel that something is there! How cool is that!"

"That's really cool," I say, turning to face her. Then I laugh.

"What?" she says. "I'm a total science nerd."

"No. It's not that, that's actually really cool," I say. "It's that"—I grin in the dark—"you have sea sparkles in your hair."

"No way!" Cricket runs her fingers through her wet, sparkly strands. "Who needs shampoo!" She giggles, and I do too.

After ten minutes or so of walking, we finally reach the lighthouse.

"Holy moly!" Cricket sighs. "The rope."

After bashing my knee on the dirt bike that I walked into, I feel around in the dark and finally grab a flashlight from one of the shelves and point it toward the path of the rope: a spotlight for the climb.

Cricket goes first.

It takes her a while, and a few choice words: "@#&!?, this rope is nuts!" But she makes it all the way up. I keep the flashlight in spotlight mode until I see her sitting on the edge of the trapdoor. Then I stuff the light—still on—down the collar of my shirt, with the beam shining into me. I'm like a glowworm, inching my way up, holding on tight, and pull by pull, I haul myself up into our secret hideout nest, crumple onto the floor, pull the rope up, and flip the hatch shut.

# 61

It's dark. All the windows are cranked open, and there's a chill in the air. Cricket and I say nothing. We both silently stumble the few steps across the wooden floor and flat-out collapse face-first onto our beds. I can feel the wet suit and all of Sunny's gear underneath my stomach and chest, but I don't care. I yank it out from under me, drop it on the floor, reach down around my feet, and pull the blanket over me. I can honestly say I have never in my life been this tired. Also, it's so still and so quiet.

"Liv?" Cricket whispers.

"Yes?" I giggle facedown into the mattress.

"Can you believe that we're finally here?"

"Not really," I say.

I hear some shifting on her side.

"Hey," she says in that same soft tone. "Do you think I sounded stupid to Jemma?"

I turn toward Cricket and peer through the dark. "What? No, not at all," I whisper back.

"Yeah. Okay, good. I think it's just, like—" Cricket stops talking, and I hear her move around and turn over so that she's facing me now. "She's so awesome that she's kind of a little intimidating. Do you know what I mean?"

"Yeah," I whisper.

There's a long pause. "I want to be like her one day," Cricket whispers.

I look into the dark. "You kind of are."

"Not even," she whispers back. "There's a bunch of stuff I haven't told you yet."

I want to say, *Me too. Me too!* My heart starts to pound, and for one millisecond I think about telling her the truth. Telling her who I really am. What happened. What's going on. Only, I do not do that, and I'm pretty sure I never will. I just can't. And now I'm lying here hating myself.

I flop over and turn away.

"Hey," says Cricket, suddenly sounding more awake. "I wonder who you remind her of. She looked kind of sad when she said that. Almost like, hurt in a way. Did you get that vibe?"

"I guess, maybe" is all I say.

"I wonder what that was all about," she whispers.

"No clue," I lie.

Cricket's quiet, and then I hear her flop over. "Oh my gosh," she says. "I really need to go to sleep." She lets out a big, long, tired breath. "Okay, for real. Night, Liv."

"Night," I whisper back.

**62**

**D**id you think I'd fall asleep that easy?

Nope.

Not so fast.

Let's switch places for a sec: if you are me right now, you are lying flat on your back, eyes wide open, staring up into the night. You are still awake! Sure, you can hear the waves in the far-off distance, but besides that?

It's scary quiet!

It's crazy dark.

Whatever, right? Tell yourself that you're tough. You're strong. You are used to being by yourself, but here, twenty feet up in the sky, the windows open, the breeze coming in, your mind just runs. What are you thinking about? What are you not! A whole bunch of random thoughts: *How nice Jemma is, how cool the lodge is inside. How the dinner tasted and why Sunny even left this place. Wait! Where is the real Liv? And what is she like? Is Sunny okay? Did Ms. Martinez really call the police? Were you totally weird at dinner?*

You are more tired than you have ever been in your life, your arms hurt from climbing up the rope.

Sit up.

Stare straight ahead.

Take a deep breath.

Try lying on your back, on your side, blanket on, blanket off. Make loud sighing noises like, *"Arghhh!"* Take your pillow and slam it down.

Nothing works.

Pull your knees to your chest.

Breathe.

Guess what? While you are curled up in a human ball, blanket on, breathing in and out, you suddenly hear a high-pitched scream!

Your heart is racing now!

Stay perfectly still and tell yourself that you aren't one of those people who hears weird sounds and panics (*you are*), that you don't immediately think of the worst-case scenario (*you do*). You tell yourself that the noises you hear are the wind, but—

That's not what wind sounds like.

You look into the darkness and you whisper, "Cricket, quit it. Is that you?" You wait for her to speak. "Cricket?" you say again. "Stop messing around." But—

Silence.

Now you sit up again.

Sit up straight with your back against the wall. Pull your covers up to your chin. Hug your knees. Yes, your heart is pounding, loud. Suddenly everything looks scary—the lump of clothes on the floor is like, a monster or something. Tell yourself to calm down. "Calm down," you whisper out loud.

Which is EXACTLY when you hear another loud, ghostly, eerie-sounding screech! I'll just tell you straight up: you jump, no, *leap* out of bed and jump up onto Cricket's bed. You are standing right on top of her feet.

"Cricket!" I think you kind of squeal.

You might have sort of kicked her.

"Someone is out there," you whisper.

"It's just the wind," Cricket says into her pillow. "Go back to sleep."

You say, "No really, Cricket, something is out there!" And when she doesn't answer, you do not move one single inch. You just stand frozen on the end of her bed and watch the darkness. Until—

It happens AGAIN!

A spooky, ghostlike, raspy scream, it's like some sort of Halloween soundtrack, except it's *real*. Guess what? Now Cricket believes you.

It takes only a second, and she's up on her feet. The two of you huddle together at the end of her bed, shrieking and almost crying, you're laughing so hard. "It's coming from over there!" you manage to whisper, pointing in the darkness to the windows above your bed. You feel around the end of the bed for the flashlight, and when you find it, you spring from Cricket's bed to yours.

"Ready?" you whisper, and now you turn the flashlight on. Go ahead, it's in your hands. It's bright, you have to squint, but you are pretty sure you see: a flash of wings, and lit up by the flashlight's single beam is—

And you say, "What in the world!"

Cricket whispers, "They are *so* insanely cute!"

There are three of them in their little nest, frozen by the bright spotlight, too scared to even squeak. They are so little and fluffy and snuggled as close together as they can possibly get. That's right: you have basically been freaking out over a nest of tiny baby owls! They're just fuzzy little babies covered in soft, fluffy whitish feathers, and they're staring back at you with these big, round eyes. They look absolutely terrified.

Cricket whispers, "We should turn the flashlight off."

That's you. Do it. It's in your hand. You quickly click the flashlight off. And you're glad you do, because the tiny, cuddly baby owls are more freaked out than you. And it's crazy, because you were scared, but as it turns out . . . *you* were the one who was scary!

## 63

In the morning, I wake up with my face smooshed into the pillow. I turn my head and crack my eyes open a teensy bit and: *Whoa! SO MUCH SUN!* I immediately squeeze them shut. Then I roll over on my side and open them again.

The room is breezy and quiet and beautiful, and there is Cricket across from me, sitting up in her bed, reading. She's wearing eyeglasses with thick black frames, and she's got all sorts of crazy bedhead hair, pushed back by a pink sleeping mask propped up on her forehead like a headband.

"Morning," I say, and my voice kinda cracks.

"Buenos días, roomie!" she says, looking up from her book and smiling at me. She sounds very awake and *very* cheerful.

My brain isn't super working yet.

I raise my arms over my head and stretch.

I sit up and look around the room: all the windows are open and there's this nice breeze coming in. It feels so good. I'm in the middle of yawning and rubbing my eyes, when I remember the baby owls from last night! I turn to look, and there they are:

one

two

three of them

sleeping all cozy under the mom—

*They are so stinkin' cute!*

The nest is set right on the ledge of the lighthouse overlooking the bay and, farther out, the ocean. *What a view!* If I built a nest, I'd want it there too! I flop back into my pillow and exhale a big breath. This is so wild. *I'm here. I'm safe. I have a family. Whatever, I'm pretending to be someone I'm not—but . . . I mean, it's working so far!*

I sit up again.

I look over at Cricket. She's put her book down, and she's up and making her bed, plumping her pillow and smoothing the blanket flat. Her black-framed glasses are now folded on the nightstand, atop her stack of books. Her side of the room looks very inviting and cozy.

My side of the room is a wreck!

Sunny's stuff is now half on my bed and half in a heap on the floor. You cannot walk without tripping over boots or stepping over wrinkled clothes. It's weird, because I'm usually the one cleaning, and now I'm messy! It's never been like this for me.

Cricket moves over to the end of her bed. She's bent over, searching through her pack. I watch her as she pulls out her wet suit.

"Are you going for a swim?" I ask.

I can tell by the way she looks back at me—this look I'm starting to know—that something is up. I grin and go, "What?"

"Go check out that view," Cricket says, and nods toward the windows above the Viking's trunk, between our two beds.

"What am I supposed to see?" I ask, peering down at the bay, searching for some kind of amazing fish, or bird . . . Then I see it! It's not low, it's *high*! Mounted to the side of the lighthouse, jutting out over the bay.

I drop my jaw. *I can't believe my eyes!*

# 64

Jumping off the second story of the lighthouse, plunging fifteen feet straight down to the water, is nothing that I ever imagined I'd do five minutes after waking up. But here I am with my wet suit on and jittery butterflies in my stomach. The "diving board" is a simple plank of wood that you can only reach if you are brave enough to climb out the window (we do) and step out onto the small deck that wraps around the top of the lighthouse (we do that too). Which is how I am standing here right now, high above our secret cove, knees knocking, peering out at the long wooden plank diving board that sticks out ten feet over the bay. My wet suit is all black and tight as heck. Cricket has hers on too—black with white flowers down the sleeves. She looks like a pro surfer you'd see on TV.

"That is for sure deep enough to jump," Cricket says, standing on the edge and peering down.

"Uh-huh." I tremble, inching forward and looking below: the drop is straight down into a deep pool of clear blue water.

This is nothing like the diving board at the Clarksville Country Club, where Emi has her birthday party every year. There's no single-file long line that snakes around the lifeguard chair, where you have to stand and wait for your turn. And the board is not white and springy or made of plastic. And it's not two feet above the water. This one, I'm guessing, Sunny and Jemma made when they were my age, and it's more like those platforms you see Olympic divers do five somersaults off.

It's high.

I look over at Cricket.

She smiles back at me.

Then—

"Sometimes you just have to go for it!" Cricket says, maybe more to herself than to me. She steps forward onto the plank, then walks across it like a balance beam, hesitating for a second at the tippy end and looking down at the bay. "Oh snap, this is high!" Cricket laughs, then—

She pushes off, springing up into the air and leaping out over the bay's blue water—a blur of red hair flying, arms flailing, free-falling, and hitting the water butt-first, with a huge splash. I look down and hold my breath until I see the top of Cricket's head burst through the surface of the water. "It's COLD!" she shrieks. Her hair is shellacked back, and she looks up at me standing on the deck. "IT'S AMAZING, LIV!"

It's only a split second, but I have three thoughts: One, *This is totally nuts!* Two, *It's going to be freezing.* Three: I don't even remember three, because I'm just like, screw it. I walk down the plank, spread my wings, and jump!

# 65

A nanosecond later I'm flying through the air and plunging straight down into the freezing-cold, deep water. And when I pop my head back up through the surface, the bright sun hits my face, and I see the mountains, the trees, the lodge above the beach. My very first thought is how alive I feel! The salt water washes off everything, the last seven days, the sticky layer of sweat. I am smiling so big. I look over at Cricket a few feet away and say, "That was the most fun thing I've ever done!"

Cricket holds up her hand and we high-five. "What a rush!" she says.

For the next few minutes, we float on our backs, faces to the sky, soaking in the sun and the bay's dreamy water.

"Liv," Cricket says, breaking the quiet.

"Yeah?" I say.

Cricket turns her head to me. "You're a certified lifeguard, right?"

"Uh-huh," I hear myself lie. We drift in the water on our backs, and my mind is racing. *A lifeguard? This is bad. I mean, that kind of lie can actually hurt someone.*

It's unusually quiet, until—

"Wait. Do you swim high school or club?" Cricket asks. I have no idea what she is talking about, and so I go, "Huh?"

"Do you swim high school or club?" she repeats.

"Club," I lie again.

Now the two of us are neck-deep in the water, face-to-face.

Cricket dunks her head under, then pops back up. Water is

dripping from her eyelashes. "Do you think you want to swim in college?" she asks.

"Swim in college, oh, I mean—" I stop. Obviously, the real Liv is some sort of swimming star. I shrug and go, "Who knows!"

Cricket splashes me. "You're so humble, Liv! Don't think I didn't google you!"

"You googled me?" I say, and now my insides sort of shake.

"Oh yeah!" Cricket splashes me again. "State swimming champ!"

*Oh God.*

I can feel the blood rushing to my face.

Cricket gives me this same crazy look that I'm starting to know.

Eyebrows raised.

Her face lit up.

And she goes, "You up for a little swim?" Then, before I even answer yes or no, Cricket turns herself toward the giant turtle-shaped rock in the middle of the bay and says, "One, two, three . . . GO!"

## 66

You should probably know this: I learned to swim when I was seven and a half. Sunny was dating this guy, and his apartment complex had a pool. The lifeguard taught me. I was always there alone for a whole lot of hours. I'm not terrible, but I'm *definitely* not a state champ.

I point myself toward Turtle Rock and start out swimming hard and fast. A minute in, I'm trying to catch my breath. I slow down to the water's pace, I stop fighting and thrashing and get my breathing into a rhythm, until I feel like I could just go forever, and soon I'm pulling up right next to Cricket. We swim together, trading the lead, and touch Turtle Rock at the same time. I reach for the rock and graze it with my fingertips. I turn to face her just as she turns to face me, and we both shout, "TIE!" and gasp for breath.

Cricket climbs up onto the Turtle's back—

I'm right behind her, hauling myself up and collapsing on the warm stone. My face, hands, and feet are numb, and snot is dripping from my nose. My teeth are chattering. But the stone feels so good and warm against my cheek. My whole body feels lit up. I am breathing so hard. My heart is pounding in my chest. All talking has stopped. And for the next few minutes I lie on my stomach on the Turtle's back until I finally roll over and sit up. My whole body is shaking. *I thought I couldn't do it and I did it*, I think to myself, and I'm grinning really big. I'm sitting on a tiny island the shape of a humongous turtle, surrounded by the turquoise water in the bay. I glance over at Cricket, lying flat, face to the sun. She actually *really is* a mermaid—her red hair is all slicked back—she's strong!

Now I lie back too and close my eyes.

It's just stillness, and the water rising and falling in the bay. No police sirens or blaring TVs to fill the morning quiet . . . I'm not used to this kind of silence. After a long time, Cricket lets out a sigh. "This is *heaven*," she says. "I love it here so much!"

"Same," I say, turning to give her a smile.

Cricket smiles back, and her eyes light up. "Hey," she says squinting into the sun. She has that look again, and I know whatever she's going to say is going to be a little bit nuts. "Yeah?" I wait.

"Let's do this every morning. It can be our tradition!" she says, and looks at me. She's serious. "Deal?"

I don't have to think too long: Turtle Rock is my newest favorite spot. I smile back at Cricket and say, "Deal!"

## 67

I push my toes off Turtle Rock to dive headfirst into the cold, deep water, then swim underneath, holding my breath for as long as I can, and when I come up for air, my face feels warmed by the sun. I can breathe again. And when I swim back to the lighthouse, it feels like I'm going home, swimming toward a beacon rising from the bay. The return trip is way easier.

At the lighthouse, from the water, I spot another way back up to the narrow ledge that we launched ourselves off. We don't have to climb over the rocks and back onto the shoreline in our bare feet and haul ourselves up the rope.

Nope!

There's a steel-rung ladder attached to the side of the lighthouse, which runs straight up. For the next thirty minutes, we have so much fun climbing up the ladder and jumping out into the bay. We both give each other style points for jumps. Cricket does a spread eagle, where she touches her toes, a straight-up TEN! I get three sevens and one nine for a cannonball with a really big splash.

After we climb through our own open window into our light-house room, I take the best, coldest shower of my life. There's something kind of awesome about working for the water you use, cranking the bucket up with my hands, soaping up real good, then dumping the bucket out on my head. It's cold, but I don't care. And when I get out, I dress in whatever I want and I don't really worry about it, even if it looks dumb. I dress for work:

—cutoff shorts

—a T-shirt

—a button-down flannel (like Jemma, I roll up the sleeves)

—tall rubber boots

And for our commute to work, we make our way along the Sunshine Coast, across the beach, past the docks and the dollhouse cabins, stopping at the waterfall spigot to fill Cricket's bottle with glacier water, taking turns passing it back and forth and gulping it down. Then—

We head up the steep stone steps to the lodge.

On the deck that faces the bay, I duck under freshly washed laundry hanging from a line—blue button-down shirts, jeans, undies, white tees, and socks, each clipped to the line and fluttering like flags, drying in the bright morning sun.

Then, just before the door, I stop and hop around on one leg, yanking my tall rubber boots off one by one and setting them in line with everyone else's. Cricket glances at her watch. "Nine twenty-three a.m.," she says, glancing back up. "I'm starving," she whispers.

"Me too!" I nod.

This time, I don't knock.

I slide the large wood-framed glass door open and step inside the lodge. It's the first time I've been not just on time, but early, for anything in my life.

# 68

The second I walk through the door, Lulu, a shaggy blur of white, comes running, skidding across the wood floor, slobbering on my bare knees, looking up at me, tongue out, panting. "Hi, Lulu," I say, and this time I'm a little bit less afraid. I lean forward and give her a scratch on the top of her head. Then Lulu, half-dog, half-wolf, sinks down and offers me her paw! *Okay, that's it—I'm in love*, I think as I gently take Lulu's foot and give it a shake. The bottom of her paw is velvety and rough, and it's official: I have another new best friend.

Two feet away, Cricket has dropped to her knees and she's nose to nose with Zeus, who is giving her kisses. "Oh, yes," she says, giggling, "I missed you so much!"

Lulu begins licking my legs and knees. I stand up straight and glance around the lodge: last night's cozy, candlelit scene is flooded with morning sun. Everyone is awake!

Till is walking in from the back of the lodge, carrying in an armful of firewood ready to burn. The second he looks up and sees me, he gives me a big smile. "Sorry, Liv. If she's bugging you, you can just say, 'Off!'" he says. Lulu is still at my feet. "Oh, it's okay," I tell Till. "We're friends!"

I watch Till unload the split wood onto the floor, then begin to stack it in neat rows, bark facing down. He's dressed in jeans with patches on the knees and a button-down flannel with wood splinters all over his chest and sleeves. His cheeks are rosy and his eyes are bright, and I get the feeling that even though it's only a little after nine a.m., at Great Bear Lodge this is more like lunch! Till just has this glow in his eyes, like he's already chopped and stacked firewood, washed the docks, foraged for berries, and surfed at sunrise.

In the kitchen, Nash looks up from the counter, where he's slicing a loaf of bread. "Morning!" he calls out to us, and smiles.

Jemma is sitting at the Viking's table. She has her right hand cupped around a mug of something that's steaming hot, and she's studying papers, spread out in front of her. "Morning, girls," she says, glancing up.

"Good morning!" I say, and I'm almost startled at how happy my voice sounds. But that moment doesn't last too long, because Jemma says, "Liv, I'm just looking at your paperwork and—" She suddenly stops. Maybe because she sees how terrified I am right now. "It's okay," Jemma says, and smiles. "I just have a few questions." I walk toward her at the table. Lulu follows me.

"Have a seat," Jemma says, nodding toward the same spot at the table where I sat last night. I scoot down the bench. My heart is beating fast. I look at Jemma across from me. She's in the same outfit: denim shirt, sleeves rolled up. Her long, dark hair is tied up in a loose knot. No makeup. All business. I watch her and I take a deep breath. Under the table I am grabbing my knees with both my hands, bracing myself.

"Okay," Jemma says, looking back down at the papers. She sorts through them until—"Here it is." She picks up a single sheet. " 'Parent/Guardian Emergency Contacts,' " she reads, and hands it to me. "You need to fill this out."

## 69

When Jemma removes a sheet of paper from the real Liv Hogan's folder and hands it across the table to me, I take it and I flash her a smile and I go, "No problem!"

"Great," Jemma says.

"Sure," I say, and I shrug a little, like, *No big deal, of course I know Liv Hogan's mom's and dad's names and phone numbers. Duh.*

No.

I do *not.*

I stare down at the blank form. My face is hot. I glance up at Jemma. I go, "Do you need all these phone numbers?"

Jemma looks confused. "You live with both parents, right?"

"Uh-huh," I lie.

"Can you put their different work numbers and just your home phone?" Jemma says, and she passes over a pen.

And I go, "Oh! Yeah. No problem."

Jemma keeps her eyes on me. "Your dad's a law professor? Am I remembering that right?"

"Uh—yeah." I nod.

"And your mom?"

"My mom?" I repeat. "Um, my mom is a—" I stop and watch Jemma as she looks down at the real Liv Hogan's file. Then she looks back up and says, "Oh that's right, she's a physician."

And I go, "Uh-huh," and nod my head.

"I remember now, she's a surgeon, correct?"

"Yep." I smile. "A surgeon," I repeat proudly—which is so messed up. I'm proud of a mom that isn't even mine.

"You know, Liv," Jemma says, and she watches me for a sec. "I know all this planning might seem like a hassle, but there is a purpose behind it."

"I get it, no worries," I quickly say. I know how to make grown-ups happy. I know how to go along with stuff. You just nod a lot—act like you get it even when you don't. Then just like, do what you have to do. I've done this all my life.

Jemma stands. "Can I get you anything to drink, Liv?"

"No, thank you," I answer. "I'm good."

She raises an eyebrow. "You sure?"

"Yeah. Thanks, though," I tell her. The second Jemma turns and walks toward the kitchen, I know what I have to do—

I look over at Cricket and Till, across the lodge by the fireplace. Both of them are laughing and playing with the dogs. Then I glance at Jemma and Nash, standing in the kitchen, turned away from me.

My heart is pounding.

*It's now or never!*

The theft itself only takes a second.

I sit up a little in my seat, reach over the table, and grab the real Liv Hogan's file from the neatly stacked pile in front of Jemma's empty seat. Then I shove the folder behind me, and down the back of my shorts, under my T-shirt. Last, I scooch down the bench and get up from the table.

"Excuse me, Jemma?" I say, and Jemma looks up. She's standing in front of the stove. "Is there a bathroom I can use?"

"Of course!" Jemma answers. "It's right there," she says, pointing.

"Thanks," I say, and I try and look relaxed, which is hard because I have the real Liv Hogan's application file shoved down my shorts.

"Liv?" Jemma calls, and I turn to face her. "Is the form all set?"

I shake my head and put my finger up like, *One sec!* Then I whirl around and head straight for the bathroom, walk inside, and shut the door.

## 70

The bathroom is small. It smells good, like homemade soap, or maybe it's the yellow cedarwood. There is no tub. No shower. No mirror. Just a simple sink, a composting toilet, and a window that faces mountains.

The first thing I do is sit on the edge of the toilet seat.

Not to pee.

To READ!

I am holding the answers to a summer of freedom in my lap!

I have maybe five minutes tops to memorize what's in this folder and put it back. My heart is pounding in a way your heart tends to do when you are doing something that you know is *wrong*, but whatever—I want to stay!

"Let's see who I have to be," I whisper to myself. Then I flip open the folder, thumb through the loose papers, and scan each page for what I need. The first few pages are not any help.

"Medical Form," I read out loud.

"Physician's Release," I breathe.

"Allergies: horsehair, dust." I let out a quiet laugh. *I've never been near a horse in my life!*

I flip to the next page.

Then—"Yes!" I whisper, and I sound like someone who just won a very large prize: *more time with these people, and this life!* I zoom in on the single piece of paper that I need:

NAME: **Olivia Grace Hogan**

ADDRESS: **100 Linden Road, Atherton, California, 94027**

PARENT/GUARDIAN NAME: Kate O'Hara Rutherford
OCCUPATION: Chief of Pediatric Surgery,
    Stanford Medicine
PARENT/GUARDIAN NAME: Charles Hogan
OCCUPATION: Lawyer, Professor of Law,
    Stanford Law School
APPLICANT'S CURRENT SCHOOL: Phillips Exeter Academy
AGE: 16
YEAR IN SCHOOL: 11th grade

COMPLETED COURSEWORK
Accelerated Chinese III
Advanced Readings Latin—Intensive
Absolutism & Revolution,1660–1800
Calculus (enriched)
Advanced Physics
American Slavery, American Capitalism
Indigenous Peoples of North America
German Two Years in One
Author Immersion: Herman Melville
Hinduism and Buddhism
Greek Poetry—Intensive
Existentialism
Postimperial Chinese Literature
Reading Seminar: Chimamanda Ngozi Adichie

ACTIVITIES
Robotics

Environmental Action Committee (EAC)
Symphony Orchestra (violin)
Girls' Varsity Swimming (New England Prep Champions)
Girls' Varsity Hockey
Exeter Student Service Organization (ESSO)

A summer at Great Bear Lodge will stretch your limits.
Please check the technical and interpersonal skills you feel
competent in:

☑ **Mountaineering** ☑ **Rock climbing (belay and
rappel, safety and etiquette)** ☑ **Leave No Trace
Methods & Ethics** ☑ **Tide chart calculations**
☑ **Experience living and working in remote, rugged
setting** ☑ **Carry heavy pack** ☑ **Paddle open water
(portage)** ☑ **Rappel down rock faces and walls**
☑ **Basic wilderness first aid** ☑ **Map and compass skills**
☑ **Problem solving** ☑ **Self-confidence**
☑ **Communication** ☑ **Leadership** ☑ **Character**
☑ **American Red Cross Lifeguarding**

I'm sitting here staring at this page and thinking, *I don't know the
real Liv Hogan, but I am nothing like her, that's for sure*, when I hear:
"Liv?"

It's Cricket.

"Are you okay in there?" she asks.

"One sec!" I say, and as I say it, I stand up, shove the folder in the
back of my shorts, and pull my T-shirt down over it. When I open
the door, Cricket is standing outside the bathroom, facing me. "You
okay?" she asks again, and she looks at me funny.

"Yeah," I say, and laugh. "I'm fine!"

"Okay, good," Cricket says. "I've gotta pee!" she giggles, brushing past me into the bathroom.

I stand just outside the door and take a quick look around the lodge: Till is feeding the dogs. Nash is still making breakfast. I don't see Jemma anywhere. When I'm sure no one is looking, I go for it! I walk straight to the table and slip the folder back onto the stack, and just as I do, I hear, "Liv? What's up? Is there a problem?"

I look up and see Jemma watching me.

Now I panic.

My heart starts beating so hard.

"No, no. No problem," I say, trying my best to sound like everything is perfectly okay. I sit down on the bench and scooch back to my seat at the table. "I just want to make sure I fill out the forms correctly."

"Liv, it's okay," Jemma says, and now she smiles. "We're not going to grade you on the forms." She pauses. "We do this to keep you safe."

I nod.

Jemma sets her cup of coffee on the table and takes a seat. She reaches for her mug and takes a sip.

Question: Do you think dogs can sense danger?

Because, right this second, Lulu suddenly appears under the table and places her head in my lap. It's heavy and warm. I rest my hand against her soft, furry ear and pet it, trying to calm myself. Then I stare down at the blank form, grip the pen, and write everything I just memorized as neatly as I can. I jot down the names of the real Liv's parents:

*Kate O'Hara Rutherford*
*Charles Hogan*

The only thing I have to make up are the phone numbers. Easy!

I quickly double-check my work, make sure I spelled the names right—*yes, I did*—then pick the paper up and hand it back to Jemma. "Here you go!" I say, and grin.

"Thank you, Liv!" Jemma takes the sheet of paper, looks down at it, then looks back up and says, "Great, we are all set!"

For a second, we look at each other.

I can't explain it, but when Jemma looks at me, I can *feel* it. I feel it right in my heart. It feels so good and it also feels so scary. I'm so afraid that I'll have to leave. That she'll figure out my lie. That pretty soon, she'll hate me.

## 71

"**S**mell that?" Cricket breathes. "*Mmmm!*" She's eyeing the heaping plate of crispy fish skin that Nash just set in front of us. Breakfast.

"It's a delicacy," Cricket whispers.

I look around the table. Raw sliced salmon, salmon eggs—these little balls the size of pearls that jiggle like jelly, and the fish skin.

"This is the first sockeye salmon of the season," Till says proudly. "We don't waste any of it: the head, eyeballs, offal—the edible internal organs—the heart, fins, skin, the bones for soup, the eggs," he says, looking right at me. "If you're going to kill something or take something's life, make sure you use it all up."

For a few seconds, it's very quiet.

I straighten up in the seat.

I glance at Cricket, then Nash.

Nash gives me a quiet smile and says, "So, in our culture, salmon is a source of wealth." He pauses. "It's the lifeblood of every living creature on Great Bear. Salmon feed plants, bears, wolves, birds, and us. Salmon is life. We treat it with the deepest respect."

The table falls silent.

Now we hold hands.

This time I know to reach out and connect to Cricket (on my left) and Nash (across the table). I don't close my eyes. I just sit quietly. Till recites the blessing: "We give our thanks today for all life that nourishes us." He pauses and looks around the table at each of us, then goes on, "For sun and rain, for sea and sky, for our friends who sit by our side." He flashes a big grin, and a second later—just like dinner last night—hands are reaching and there are the sounds of passing dishes, then silverware clinking against the plates as we get to the business of eating.

## 72

**W**hat I'm thinking here is: *I have no idea how to eat this food.* I glance up and copy Nash, loading up strips of salmon on a thick slice of homemade bread. Then, just like he does, I sprinkle on a spoonful of little jiggly orange eggs. Finally, I lift it to my mouth and take a big bite, and as I begin to chew, I immediately want more. The only way I can sort of describe it is—I guess it's like . . . to eat a piece of fish from the river, right here on Great Bear . . . it tastes like life! Like my muscles are getting stronger with every bite. Maybe I'm under the spell of this magical place, but as I chew, I swear I feel the fish's energy moving through my veins. I glance up at Nash, the fisherman and the chef, his wild eyes, his jagged scar across his cheekbone.

Nash gives me a quick wink as he chews.

*I really love my uncle*, I think to myself, and smile back. Then I pile another slice of fish onto my thick, crunchy bread and top it off with a heaping spoonful of the perfectly round, salty-squishy-shiny eggs, and use a knife to slather on some homemade honey mustard— and last, my favorite part: the crispy salmon skin. Honestly, it's *so* good! The little eggs pop in my mouth, the salmon is kind of sweet like candy. The bread is so good. Everything here is like, the most delicious thing I've eaten in my life!

There's a really nice light streaming through the open kitchen window. I can hear seabirds calling in the distance. The chatter at the table is mostly the sounds of eating: the clinking of forks and knives, the setting down of cups.

And ten minutes later, all that is left on my plate are a few tiny crumbs and a smear of bright yellow mustard. For dessert, Nash pours us each a hot cup of fish-head broth. I take a small sip and then another. *It's not so bad!* It tastes like some sort of healing potion that's making me strong. Medicine. *I could eat this breakfast every single morning for the rest of my life*, I think to myself, and set my cup down. I look around the table, first to Cricket, then Till, then Jemma and Nash. "Thank you," I say.

Nash cracks a smile. "Sure, you bet."

Everyone stands and helps to clear the table and just gets on with it. Nobody has to ask. Till moves to the sink and begins to wash plates and glasses and bowls and cups. Jemma is putting things away. Nash helps to clear, then quietly slips outside to work.

Cricket sweeps the floor around the table.

I want to help, but I'm not sure what to do. I walk over to the sink, and I pick up a dish towel and just start drying dishes.

I don't mind it at all. This isn't anything like cleaning up after Sunny. First of all, everyone helps, and second: the view! Just outside the kitchen window, everything is so alive—the mountains, the trees, I can hear a fast-moving creek, the waterfall. It's almost like I'm standing outside. I can see for miles. I have a bird's-eye view of the beach, the bay, the ocean. I watch Nash, with Zeus and Lulu trailing behind him, walk past the dollhouse cabins, across the dock, where he sets down a toolbox by the small boat that's tied up. He kneels and leans forward, getting to work on the motor.

I'm pretty sure I've been drying the same red bowl for five minutes, watching out the window, when I hear—

"Liv?"

It's Jemma.

When I turn to look, she's standing two feet away, holding a tray. On the tray is a steaming cup of fish-head broth and a small blue plate with a single piece of toast. "Can you give me a hand for a sec?" she asks.

"For sure! Yeah. I can," I say, surprised at how eager I sound.

I set down the bowl and dish towel and follow Jemma across the lodge—past the fireplace, past the ladder that goes up to the loft, past the cushioned seats you can watch the ocean on, past the guitar hung up on the wall. Jemma's a few steps ahead of me, carrying the tray of food, when she suddenly stops in front of a sliding door and gestures for me to open it. I slide the heavy panel open, and I'm not even one step inside when I look straight ahead and hear myself say, "Oh my God."

## 73

There is another person here!

Sitting, propped up by pillows, in a bed that faces the ocean, is a very old lady with clear blue eyes, and as soon as I step into the room, she looks up at me and her face comes alive. She has weathered, deeply tan skin, a lot darker than mine, high cheekbones that are kind of sunken in the way old people's faces get when their skin sags, and a full head of pure white hair, parted in the middle and combed back.

I stand motionless in the open doorway, stunned.

My mind is racing with a million thoughts, like, *This explains where Jemma goes when she disappears. Who is this lady? Why is she here? I think she might be ninety-nine or a hundred years old!*

When—

"Good morning, Ms. Birdy!" Jemma sings out. She puts the tray down on a wooden table beside the bed.

I think, *Ms. Birdy? Did I hear that right?* I glance toward the lady in the bed. If she were a bird, she'd be a beautiful one. She has jewel-like eyes and a small angular face, and she's wearing a faded yellow short-sleeved nightie. She's all tucked in bed, under a colorful hand-stitched quilt pulled up to her chest. She's very petite and sort of shrunken—I can see the shape of her collarbone poking out under her skin.

"It's a beautiful morning," says Jemma. "Let's pull back these curtains!" She walks to the window and pulls the sheer curtains back, and even more light floods the small, bright room.

Jemma sits down on the edge of the bed. "How about I lift you up a little so you can have some breakfast?"

Ms. Birdy nods.

Jemma leans in and gently holds Ms. Birdy by both her shoulders, pulling her slightly forward and placing another pillow behind her back. "There you go! Comfy?" She waits, and Ms. Birdy's eyes brighten. "We brought you your favorite broth—Nash made it just for you. Would you like some?"

Ms. Birdy nods, and Jemma reaches toward the table and picks up the steaming cup of fish-head broth. Jemma smiles. "It's hot," she says, as she tenderly helps Ms. Birdy steady her hand and bring the cup to her lips.

It doesn't feel right to stare. I look away and around the room. It's simple and sparkling clean. A deerskin blanket on a very old chair, books neatly arranged across the top of a wooden dresser, and a simple glass jar filled with pink wildflowers.

Outside the open window, I hear the waterfall in the distance, crashing off the cliff to the beach below.

"Ms. Birdy," Jemma says, and I turn and look. She puts the cup of hot broth back on the table beside the bed. "I want you to meet someone special." Now Jemma turns to look at me. "This is Liv. She's going to be with us for the whole summer."

I don't know what to do. So I go, "Hi, I'm Liv."

Then I walk over and stop just before the bed. Honestly, I've never been this close to anyone this old. I don't have grandparents. I'm nervous, okay? I don't know what to say.

Ms. Birdy smiles up at me. She is missing four front teeth. She has that kind of translucent skin that old people have; her skin is loose and it kind of drapes over her bones.

"Liv is sixteen," Jemma says. "She's come to us from California."

Ms. Birdy slowly lifts her arm and reaches out for my hand, still smiling up at me and searching my face.

I glance at Jemma, like, *What should I do?*

"It's okay," Jemma says. "She's connecting with you."

I take a step closer to the bed. I hold out my hand to Ms. Birdy, and she laces her fingers between mine. She's still staring up at me. "Sagagyemk," says Ms. Birdy. Her voice is scratchy and weak.

"I know," Jemma tells Ms. Birdy. "I think so too."

"What did she say?" I ask.

"Sagagyemk," Jemma repeats, and then she turns to me. "Ms. Birdy is one of the last fluent Sgüüxs-speaking elders. She is a wisdom keeper."

"Sagagyemk," Ms. Birdy repeats to me.

I smile back. Then I glance at Jemma and ask, "What does that mean?"

"Sagagyemk," Jemma repeats. Then she goes, "It means sun, sunny, or sunshine."

Suddenly my heart begins to race. *It hits me just now—Ms. Birdy must somehow know Sunny.* My throat tightens. I look back at Ms. Birdy. Her eyes wrinkle as she smiles up at me. She grips my hand a little bit tighter.

After a while, the room grows quiet.

Ms. Birdy closes her eyes.

I listen to her breathing.

Jemma is still sitting on the edge of the bed.

I'm still standing, my fingers interlocked with Ms. Birdy's. My palm is getting sweaty and sticky. My head is hot. I feel almost sick inside. All the lies I've told . . . these people have been so kind to me. I look up at Jemma and finally ask what I want to know most. I just get up my nerve and whisper, "Is she your mom?"

Jemma looks surprised. "My mom?" She laughs quietly. "No, my mom wasn't able to raise us." She pauses. "This incredible woman did." After a minute, Jemma says, "Without her, none of us would be here . . ."

More silence.

I look at Jemma and then Ms. Birdy—her eyelids are closed; her grip is weakening in my hand. I think she may be asleep.

"Wait, so who is she?" I finally ask.

And Jemma says, "She's our grandma."

## 74

**O**utside Ms. Birdy's room, I don't say a word.

I silently follow Jemma across the lodge. She heads straight for the kitchen. I stop when Till calls out, "Team meeting," from his spot on the "couch"—a chunky wooden bench, hand-carved by the Viking, lined with furry sheepskin cushions.

Cricket is sitting a few cushions away from Till, and when she sees me, she shoots me a look like, *What just happened?*

I look back at her like, *All good!* My hundredth lie, it seems. Then I sink to the floor and lean against the bench. Don't think I'm sitting here all chill. I'm clenching my teeth. And I'll tell you why in a sec.

I watch Jemma grab two chairs from the kitchen, one for her and one for Nash. A few minutes later the two of them sit facing us. There's a different feel in the air. It's hard to explain. But I can tell things have shifted from *Welcome to Great Bear!* to *Let's get down to business!*

"All right." Jemma looks up from the pad she's holding. "Here we go," she says, eyebrows raised. "Our first guests of the season arrive by floatplane in just fourteen days!"

I watch Jemma and nod my head like I'm listening carefully, but it's hard to pay attention to what's going on around me right now. I mean, I just met my great-grandmother for the very first time and she doesn't even know I'm me!

Nobody does.

"There are a lot of moving parts," Jemma continues. "We have a ton of work ahead." She pauses. "We will be pushed mentally and physically. We will get to know each other, and get to know ourselves a little better too." There's another long pause and Jemma looks at me. "There's a special thing about working together: we are really going to need to trust each other." She takes a breath. "Part of trusting each other is agreeing to our safety plan." Now Jemma turns to Nash.

Nash sits there in his dark jeans patched at the knees, a knife clipped to his belt, and a flannel with the sleeves rolled up. He sits tall in the chair. And when he speaks, he looks straight at you. "Hey, guys," he says, and grins. Then his smile fades. "My most important job on Great Bear is to create a level of safety. We're a team and we rely on each other. Our rules are a lifeline to keep everyone—"

I don't really hear a word after that.

I stare up at my uncle's face. His lips are chapped. Now that I've met Ms. Birdy and know who she is . . . I can see a resemblance: bright eyes, sunken-in cheeks, angular jaw. I look at Nash and wonder if I look like Ms. Birdy too. Nash pauses and moves his eyes from Till, to Cricket, and finally, to me. "The way I see it," he goes on, his voice softer now, "we are responsible for each other, and to do that, we have to be responsible for ourselves."

I'm looking straight up at Nash, but I feel like I am spacing out. I watch his mouth move, but I don't have any idea what he is saying. Every word is like background noise. I try to listen. I swear I do. But inside, the same stupid question is shouting in my head: *Why did Sunny keep all this from me?*

I work to keep my anger down.

My chest tightens.

I look back up at Nash, and as I do, he gives me the slightest

reassuring nod and says, "Back when I was a kid, I learned everything the hard way. Out here, you can never underestimate all the
little factors—the tide, the swells, the cold water . . . bears, wolves,
cougars, rip currents. Things can turn dangerous"—Nash snaps his
fingers—"like that."

It's dead silent.

Half of me is listening, but part of me isn't really here. I'm kind of
sitting, staring into space, when Lulu suddenly appears, pressing her
nose right into my chest. I hear bits and pieces, sentence fragments
of Nash speaking: "Expect and plan for the worst . . . check your tide
chart . . . four hours by boat from any help . . ." Mostly I just stare into
Lulu's eyes, and reach behind her ears, and give her a good scratch.
Lulu settles on the floor, pushing her head into my lap.

I sit up a little bit.

Again, I look at Nash.

"Our bay is protected, it's calm," Nash says, and he catches my
eye. "The west side of the island, up along the coast, is really rugged,
with lots of swell—the weather changes fast, and if you fall into the
ocean water, you have maybe half an hour to survive. The water is
cold, and if you don't have a life jacket, you will have a lot less time
than that. Don't get trapped by the tide or changing weather. It can
look like it's nice and calm, and then a big surge comes in." He waits.
For a long moment he's quiet.

He looks at each of us.

His shoulders are broad, and his arms are strong. His face, even his
scar, is tan. When he smiles at me, it feels almost like a hug, and maybe
that doesn't even make sense, but that's how it feels. It just does.

"If you go anywhere outside our protected cove down below,"

Nash begins again, "take this gear pack with you." He reaches down for the two small red packs sitting beside him, grabs them, and hands one to me and the other to Cricket.

We each get our very own small red pack. Jemma hands us each a fluorescent orange life vest for when we go on the Zodiac boat.

I immediately slip my arms through the vest. It fits me perfectly. I glance down at the red pack in my lap. It's crazy—I came here with nothing, and now I have my own official Great Bear pack, with LIV hand-stitched on the front zippered compartment. Nash takes us through all our new gear and supplies—including a "bear banger" that he teaches us how (and when) to use, a flashlight with two modes: bright and dim, and a small multi-tool knife that is so cool!

After we settle down from what feels like a gift that I didn't even know I was getting, we get back to our safety briefing, and I'm all glowy and grinning.

"One more thing to know," Nash says. His voice is firm.

I look up from all my new gear.

Lulu jerks her head up and looks at Nash too.

Nash leans toward us in his chair, almost like he has to make sure we hear this. "Part of our culture is a sense of responsibility that's bigger than us." He pauses to look at all of us for a good long time. Then he says, "*Always* tell someone where you're going—we call it a 'sail plan.' Tell someone where you're going and what time you're expected back. I do it, Till does it, Jemma does it. We do it all the time." He turns to Jemma and demonstrates. "J, I'm going up to the Bear Tooth River to fish. I should be back by"—he pauses and looks down at his watch, then back up at Jemma—"five or so, no later."

"Thanks for letting me know! Have fun," she says, going along and laughing.

"Just tell someone your plan," Nash says, turning back to us. "It's what we do here. Tell me or tell Jemma. One of us should always know where you're going and when you'll be back, so if you're not back on time, we will come looking." For a moment it's quiet, then, "Understand?" he asks.

"Roger that!" Cricket says, sounding excited.

"Uh-huh." I glance up at Nash and nod, then get back to the zipper on my life jacket. It's caught on a piece of thread. I fiddle with it, give it a little tug, and finally zip it up, snug.

Now I'm sitting on the floor of the lodge in my life vest. Lulu puts her head back in my lap. I look up at Nash.

"Listen, and I mean this," Nash says, and he's not smiling. "Around this area, by the time a helicopter or a boat from the coast guard gets here, it's too late. They won't be able to assist. We need to make good choices at the outset. If you're not certain, ask." He waits. "The ocean can be the best thing in the world, or it can kill you . . ." It gets real quiet again. He looks me in the eyes and goes, "There's never bad weather, just bad choices."

# 75

The next ten days—before the first guests of the season arrive—fall into the dreamy rhythm of Great Bear. It's like a heartbeat, a slow, steady song. Some days, a sweaty, miraculous blur. A cold plunge. A clam I dig out of the flats at low tide, tip my head back, and slurp down. Raw. It's like I have been sleeping for the longest time and I'm just now waking up. Something in me feels like it's changing. I don't know how to explain it . . . It's something that I can't really describe except, you can't miss what you didn't know. And now I know.

On Great Bear, I am never alone.

I'm within one foot of a living being at all times . . . not just humans, but Zeus and Lulu, roaming free on the beach, chasing seabirds or running after driftwood I hurl. Each day I tilt my head up and crane my neck and stare at the biggest, tallest, widest trees that I have ever seen, Sitka spruce and cedar that have been alive for one thousand years at least! Even in the rain and sweet-smelling mists, knee-deep in mud—I am surrounded by life.

For the first time in my life, I can count on eating three meals a day and feeling safe. Jemma, Nash, Till—they each treat us so well. I wake up with the sun, very early in the morning. My alarm clock is literally sunbeams that scatter golden sparkles on my face, like one of those baby mobiles that hang over cribs, projecting light.

I wake up to that!

I'm not lying.

I open my eyes, and I swear to you, the first thing I do is smile.

In thirteen years of life, I have been homeless plenty of times. Sunny and I have lived in an abandoned minivan, trailers with no running water, motel rooms with toilets that didn't flush.

There were always bad smells.

Sewage.

Crumbling ceilings, mold.

I've never lived anywhere I could sit up in my very own bed, turn my head, and look out the window at the sky, the water, the endless ocean, and watch the world wake up. The light is insane. The colors are reddish, pinkish, yellowish, then pale blue.

Each day starts off at six a.m.: "Mermaid swim sesh!" as Cricket says. We haven't missed one single morning swim to Turtle Rock. And listen, I never thought I'd be the type of person who wakes up with the sun, climbs out my own window, and willingly runs down a worn wooden plank and jumps off into deep, cold water!

But, apparently, I am.

I wake up every day with a purpose.

I feel myself getting stronger. I'm standing a little bit straighter. Holding my shoulders back a bit—maybe it's the rope, maybe it's the swim, maybe it's the fact that I'm never hungry here. Maybe it's all three. The thing I love best so far is that every morning is the same. There are no surprises.

We swim—sometimes race—to Turtle Rock, bask in the sun, catch our breath, swim back, climb up the steel ladder and back into our small, square room that sits atop the lighthouse. Could there be a better feeling than after you do something hard like that? Honestly, I don't really think there is.

I'm really settling in. I'm reading a book that I borrowed from Cricket's stack. I've folded all my new clothes and put them away. We keep it nice and neat up here—

Shoes off at the hatch.

Flashlight on the Viking's trunk.

Sawdust for number two.

Cricket gives me an extra toothbrush, and the days go by fast. I have never slept so well for so many days in a row. The spooky, wild night sounds don't scare me anymore. The little baby owls are growing, and maybe I'm crazy, but I feel like they know me! When the mom—or it could be the dad—leaves, the little chicks and I look into each other's eyes, smile (me) and make soft, squeaky sounds (them). And OH! In the back of Sunny's journal, I've begun filling in the pages with lists of animals and birds that I've seen. I use a field guide I found on a shelf at the lodge to help me identify them.

So far, it's:

A bald eagle perched high in a giant red cedar tree,
    outside the lodge kitchen window
Seals!
A sea otter on Turtle Rock
A fox trotting along the beach
A whale, a black-and-white orca with big dorsal fins
Pacific white-sided dolphins
Hummingbirds
Barn swallows
The craziest dragonflies I've ever seen
Trumpeter swans
Black-tailed deer
A mink, looking for crabs under the rocks
Rhinoceros auklets—*dang! For real, look that one up!*

I see plenty of animals eating each other: an eagle ravaging a baby shark; a small, adorable bunny snatched by a hawk; a sea wolf tearing a salmon apart, clutching it in its mouth while the fish wiggles around. At first it sort of shocks me. There's blood. But then I think about it . . . I mean, I do it too. Who decides who is allowed to eat who?

I haven't seen any bears around the lodge or our cove, but once, with Till and Cricket, I saw two cubs chasing each other on the beach, their mom eating the mussels and the crabs under the rocks.

I found one bald eagle feather by the dock.

My uniform lately is: tall rubber boots that can slosh through cold river streams and ocean water, jeans with patches on the knees, one of Sunny's old T-shirts, a hat (for when I'm working outside). What I wear, how I look, I haven't even really thought about it once. It takes me three minutes tops to get going and get dressed. "Tangled hair, don't care!" is my new slogan—well, mine and Cricket's. Sometimes I brush, most of the time, nope! My hairstyle is now officially wind-tossed and snarled. Bucket shower, ponytail it, and hustle to the lodge.

These days I am smelling like pine cones and ocean.

For breakfast, lunch, and dinner, each and every day and night, we feast! Nash transforms the clean, fresh bounty of Great Bear into the most delicious meals that I have ever eaten.

After breakfast each day, Cricket, Till, and I do chores around the lodge and the cabins. We get everything ready for the guests: we chop wood, scrape barnacles off the bottom of the boats, power-wash the docks, paint along the rails of the cabin decks. And in the garden out behind the lodge, we kneel in the dirt and dig our hands into soft, warm soil. We harvest: potatoes, onions, cabbage, kale, asparagus, and bucketsful of berries. Bugs buzz around my face and up my nose. I have so much dirt underneath my fingernails. Nash has been teaching us how to compost with bull kelp we collect from the beach and spread on the garden beds. He says, "Soil is life. Nature is doing all the work; we're just helping."

We do pickling, jarring, canning, curing for the winter months— even though it's the start of summer. It's all part of life around here. They'll never ever run out of food. No stores, or deliveries, it's all right here on Great Bear. They are 100 percent self-sufficient. We harvest all our own food. And I watch and learn how to really use it up. Nash doesn't waste anything. Not a drop. We learn to forage for salmonberries, fiddleheads, golden chanterelles (do not pull or pluck or even yank them out of the earth; you carefully cut with a pocketknife at the base). It's sort of like a scavenger hunt. We dig for clams and collect oysters, fresh bull kelp, and red nori. We only take what we will eat. Nash says, "Don't be greedy and take more than you need."

We've cleaned all five cabins top to bottom: floors, walls, bathrooms, dusted and scrubbed. It's hard work, but I like working hard. We get down on our hands and knees. And we aren't using stuff from Walmart. There's no bleach, or blue spray in a bottle. Everything on Great Bear is homemade. Jemma uses vinegar, rosemary, lavender, and water with a little handcrafted soap and good old-fashioned elbow grease! Now the scent in the cabins is even more unreal. The cedarwood, plus the lavender and rosemary scent—each small cabin has the best, coziest feel, right down to how we make the beds. Jemma's method: lambswool cotton pad, then fitted sheet, then the top one, make sure the sheets are square and all tucked in tight, finish with the warmest, softest patchwork quilt, made by Ms. Birdy years ago. Two pillows centered at the head of the bed. Fresh towels folded square and tidy, then hung up. Some people might not think house-keeping is a good job, but I do! When we're done, when everything is scrubbed and clean, it's just a feeling of peace and calm.

Making beds every morning, even mine . . . just makes me feel like I've accomplished something. Jemma says, "Ms. Birdy always told us, first thing you do every morning is be grateful you woke up, then make your bed." So that's what I do now.

Nine days in a row: I'm on a streak.

After lunch, Cricket and Till and I each have different jobs.

I bring the hottest black coffee on a tray along with a poached egg with a side of toast and jam—the same thing every time—and serve Ms. Birdy. A good day is when I can help her to eat half of the toast and the egg.

I sit with her, right beside the bed in the old wooden chair, or on the edge of the mattress, and I lotion her arms, her hands, and her calves. At first, it's a little bit strange to be putting lotion on her, but I mean, she *is* my great-grandmother, even though nobody knows, and . . . she likes it so much.

It feels good to help.

I help her with the bathroom too. It's a little far away, so there's a walker that Nash crafted out of wood, with felt pads stuck to the bottom, so it glides when she pushes. It takes us at least four to six minutes to walk ten feet.

We have to stop and rest.

Jemma told me that sometimes people with dementia or memory loss forget simple things, like how to walk. A lot of times they forget the mechanism to stand up, so you've got to help Ms. Birdy get started.

Jemma taught me this little trick, to stand with Ms. Birdy and sing "You Are My Sunshine"—the song—and together Ms. Birdy and I march to the beat as I sing, "You make me happy when skies are gray." She won't take a step without that song. If I stop, she stops. Which is kind of crazy, because Sunny used to sing that to me.

And I didn't remember that till now.

Other little things I do with Ms. Birdy are: Keep her nails short and clean. Brush her hair and teeth. She has eleven teeth left. I counted. I brush them for her. Since she can't stand at the sink, I bring a chair in so she can sit by the sink and bring a little bowl she can spit out in.

Jemma says hearing is the last sense to go. She says Ms. Birdy might not look like she is listening, but she can hear me. I've been reading to her every day. And when she speaks in her heritage language, Sgüüx̲s, Jemma has been helping me record Ms. Birdy teaching us Sgüüx̲s words. I use a small tape recorder that's about thirty years old, but it works. So far I have recorded eight Sgüüx̲s words. I don't want to forget them.

> mountain - sga'niis
> sea - l̲axmoon
> salmon - hoon
> wolf - gyibaaw
> sky - l̲axha
> bear - ol

grizzly bear - mediik
grandmother - 'ntsi'its


Ms. Birdy almost always falls asleep when I'm reading with her, but as soon as I stop reading, she opens her eyes again. And if she's holding my hand sometimes, I might feel just a little squeeze. Very slight.

But I feel it.

## 76

In our free time, Cricket, Till, and I explore wild places around the coast. Pretty much anything you can think of, we do.

Climb.

Swim.

Paddle.

Hike and scramble up big granite boulders, then leap off, sinking into plush carpets of lime-green moss. We trek through old-growth forests on winding trails that Till and Nash have cared for and made, hiking past towering, ancient red cedars—the most enormous, beautiful trees I've ever seen. Some are a thousand years old! Still here, breathing.

Just a little ways up behind the lodge is a creek that we call Nature's Waterslide. Till, Cricket, and I slosh through the creek, sit on our butts, and shoot down the smooth, slippery rock. We slide all the way, directly into a perfect pool of cold, clear water. I must have done it twenty times the other day! It's the most fun thing in the world! There's a certain feeling before I try anything—like butterflies. But once I get through my nerves and just do it . . . it's the best rush.

On Great Bear you are never, ever bored—even when we're resting, we do stuff. Till has been teaching me and Cricket how to crochet! For the first few days, it doesn't click for me . . . but now I'm starting to get the hang of it! And when I crochet, I feel my mind just sort of relaxing. I don't even think. I am just like—totally into it, in sort of a trance. All you need to do it is a ball of yarn and a hook, whittled out of a cedar branch by Till. He does it all: the soft wool is sheared off the sheep that graze up in the valley on the mountains, and then there's about a dozen more steps he takes to spin the wool by hand and transform it into yarn. He dyes it using tinctures from rose petals, sunflower seeds, onion skins, and turmeric root into colorful balls of yarn: pink, blue, orange, violet, and the brightest yellow. I swear, Till can do anything. He's the smartest, nicest kid I've ever met.

Twice, we climb up the mountain behind the lodge. We are hardly even a quarter of the way up when we stop, but still—we have the most insane views! You can see for miles: small, uninhabited islands and fjords, surrounded by the never-ending ocean.

We are so high up that it's a lot colder up there, and it feels like the sky is so close that I can reach out and touch it. Up above the forest, in the valley, we swim in freezing alpine lakes, return to the lodge, and warm our toes by the fire. Play with Zeus and Lulu and laugh. I've laughed more in the last nine days than my entire life. Till is 100 percent jokes. Cricket only has to look at me a certain way to make me crack up.

We are always together.

Jemma calls us the three bears.

Walking back to the lighthouse, across the Sunshine Coast with Cricket and Till, and Zeus and Lulu skipping ahead, I realize something—even though they all think I'm this girl Liv, I've been really actually feeling like me.

*Me.* River Ryland.

I just feel so at home. It's like . . . this place is a dream I didn't even know I had. Like, how do you wish for something you don't even know?

I look up when I hear Till shouting, "Liv!" and see him running back to me. Cricket's stopped up ahead, playing with the dogs by a huge driftwood log.

Till stands in front of me now, face-to-face.

He's a little out of breath. And he goes, "Hey," and smiles. "You okay?"

"Yeah." I nod.

"Okay, just checking." He has this twinkly look in his eyes. Then he spins around and runs back toward Cricket, Zeus, Lulu, and the lighthouse.

"Oh man," I say, and I let out a soft laugh because now I'm standing on the Sunshine Coast talking to myself, or maybe I'm talking to the bay, or the ocean, or the osprey circling above the crystal clear water for fish. What I do is shake my head. And what I say is, "I never want to leave."

# 77

Three days before the guests arrive, after I work clearing a trail with Till and Cricket, I am reading with Ms. Birdy when Jemma pops her head into the room.

"Liv." She whispers, because I'm sitting in a chair next to Ms. Birdy's bed and Ms. Birdy is almost asleep. "Can you come sit with me in the kitchen?"

The second Jemma's eyes connect with mine, I begin to panic. *Did she figure out that I'm not Liv? It's over*, I think.

I follow her to the Viking's table.

We sit.

I'm in my seat.

She's across from me.

Two cups of tea between us.

I don't take a sip. I even kind of push it away a little. I can't drink at a time like this! Like always, I prepare for the worst. I can barely look up at Jemma. I sit back in my seat, cross my arms, and try to ride it out.

Take the silence.

Not flinch.

Oh my gosh. Can you imagine my heart right now? I'm just like, I can't really help it. A million things flash in my mind . . . *I don't want to go; I don't want to leave. I love it here. Please, God, please.*

Jemma is quiet. She keeps her eyes on mine. Somehow, I manage to look back at her. I bite my lip a little. I force a smile.

And Jemma says, "Liv"—long pause—"I want to tell you—"

My throat is tightening. I drop my head and close my eyes.

"Liv?" she says.

I lift my head and now Jemma gives me the softest smile. Jeez. I look away. If I don't, I'm going to lose it.

"Hey, it's okay," she says softly.

More quiet.

"Listen, Liv, I promise you, if there was something wrong, I would tell you and we would talk it out." She waits a bit and then she goes, "Hey—"

I glance at Jemma.

"You're not in trouble."

"I'm not?" I say.

"Not at all!" Jemma says. "I just wanted to tell you how much it means to me that you've connected with Ms. Birdy." Jemma keeps her gaze right on me. Now that I realize she's not angry, or mad—

I breathe in.

I feel my shoulders relax.

"You've tackled this job with so much love," Jemma says. "For such a young person, I'm so impressed at how you've been able to adapt and the loving connection you've made. You're a natural care-giver, Liv. You are a nurturer. You have a lot of inner wisdom. You lead with your heart. You're strong." Now she gives me a long, quiet smile. Then she says, "You must have a very, very special mom."

## 78

Two days before the guests arrive, we are walking back to the lighthouse along the coast when I declare an adventure. I turn to Cricket and shoot her one of her own trademark mischievous looks.

This time she's the one who says, "What?" and laughs.

I go, "Let's find Treasure Beach!" And I don't have to say it twice. She's all: "YES!" We look at each other like this is quite possibly the greatest idea ever!

According to Sunny's journal and her illustrated map, there are not only treasures on Treasure Beach, but just beyond it, circled with a colored pencil in bright red, is an arrow and an X marks the spot, with neat handwriting that reads, *Secret hot spring!*

We don't have to think too hard.

There's no planning it out, or stress.

Ten minutes later we are walking around the lighthouse point, following the shoreline away from the lodge, pushing at a pretty good pace out along the beach. We've never been this direction along the coast. It's gorgeous. The tide is low and we are walking in the packed sand along the ocean. It's so quiet, so peaceful. There's just the right amount of breeze and the sun is out and shining.

I'm in my jean shorts and white T-shirt. Cricket has shorts on too, and a tank top. We skip, run, and splash in the low tide. But just over the next bendy point, Cricket suddenly stops in her tracks.

I'm a little bit ahead of her, wading through ankle-deep ocean water.

I look back over my shoulder, then turn around to face her.

I cup my hands around my mouth and shout, "What are you doing?"

"Liv," she yells. "We have to go back."

"What? Why?" I shout.

Now we walk toward each other and meet halfway.

We stand with our bare feet in the water, facing each other.

"Sail plan," she says.

I go, "What are you talking about?"

"We forgot to tell Nash or Jemma where we're heading or when we're expecting to come back."

And what do I do? I kind of laugh. Then I shrug and go, "Don't worry about that. No one cares. It makes no difference."

Cricket's face looks suddenly nervous. "Are you sure?" She waits and I nod, and again I laugh a little. *I mean, I've never had to tell anyone where I'm going in my life. Nobody cares.* I don't say that, though.

What I say is, "We're pretty far out, and we'll be really careful."

Cricket looks unconvinced. "I feel like they want to know, though," she tells me. "We didn't even look at the tide charts. We don't have our life jackets or our red emergency packs."

I don't say anything. I don't want to go back! We look at each other. The wind blows, the water trickles in. "We're already so far!" I say, and I wait. I give her a smile.

Then Cricket puts her hands on her hips and goes, "What if we see a bear?"

"We're not going to see a bear." I laugh.

I've got Sunny's old backpack strapped to my shoulders. I stuffed her old journal in it, and I have one extra hoodie packed. Cricket has her water bottle clipped to my pack.

I point this all out. I say, "We'll be fine, I promise!"

Cricket goes, "Are you sure?"

I nod toward the beach. "Look," I say. "It's low tide, it's so calm." Now I spread my arms out wide. All around us is sun-drenched flat white sand and calm waters. I tip my head back and say, "Pure blue skies!" I grin at Cricket, and then I reach for her arm and pull her forward. "Let's go explore," I say. "Come on! It will be an adventure!"

After an hour of walking up the coast, we stop on a small, crescent-shaped beach that we are convinced is Treasure Beach and set out to discover all the life and gems revealed across the sand when the tide is out. We turn over rocks and see tiny, tiny crabs scattering away. We stumble upon these amazing tide pools, real-life aquariums, surrounded by boulders covered with barnacles, and orange starfish clinging to rocks.

"Holy moly!" Cricket says, crouching down, mesmerized, staring into the water at a purple sea urchin. "Ooh, this thing's moving!"

I crouch down and stare into the water too.

It's unreal.

Squishy blobs of gold and green. Spiky sea stars, sea glass that's worn and smooth, transformed from broken bottles to treasures! I bend, cup my hand, and dip it into the sea, letting the sand and water sift through my fingers, and—"Look at this ruby one!" I say to Cricket, but also just to me. It's *incredible*. Left in the palm of my hand are these real, tiny shimmery gems.

Cricket looks up and says, "Hey, we should think about heading home soon. I don't know what the tides are doing, and I want to make sure we can get back on the beach and not have to run in the waves."

"But we can't come this far and not find the hot spring!" I say.

Cricket laughs. "A hot spring does sound really good right now." She grins and goes, "And we'll be quick, right?"

"Yeah! We can be quick! Totally!" I say, and I dig through my pack, fish out Sunny's old journal, and open it to the right page. My fingers are wet and cold, but still, I hold the map up in front of me like we're trying to find an ancient ruin. I am trying to match Sunny's illustration to what is actually before our eyes.

It's a pretty good map.

"I think we have to go up there," I say. I'm pointing toward the line where the mountain meets the sea, and a gap in the forested cliffs, a narrow channel, with a creek that runs into the ocean.

Cricket is next to me, and now she takes the journal in her hands and holds it up. "Yeah," she says, looking at the map, then looking at where I'm pointing. She turns to me, eyes all wide and sparkly. "Let's go!" she says. And now we are running.

Well, wait.

You can't exactly run on slabs of stone and rock. You have to step carefully, and kind of scramble up and over them. There's some pretty large gaps and holes between the granite slabs that would not be fun to fall in. Stuff is washed up on the rocks—tons of giant driftwood logs, worn smooth by the ocean and the rain and the sun. There are fresh piles of fish guts, left by bears or sea wolves, and half-eaten salmon with their heads bitten off. It sounds gnarly, but honestly, it doesn't faze me that much. Twelve days in, I've got a bit of a different view. I mean, bears have to eat too. I plug my nose at times, but Cricket and I forge straight ahead.

"Oh shoot," Cricket shouts. I'm not sure why. She's up ahead of me, standing on a boulder.

"What's up?" I holler out.

"I think this is a dead end," she yells back.

I stop, unstrap Sunny's backpack, and take out the journal again. I hold it up in front of me with both hands. I look all around. It's like solving a puzzle. Or maybe more like *Where's Waldo?* Basically, even though we are just about one football field length off the beach, we've entered a full-on coastal rain forest. Even the mountains we climbed with Till were not like this.

There's no path.

Cricket and I are walking up the bottom of a narrow gorge between two sloped granite cliffs covered with forest. The ravine is flooded with sparkly beams of light filtering through branches. I'm stepping from one giant slab of stone onto another, pushing my way through a maze of tall tangles of ferns and about a zillion downed, decomposing logs covered with fluorescent green moss. I look and look for the hot spring.

I look to my right. And I look to my left.

This ravine is super dense.

Meanwhile Cricket is hopscotching back, leaping from giant rock to giant rock, until soon we are standing together again, searching for the hot spring that Sunny circled in red.

It's so still and quiet.

I turn to Cricket and whisper, "This map is no good. It doesn't even work anymore." Then I shake my head, and . . . guess what? That's exactly when I hear it . . .

# 79

Wait. No, Cricket hears it first, actually. My bad. Her eyes go wide and she says, "Hey, do you hear that?"

I'm searching the ravine floor, trying to see this ancient hot spring, when I hear it too. It almost sounds like a wind chime. This light tinkling sound that breaks the quiet. It's so soft you could totally miss it. "Where is that coming from?" I whisper. My head's on a swivel now.

Cricket takes Sunny's journal from my hands. She holds it up in front of us. She looks down, studying the illustrated map.

I go, "It's not here." I shake my head. "It was dumb to think it was."

"*Shhhhh*," Cricket says, glancing up from the journal.

Then, almost at the exact same time, we both see it.

It's just ten feet away.

"Oh my gosh!" I say, and drop my pack. And within seconds we are squealing and hugging and shrieking, "YES!!!!!!"

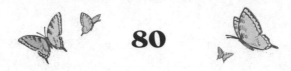

## 80

We strip off our clothes right down to our undies and bra (me) and surfer-girl bikini (Cricket) and leave our clothes in a heap beside my backpack on top of the giant boulder.

Then we leap from boulder to boulder, laughing and shrieking the way you do if you are half-naked in a ravine in a coastal rain forest and there are no other humans, just birds watching, possibly deer.

Hopefully, no bears!

We stop and look down: the huge boulders create a natural pool. It's like—

"Perfect!" Cricket says. Then she crouches low and reaches in to check the water. "Always check to make sure the water isn't boiling hot," she explains. "The best hot springs have a mix." She nods up the ravine toward a gurgling creek flowing over the rocks. "Cool water from that creek mixes with the hot water from the ground . . . and voilà!" Cricket sits down on the edge, sinking into the hot spring until the emerald water is up to her chest. "Heaven!" she says.

I slip into the water too. "Oh, whoa, it's hot" is what I say, shocked at the wonder of it all. I mean, we are in a forest, beside the Pacific Ocean, in a pool of crystal clear hot water that is gushing out of cracks in the earth! "This is unreal," I say, sitting on a smooth, narrow ridge. It feels like a hot tub, but it's just nature! Cricket's on the other side, opposite me. The walls of the hot spring are solid granite, probably millions of years old.

Cricket sighs. "It's the perfect temperature. Amazing!"

I breathe in. "I never want to get out!" I say.

Cricket tips her head back and shuts her eyes. A second later, "Liv," she says. Now she opens her eyes and smiles.

"Yeah?" I laugh.

"You're seriously my best friend," she tells me.

"Same," I say, and giggle. Hot steam is misting up into the cooler air, we are by thousand-year-old cedar trees, and if you stand up (I don't), you can see the ocean and the beach. For the longest time we just sit and soak in the quiet.

Cricket breaks the silence. "You know what," she says, and she sort of whispers, the way you do when you are in a place that's beautiful and silent. "This is by far the prettiest place I've been in the whole world."

I go, "Yeah," even though the truth is I haven't been anywhere but here, but I don't say that.

For the next who knows how long, we soak. We talk and laugh. Cricket gives me a lesson on how hot springs work. "Okay," she begins, looking excited. "So. The water from streams and rain percolates down into deep cavities underground and comes into contact with molten rock." Cricket pauses. "Then the magma—the rock at the core of the earth, *many* miles below the surface—heats the groundwater, and then"—her passion rises as she talks—"that hot water circulates all the way back up, resurfacing as a spring that's hot! A thermal spring is literally heated by the earth."

"That's amazing," I say.

Cricket sighs and goes, "I know, right?"

And I ask, "How do you know this stuff?"

Cricket says, "Honestly, I'm really curious about the earth and how things work. What can I say?" She grins. "I nerd out on geo-chemistry."

"Cool," I say.

"No!" Cricket laughs, and she goes, "HOT!" She waits. "Get it?" she says, and we both crack up.

Then we bliss out. The hot spring is like a hot bath that is just the right temperature, except the water never gets cold. And if you do get too hot, you just get up, run over to the creek, and soak in that, then dip back into the hot spring!

There's no better spot than this!

Why leave?

The sun is streaming through the trees, hitting my face. It's really easy to lose track of time. We soak until—after who knows how long—I notice my fingers are shriveling up, and wrinkled. Also, the air is getting a little bit colder and the light has changed. I suddenly get an uneasy feeling. It's in my gut.

"Hey," I say, and boost myself out of the hot spring and step up on the granite rock. "We better hustle out back to the beach," I tell Cricket. I tip my head back and look at the sky. "I think there's a storm coming."

We don't sit around.

We move *very* fast!

Cricket quickly gets out of the hot spring, and one at a time we leap from boulder to boulder back to gather our gear, throw on shirts and shorts, and begin to retrace our path to Treasure Beach. Very quickly the weather is changing. All that heat and warmth and bliss gives way to a chilly cold blast of air. I look ahead of us, through the narrow ravine we are in out toward the ocean. My mind realizes

what's happening before the words come out of my mouth. I feel
terror in my chest. The ocean looks angry. The tide is rising fast. I
turn to Cricket and try to look calm, but what I say is, "We've got
to run!"

# 81

We make it out of the ravine, but we are trapped where the forest meets the ocean, standing huddled together on a very large boulder the size of a garbage truck. We are surrounded by quickly rising water.

It begins to rain.

It's very slippery.

I leap down and land on the beach and try to see if we can make it back by walking along the shoreline, but quickly, I'm thigh-deep in freezing-cold salt water. There's no way we can get back the way we came. In the rain and the wet, I scramble and barely pull myself back up onto the boulder and try to think fast. The only other option is to climb the cliff behind us and somehow walk into the forest. Try to push through the bush. I turn to Cricket—she looks so scared—and shout through the drenching rain, "It's okay. Stay here!"

I reach up and grab a branch that's sticking out and push off the rock as hard as I can and pull myself up onto the side of the cliff. But right away I hit thickets and sharp pricker bushes and crumbling rock. To make matters worse, I'm losing my footing. Something in my gut tells me to go back. I carefully lower myself down onto our rock—

I look all around.

We are now officially surrounded by water from the incoming tide. The water is almost halfway up our boulder, and rising fast.

Cricket is sitting. She's hugging her knees, and her head is down. At first, I think she's resting. Then she looks up and—

"Oh my gosh." I rush over to her, and I have to shout through the rain. "Cricket, you're bleeding!"

## 82

We are trapped on a boulder with rising ocean water.

Cricket is now looking up at me, holding her head. Blood is streaming down her wrist and arm. I'm still trying to figure out what happened. I crouch down. I position myself so I'm facing the sea. I don't want to turn my back on the water. The first thing I do is take off my T-shirt, ball it up, and use it to put pressure on the wound. "What happened?" I shout over the surging waves.

"I don't know," she yells. "I think I got cut when I slipped."

I lift up the T-shirt for a second and look. There's a gash on her forehead just over her right eyebrow. It's bleeding a lot. I glance at the ocean. I look at the sky. It's eerily dark, and big, thick clouds are moving in. I am acting as calm as I can, but inside, I'm frantically trying to figure out what to do. It's not just the tide, it's a storm, and it's heading for us.

Cricket takes over holding the balled-up T-shirt to her head. "Hold it tight," I yell. Then I dig into my backpack for my hoodie and carefully help Cricket slip it over her head and put her arms through the sleeves. Her hands are trembling. She's a little bit dazed. I think she's dehydrated.

I grab Cricket's water bottle, unscrew the top, and hold it to her mouth. "Can you take a few sips?"

Cricket opens her mouth and takes three or four large gulps. She's definitely thirsty.

I am too.

I take three big sips.

"We're going to sit tight," I say, and now I have to kind of almost shout in her ear, the waves are so loud. "We're going to be okay!" I tell her. I screw the water bottle top on tight, place it in my pack, and strap the bag to me so it doesn't get swept up into the sea.

"We'll wait until low tide, and then we'll get out," I tell her. I am half telling her and half telling myself. I do the calculations in my head. After twelve days in Great Bear, at least I know this: there are two high and two low tides each day. There is about a nine-foot difference between high and low. I peer down into the water and try to get a sense of whether it's reached nine feet or whether it's going to get higher.

I glance over my shoulder. The ravine we were just in is filled with a surge of ocean water, and immediately behind our boulder of stone is the steep, cliff-like mountain that goes straight up—a maze of thick prickly bushes and fallen logs, tree trunks that are so big it would take ten of me to hold hands in a ring around them. *No. No way can we get through that,* I think to myself. *Going into the woods in the dark would be the worst thing to do. The smartest thing is to stay on this rock.*

We are caught by the afternoon high tide. It must be around six p.m. It's gonna be dark before the dead low tide, which will probably not come until—I count five or six hours out on my fingers. Midnight.

We need to wait until the tide drops.

I glance at Cricket. The blood from her forehead is running down her chin and neck. "How's your head?" I shout.

"Okay," she mouths, but I can tell by the way she cringes that she's worried. Cricket takes the balled-up T-shirt off her cut. "How does it look?" she asks, turning to face me.

I get up on my knees to take a look at the cut. "Oh, okay," I say. "The pressure is helping," I tell her. I work to make my voice sound calm and not as freaked out as I am. The gash in her forehead is gnarly. I'm pretty sure she needs stitches. Things are getting worse, not better.

"I'm scared!" Cricket cries.

"I'm scared too," I say. "But we're going to be okay," I tell her. Then I take the shirt from her hands, use my teeth to rip a long cotton strip, carefully lay the cloth over her forehead, and tie it tight around the back of her head. I try to get her to laugh. "You look like the Karate Kid," I tell her, and try to smile.

Cricket is not laughing.

Neither am I.

I sling my head back and squint up at the sky. The rain is driving down on us and it's getting dark fast. Not sun-setting dark—it's too early for that. It's storm clouds, turning more than half the sky a dark, brooding black. Out of nowhere I see lightning crackle and flash across the sky. Then I hear a blast of thunder, a boom so loud I feel it rattle in my chest. The storm isn't in the distance—it's over our heads.

# 83

"We're going to die!" Cricket begins to sob. She just loses it. "Liv, this is too much!" I've never seen her like this.

"We're going to be okay," I try to reassure her. "We're going to get out of this!" I tell her as the lightning and thunder give way to pelting hail. Small balls of ice rain down on us, bouncing off the rock.

Cricket is freaking out. "We should have told Jemma or Nash or Till where we were going and when we were planning to be back!"

In seconds, the hail turns back into a cold rain. A waterfall of blood is streaming down Cricket's face. She turns to me. "Now how is anyone going to find us?" she cries. "They might not even know we're gone!"

She's afraid. But the thing is, she's right.

My ears are still ringing from the thunder.

We are in high tide, sitting beside an ocean of open water in the craziest lightning storm I've ever seen. The wind is unbelievable and getting worse. Twilight is fading fast. I keep telling myself I can do it: *I can do it . . . I've been through worse.* And something inside me just kicks in. I grab Cricket by both her shoulders. "We're gonna figure this out," I yell. "We're not gonna die!" Maybe it's the adrenaline, or a lifetime of practice dealing with sketchy situations with Sunny.

*Of taking control.*

*Caring for her.*

*Trying to solve her problems.*

I switch to full-on survival mode. I stand up on the boulder. I'm more focused than afraid. I need to figure out what to do. Figure out our next move!

I look around.

I have an idea.

The first thing I do is move Cricket and me out of the wind and rain. I help her scooch over a bit, until we are sitting in a small crevice in the stone, huddled together underneath a hollowed-out downed log, which keeps the rain from falling on us. This is the best we're going to do to stay dry.

Cricket is soaked and shivering.

We sit shoulder to shoulder, sheltered by a log, staring out at the rising water. "We're gonna be okay," I tell Cricket over and over again. I'm telling myself, *Breathe in courage, breathe out fear.* I read that once. But when I glance at Cricket, her lips are turning bluish purple. She's shaking. I take my backpack off and drape it over her—any layer might help.

"Now what do we do?" Cricket cries. Her teeth are chattering together.

I yell two words: "We wait!"

# 84

After hours of waiting, soaked and shivering on our boulder, under my not-very-great, now-leaking shelter, the light is nearly gone. Worse, Cricket is convinced we are going to die. "We have no way to get out!" she cries.

Her hands are frozen.

I try to warm them with my hands, but mine are pretty freezing too. "You're okay, you're okay!" I yell to Cricket. I look right into her eyes. "We're going to be okay. I promise!" I tell her.

But inside, I'm not so sure.

We're two tiny specks on a giant slab of stone sandwiched between a towering forest and the Pacific Ocean. If anyone does come looking, they'll never see us. I know I have to figure out a way to warm us up—keep us safe before it's pitch-black. I begin frantically riffling through my backpack, Sunny's old bag, hoping Sunny left something in the pockets that might help.

I unzip the three zippered compartments on the front and side and dig my numb fingers around and—"Nothing!" I mutter. *Come on, Sunny*, I think to myself. *For once, please help me!* But soon—

There are no zippers left to unzip.

No pockets to check.

In a last-ditch effort, I open the top of the pack, reach in, and dig around the main compartment for any glimmer of hope. My fingers run over the sides of the journal, then—

I feel something!

I fish it out.

In the fading light, I have to hold it up close: it's a very small container made of metal, about the size of a lipstick case. I grip it with my frozen fingers. But the top won't budge. I breathe in and try to calm down. Try to hold my hands steady. I go at it again. I'm so cold it's hard to unscrew the top, but I do, and inside the small container are—

"Matches!" Cricket shrieks.

We both scream, "Yes!!!!!"

I don't just sit here. I pop up on my feet and get to work gathering something to burn. I reach up as far as I can toward the steep mountainside behind us, scavenging for kindling to burn. I do this five times. I gather dry moss, twigs, and a few large branches that have fallen. The branches snap easily in half. I hold them to my nose and sniff; they smell like the lodge. *Cedar*, I think, and I hope it's dry. The hollowed-out log that we are sitting under is also pretty dry underneath. I pull chunks off. It's dead and dry. Last, I organize my wood into piles: the moss, and twigs, pine needles, pine cones, sticks the size of pencils, and the bigger stuff: snapped-in-half fallen cedar branches and chunks of the hollowed-out log.

Finally, I make a bed of pine needles to keep the fire off the damp, cold rock and let air come in underneath. *That will make everything burn*, I tell myself.

The whole time I'm in fire-maker mode, I keep talking to Cricket. Joking. Trying to keep her spirits up. "We're tough, we're survivors," I tell her. "We're mermaids, right?" I glance at her and she cracks the slightest smile. I pile the chunks of wood, stacking the pencil-size pieces of cedar sticks together.

"We're gonna have a great story to tell," I say, and give her a little nudge. "We will never forget this in our entire lives."

Then I get up on my knees. I bend forward to shield the wood and strike the match on the strike pad on the side of the container. The first one is a dud.

"This better work," I whisper to myself, and . . .

Match #2 lights for a millisecond, then gets blown out by the wind. "@#$!" I take a deep breath. I calm myself down. Cricket scooches closer, and the two of us huddle together to protect our small stack of wood from the wind and the rain. There are three matches left.

I glance at Cricket, then back at the match. "Here goes," I whisper as I strike #3 and—

"Yes!" We both let out a cheer.

Now with the lit match between my fingers, I carefully steady my hand and light the one thing I haven't mentioned yet—ten crumpled-up pages of Sunny's journal I tore out and stuffed inside the small tower of branches and wood. As the paper burns, it ignites the small sticks, moss, and cedar that are underneath it. I get down on my stomach, on the cold, damp rock, and blow very gently on the flames. As the fire gets going, I add branches of dead downed wood. "You did it!" Cricket shrieks.

Hold on. I don't celebrate yet.

It's just a little fire. And we need BIG. I feed the flames with sticks and moss, cedar branches from my collection. Then, finally, I add on the bigger chunks of the hollowed-out log. The flames grow. The heat feels so good!

I get down low and close and blow on the very base of the fire, to help it burn. Soon, the larger branches and chunks of wood begin to turn to coal. "I'm starting to feel my fingers," Cricket says, holding her hands up to the fire.

I give her a quiet smile and glance at her face: the Karate Kid strip of T-shirt is down around her neck, the gash on her forehead has stopped bleeding, but her face is stained with streaks of red blood.

We sit back, huddling in our makeshift fort, on our boulder. We are completely surrounded by high tide. But the darkness is now lit by fire. We have warmth and we have light.

Cricket breaks the quiet. She goes, "Liv, you're really good at taking care of people. You're like a mom! How are you so good at this?"

I don't answer . . . Telling her the truth about me is not an option right now. It's still cold and pitch-black, and the ocean is all around us.

What I do is: I sit back and rip more pages out of Sunny's old journal, feeding them to the fire and watching them ignite—until after a while, Sunny's journal only has three pages left.

No more drawings.

No more maps.

No more possible tattoo sketches.

No more quotes.

I burned all that seventy pages ago. I don't even care that the pages are disintegrating before my eyes, turning into tiny glowing red embers that float up into the night. *If Sunny hadn't kept everything from me, I wouldn't even be here. I hate her right now*, I think, and feel my throat tighten. At this exact same second, Cricket pops up to her feet. "Light!" she screams.

I scramble up too.

I have to squint, it's so bright.

A giant searchlight beam swings to our left and then to our right, then stops on me and Cricket jumping in the air, waving our hands wildly overhead. "We're here!" I scream in pure elation.

"We made it!" Cricket cries.

It's quite a ways away—

A big searchlight, like a real bright flashlight.

It's not on a helicopter.

It's on a boat.

It's Nash.

## 85

The rescue is a blur. Super choppy. Sideways rain, crazy wind. At first, Nash can't even get the boat close to the shoreline, the swells are so big. The boat bobs in the water, beaming the spotlight on us, until finally, there is a break in the waves and the Zodiac motors in alongside the boulder so that Nash can get to us.

It's Nash and Till, wearing bright orange heavy-duty storm gear and life vests. Till takes over steering and Nash does the dangerous part: getting from the boat to me and Cricket on the rock.

I stand on the ledge and watch. Nash is quick, like a rugged, real-life Spider-Man, the way he scales the vertical side of the rock using only his hands, clenching cracks and nubs, reaching and pulling himself up the steep sheet of granite rock to reach us on the top. Then he's here. Standing in front of me.

Nash is soaked. He shakes his head and his eyes catch mine. "Man, am I happy to see you!" is the first thing he shouts over the crashing waves. Then he yells, "Are you okay?"

I yell back through the wind, "Cricket's head!" and touch my own head with my hand. His eyes shift to Cricket. "We'll take care of that," he yells out, and gives me a reassuring smile through the cold wind that's picking up. "Let's get you home!" he shouts.

Nash makes fast work of getting Cricket, then me, buckled into life vests, calling out instructions and giving hand signals to Till, who is looking up from the boat, trying to keep it from smashing into the rocks.

Cricket is evacuated first.

Nash scoops her up and carries her, with her hands wrapped around his neck, somehow lowering himself with one hand, working his way down the boulder with Cricket clinging to his neck.

This isn't a joke.

This is life or death.

Now I am alone on the rock. My hands are shaking. I glance down. My fire is out. I don't move. Not even one inch. I'm terrified right now. I don't want to get knocked off my feet or slip into the deep, dark sea—a stew of downed logs, probably sharks, roaring waves. I do not want to get swept away! *There's nothing like almost dying to make you want to live.*

"Liv!" I hear Nash yell. He came back for me, and he's now in front of me, reaching for my hand. I grip onto his in a full-on lock, like I'm never letting go. Getting off this boulder onto the boat is probably the scariest thing I have ever done in my life. "Hold on as tight as you can," Nash shouts to me. I follow his instructions word for word. I hold on for life. The two of us stand together, linked by our hands, on the ledge of the boulder. I look straight down.

Suddenly, this seems crazy!

I panic. There is a pretty big gap of ocean between the narrow ledge I'm standing on and the Zodiac boat down below us. I don't see how I can make it. It looks impossible. The swells move under the boat, whipping it up then dropping it down. The dark, monster waves are roaring loud.

Nash grips my hand tighter. I glance at his face lit by the glow of the spotlight shining from the Zodiac. I hear him shout over the stormiest waves, "Trust yourself, Liv!" Then, on his signal, hand in hand, we jump.

# 86

On the boat, it's like the ocean is alive.

It's dark, it's night.

Nash pilots the Zodiac away from our rock, into the open ocean. The boat pounds through the waves. Till sits between Cricket and me, and my arm is looped through his arm. Till takes off his gloves and gives them to Cricket. Then he takes both my hands and tries to warm them in his. There's no talking. I can feel the rush of air, the bone-chilling cold. The ocean lashing against the boat.

The thumping of the waves.

The three of us hold on to each other tight.

And when we finally swing around the point and turn right into the bay, the swells smooth out—our cove is protected from the wind and the waves. There are still booms of thunder and flashes of light across the dark sky, and as the boat slows down, I look up and see the shapes of the five dollhouse cabins, the silhouette of the lodge nestled above them, the dark shades of the mountain peaks surrounding us.

Home.

I can't even describe my relief. My grip loosens around Till's hand. *We made it*, I think to myself. My teeth are chattering together like some emergency Morse code. In the stillness of our secret cove, Nash cuts the motor, and we glide silently toward the shore. Till jumps onto the dock and ties the Zodiac up, wrapping ropes tight, tying knots. Then all four of us head up the steps to the lodge. Nobody is talking. I'm exhausted. I've got Nash's huge bright-orange jacket wrapped around me like a blanket. Cricket has Till's on and zipped all the way up to her chin. The second we reach the deck of the lodge, Jemma rushes outside, and I am thinking, *It's over. I'm gone. She's going to be so mad. This was all my fault. Everyone is going to hate me now* . . .

But—

What Jemma does is wrap her arms around us. "I'm so glad you're safe," she says, pulling us in. Cricket is uncontrollably sobbing into Jemma's shoulder. I feel this hurt in my chest. I try so hard to push it back. For some reason, I don't cry.

It's like, if I do, I won't stop.

## 87

"Liv?" Jemma says, walking toward me. "Hey, you should probably get out of those wet clothes."

"No, I'm good," I say. Not true.

I am sitting on the stone ledge in front of the fireplace.

Pretty sure my lips are blue. My teeth are still chattering together, and they won't stop. I'm shivering. Dazed. Just in shock, I guess. Everything happened so slow and so fast—if that even makes any sense.

It's like, I almost died.

Now I'm alive.

I'm still pretending to be Liv Hogan.

They still don't know who I really am.

Everything is feeling especially scary, and nervous and also pure relief. All three.

Soon—a minute, five, I really have no idea how long I sit in front of the fire—I'm in the bathroom. My wet clothes—my tangled-up bra, my underwear, and shorts—are now in a heap on the lodge's bathroom floor. I'm naked and trying to dry off, wrapping myself in a towel, when I hear a soft knock.

"Liv," Jemma says, and I get out of view and open the door a crack, just enough for Jemma to hand me a neat stack of folded dry clothes. "These should fit," she says.

I take the clothes and shut the door. I crumple to the floor and sit with my back against the wall. What do I feel? I feel doom. *This is just going to get worse. I blew it. I'm going to get fired. I know it. I hate myself so much right now.*

"Liv?" I hear. It's Jemma again.

"Everything okay in there?" she asks.

I'm silent.

"Yeah," I finally manage.

I don't say more.

I can't.

I'm sitting on the bathroom floor, trying not to cry.

Eventually, I get up. I put on Jemma's too-big-for-me flannel pajama bottoms and her cozy crewneck thermal, then pull a pair of thick wool socks over my feet. I tug them all the way up to my knees. I wiggle my toes. I can feel them again.

Before I walk out, I put my ear to the door like a nurse with a stethoscope listening to a heartbeat. *Is it safe? Are they mad?* I listen for yelling, for trouble. For a dish to break or a door to slam. But that's not what I hear. What I hear is Jemma asking everyone if they'd like soup, Till coming in from outside, the thud of an armful of chopped wood being set down on the floor—then the fire snapping from a fresh chunk of alder. And I hear Cricket. She's back to herself—I smile when I hear her laugh. I hear Zeus and Lulu, their paws scratching the floor. I hear Nash's gentle, steady voice. "Looks like you got cut by some barnacles on a rock," he says to Cricket. "They can be really sharp. You can get a good slice."

It takes a second.

I take a deep breath, put my hand on the driftwood knob, push the door open, and finally walk out.

## 88

I emerge from the bathroom dressed in Jemma's cozy pajamas. I take a few steps forward, and the first thing I see is that the middle of the lodge is now a makeshift emergency room. Nash has a headlamp on, and Till is arranging the contents of a first aid kit on a tray: gauze, scissors, a syringe, a whole mess of sterile bandages in small white packages.

The patient, Cricket, is lying flat on top of one of the Viking's sturdy benches. She has on Till's flannel shirt, buttoned up, and pajama bottoms tied at the waist. Her long hair is strung out all over the place like a mop, hanging off the end of the bench.

"Good news," Nash says, sounding relieved as he closely examines Cricket's cut and head. "So. No broken bones, no concussion."

"And the bad news?" Cricket asks, looking up.

"You've got quite a gash on your forehead," Nash answers. His voice is sure and steady. "It's a pretty decent cut. We're gonna need to stitch it up."

"Stitches?" Cricket says, wincing. "Oh man, how much is this gonna hurt?"

"I'll numb you up with some lidocaine," Nash says, and he's very calm. "But you'll still feel it. It's gonna hurt, no doubt about that."

"My guy's amazing," Till pipes up. "He can suture you up from the back of an SH-60 helicopter," he says proudly. "He knows his stuff."

Nash is all action, no talk.

He's completely focused on the task at hand: filling a syringe and washing out the gash on Cricket's forehead. "Okay, Cricket, here we go," he says. His voice is gentle. "Tiny needle. You're gonna feel a little sting."

"*Ow!*" she cries.

Till offers Cricket his hand to squeeze, and she grabs on. I feel bad that I don't offer to help, but I don't think it would be a good idea. I can't watch this and not cringe.

"Oh man," Cricket breathes. "This really hurts."

Till goes, "Keep breathing."

Nash keeps quietly working.

For a quick second, I glance toward Ms. Birdy's room. The light is on and the door is open. I can hear Jemma helping Ms. Birdy with something. *Gosh. I'm so stupid! I made everyone worry when they already have so much on their plate.*

"OW!" I hear Cricket and turn to look. Nash is sewing a row of stitches through the gash above Cricket's right eyebrow, pulling together the wound, one stitch at a time.

"You're doing great, Cricket," Nash says, coaching her through. "Do you think you can hold very still?"

"Uh-huh," Cricket says, her eyes watering now.

I watch as Nash pulls the cut together. The edges line up. Then he uses a small scissor-like tool to tie the tiniest double knot and snip the ends.

"Three down, five to go," Nash says. "Okay. You're going to feel the needle going in and coming out again." Nash is so steady and solid. He looks like he's done this a thousand times. "Just a little tug, and a knot." It's quiet for a few more minutes until there is now a neat row of eight dark threaded stitches. "That's it," Nash says.

Till assists with the last steps: applying antibacterial ointment, covering the stitches with a bandage, dabbing Cricket's cheeks with a clean washcloth to gently wipe away dried blood.

Cricket's smile is back.

Till is his goofy, warm self: "Bashed my nose and mouth surfing, my lip was so swollen," he tells her. While they talk, I am standing here and watching Nash take off his surgical gloves and clean up his tools. After a minute, he glances up at me and catches my eye. "How ya doing?" he asks.

I want to say I'm sorry, but I open my mouth and nothing comes out.

Nash gives me a nod. "You're a kid and you're learning," he says. And he's quiet. "Sometimes that's the way you do—you learn the hard way. That's the way I learned too."

## 89

At the Viking's table, I slide all the way down the bench. Even though I'm the only one here, I sit in my same spot. Jemma sets a steaming cup of Nash's fish-head broth in front of me.

I pick up the cup with both hands and lift it to my lips.

I blow on it just a little bit, then take a sip. I can feel the heat slip down my throat, warming me. I feel myself thaw. My stomach gurgles, my shoulders kind of soften.

My cheeks tingle.

I'm suddenly so sleepy.

Jemma looks over at me from the kitchen, and when her eyes meet mine, she gives me a look that feels so good. It's not a grin or a laugh; it's like this deep relief feeling. It's hard to even explain because I've never in my life had this feeling before. "That must have been really scary for you," she says.

"Yeah," I say, and my throat tightens.

I look back at Jemma.

She keeps her eyes on mine. And for a second I think, maybe this is what it feels like to have a regular mom—who cares about you and worries when you're gone. I'm honestly not really sure. All I know is she doesn't leave and she doesn't yell and it feels so good. Honestly, I have to look away because it makes me think, *This is what I missed.*

## 90

Jemma turns off the lights in the kitchen. "You two are sleeping here tonight," she tells me and Cricket. "We'll talk about everything tomorrow after breakfast."

God, I'm so relieved. It feels so safe and cozy here in the lodge. I'm still a little bit rattled by everything. And I can't really imagine walking along the coast back to the lighthouse and hauling myself up the rope.

Till is already asleep in front of the fire, curled up with Zeus and Lulu and a blanket. Nash quietly climbed up the ladder to the sleeping loft an hour ago.

Jemma helps us get settled in front of the fire. She brings us pillows and a pile of blankets. "I'm just right here if you need me," she tells us, pointing toward Ms. Birdy's room. "Good night," she says.

And that's it.

I watch Jemma walk into Ms. Birdy's room. I didn't realize she even slept there, but it makes sense. Ms. Birdy needs help. Like, if she has to get up at night.

Cricket immediately drops onto the Viking's carved-out couch with the fuzzy cushions and snuggles up under a wool blanket pulled up to her chin. Her eye is pretty swollen, and she has all those stitches . . .

"Whoa," she murmurs, "my forehead is throbbing."

"I know. I'm sorry," I whisper. Then I wait. "I should have listened to you," I say softly. "If I had, this never would have happened."

I wait for Cricket to say something.

But—

I just hear all the little sounds of the sleeping lodge: the crackling fire, the wind against the glass.

"Cricket?" I whisper into the dark.

"Cricket, are you awake?" I try.

She's out.

Me? I'm finally warm and cozy, atop the thickest, softest sheepskin rug. I'm closest to the fire. A few feet from Till and the dogs.

I can't sleep.

I lie awake staring into the shadows for the longest time. I scrunch up into a tight little ball. I just stare into the night and I listen to the darkness, the snapping of the flames. I don't toss and turn, but I am wide awake. My mind is racing, going over the facts in my head: *I broke the rules. I put everyone in danger. Like, really—the whole deal was my fault. I'm still pretending to be Liv Hogan!*

I let out a sigh so loud that I almost think I'm trying to wake everyone up. I don't know what to do. I have ruined the one good thing I had. There's no way Jemma's not going to hate me soon. I picture every scenario in my head, but no matter what, it always ends with me letting everyone down. I know what I have to do. I have twenty-four hours before the first guests arrive. I have to get out of here before I get fired or before they figure out that I lied.

# 91

In the morning, I wake up when it's still dark outside. The lodge is so quiet. The fire is only orange embers and coals. It takes a second for my eyes to adjust. Lulu and Zeus are passed out, and so is Till. I sit up and look over at Cricket, curled up in her blanket, still sound asleep.

I know what I have to do.

I only have a little bit of time. I get up. I walk, or more like creep, over to the kitchen counter and hope the floorboards don't creak under my feet. They do. My heart immediately starts racing. I am holding my breath.

At the kitchen counter, I pick up a stack of Jemma's folders and begin hunting for what I need. What I need is the ferry schedule. Tomorrow the guests arrive. I have to get out of here before this whole Liv Hogan lie blows up.

It's not in the first stack of folders.

I put those down and look all around the kitchen. I've got to find this. I open cabinet drawers and riffle through neatly organized old guest books, envelopes filled with old letters, stacks of paper. Jemma's to-do lists, written by hand. Yes, I feel bad. This isn't my stuff. But . . . *I have to get out of here.* In the third drawer down, I find what I am looking for: a tan folder labeled FERRY SCHEDULE. I grab it and flip it open, scanning for the next time the ferry is due. Only—

It is not due into Great Bear until a week from today.

Now I remember: Jemma told us that our first guests of the season are arriving by floatplane, and in a split second my whole get-out-of-here-before-they-know-I'm-not-Liv-Hogan plan crumbles.

This hopeless feeling floods my chest. I obviously don't have a way to fly out. I don't own a helicopter. I can't swim through hundreds of miles of open ocean. I'm on one of the most remote islands on the Pacific coast, the farthest north you can even go. I feel sick. And I'm thinking, *This is it. I know they're going to find out what I've done. Who I am. They'll hate me. I know they will* . . . I really can't bear the thought of it. That's when I hear: "Can I help you find something?" and I look up.

## 92

Jemma.

She's standing in front of me with her arms folded across her chest.

I'm holding the folder, and I close it fast.

I freeze.

I don't move.

We just sort of stand here in the kitchen and look at each other. She waits for me to say something. But I say nothing. I do nothing. I just stare back at her.

She holds my gaze. "What are you looking for?"

"Oh—um," I stall. I find myself shaking my head back and forth. My heart is beating so fast and so hard. What do I do? I LIE AGAIN! I'm beginning to think I'm the worst person in the world. The words just come out of my mouth. It's automatic—

"I was just, uhhh—" I stop. I drop the folder back into the drawer, close it, and look up at Jemma. "Yeah. Um. I couldn't sleep. So— well . . . I was just trying to tidy up," I say, which is such a stupid lie. I mean, it's like four in the morning. The sun hasn't even come up yet and the lodge is the most cared-for and organized place I've ever set foot in. There's nothing messy about it.

Jemma's dark hair is hanging down over her shoulders. She looks at me for a long time. "Hey, what's on your mind?"

I shrug my shoulders and I go, "Nothing." My billionth lie.

"Do you want to talk about anything, Liv?" she asks me. "What's going on? What do you need?"

I want to cry.

I want a hug.

I want to tell her that I'm not Liv Hogan. But I'm so afraid that if I tell her, she'll make me leave. So—I look everywhere but back at her. The lodge is brightening with a soft, rising pinkish light. And when I finally glance back at Jemma, she's still standing in front of me, arms folded, waiting for me to answer. I can see her eyes now, and the dark circles under them.

"Liv, I understand if you're feeling shook up." She pauses. "Last night was a lot. We'll get through this. We'll talk it out and we'll keep talking." She waits.

I say nothing. Not a word.

"I get why you might feel scared," she goes on, "but . . . leaving isn't going to work and—"

"I wasn't leaving," I blurt out. Of course, I'm lying.

"Good," Jemma says. "We all have hard times. You don't have to run. No matter what, we can *always* talk it through."

## 93

That whole we'll-talk-about-it thing?

It is happening now.

After breakfast.

After chores.

After reading with Ms. Birdy and helping her sit up, change clothes, and wash.

In the lodge, next to the stone fireplace, we "circle up"—that's what Till calls it. At first, I sit on one of the Viking's benches, but Jemma says, "Liv, come join us," and pats the floor beside where she sits. And so, I do. I walk over to the circle and sit, cross-legged, like I'm gonna do yoga. Except this isn't yoga.

This is serious.

This is the TALK.

About yesterday.

About me screwing up.

The glass doors are pushed open, and sun is streaming into the lodge. The air feels so good. Sunshine is bouncing off the wooden beams, scattering light on everyone's cheeks.

I fidget with my hands, twist my hair around my finger . . . fold and unfold my arms. A full minute of quiet goes by—

I glance at Cricket to my right.

The side of her face is swollen, and she woke up with two black eyes. She is holding an ice pack to her head.

Finally, Jemma breaks the quiet. "I'm so relieved that we are all here together this morning and safe," she begins, "and I'd like to better understand what happened." Jemma glances around the circle and stops on me. "We are not here to blame or punish," she says. Her voice is even. "So, let's talk about yesterday."

Jemma reaches for an actual deer antler that she has set behind her on the floor. She places it on her lap. "I found this yesterday morning by the river." She carefully holds the bone-white antler, curvy with three branch-like points, in her hands. "Antlers grow back after they shed. They remind me of the ability we all have to begin again." Jemma pauses. "What I'd like to try is to pass this antler around the circle and have all of us share how we feel." She takes a breath, then continues, "Whoever holds the antler, we give them all our respect and attention."

It gets real quiet.

"Ready?" she asks.

We all kind of nod.

Jemma passes the antler over to Till. He takes it and holds it in his hands, with great care, like the antler is a gift. I haven't seen Till like this. His jaw is tight. He's quieter than usual. "Yeah. It's just—um, yesterday, it kind of definitely made me think—you know, everything that happened . . . it's partly my fault." For a second he's silent. Then he goes, "I was up here, out on the deck, and I saw you guys way down along the coast. You were just two little dots but I knew it was you, and um"—he lets out a sigh—"I just had a bad feeling . . . kind of warning me, like maybe I should run and catch up to you, check to make sure we knew where you were going, stuff like that." Till shakes his head, like he's beating himself up. "I should have listened to that voice in my head." It gets very quiet. Till's eyes look so sad. Nash leans over and throws an arm around Till's shoulder and whispers, "I love you, bud." They lean on each other, and Till hands the antler back to Jemma.

I wait.

I watch.

I try to swallow.

I keep my eyes on Jemma as she lets out a long breath. "I was tossing and turning all night, rethinking everything, replaying it all in my mind." Jemma shakes her head. "The reality is: I made a mistake." She looks right at me and Cricket, and now my heart jumps. "Having you two stay way out on the point. It's my responsibility to make sure you are safe. The lighthouse . . . it's too far away."

Silence, then: Cricket's hand shoots up. "Can I go next?" she asks, and Jemma hands the antler to Cricket's outstretched hand. She's sitting right next to me, so I turn and look over at her face, her two black eyes, the bandage over her cut. "I mean, I'm just like—" The second she begins, Cricket's eyes fill with tears. "We put ourselves in a really sketchy situation . . . I feel so awful that we did that and put you all at risk." Cricket pauses to wipe her cheeks. "I wish so bad that I could redo everything—" She turns to face Jemma. "I would have totally told you guys where we were going and when we were planning to be back. I would have checked the tides." Now Cricket looks at me. "And Liv, I'm not blaming you at all, because I was right there with you, I did it too, but—when we first set out, remember when I stopped and said we should turn around?"

I look at her and barely nod.

"You know, I had this feeling we should turn back." She pauses to sniff back tears and wipe her eyes again. "I should have insisted. That's totally on me." She takes a breath. "It's like, a deeper part of me knew, and I didn't trust my instincts."

My head is getting hotter and hotter . . .

My chest is tight.

Cricket passes the antler over to Nash.

He's sitting directly across the circle from me, in his gray hoodie and work jeans. His cheeks are wind-chapped and he looks tired, worn-out—probably from searching for us last night. He has a small cut on his chin, and I wonder when that happened and if it was because of me and having to rescue us.

Nash is quiet for a long minute.

We all watch him.

We wait.

He turns the antler over in his hands. This when I notice that his knuckles are all scraped up. I scan his face, his scar along his cheekbone, his eyes. He's so soft-spoken and strong.

Then—

"Dead honest," he finally says, and his voice is hoarse. "Last night, I thought we'd lost you. We're just really fortunate that you're here— we're just so lucky. You always think of that after, you know?"

Silence.

"I'm not different from you guys," he says softly. "At our core, we're all human, and"—he pauses—"I've definitely been irresponsible before . . . I was just a kid. I just wanted to do what I loved to do . . . ride waves, cruise all day, go fishing, make a fire on the beach . . . I wasn't really thinking about how stuff I did would affect anyone else." He and Jemma share a glance. "Most of the time, I did whatever I wanted . . . We didn't really have a lot of rules to keep us safe," he says, his voice starting to crack. "So. Yeah. Uh—" Another pause. "One day, I went out surfing . . . It was winter, some really heavy waves . . . and—I got caught in a big storm, fifty-foot seas and rain, howling winds. It's nature. It just got worse and worse." Now he looks square at me and goes on: "The people who came to find me capsized way offshore and, um—" Nash goes quiet, then says, "They didn't make it"—he swallows hard—"and I'd do anything to change that."

I watch a single tear run down Nash's cheek. He doesn't wipe it away. He looks straight ahead. He doesn't even blink.

Now he looks at me. "Yesterday was tough. We didn't know where you were; we had no idea where to even look. It was scary." Nash shakes his head. "There are miles of coastline, open ocean. You could have been anywhere." He pauses and his face tenses up. "I don't know," he goes on. "I must have rushed through the safety talk. Maybe I wasn't clear enough? I mean, I should have really drilled into your heads that you always have to tell someone where you're going. *Always.* We're just so lucky that you're here," he says again. "You could have died out there. And not only you, but me and Till—something could have happened to us too."

Now my stomach is in knots.

Nash holds the antler across the circle to me. There is a sadness in his eyes, and for a second I see it, when his eyes connect with mine. As soon as I have the antler and take it from him, I pull it toward me, then set it down on the floor.

I can't even hold it.

I sit for a good minute without saying a word.

I don't look at anyone. I just sort of stare off into space. It's like,

*I can't lie anymore. I don't have anything left. I don't know what to do.*

I steal a quick glance at Jemma, then Till, combing his hand through his thick curls. I look over at Nash, then Cricket—all eyes are on me.

My heart is pounding in my chest.

I mean, it's like—what choice do I have?

It only takes a split second—

I get up and bolt.

# 94

Do I really run?

Yeah. I do.

I bolt out of the lodge, across the deck, down the steep stone steps, and when I hit the beach, I dig my bare feet into the sand. I hurdle over piles of seaweed and driftwood. I run and run, all the way to the dock, past the dollhouse cabins, past the boats tied up. I run until I can't run any farther. I finally stop at the end of the dock. I'm breathing so hard. I stand there, bent forward with my hands on my knees, and look out at the turquoise water and the ring of mountains surrounding me.

I sit down and let my legs hang over the edge of the dock. I lie back flat on sun-warmed wooden boards, staring straight up into the sky.

I am *not* crying.

I am holding everything in.

That's what I do.

I've done it my whole life.

I just turn off.

Shut down.

I just sort of stop any feeling from coming up. It's like I put an imaginary cork in my throat. That way nothing can spill out. And I lie like this for a while—until, out of nowhere, I feel the dock vibrate underneath me.

Footsteps.

I whip up, glance over my shoulder, and look back toward the beach. Jemma is walking down the dock straight for me.

Right away my heart begins speeding up.

"Hi," Jemma says, walking to me at the end of the dock.

I force a smile, then turn away and face the water. Out of the corner of my eye, I see Jemma sit down on the dock a few feet away from me.

Neither of us says a word for a minute or two.

I don't look at her.

I stare straight ahead toward Turtle Rock and the sea lions playing and lounging on top.

"Look, Liv. You're not in trouble. We all make mistakes. That's how we learn and do different next time."

I stay quiet.

"You know—" Jemma turns to me. "You made choices that were really dangerous to your own safety." There's a pause. "We have to talk about that. We really need to be able to count on each other."

I don't say anything.

And Jemma says, "I'm just curious . . . is this about something that happened before you got here? Like, at home?"

I stare straight ahead.

I bite my bottom lip.

"Liv?" Jemma says again, and waits. "You don't have to be scared to say anything to me. Whatever it is, I can handle it. We can always figure it out together."

I try to swallow.

And Jemma says, "Is there something else going on?"

"I just—" I begin, then I stop myself.

I drop my head.

And when I look up, Jemma's looking straight at me. "Liv," she says, and her voice is steady and kind. "Saying how you feel—the other side of that is we'll all grow even closer, not farther apart. You can really trust that. It's okay to ask for help."

My throat is so tight.

I feel like I can't breathe.

*I have messed up in so many ways. I feel horrible. I feel guilty. Yesterday I almost caused people to die—all because I just wanted to have fun? And on top of that, I'm lying about who I am. I am terrified to tell Jemma the truth.*

*To lose everyone.*

A minute passes by, and Jemma places a light hand on my shoulder. She keeps it there for a minute. I turn to face her, and for a split second, our eyes kind of lock, and that's it.

I know what I have to do.

# 95

On the dock, I sit up a little straighter.

I take a deep breath.

I glance at Jemma sitting a few feet away from me.

She smiles back.

In my head I'm just telling myself, *I can't do this anymore . . . I have to tell her who I really am. . . . how I didn't mean for any of this to happen, how when Cricket thought I was Liv, I just like, let her think it!*

But when I open my mouth—

I don't.

I can't.

Instead I look away again. "I should just go," I blurt out. "I'm sorry, Jemma—I just—I really messed up. I can take the next ferry out and—"

"Go?" asks Jemma, sounding puzzled.

I nod.

"Listen. I'm angry that you didn't tell us where you were going, but it's okay. We can talk about it and figure it out together. We don't want you to leave at all." She waits for me to turn and look at her, and when I do, she breaks into a smile and repeats the words: "Not at all, not even a little bit. It feels like you are part of our family now."

I can barely swallow.

Again, I turn away.

I face the water.

"Ms. Birdy adores you. Till has been so happy to have you and Cricket here. Nash keeps telling me what a hard worker you are."

I go, "He said that?"

Jemma just smiles. "He did."

She takes a breath. "And for me to be able to not worry about leaving Ms. Birdy alone, to know she's in your care even for a few hours a day . . ." Jemma sighs. "You've been such a big help to me. It's real hard work, and I am so grateful for you," she says. "Trust me. We need you now more than ever."

Something is suddenly different about the sound of Jemma's voice. I look over at her. The look on Jemma's face makes me think there's something that she's not telling me.

"Listen, Liv," Jemma finally says, and her voice is sure and warm. "We can't change the past." She pauses, and we look at each other. "We don't get yesterday back. But we have today. That is in our hands." Jemma's eyes brighten as she looks at mine. "What do you say we try again?"

## 96

When Jemma and I walk back into the lodge, everyone's there waiting. They didn't give up. Zeus and Lulu are so excited to see me, they treat me like a celebrity. They know me now. I crouch down and rub their ears, let them kiss my face. Across the room, "Liiiiv!" Till calls out. He immediately puts down his book, pops up to his feet, walks over, arms wide, and hugs me tight.

"Yay!" Cricket says. She doesn't get up. She's got an ice pack on her face, but she waves with her free hand.

Nash comes right over to me and Jemma. "Hey, you okay?" he asks me.

"Sort of," I say.

Nash is quiet. He looks me dead in the eyes. "Hey, I'm so sorry if what I said made you afraid. This isn't about blame. Let's talk it out. That's how we learn, so we can do different next time."

# 97

**B**ack in the circle, everyone gets quiet. Jemma says, "Okay, let's keep talking. What did we learn so we can do things differently next time?"

Nash reaches for the antler first. "What I learned—" He turns the antler in his hands. "A lot," he says, and grins a little. We all kind of laugh.

Nash has got this thing about him: he's so big and strong and tough, but he has this softness in his voice. You just want to listen.

"To start," he says, "I went through our safety talk too quickly. I didn't check to see if you understood. I take responsibility for that— that's something that will change." He looks at Cricket, then me. "What do you two think about making a plan to help me give the safety presentation to the guests this season?"

"Heck yeah!" Cricket beams.

"Sure," I say, and nod.

I kind of relax.

I sit up a little straighter.

Nash passes the antler to Till.

"What would I do differently next time?" Till repeats the question. "Easy. Trust my gut feeling, and if it seems wrong, it probably is."

Jemma goes next. She holds the antler in both hands. "My number one focus is keeping you safe. And look, the lighthouse is much too far away to check in with each other." She looks at Cricket and then at me. "I'm going to have you two stay in the lodge for the summer. I care about you and I want you to be safe. That's my job. I don't want you to be alone or out there by yourselves. I'd feel better if you were here with us."

Cricket goes next. Right away she tears up. "I'm *always* going to tell someone where I'm going or when I'm going to be back," she says. "I'm gonna speak up," she goes on, "even if it makes someone else not happy." Cricket sniffs back tears. Then she hands the antler to her left—

To *me.*

It's my turn.

This time, I take the antler and I don't let go. I hold on with both my hands. I take a deep breath. I glance at Jemma.

She nods me on.

"It was my fault," I suddenly say, my voice tightening. "I just didn't think, I mean—" I stop. I let out a big breath. I start again. "I'm the one who told Cricket not to bother telling anyone where we were going or when we were supposed to be back. That was *me.* I did that." I go silent. I glance at Till, then Nash. I take another deep breath. "I guess . . . I don't know—I just didn't think we needed tide charts, or to let you guys even know where we were headed." My eyes fill with tears. "I didn't think my decision would affect any of you. I just didn't think I mattered. But—I mean . . . we all could have died out there—" My eyes jump to Cricket, then Nash, Till, and to Jemma. Each of them meets my gaze. "I get it now," I say, tears running down my face. "God. I'm just so sorry," I say.

After I say it, I feel my whole body relax—that wasn't me lying, or me saying what I think people want me to say. That's really how I feel. I don't know what's gonna happen. I don't have a plan. I just know that I love it here and I don't want to leave.

I hand the antler to Jemma, and she takes it and sets it back beside her. "Are there any questions that I didn't ask that I should have?"

It's real quiet.

We all look around the circle.

Nash speaks up. "I do want to say one thing: Liv, you and Cricket showed a lot of courage last night. You had some good survival instincts. You stayed put, you found shelter, you built a fire. It was those decisions, and staying calm, that saved your life." Nash looks at me. "It's tricky," he says softly. "We learn by messing up. Sometimes the bravest thing you can do is trust your instincts and know it's okay to ask for help."

"Could not have said that better," Jemma says. She and Nash share a quiet smile, and then she looks around the circle at each of us. "Does anyone else have anything they want to add?"

"Just one thing," Till says. He's got this huge, big grin and his eye twinkle is at an all-time high. And he goes, "Can we have a group hug?" and we all burst out laughing.

We stand up, right here in the middle of the lodge. Our circle is now an arm-in-arm giant hug. My face smooshes up against Nash and his hoodie, which smells like woodsmoke. I take the biggest, deepest breath. I just feel home.

# 98

Ten minutes after our group hug, I am wrangling my hair into a pony and pulling on my tall rubber boots. I'm dressed in my shorts from yesterday—which Jemma somehow found time to wash, then hang on the line, outside in the sun. I still have her thermal crewneck on. It's comfy and it fits. I push the long sleeves up.

"Ready!" I call out.

"Just looking for socks," Till answers from the upstairs loft.

"One sec!" says Cricket from the bathroom.

And then we're off! Our mission, to quote Nash when he invited us along, "To get out in the mountains and clear our heads."

And just like that: I'm heading out the lodge's back door, straight up into the forested mountains on a trail made by bears.

"Bears?" I ask.

"Yup!" Till says.

Till calls this the Cathedral Trail, nature's church. I get it. We are zigzagging over a narrow, muddy path, past the tallest, oldest, most gigantic trees I've ever seen. The trunks tower into the sky. Ancient red cedars, hemlocks, Sitka spruce. I know their names now. This is an old-growth forest. Misty and cool. Walking through it feels like I'm in some sort of magic, secluded, prehistoric world. A mountainside that rises straight out of the Pacific Ocean: nothing is flat, it's all ups and downs, thick lime-green carpets of moss, covering everything, and roots that look like bulging monster veins, pushing up through the ground. I scramble over massive fallen logs, sink my boots into deep, gooey mud, leap fast-flowing creeks, cross high wooden bridges over marshes and streams.

At first, we talk. Wait, not Nash, he's up ahead. Till and Cricket and I move like a little pack of wolves. Together. We all fall into a single line. In sync. I stop thinking. It's feels good. Safe.

When we do talk, we talk about the coolest stuff. Till is a real-life Google . . . except he's never even *used* Google! He knows so much. Like what? Okay. How about this: How trees are the lungs of the earth, photosynthesis and how it works. How carbon sequestration in soils and trees could slow climate change! How trees actually "talk" with each other through a system of underground mycorrhizae-linked networks, sending signals from tree to tree, communicating their needs!

Um. Whoa.

And trees can transfer their legacy from the older trees to the younger ones. Sort of like elders in a family passing stuff on to the generations after them. They regenerate by what they leave behind.

More? Yep.

Did you know that nature has healed itself for hundreds of millions of years? The forest cleans the air, the rivers and the salmon feed the forest. It's symbiotic.

We stop and crane our necks back and stare straight up at the canopy, 150 feet over our heads. Splashes of light shower down, making all the wet, mossy lichen sparkle. It's so quiet. So mystical. I can hear the tiniest sounds—

*Creatures scurrying . . .*

*An eagle flapping its wings . . .*

*Water trickling somewhere close . . .*

And Till drops this: "You know, humans aren't alone," he says softly. "We aren't separate beings. We are all related, everything is connected . . . nothing survives on its own."

We walk. And walk. Up and up and up, up, up. Little by little, all three of us fall into this good-feeling quiet. Something happens hiking up the mountain trail that is just so soothing. The cool air, the rhythm of my feet, the sound of songbirds singing. It all puts me into a spell, quiets the thoughts in my head, and soon, everything fades away—replaced by the music of trickling water melting from the mountain's peak and finding its way down.

We stop only once, to fill our water bottles by an ice-cold stream, gulp the glacier water down, and eat handfuls of huckleberries right off the branch. Then we begin again, our lips and hands now stained with purple berry juice. We walk single file with me leading in front, through sparkly beams, sunlight filtering through the trees. Nash is still pretty far ahead of us. And as we get farther and farther up, higher and higher, something feels different. The trees are a little shorter and windblown, there's less moss and more gravelly rocks—and when I step out of the forest, I look up and say, "Oh my gosh."

We walk out of the forest into what feels like a dream: a hip-high grassy meadow covered with a blanket of a trillion wildflowers. There are butterflies, and swarms of tiny, pale pink moths, fluttering and bouncing above the orange flowers and tall grass.

"This is unreal," I say softly.

"Incredible," Cricket breathes.

"This is one of Ms. Birdy's favorite spots," Till says, gazing toward the meadow. I glance over to Till and then I suddenly look down—

"You guys," I whisper, and stay completely still. A crazy-beautiful butterfly is crawling up my arm, just above my left wrist.

The three of us stand entranced, watching this pale blue creature with bright orange and black spots on her wings.

*This place is so full of magical things*, I think as I watch her wiry, striped antennae make the slightest moves. Then she flaps her wings a few times and flutters up and away.

Cricket sighs. "I freakin' *love* this place!"

"Same," I say, and smile.

Till just looks at the two of us and grins.

And we march on—

Swooshing through the high grass, following the edge of the butterfly meadow to a slight hillside, where we slip and slide down on our butts, giggling and laughing as we help each other up.

Then I stop.

We all do. Why?

After walking through a forest, then along the edge of an alpine meadow, we are rewarded with this: a hidden waterfall, spilling over boulders, rushing downstream, cascading over staircases of rock, curving and winding and feeding into a narrow river of crystal clear water that rushes right by our feet, making its way down the mountainside to the sea. And it's right here, on a flat section of the river, between two waterfalls, where the rocks come right up to the banks, that I spot Nash, who gives us a nod, takes off his pack, and sets it on a nice, big, flat, smooth, sunny rock. Then he looks up, cracks the biggest smile, and says, "This is the spot."

**101**

I slosh through the water in my tall rubber boots. I'm gripping the rod with no reel that Nash crafted out of wood, then tied a single piece of thread and a bit of wolf hair to the tip. No high-tech rods or fancy gear. We have everything that we need right here.

Nash keeps it simple. There's no big lesson.

He smiles and says, "Get out and get wet."

"Anything else?" I say, and laugh.

"Think like a fish," he says with a wink.

So here I am, standing on a boulder, flinging my rod back and forth. Practicing casting a little bit. Staring down into the water, looking for where a fish might hang out.

Till is on a boulder close to mine. "That line is solid. It floats and casts really well," he tells me. "You're doing awesome, Liv!"

I cast and wait.

I breathe in. I peer down into the swirling water, looking for anything I can see that's moving. I see a sunken log, a whole lot of rocks, but no dark shapes or finning tails. I hear Nash helping Cricket a little upstream.

"Pick it up and cast right back out," he's saying. "There you go, good work. It's all in the arm!"

I follow that tip. I use my arm to bring my rod back, then cast it out into the water. And—

*Oh my gosh.*

There's a JOLT on my line. It goes tight, and suddenly I'm connected to this force of life.

I hear Nash holler out, "Yes, Liv, let her run!"

Till yells, "Do what the river tells you to, Liv!"

What happens next is I go from standing on the boulder to sitting in the river on my butt, holding my rod with both my hands, water filling my boots. I'm fighting to stand. I'm soaked up to my chest—this river is cold! And I'm laughing so hard, and also, I'm trying to hold on because—yep, that's right—there is a *fish* on my line!

"Stand strong. That's it! Good work, Liv!" Nash calls out. "There you go, hold the rod tip high, that will tire her out."

Now I'm back up on my feet, holding on. The fish is big, and it cuts through the water and uses the current to try and swim away—

I scream, "What do I do?"

"You're doing it," Nash says. "Just keep the line tight and slowly walk backward. There you go—try and bring her into the shallow pool over by the waterfall."

"Go, Liv!" I hear Cricket say. Then I zone in. It's just me and the fish. She's fighting and thrashing in the shallows, swimming left and right.

"You got this, Liv!" I hear Till say.

I'm pulling in a salmon about as big as the length of my entire arm! I back her into where the water hugs the river's bank.

"Ooh, man!" Cricket says in awe. "One or two casts. Look at you, Liv! You're a champ!"

Till is crouched down, reaching to help me keep the line from getting tangled as the bright silver fish fights.

Nash grins. "That's a nice Chinook. You're a natural, Liv!"

"Now what?" I ask, locked on the salmon's shiny black eyes. "I mean, should we release her?"

"Release her?" Till says, fast. "Would you want a hook in your mouth just for sport?"

Nash pulls the salmon from the water, cradles her in his hands, and unhooks her from the line—and I don't know what I'm thinking, because I like to eat salmon, but seeing this up close, it's a whole different view. I watch as Nash takes out his knife. He's very careful, and it all happens fast.

I wince a little as I watch.

"This is the most humane way to do it," Till says, throwing a glance at me. "When you puncture the brain, it puts them down quickly—then you snip one of the gills, and that causes the blood to flow out."

Nash glances up. Pretty sure he can read the look on my face, which is kind of like . . . *This salmon I caught was just alive, and now . . . it's not.* It's silent for a moment. Then Nash speaks directly to me. "In our culture, we believe this salmon offered itself to you. We receive them with respect." He cradles the silvery fish in his hands and places her in mine. "Salmon are as close to medicine as you can get. They nourish us. It's lucky to get just one." Nash pauses. "They feed the forest and give us life—she chose you, Liv. It's an honor."

## 102

For the hike back to the lodge, Nash gives me his backpack. I will carry the salmon strapped to my shoulders. Catch and carry. This is my job. I kind of love it. I feel proud.

Before we begin our long walk back, I take one last look at the river and—"Guys!" I whisper a little too loudly. And I freeze. There is a big bright-white-coated bear wading into the water's edge, standing on a boulder, fishing for salmon! Behind her to her right are two of the most adorable little bear cubs—one white, one black—playing along the river on a fallen log. Cricket whispers, "Wow! Is that a Kermode bear? Aren't they really scarce?"

Till nods. "A Spirit bear, a black bear with white fur. She's feeding her cubs," he whispers in in awe. "They're pretty rare to see. A lot of people think the Spirit bear is a good omen, a very strong symbol of something that is very sacred."

We watch in silence.

The mama bear chomps off a fish's head. Even from the other side of the river, I can hear the crunch. My eyes go wide. And just now, the mama bear stops eating and looks up. I swear her eyes connect with mine. I instinctively grab onto Nash's arm.

"It's okay," Nash says softly. His arm is sturdy and he stays perfectly still. "Keeps you humble, for sure." He gives me a quiet nod. "We're just one more creature here on earth."

Cricket backs away. "Is she gonna come after us?"

"No," whispers Till. "As long as she's between us and her cubs, we're good." He pauses as we watch her fish. "The most dangerous is a mom, because she will do *anything* to protect her young."

"That's the way it should be," says Nash, and he quietly turns and the four of us begin the long trek back.

# 103

We're in the kitchen. "Okay," Nash tells me. He's holding a very sharp knife in his right hand.

I glance down at the salmon set on a wooden board beside the sink. I've gone from girl who eats dry ramen noodles on the floor with her back against the door to girl who is learning how to carve the wild salmon she just caught—and I love it. I love who I am.

"We start off making a cut behind the head," says Nash, breaking down the fish with his hands. "Then"—he pauses to work—"we run the knife down the body against the backbone, flip it over—and that's it."

I stare at the perfect bright orange flesh. The salmon's shiny black eyes. I'm not gonna lie: I still feel bad.

And Nash says, "We harvest the head, the skin, the bones, the meat, and the eggs." I watch him carefully remove the intact sack of eggs from the salmon's belly. "Nothing is wasted," he says. "That's how we respect the life she's given us."

## 104

After three hours of work prepping for our big feast, Cricket and I have one last job: get our things from the lighthouse and bring them back to the lodge. The two of us head out the lodge's sliding glass door, which opens to the deck overlooking the turquoise-blue water in the bay and Turtle Rock and, farther out, the sea. We're at the top of the stone-slab steps, making our way down to the beach, when Cricket gives me this look, and before the words come out of her mouth, I know what is about to go down. Picture this scene in slow motion with your favorite song.

Cricket says, "Let's race!"

I say, "It's on!"

I'm barefoot, my hair is flying all over the place, the sun is shining on my face. Cricket is already breaking out ahead of me. She's fast! But on the narrow strip of sand that leads out to the point, I catch up. We are two horses galloping side by side, bodies in motion, arms pumping, toes sinking into the sand. I forget myself, I'm in the zone, I've found a whole different gear and I'm locked on the goal. We battle, trading leads all the way down the Sunshine Coast, and we don't stop until our shoulders and outstretched arms collide as we reach for the wooden beam of the lighthouse, touching it at the very same time.

Cricket calls out, "Tie!"

I say, "_____!" (nothing) because I'm currently bent over with both my hands on my knees, sucking in air.

"That was amazing," says Cricket.

"That was so fun!" I say.

And soon, we're pushing the lighthouse's big heavy door until it slides all the way open; and just like our very first day here, a bajillion bats zoom out, startling us, and we laugh our heads off and duck for cover.

I go first. I walk across the wide-planked wooden floor that my great-grandfather, the Viking, built and sanded with his own two hands. The wood feels good under my bare feet, smooth. I take a deep breath. I love the musty scent of the lighthouse. The afternoon sun is a spotlight flooding the entire first floor. I have to squint. I rub my hands together like a gymnast with no chalk. Then I step to the single rope hanging from the rafters, jump up, and grab on.

"Grip it and rip it!" Cricket cheers me on.

My shorts are still damp from my river "bath," and I'm kind of beat up from the last two days, but the climb up into our top-floor hideout, the pull and the reach, is so much easier than day one. I haul and lift my body up and push through the open trapdoor, then collapse back onto the sunny wood-planked floor. My chest heaves up and down and I'm smiling so big, 100 percent—it feels like a straight-up accomplishment! It's so cozy and comfy climbing up into this place. It's so protected, it's amazing up here. I sit up and watch Cricket pull, inchworm-style, up, up, up. "That's it!" I say, when she reaches the top.

I close the secret trapdoor of our fort in the sky. We stand. Cricket takes a few steps across the room, then falls face-first onto her bed. I belly flop onto mine. "Oh man," I mumble straight into the pillow, "I love this place."

There's a long minute of silence while we both breathe in that awesome feeling when you've had the longest adventure ever and you're finally home. Actually, I haven't ever felt that, until now. It feels so good. I stay perfectly still and just breathe it all in. I listen to the owl babies chatting outside my window. I glance over at Cricket, lying spread eagle on her bed. Her eyes are closed and her mouth is a little bit open. "This is heaven," she says.

## 105

A minute later, I'm tiptoeing to the bookcase door, sliding it open, and stripping off my clothes. Next, I take the most freezing shower of my life! *Holy ice cubes*, I think, and laugh at how much has changed and how lucky I am. I towel off and slip into clean clothes. What am I wearing? Glad you asked! For our celebration tonight, a bonfire on the beach, I go with layers. It's funny, but somehow, I've started hearing Jemma's reassuring voice in my head. She says things like: *What do you need to keep yourself warm?* I go with:

Layer one: knee-high socks, undies, bra.

Layer two: Jemma's thermal crewneck, which I slip back on.

Layer three: Sunny's cozy wool sweater and her old jeans, with the sewn patches on the knees.

Now Cricket's up. "No shower for me," she says.

I go, "Why not?"

"Can't get my stitches wet."

"Oh yeah, sorry," I say, and give her a sympathetic look. "How is it? The cut, I mean."

"Actually, pretty good," answers Cricket. "This place is like a magical elixir. Look at my stitches. They're healing so fast!" As she talks, she is expertly weaving her hair into a crown of braids with a pony in the back.

I watch, then ask, "Hey, will you braid my hair like that?"

"Absolutely! Sit!" Cricket pats the end of her bed.

I plop down onto the edge. She kneels behind me and gets to work, using her fingers to comb through my hair. "I'm not very delicate," she laughs, gathering my long, wet hair and raking it back. "Let me know if this hurts."

She separates my hair into clumps. "OW!" I squirm, and we both crack up. After a minute, Cricket says, "Liv?"

And I go, "Yeah?"

And she goes, "Do you like Till?"

"Of course!" I say, confused.

And Cricket says, "No, I mean, do you *like* him, like him?"

"What?! *Nooooo!*" I say, and now I'm shaking my head back and forth, which only makes us both laugh because Cricket is trying to braid.

I say, "Why are you asking me this?"

"Well, it's just—" she begins, and then stops.

"What?" I say. "Tell me!"

"Okay, I'm just gonna say it." She waits, then: "I have the *biggest* crush on him!"

Now I'm really smiling big.

Cricket begins speaking very fast. "I mean, he's just so smart and adorable and quirky, in like, the best way—and his dimples, oh my gosh! And his eyes! They're like, this crazy-blue like the sky. Are you sure you don't like him, Liv?"

"I'm *sure!*" I say quickly, and laugh. "I mean, I love Till," I say, "but not like *that.*" I try to stay still as she twists and weaves and tugs my hair. "I can totally see it—you two, I mean."

"Really?" Cricket says, sounding happy. "He's like, one year younger than I am, but I mean, he's way more mature than most guys I know."

"That's for sure," I say, nodding.

"He's fifteen, going on sixteen in one month." Cricket ties the last braid with an elastic, then pulls them both back into a pony.

I turn around and smile at her. Her cheeks are bright red!

"Stop!" she laughs. She is blushing so bad. She quickly changes the subject. "Look at you." She beams. "You're lookin' like a boss with your crown-braid pony!"

I laugh. I stand up. There are no mirrors on Great Bear. I haven't really looked at myself in a long time, and I don't even care. "Liv, seriously, you are rockin' it! You look like some sort of ancient warrior goddess, ready for battle!"

I run my hands over my braids, and I get this good feeling like, I'm ready for *anything*.

"Let's go!" I say.

**O**n the beach below the lodge, under a setting sun, we sit on ocean-worn logs that we pull around the fire as seats for our feast. And listen, if you've never had salmon that you caught yourself, then cooked over an open fire that you made from driftwood you gathered on the beach . . . Well, do it. Do it soon.

Cricket, Till, and I get the fire going good! The flames are shooting up into the quickly falling night. The menu for our last dinner before our guests arrive: salmon, pea greens, wild onions, chanterelles that we forage in the forest around the beach, and oysters that we harvest from the bay, shuck with a knife—prying the shell all the way apart—and eat raw.

Before we dig in, I reach out to my left (Cricket) and to my right (Jemma). After two weeks here, I don't even think twice about joining hands. I listen to the blessing by Nash. "Here's to strong women." He pauses. Till pipes in, "I second that!" We all share a soft laugh, and I feel Jemma and Cricket both grip my hands a little tighter.

Nash continues, "The first guests of the season arrive by a float-plane charter tomorrow." He looks at each of us sitting, linked together, around the fire. "Over the last two weeks, we've built a family. Look around you," he says, and I do. I share quiet smiles with Jemma, Cricket, Till, and Nash. Nash takes a breath and then says, "Please remember, no matter what, you've *always* got someone who will watch your back."

We eat our feast until there's nothing left. Literally. I lick my fingers. No crumbs. Nothing goes to waste. Then we sit around the bonfire and watch the darkness move in fast. We talk and laugh about all kinds of stuff. The topics bounce, in that easy way that happens when you get to be yourself.

Cricket asks Nash what the military was like.

"Not much to say," he says, with a quiet shrug. But Cricket keeps at it. "Well," she says, "did you like it?"

Nash looks up. "Honestly, it made me grow up really fast," he answers, then goes silent. We wait. There's some fire crackling and the sound of waves. Then Nash begins again. "I guess sometimes you're lucky enough to figure out what is really important in life," he says. He looks off in the distance, then back. "It's always just been this place for me. The mountains, the ocean. You can find peace from what is here, what we've been given." Nash goes quiet again. The fire snaps, and we all wait in that way you do when someone who you just like listening to is telling you a story. "You know," he says, placing a chunk of wood on the hot coals, then looking around the circle. "A lot of people say that coming here helps them to see the world with fresh eyes." He waits. "It's a gift we give our guests, but really, they give it to us just as much. Each time they visit, it reminds me—"

"Reminds you what?" asks Till from the opposite side of the fire.

Nash flashes his dimples. "Sometimes you have to get away to find yourself."

# 108

**B**y now the night sky has turned a bluish black. Embers from the fire shoot up into the night and snow down onto the beach. Till tells us all sorts of crazy stories: all the people who visit Great Bear, guests he has met, mostly fishermen, who come back year after year. This one time, one morning when he was surfing, three men in suits came by helicopter who want to bulldoze the mountainside, to drill for oil and gas and build a pipeline right through Great Bear. "They claimed they had the right-of-way. They had all these official documents and—"

"What! That's insane!" says Cricket. "What did you tell them?"

Till sighs and says, "Well, we are—"

"Tillman," Jemma says, and she looks at Till quickly and he stops. Jemma stands. "I'm going to check on Ms. Birdy," she says.

"I can run up," offers Till.

"No," says Jemma. "I'll be back down in a little bit."

At this moment Nash is quietly clearing the empty plates and stacking them with a low-key easiness that is just him: when he helps, he is all action, no talk. And I look up and watch him catch up with Jemma, and they walk together up to the lodge.

Now it's just me, Cricket, and Till and our gigantic bonfire, with sparks that shoot up into the night. We are sharing the same driftwood log, sitting close, shoulder to shoulder. Cricket's in the middle.

I stare into the fire. Looking into the flames makes the darkness even darker. In the distance I can hear the ocean waves.

After a little while, I slide off my seat and lean back against the driftwood log, feeling pretty good about leaving the lovebirds sitting together side by side. I glance at the two of them, arms slightly touching.

Till has his head tipped back and he's staring straight up at the sky full of stars. "That's a three-hundred-fifty-light-years-long river of cosmic snowballs up there," he finally says in awe.

"Oh my gosh," I say. Now I'm looking up at the dusting of glittery light spreading across the sky.

"Holy wow!" says Cricket. "It's like a fireworks show up there!"

It's silent for a long time. We sit, watching the stars fill the night.

"This is the most magical thing I've ever seen," I whisper, and wonder why I've never seen this before. I mean, we all have the same sky.

The bonfire has died down a bit, though it's still plenty hot and snapping some.

"Guys?" whispers Cricket, gazing up. "Do you think stardust is like some sort of signal from another galaxy? Like, maybe it's a message . . ." Her voice trails off.

"Yeah, or a secret map," says Till in a hush.

"A storybook," I whisper.

"Whoa, yes!" says Cricket. "The stars are kind of a storybook. They've seen so much."

Till says, "I always wonder what all the stories are that I don't know."

We roll the driftwood log out of the way, and the three of us get flat on our backs. Three in a row. Close. I can feel the dampness of the sand under my shoulders, and the heat of the fire covering me like a blanket.

More quiet.

"Big Dipper," says Cricket. "Little Dipper, North Star!" she calls them as she connects the dots. "Ooh, I love Orion, the hunter—do you guys see his belt? Look, you can really see his sword!"

Till joins in. "See Pisces, the two swimming fish—see that bright one?" He waits. "That's like, two hundred ninety-four light-years from Earth."

"Whoa," says Cricket.

"Whoa," I say.

Then: "I just saw a shooting star!" Cricket whispers loudly. "Quick, look!" She points her finger up. "There's another one! Another one! You guys, it's raining stars!"

It really is. There's a second where I glance at Cricket and catch Till's eyes and together we share a smile. Cricket is just the most fun and alive human that I've ever known.

"Make a wish!" she calls out in delight each time she spots a falling meteor streaking through the night. "Make a wish, make a wish! Did you see that one? Make a wish!"

I watch the glowing trail of cosmic dust streak across the sky. And I don't have to make a wish. One that I didn't even know I wanted has already come true. On a beach, under a trillion stars, lying on my back, next to the kindest best friends a girl could ever have, for the first time in my life I finally feel like I belong.

## 109

We interrupt our stargazing sesh, gather more driftwood, and throw huge chunks of wood onto the fire and get it going again. Now I'm getting cozy and all warm when I look up from the fire and see Jemma walking toward us, with Nash right behind her. She's headed down the steps from the lodge, carrying a tray with both hands. You're probably wondering, how do I even notice her in the dark? Good point. On the tray that Jemma is carrying with both hands are glowing lit candles poking out of a cake. I watch and wonder, *Whose birthday is it?* And on cue, as Jemma gets closer, and everyone begins to sing, I do too. "Happy birthday to you," I sing, and scan the faces around the fire for a clue. Till is all smiles. Nash sits down across from me and his eyes are lit up and sparkling. Cricket is singing very loudly and grinning at me. Then, wait. What?

*Oh God.*

Jemma places the cake, lit with seventeen candles, directly in front of thirteen-year-old *me*. She kneels in the sand and cups her hand around my shoulder, leans in close, and says, "Happy birthday, Liv!"

# 110

*I'm such a jerk.*

*I am a liar.*

*I am the worst person in the world.*

These are all things I am thinking as we finish singing, and Cricket starts cheering, "Blow them out!"

"Make a wish!" says Till.

I lean in and I do: I make a wish, on a birthday cake for a girl I'm pretending to be. Oh, it gets even worse.

I manage a bunch of awkward looks. I say, "How did you even know?"

And Till goes, "We've been planning this all week! It's on your application."

And I say, "Wait. What is?"

"Your birthday!" he laughs.

Everything happens so fast: first, speeches and toasts. Cricket and I are presented with our very own Great Bear Lodge uniforms, which are pretty much just simple hoodies with a patch sewn on the front, but I pull mine on over my head and swear I'll never take it off. Nash gives me a wink and says, "It's official, Liv: you're part of the family now."

And here come the gifts! Till surprises me with my very own hand-crocheted vest. It's blue with pink specks. "The buttons are off my dad's old shirt," he tells me proudly.

"Thank you, Till," I say to my cousin, who has no idea we're even related or that I'm *not* seventeen and it's NOT my birthday.

He walks up to me and gives me the biggest hug. Then, as if that's not enough, we all sit back down around the fire, and Cricket turns to face me and says, "Close your eyes," and so I do.

I can tell she's placing something around my neck. "Okay!" she says.

I look down at a necklace made of a string of orange and pink crystal-like chunks of rocks we found on Treasure Beach.

"Agates have a crazy ocean and forest energy," Cricket says, beaming. "They're like little orbs of magic for the goddess that you are!"

I look at her in disbelief. I ask, "When did you even make this?"

"I have my ways!" she says, smiling.

Next, Jemma tells me to close my eyes again. Then: "Okay," she says, signaling for me to look and—

"Oh my gosh, seriously? Aren't these yours?" I ask in shock, because I'm the lucky recipient of Jemma's fuzzy sheepskin slippers.

And Jemma smiles and says, "Now they're yours."

We look at each other. "Thank you so much, Jemma," I manage, but then I have to stop because there's a lump in my throat. *Nobody has ever done this for me before. A party? Presents?* I swallow hard. I look at the faces around the fire. Have you ever felt like, so much guilt and so much joy at the same time? I feel love and I feel so completely afraid of losing them—Jemma, Till, Cricket, Nash. I feel so many feelings that I've never felt.

"Um, I, uh—"

Jemma looks at me and asks, "Is everything okay?"

"Totally!" I lie. "I've gotta go to the bathroom," I suddenly blurt out, and leap up. Then I proceed to back away, flash a smile, and spin around, moving toward the stone steps as calmly as I can, as if I'm really Liv, the birthday girl, as if I really am just turning seventeen and not thirteen-year-old me, the worst person in the world.

## 111

In the dark, I take the stairs two at a time. I suddenly feel like I can't breathe. Like the whole world is crashing down on me.

I yank off my boots, slide open the wall of glass, and step into the lodge. I don't really have to go to the bathroom. You get that, right? I've gotten myself in such a mess. They think I'm Liv. They gave me presents! They trust me. I hate myself so much right now.

"Jemma?" I hear.

"Ms. Birdy?" I call out her name. "Ms. Birdy, it's me," I say, and walk straight for her room. When I enter, the light on her bedside table is on. She's sitting up in bed, propped up with tons of pillows and covered with a heavy cotton quilt. "Is everything okay?" I say softly, and sit down on the very edge of her bed.

Ms. Birdy looks right at me, her eyes lighting up. "Sagagyemk," she says, speaking Sgüüx̱s. She's calling me Sunny.

"No, Ms. Birdy," I say quickly. "I'm not Sunny. I'm—" I stop. "I don't even know who I am right now," I say, and lean over closer. "Ms. Birdy," I whisper, "I really messed up. I've lied so much."

She looks at me quietly, then lifts her hand. It's trembling. She reaches for my face. I gently take her hand in mine and hold it to my cheek. It feels so good to be close to her. She seems so happy to just look at me. So happy that I'm here. I just sit with her in silence. I look into her eyes. They're darkish turquoise blue, same as mine. Now I know where they came from. Who I came from. I begin to breathe when Ms. Birdy breathes. It calms me down. She looks at me and I look at her. We smile at each other. And it doesn't feel scary; it feels so good. The lodge is so quiet. There's not a single person here but me and my great-grandma, who doesn't even know I'm me.

There's something I want to do. I don't know if I'll get another chance. "I love you, Ms. Birdy," I say in the quietest whisper. Then: "I'm River." I wait. "I'm your great-granddaughter. I am Sunny's daughter," I tell her, and as I say those words, a single giant tear spills down my cheek. Ms. Birdy smiles up at me. I feel like she already has one foot in another world, but somehow, she keeps her hand against my face and wipes away my tear.

# 112

**W**hen I tiptoe out of Ms. Birdy's room, I have to quickly wipe the tears from my eyes.

Jemma is in the kitchen, and she looks up. "Everything okay?"

I say, "Oh. Yeah," and I smile at Jemma. "Totally," I lie.

Jemma loads me up with a mound of cozy quilts, folded and stacked. "Sleep well, and happy birthday," she says, reaching out her arms. Jemma's hugs are strong. It's like, she hugs you heart-to-heart, and it feels so good that it also feels scary. *I don't want to lose Jemma. I don't know how long I can do this. Not be me.* I step back and put on this fake, super-cheerful, I'm-Liv-and-it's-my-birthday voice. "Thank you so much, Jemma!" I say, and I force the kind of try-too-hard smile that you do when you don't want someone to know you're really about to completely fall apart.

Zeus and Lulu and a sky full of stars accompany me and my stack of seven heavy quilts back down to the beach. We arrange our slumber-party quarters close and in a row.

Me.

Cricket.

Till on the end.

A mound of quilts draped over us.

I pull the worn edge of one of the quilts up to my chin. I breathe in cool mountain air, listen to the crackling fire still burning in the night. I have the worst ashamed feeling lodged in my throat. I try to listen for the baby owls out on the point, the water lapping at the bay, anything that will make this awful sinking feeling go away.

And Cricket suddenly whispers, "You know what? I love you guys!"

"I love you guys," echoes Till.

"I love you guys too," I say softly, and I look up at the stars.

The lying is just too much. I never planned on loving people like this. I never knew how scary it was to trust. I stare at the trillion stars in the night sky. I want to remember everything about Great Bear. The scent of the fire, the sound of the waves, friends who I can count on sleeping just a few feet away. In the dark, silent tears roll down my cheeks. *Who does this? What's wrong with me?* I swear Lulu is some sort of psychic dog. She comes over and lies right on me. I make room for her under my blanket. She's so soft and warm. She smells like salt water and tree roots and kelp and burning wood. Or maybe that's me. I feel safe under her weight. I feel her breathing. And finally, I sleep.

# 114

**W**hen I wake up, the air is kind of cool and damp, the sun is just rising, and it's so dreamy quiet. It's crazy, but my favorite sound these days might be listening to silence. I'm pretty sure I fall back asleep, because the next thing I know I hear Till's voice. "Hey," he says. He has his hand on my shoulder and he's shaking me a little bit. I open my eyes, and about three feet away from my face is Till and his long eyelashes and his zillion freckles spread across his cheeks. His hair is wet and he's changed into fresh clothes. I'm still pretty groggy. I glance past Till at the far end of the beach—there are three coastal wolves watching me.

"Come on," says Till, and something about the urgency of his voice makes my stomach drop.

Now I sit up. I go, "What's wrong?"

Right away he says, "You gotta go up to the lodge."

I say, "Why? What happened?" and move to my feet.

"Come on," he says, and looks away and up toward the lodge. Something feels different. Something feels really wrong. My heart is pounding now. My mind begins to flood with a million things. *What time is it? Why are we leaving Cricket sleeping on the beach? Oh dang! We forgot to move our stuff from the lighthouse to the lodge! Are the guests here? Did we oversleep?*

I'm right behind Till on the stairs up to the lodge. "Is everything okay?" I blurt out. Till stops for just a second and looks over his shoulder at me, and in an instant, I have the worst feeling wash over me. "Is it Ms. Birdy?" I ask, and my heart just drops.

"Just hurry," is all Till says.

I smell her before I see her. It's her cigarettes. And when I do see her, she doesn't even come near me. There's no hug. No "I'm so glad you're okay." Sunny's not like that. Do you believe me now? She's not a regular mom. She's standing in front of the kitchen counter. Her long blond hair is loose and down. She's wearing dark ripped jeans and a tight white T-shirt and her black leather boots with chunky heels. She folds her arms tightly across her chest, and the second our eyes meet, I get the worst feeling inside me and I brace myself.

Nobody is speaking.

There is a tension in this kitchen that I've never felt. The tension is spelled S-U-N-N-Y, and she just stands there stone silent and then she finally says, "River, get your stuff."

I can't look at anyone.

I can't even speak.

I don't have the courage to say one word. I stand there, completely still. I do not move. I can't look at Jemma. I can't look at Till, who is standing beside me, or Nash, sitting at the Viking's table with a mug of steaming broth cupped between his hands. I can barely breathe. I can barely even swallow. *How did Sunny even get here? I don't even care.* And right here, right now, I sort of just feel like any hope I had is gone.

I feel Jemma touch her hand to my shoulder. "River." My aunt says my real name for the first time, and she waits for me to look. "How about you and I go to the lighthouse and pack up."

# 116

**I**f you think I suddenly bawl my eyes out and beg Sunny to let me stay? No. Sunny's like a time bomb but you don't know the time. I know better than to try and say what I feel or think. I do what I do best. I run.

I run and I don't stop until I see the lighthouse and finally slow to a jog. I push the heavy door open all by myself. I somehow get up that flippin' rope.

I stand in the middle of my favorite room on earth with the sun streaming in, and I reach up and take out my goddess braids. Then I strip off Sunny's stupid clothes. I leave everything I gained. I take my Great Bear hoodie and Cricket's magical orb necklace off. The vest Till gave me that he crocheted himself, with his dad's four red buttons that go up the front. I promised myself I would be different. I would do everything different than Sunny, but now I am just like her.

I leave the same way I came.

I step back into my stupid jeans with holes in the knees. Slip my head through my T-shirt that I haven't worn since the bus—

"River." I hear Jemma and quickly use my hand to smear the tears from my face.

A minute later, Jemma's standing up here. She moves to the windows that look out on Turtle Rock and the bay. "Wow. I really haven't been up here since your mom and I were kids. We would stay up here all summer, jumping into the bay, swimming to the rock . . ." She turns around to face me. "You remind me of her so much, only—"

"Jemma," I interrupt, "I shouldn't have—" I begin to say I'm sorry, but then I stop. I can hardly talk, because if I do the tears in my throat are going to come out.

Jemma keeps her eyes on mine. She gives me the softest smile. "Hey, let's take a breath," she says. She takes the half-full water bottle from beside Cricket's bed and hands it over to me. I lift it to my mouth and drink three small sips. I breathe.

I sit down on the edge of my bed.

Jemma sits on Cricket's across from me.

I look at her and she looks at me.

"River, listen," she finally says. "I'm disappointed in this situation, not in you."

Tears fill my eyes and I look away.

"I'm sorry this is so hard," Jemma goes on. "I know your mom. I get why you might feel angry—"

"I'm *not* mad," I say fast.

"Well, it's okay if you are." She waits. "Anger is just telling you that you want something to change."

"I'm *not* angry," I lie.

"Well, I am," says Jemma. "Your mom is a grown-up, and she should be figuring out her crap and taking care of you. You deserve that."

"But—" I stop. I look right at Jemma. "How can you not hate me?"

"Hate you?" She looks at me and shakes her head, and then the slightest smile overtakes her face. "I love you even more. Nothing will ever erase your time here. That was real. I wish you could have asked for help. We can always talk things out. I'm here for you, no matter what."

Now tears are rolling off my cheeks and down my neck. For a long moment it's just quiet. The sounds of the ocean and seabirds, sunshine filtering in, and Jemma smiles at me and says, "You know, I met you once."

I look up at her.

"You were just three weeks old when Sunny came back with you. She stayed for one month. Till was two years old. Nash was around your age. Ms. Birdy was healthy then. We wrapped you in wolfskin and dipped your face in our most sacred river, way up in the glaciers." Jemma laughs softly. "Oh, you cried so hard, and then you were so peaceful."

"Why'd you dip me in the water?" I ask her.

"So you would grow to be strong."

## 117

It's almost like, the universe knows what's happening. As we stand on the dock and wait for the ferry guys to finish whatever they're doing to get the boat started up, the fog and a cold rain roll in fast.

Everything is already bad. Then I realize that the guy on the boat with the ferry guy is not a part of the crew. He's—

*Ugh.*

He's with Sunny, and he looks like the head of a motorcycle gang or a UFC fighter who hasn't shaved or cut his beard off in years. He has long, dark hair slicked back and tucked behind his ears. He looks kind of mean. That's Sunny's type.

After a minute of awkward standing and waiting, Jemma steps right up to Sunny. I can tell by the way Jemma holds herself that she is angry. I kind of stay close to Till. We don't talk, but his shoulder brushes mine.

"You've got an amazing kid," Jemma tells Sunny. They are face-to-face. Jemma glances at me and back to Sunny. "She's probably the toughest kid I've ever met."

Sunny shakes her head and lets out a laugh.

"What's wrong with you?" Jemma says, and now she gets a little bit in Sunny's face. "When are you going to wake up? Stop fighting the world and start fighting for your daughter."

Now Sunny gets heated. I can tell. Her jaw is clenched and her eyes kind of flash. She glances at Scary Motorcycle Guy, then back at Jemma. "You have no idea what you're talking about and probably should stop talking—"

Up until this moment, Nash has been helping the ferry pilot

untether the boat from the dock, but I watch him suddenly drop the line and move quickly to step between his sisters. "Laurel," he says softly, using Sunny's real name. He looks right at her and says, "I think it's time for you to go."

Just exactly then, I hear yelling and turn to look. Cricket comes running toward us from the beach. She's waving her hands over her head. "Wait! Hold up!" she shouts, and when she gets to the dock, she runs straight for me and gives me the tightest, longest hug. Her hair smells like bonfire, and she holds me so close and whispers straight into my ear. "Till told me a little, and I don't know what's going on, but"—she pauses—"I would not have made it without you being here."

"Yeah, you would have," I say.

Cricket just squeezes me tighter. "You have no idea. You're braver than I am." When she lets go, she plants her trucker hat squarely on my head. "It's official, *you're* actually a mermaid," she says, and her eyes light up and she hugs me one last time. "I don't care what your name is," she whispers. "We're friends for life."

The rain begins to pick up, and the motor of the ferry revs to a start. I don't even get to hug Till or Nash or Jemma goodbye. Sunny takes my wrist and pulls me toward the boat, and as soon as I step on, the boat begins backing up. I look at them all gathered together on the dock and my heart feels like, the worst hurt. Jemma and Nash and Cricket and Till get smaller and smaller until I can barely see their faces: they're just small dots. I squint to try to see the lodge and the mountains through the rain and the fog. I can just make out Zeus and Lulu barking and chasing the boat as we move out along the coast. And Sunny says one thing to me as the ferry motors out of the bay. "Get a good look. We're never coming back."

## 118

I'm going to skip the worst boat ride of my life and the fact that I threw up three times and pick this up in Scary Motorcycle Guy's rusted-out pickup truck, which smells like cigarettes mixed with gas, and where I am currently sitting, jammed between the door and three torn black plastic trash bags filled with empty returnable beer cans. I'm in the narrow row behind the pickup's two front seats, occupied by Sunny (on the passenger side, with her bare feet propped up on the dash) and Scary Motorcycle Guy (driving), whose name is Jax. In case you're wondering, Jax has already smoked half a pack of cigarettes. His window is only open a crack. It's night. It's probably seven hours into our trip back to Clarksville. There is not a lot of talking. Did I say this is the type of truck you see with the big monster tires, and the muffler that's on purpose loud? It is. I can feel the *ka-thump*, *ka-thump*, *ka-thump*, and the whine of the tires as we barrel down the highway. The radio is on. The only thing Sunny says to me is "I can't believe you would do this to me. You almost got me in huge trouble."

I say nothing.

"Your principal lady—"

I bite down on my lower lip.

And Sunny goes, "What's her name?"

"Ms. Martinez," I say, barely above a whisper.

And Sunny says, "Did you know she called the police?"

I stay silent.

Sunny goes, "I'm not playing, River. You almost tore my life apart."

I roll my eyes.

"You're lucky," Sunny says. "I lied my way out of it."

I don't say anything. I'm too mad to speak and too sad to cry. We are careening down the highway at eighty miles per hour in a rusted-out monster truck with some guy I don't even know. I basically just curl up in a ball, with my flip-flops gripped to my feet so that my skin doesn't touch anything in this truck. I rest my head against the glass in my little space. I close my eyes. I feel the wind from the cracked window and the little bit of dampness on my face. And I try and wish this whole life away.

## 119

We have stopped. I don't know where we are, but there's a glaring light. I open my eyes a crack and squint. We've pulled off the highway and we're getting gas. Jax is outside the truck, gripping the fuel pump, filling the tank. When I don't see Sunny, my heart kind of jumps.

I sit up. *Where is she?* I look all around. I try and breathe, but it's so gross in here. Then I hear the truck door open and see Sunny hoist herself up and into the front seat. "Hey," she says to me, like everything is normal and everything is great. She slams the door shut. Then she tosses a Snickers bar into the back. "Thought you might be hungry," she says, facing forward and kicking her feet back up onto the dash.

"Thanks," I say so softly, I'm pretty sure she doesn't even hear me. I look at the Snickers bar. I am not hungry. I can't eat. I don't even want to breathe. It's quiet, then: "What are we doing?" I ask her.

"We're getting gas and checking our Powerball tickets," she answers, and then she holds a handful of lottery tickets—fanned out like a deck of cards—up above her head so I can see. "There's only one winning ticket," Sunny announces, "and the rumor is that it was sold in Clarksville."

I sit up a little and turn to my right and look out the window at the gas station lit up in the dark. I go, "Wait, we're in Clarksville?"

"No. We have another hour," says Sunny, and as she says that, Jax gets back into the truck. The whole vehicle sinks down under his weight. He's a big guy. They lean in and kiss each other. *Gross.*

I shut my eyes.

"How many we got?" he asks Sunny.

"Ten," she says, and her voice is hopeful. That's Sunny. She loves to waste money on things like this. Things that will never happen.

Jax starts the truck, only we don't budge. We sit, truck engine idling, in the gas station parking lot on the side of a highway under a bright flood of fluorescent light that's glaring in my eyes.

Jax goes, "Okay, babe," and he stares down at his phone and together he and Sunny carefully examine the lottery tickets. How they do it is, Jax slowly reads the numbers off: "Seventeen, thirty-six, eighty-six, nine, eleven, and the gold mega ball, thirty-three," and as he does, Sunny checks the tickets one by one.

Sunny: "No."

Sunny: "No."

Sunny: "No."

Sunny: "Oh! Wait. This has—no."

Sunny: "No."

Sunny: "No."

Sunny: "No."

I sit squished in the back and have to listen to them call off the winning numbers over and over again until I know them by heart: *17, 36, 86, 9, 11,* and the gold mega ball, *33.*

Sunny: "No."

Sunny: "No."

Sunny: "No."

I almost feel bad for Sunny as I watch her do whatever Jax says. Why does she like guys like this? Jax is the opposite of Nash. He's not polite. He doesn't seem very nice, and he sort of barks at Sunny. He bosses her around. Sunny is *not* the bossing-around type. I'm not gonna lie: it *really* bugs me when he talks to her like that.

Back on the highway, Jax goes on about the first thing he would do with the money if he won. Oh, but first, he orders Sunny to turn the radio off. "Shut that off," he says. "I'm trying to talk."

I close my eyes.

I turn toward the window and listen to Jax talk about the truck he wants: "A six-hundred-thirty-two-cubic-inch big-block Ford," he says, and I watch the back of his head as he turns to Sunny, taking his eyes off the road. "Thing can pump out eleven hundred thirty-two horsepower—" He pauses to pack a wad of chewing tobacco inside his lower lip, then spits into an empty can. "It's built to pull." He laughs, and so does Sunny. I hate when she's like this, acting like she cares about trucks when I know she does not.

"Nitrogen-charged gas shocks," Jax goes on. "It's a real head-turner—you gotta have all that stuff."

"Totally, babe," says Sunny.

*Ugh.* I try and block them out.

When Sunny is like this, with random guys, it's safer to be seen and not heard. I stay quiet. In my mind, I stop trying to understand. It is what it is. I have a pit in my stomach. I try to fold my legs under me—not easy to do with my flip-flops still on—and rearrange myself. Something is poking up from underneath my butt. I dig around in my back jeans pocket and fish out two pieces of folded-up paper. And sitting jammed in the little cramped half seat, I take the first piece of paper in my hands and unfold it. It's the card Ms. Martinez gave me in her office a zillion days ago. The light along the highway gives me just enough brightness to see. I hold the small card in my hand and replay that scene in my head. *You don't have to handle this alone,*

Ms. Martinez told me. I smooth out the card and read her hurried handwritten note: *River, this is my personal number. Please, call anytime!* "Anytime" is underlined. Twice. Only, the number is sort of smeared. Somewhere along the last fifteen days, it got wet. The last two numbers may be *38* or they could be *88* or maybe *89*. I try to make them out, but I can't. I think about how actually Ms. Martinez is really pretty nice. At least she noticed, she cared, she saw what was going on. I slip the card with her smeared number back into my pocket. The other piece of paper is the folded origami envelope from the lady on the bus. Remember her?

She was so kind. I can't believe she gave me this. I honestly feel like she was an angel or something. The way she shared her sandwich and berries with me, and placed her coat on me like a blanket while I slept. That bus was freezing!

I hold the origami-style envelope in my hand and run my fingers over the creases. Something about finding this neatly folded lined notebook paper in my current situation makes me feel a tiny bit better.

The truck stops at a light.

I glance up.

We're getting closer. I recognize the car dealerships. We're on the Clarksville strip. It's so weird to be back here.

I look back down at the folded note from the lady on the bus. I try to replay the scene in my mind, the way she looked at me when her eyes met mine. I unfold the note, careful not to rip it. Inside is a little slip of paper with a note. Underneath is a single lottery ticket. That's so crazy, right? I let out the softest laugh. It's not exactly a secret: I have the worst luck on earth.

I look up from the ticket and glance out the window again: McDonald's, Burger King, Verizon, Walmart. Everything is the same. The Clarksville strip. When the light changes, I watch the neon signs blink by. In the back seat of the truck, I hold the ticket up toward the window, and under the glow of the car dealership's floodlights, I silently read off the numbers on my single lottery ticket: five white-ball numbers and the gold mega ball, and my heart starts beating so hard and my hands begin to shake. I check again and again—I read them over twenty times at least. Are my eyes playing tricks on me? Is this like, a dream? But no matter how many times I read the six numbers, there they are: 17, 36, 86, 9, 11, and 33.

Okay, hold up. Wait. I know you might be at this point of the story and be like, *No way*. Maybe you want to throw this book out the window. Hey, go ahead, but for real, think about it for a sec: the odds of winning the largest jackpot in history are one in 307 MILLION. There is *no* scenario where holding a winning lottery ticket that's worth *1.7 billion dollars* is normal, or would ever seem real. You have a better chance of being struck by lightning. *Twice.* This is the craziest thing in the world! But it is happening. And you can believe me or not.

That's on you.

Feel free to leave and go read someone else's story. This is mine. And all I know is, I'm squished behind Sunny's seat, in some random dude's rusted-out monster truck, and my mouth falls open and my hands are still shaking. I am staring at the ticket that the lady from the bus gave me. My heart is like a cartoon, *ba-boom, ba-boom, ba-boom*, pumping out of my chest. I check the numbers on the ticket seven or eight more times, maybe fifty! Honestly, it's all kind of a blur. Every time I check, the numbers are a perfect match.

17, 36, 86, 9, 11—and 33.

Oh.

My.

God.

I have won 1.7 billion dollars.

You better believe I've kept my mouth shut. I don't say one word. I carefully tuck the ticket back into my pocket, and I climb out of the truck. I watch Sunny lean over and kiss Jax goodbye. *Yuck.*

Outside the truck, standing on the gravel driveway, I wait.

I wait until Jax backs the truck up and drives away. I wait until I can't hear his stupid muffler making noise. I wait alone under the flood of parking lights, on the steps to the trailer, and hope the scary dogs next door don't come out of nowhere and charge at me. Sunny goes around the back of the trailer and breaks in through the bathroom window. A minute later I hear her kicking the inside of the bolted door and then suddenly, it flies open—

"Welcome home!" she says, and she says it like she's joking. Inside, it still smells the same: ashtray and mold. Besides an empty pizza box with a pile of half-eaten crusts that's open and sitting on the counter, everything is exactly the way I left it fifteen days ago.

Same dirty shaggy carpet.

Same bags of trash.

Same empty fridge. I looked.

The only thing different is that Sunny is here, standing a few feet away. She yawns loudly. Then she looks at me and goes, "River, don't pull that on me again, okay?" and she turns and walks into the bathroom—even though the water got turned off a month ago. And right now, I try and wrap my brain around the ticket in my pocket. It hasn't really sunk in. I mean, this is crazy! How would you feel if you were thirteen years old, your mom was totally broke, barely scraping

by, and you suddenly found out you were holding the winning ticket
to 1.7 *billion* dollars?!!!

I begin to pace around the small space in front of the green sofa
where I sleep. I start smiling like, from the inside out, do you know
what I mean? I feel tingly in my heart. *Good stuff like this doesn't
happen to us.* I don't want to mess it up. For a few seconds, I wonder if
telling Sunny is even a good idea. But—I mean, how can I not? That's
more money than I can even add up in my head. Do you know how
much that can fix our life? I'm like, OH MY GOSH!!!!! My heart is
pounding like crazy. How do I tell her? What do I say?

## 123

A minute later, when Sunny walks back into the main part of the trailer, I go, "Um. You might want to sit down and prepare for some life-changing news."

And Sunny looks at me and she's just like, "What?" She sounds annoyed. "River, I'm tired. If you have something to say, say it."

Now I am grinning. I take a breath and move toward Sunny and stop a foot away. She has her hair tied up in a knot, and she's got this mouth guard in, the kind she wears at night so that her teeth get extra white. I go, "Okay, so, I have something kind of crazy to show you," and my smile grows.

"For real, sit," I tell her.

Sunny sighs. "Just tell me, River. What?"

So—

I take the Powerball lottery ticket from my pocket and before I can even say, *Look*, she plucks it from my hand. It's kind of a blur, but I know this: the first thing Sunny says rhymes with "duck," followed by "WHAT?!" and her face looks just like, total shock. She holds the winning ticket in her hands and says, "Oh my God, oh my God, oh my God," over and over and over again.

"Where did you get this?" she finally says.

I smile. "A lady on the bus gave it to me!"

Sunny is like, "No way!"

I go, "Way!"

Then we freak out. For a long time, we are jumping up and down in a circle holding hands, while shrieking at the top of our lungs. After that? We collapse together flat on our backs on top of the mound of clothes on Sunny's bed. The night outside has the usual sounds.

I listen to the sirens.

The loud voices from a party next door.

"Rivy," Sunny whispers, which is weird because she hasn't called me that since I was little. I turn to my side and look over at her. She's facing me now. "Hey," she says softly.

"Hey," I whisper, and I smile so big.

We are lying together close.

She takes a breath and goes, "I want to tell you something."

And in an instant, I get this terrible sudden nervous feeling. A thousand things shoot through my mind. *Is Sunny okay? What did she do? Is she pregnant? Did she like, secretly marry Jax?*

Sunny keeps her eyes on mine and whispers, "I promise. I'm gonna change."

I get real quiet.

I've heard this before. I watch her eyes. The flood of lights from the Costco parking lot give Sunny's face a soft pinkish glow. She smiles over at me. "We're going to have so much fun," she whispers. Then she can't keep her excitement in. "Oh my God!" She kicks her legs up like a little kid. "I can quit my job!" she squeals. "I cannot wait until we cash this ticket in!!!!"

She exhales.

And for a second it gets quiet.

I'm kind of in shock.

And I whisper, "If I ask you something, will you promise not to get mad?"

Sunny looks at me and says, "What?" Her eyes are wide. I haven't seen her this happy in a really long time.

I take a breath and I watch her face carefully and I say, "Can it just be me and you?"

Sunny's eyebrows go up. She asks, "What do you mean?"

I whisper, "Jax," and I hold my breath, watching her face for signs that she's mad. Sunny scoots even closer. Our noses are just a few inches from each other. I haven't been this close to Sunny in a million years. It feels so good. And she looks into my eyes and it's like she's here. She's with me. For the first time in the longest time, she's really here. And her face lights up and she cracks the biggest smile and she says, "Jax who?" Then she lets out the biggest laugh and pops up onto her feet, on top of her unmade bed. She reaches her hand and pulls me up too, and together we jump up and down, holding hands. Then we dance and dance all these silly, crazy moves. We make our own music, we sing and yell, "Oh yeah, we won the lottery! Oh yeah, we won the lottery!" And we throw our arms up and squeal and laugh. Then, after all that, I watch Sunny take the ticket and place it into the box of letters. The same shoebox I rummaged through fifteen days ago. I see her tuck it in between a stack of postcards and old photos, held together with a single orange rubber band. And when she catches me watching, she holds her finger up to her lips, like, *Shhhhhh*. She gives me a wink. "Safekeeping," she says.

# 124

In the morning, I wake up with my face pressed into the mattress in Sunny's room. When I turn and look—

Sunny isn't here.

*Oh God.*

I sit up and glance across the room at the box on the floor and immediately jump up and rush over to look. "Thank goodness," I say softly to myself when I see the ticket, still right where Sunny put it, tucked in between her collection of old postcards and photos, held together by the orange rubber band.

"Morning!" I hear Sunny call out.

I walk out of her room to see her standing at the counter. "There's no way I could sleep on our big news!" she says, and her eyes light up. "You?"

"I guess I was pretty tired," I say. We share the same smile. I look around the kitchen. Sunny's cleaned up a little, and there is food. "Pop-Tarts!" she says in a singsong voice, pushing the box toward me. I use my teeth to rip open a pack and take a big bite. Then, while my mouth is full of raw cherry Pop-Tart, Sunny takes out her phone and slides it across the counter toward me. "Go ahead and have a look!" she says. She hasn't stopped smiling.

I take her phone in my hands and read the headlines:

$1.7 BILLION WINNER STILL A MYSTERY:
TICKET BOUGHT AT LOCAL CONVENIENCE STORE
IN CLARKSVILLE, WASHINGTON

POWERBALL'S SOLE BILLION DOLLAR WINNING TICKET
SOLD IN CLARKSVILLE, WASHINGTON

TIME IS RUNNING OUT FOR THE $1.7 BILLION JACKPOT
WINNER TO COLLECT—TICKET WILL EXPIRE TOMORROW
AT NINE A.M.!

I wipe the crumbs from my fingers and tap on the last headline and read out loud to Sunny:

> "What if you won 1.7 billion dollars? What to do when you suddenly come into great wealth.
> Hire a good lawyer and financial team to help you manage your newfound wealth. Don't make any quick decisions regarding your winnings! Make a strategy before you act. Impulsive decisions and trusting the wrong people can lead to misery.
> Be careful of fraudsters and people who want to take advantage of you.
> Get ready, you're about to become *very* popular!
> Remember, money isn't happiness: figure out what's important to you and develop a plan and—"

"Okay, that's enough," Sunny cuts me off. "You don't need to read any of that."

I look up. Like, *Are you sure?*

"River," says Sunny, and she rolls her eyes and laughs. "I know what I'm doing. I don't need any help!"

## 125

There hours later, we are sitting in a very high-ceilinged lobby of the most expensive deluxe hotel in downtown Seattle, the LeGrand. There are huge glittering bright red glass chandeliers hanging above our heads. This hotel is sleek, all white and crisp edges and crazy-expensive-looking, with bright yellow-gold sofas that are so luxurious-seeming that I think twice about sitting for fear I'll leave a mark. Why are we here? It's part of Sunny's plan! We're going to turn the ticket in tomorrow morning at the Powerball lottery office in downtown Seattle. We are waiting in the lobby of the LeGrand to meet up with some guy named Vic. I have no clue who Vic is. I sit on the edge of the yellow-gold couch and look around. We really stand out.

Everyone in the lobby is sharply dressed in dark suits. Crisp white shirts and ties. Women, head-to-toe polished and perfectly put-together, every last detail flawless.

By the way, I'm in the middle of eating a donut, because after the hour-and-a-half bus ride from Clarksville to downtown Seattle, the bus dropped us off three blocks from the LeGrand on a busy down-town street, smack in front of a donut truck!

I said, "Can I get one?"

And Sunny said, "Why not!"

So. I'm sitting on this fancy sofa, with white powdered sugar on my lips and all over my fingers. I'm wearing my same clothes: flip-flops, jeans, T-shirt, and Cricket's mermaid trucker hat. I am in charge of the shoebox with the ticket, which is sitting in my lap. I'm the only kid here.

Sunny sits on the same couch, combing her long hair back with her fingers, looping it into a pony, then tying it up in a topknot. I watch her separate a few strands in the front. She is not dressed like anyone here: white T-shirt, black leather jacket, tight jeans—which may be why there is a security guard with a walkie-talkie, standing by the entrance of the LeGrand, who keeps watching us.

He's staring.

I try to sit back and relax. I use the back of my hand to quickly wipe the sugar from the corners of my lips.

I smile over at Sunny.

She smiles at me.

It's really all starting to sink in.

We have a secret and it's the BEST! That's the kind of smiles we have. Like I said, we are here to meet some guy, Vic. "Vic is the *man!*" says Sunny. "Wait until you meet him. He's a friend of Jax's and—"

I go, "Wait. You told Jax?"

And she laughs and says, "Don't worry! He's not going to tell anyone. And this friend of his, Vic—he knows what he's doing. He's some big financial adviser manager guy. He reps a lot of pro athletes and YouTube stars."

I go, "Really?" I mean, I'm kind of impressed. Sunny is following the list from the article I read.

She leans over. "I told you," she says, smiling wide. "I got this!"

## 126

Minutes pass and this guy Vic, he still isn't here. From my spot on the gold-yellow coach in the LeGrand lobby, I watch a man step off the elevator and make a beeline to—

Me and Sunny.

This man is definitely some sort of security too. He is a white guy, bald, with one of those strong chins with a dimple in it. He has a very stern face and an earpiece in. Like the Secret Service or a bodyguard on TV. He is very tall and very big.

"Ma'am," he says stiffly.

And Sunny looks up at the man in his all-black suit.

"Ma'am," he repeats, "do you have a room number?"

Sunny pops up. She gets right in his face. "Are you gonna call the cops on me because my daughter and I are sitting in your lobby?" She waits. "Oh, I'm sorry," she says, her voice rising. "Do we not look *rich* enough?" She laughs.

The lobby falls quiet. People turn to watch. A few iPhones pop out. There is whispering. My head heats up.

"Ma'am," he says, stepping closer, "if you could calm down."

"Me, calm down?" Sunny fires back.

I quickly stand up and grab her by the elbow. "Come on," I say, pulling her toward me. "Let's just go."

"No!" Sunny says. Her voice is even louder now. Every single person in this lobby is staring at us. "Please, Sunny," I try again. "Let's just go," I plead.

But—no. It's a standoff.

Sunny folds her arms tightly across her chest.

The man does not move. He stares at Sunny.

Sunny stares right back at him.

From where I'm standing, I see that just inside the man's suit jacket he has one of those holsters with a gun.

My heart begins to race. "Sunny," I try for the third time.

"River," she says sharply. I can see she's not backing down, and I begin to really panic. I search the crowd that's watching us for a friendly face, but nobody is moving to help, nobody will even look me in the eye. Until—

Suddenly, out of nowhere, this glamorous lady walks toward us. Her lips are shimmery pink, her teeth are like a toothpaste ad. "Divia Gupta, head of guest services," she says, smiling at Sunny and extending her hand. "There seems to have been a terrible misunderstanding!" Then Divia Gupta turns to the security man standing alongside her and announces, "Ms. Ryland and her daughter are LeGrand VIPs!"

It's that simple. Security Man raises his eyebrows a little, then silently turns and leaves.

And just as he does, I hear, "Big things!" and look at a man walking straight across the lobby toward us. The second I see him, I just know this guy has to be Vic. He's short and stocky and dressed in a super-expensive-looking suit. He's got shifty eyes, and a really sharp haircut—with a razor-edged part.

Divia looks at the man walking toward us and says, "Mr. Vic DeAngelo just shared your incredible news!"

Right away, Vic leans in and kisses Sunny on both her cheeks. "*Mwhaa!*" he says.

Yech. I've never seen this guy in my life. He acts like he's our long-lost relative or something.

"Big things!" Vic repeats when his eyes meet mine. I do not reach out my hand. Something about Vic DeAngelo makes me step back.

I look around. Everyone in the lobby is still watching us, but now in a whole different way. They are whispering and smiling and acting like we are somebody. Like we're famous! A minute ago, we were not welcome here. It's like someone turned a switch. I go from nobody to somebody, just like that.

And we are quickly surrounded by a small crowd of LeGrand employees gathered around us. Each of them is all smiles, and they begin to clap! And Divia Gupta's eyes light up and she says, "Ms. Ryland" to Sunny and practically bows. "Please. Why don't you and your lovely daughter and Mr. DeAngelo come with me."

# 127

I love Divia Gupta. She's so nice! She hugs me hello, and then we're off on our tour. "You're an old soul," she tells me as we walk. "I can see it in your eyes!"

"You can?" I say, with a nervous laugh. I'm not sure exactly what she means. I mean, I have my mermaid hat on, and my jeans. I'm pretty sure I need a shower bad. But there's something about Divia that just draws you in.

"Where are you from?" I ask her, because she has this cool accent. It's like British, but not.

"Mumbai," she says. "It's on the beach."

"I *love* the beach," I say.

Divia says, "I do too!" and she smiles at me as we walk. "And you? Where are you from?"

I say, "Clarksville," and I feel my shoulders kind of drop.

## 128

We—Sunny, Vic DeAngelo, and I—spend the next hour with Divia Gupta and her team, who lead us on an "exclusive personal tour" of the LeGrand.

We start just off the lobby. "Here we have the fabulous Sushi Sora, specializing in five-star cuisine, featuring Wagyu beef flown in from Yamagata, Japan," Divia says. I follow along. We move in a pack, and people are watching us, whispering as we pass. Next stop: "The LeGrand state-of-the-art fitness boutique," Divia announces as she opens the door and I poke my head in. It's dark in here. And there's a guy in red shorts and a hoodie and these crazy-looking headphones with goggles, swinging his arms like he's doing karate and running in place.

"What in the heck?" says Sunny.

"What is that guy doing?" I whisper.

Divia drops her voice. "Zombie run," she says. "At the LeGrand, our fitness boutique utilizes the latest virtual reality. As you can see, our guest is hooked into headphones, goggles, and movement sensors to escape the zombie apocalypse, all while running a 10K!"

"That is crazy!" says Sunny.

Four or five minutes later, we are all standing in a very fast elevator going straight to the top of the LeGrand. When the door opens, I go, "Whoa!"

"Welcome home," says Divia. There is no door: the elevator just opens and we step off directly into the LeGrand's Royal Palace Suite on the thirty-fifth floor!

"Your palatial penthouse suite is our most luxurious crown jewel, a 2,896-square-foot suite with floor-to-ceiling windows and, as you can see, the most spectacular views of the iconic skyscraper, the Smith Tower." I walk in and just—

"Wow," I say.

Up until now Vic DeAngelo has had his eyes glued to his phone, but right at this moment he looks up. "Magnificent decor!" he says.

I don't like this guy.

Divia goes on, "Our contemporary art collection is commissioned exclusively for the LeGrand."

I look at the paintings covering the walls.

Divia stands beside me and says, "The LeGrand's Royal Palace Suite is designed by the world-renowned modernist architect Remi Gisele—the very best. You have twenty-four-hour access to our world-class chef, a living room with a fireplace and a hundred-inch TV, three bedrooms, each with sumptuous beds dressed in Lissadell linens, and blackout shades, which work via voice command. Shades down," she says, and sure enough, the shades lower, blocking out the sun. "Shades up!" Divia commands. Then there is light again. She steps toward the living room. Arranged around a low, long table made of glass are two armchairs and a huge leather sofa. Divia goes on, "We have complimentary high-speed internet, and each bedroom is equipped with this gizmo." She pauses to pick up a remote control. "This allows you to wake up in tune with nature, ocean waves, or perhaps, create your very own digital chirp, the squawk of a warble, or a wood thrush." Divia flashes her beautiful smile. "Mother Nature at your fingertips!"

She gestures for us to follow her into another wing. "Here we have your very own private spa, a professional hair salon, nail salon, a magnolia aromatherapy rainfall shower, heated marble floors, a Himalayan salt sauna, a crystal steam room, and a black-granite soaking tub."

Next, Divia leads us to the fully stocked kitchen. "Double fridge," she says, opening it to reveal packed shelves of colorful fruit, and all sorts of healthy food. Divia nods to one of her staff, who immediately puts out a gigantic tray of snacks. "Fresh pastries, cheeses, and charcuterie," Divia describes, "compliments of the LeGrand."

Sunny and I sneak a look at each other and share huge *Is this even real life?* kind of grins. Then Sunny helps herself to a piece of chocolate. I pop a chunk of cheese into my mouth.

Divia walks over to the balcony and opens the large sliding glass door. "Ladies, this is my favorite feature." She pushes a button just outside the glass wall, and a cover electronically slides open, revealing—

"A pool!" I say.

"That's crazy!" says Sunny.

Divia steps toward the pool. "Here we have your very own private outdoor infinity pool on the balcony deck overlooking the city skyline. It's fantastic at night! There is a remote lighting system as well as temperature control and underwater speakers."

I look down at the sleek, narrow pool. "This is nuts," I say under my breath. Then Sunny and I look at each other again and just shake our heads in shock.

Finally, we walk with Divia and her staff to the elevator back where we entered the suite. There are a zillion vases everywhere, filled with fresh flowers.

Divia pauses before the elevator and wraps things up. "House-keeping is at your disposal, and of course we have a nightly turndown service—"

I go, "What is that?"

Divia says, "Housekeeping will come in and turn down the sheets and fluff your pillows."

And I say, "There's a person for that?"

"Absolutely!" Divia smiles and her eyes kind of sparkle. "Ms. Ryland," she says, and she's speaking to me, and I interrupt. "Please, call me River," I say.

"Ms. River," Divia says. "At the LeGrand, our staff will go above and beyond. Whatever you need, the thirty-fifth floor is your own personal oasis. We hope you feel above it all." She turns to Sunny. "Ms. Ryland, would you like us to place your winning ticket in the LeGrand's secure safe?"

Sunny laughs. Like, *no way*. She glances at me and shakes her head. I'm still clutching the box. Sunny looks back at Divia and says, "Thank you, but there is no way I'm letting that ticket out of my sight!"

"As you wish," says Divia with a smile. "Can I have my bellmen bring up your luggage?"

"Oh," Sunny says. She looks a bit embarrassed. "Our luggage, it's—"

"It got lost!" I blurt out like the liar that I am.

"Well, that's unfortunate," says Divia. "Not to worry. I'd be happy to provide you with a personal shopper if you'd like?"

"Really?" says Sunny. "That would be amazing! River and I both need outfits—shoes, clothes, the works." She pauses to catch my eye. "A head-to-toe makeover for our press conference tomorrow morning."

I look at Sunny. "Wait. We're having a press conference?"

This very second, Vic DeAngelo, who has been quiet most of the tour, looks up from his phone. "Kiddo," he says. "Don't worry. I'll go over everything in ten." Then he steps into the elevator and looks back at his phone.

Divia gives us one last smile. She really is so nice. Sunny and I stand side by side, facing the elevator, with Divia and her team and Vic DeAngelo looking down at his phone. Divia waves at me as the elevator doors begin to close. I smile back. "Bye, Divia. Thanks!" I say.

"See you, Divia!" Sunny waves.

The doors shut.

And now it's just us.

You get how weird this is, right? This morning I woke up in a trailer with no electricity and no running water, and now Sunny and I are standing in the LeGrand's Royal Palace Suite. Tomorrow morning, we hand in our ticket for 1.7 *billion* dollars! I'll give you one guess—

What do you think we do next?

## 129

Yep! You're right!

We pretty much go nuts!

"This is unbelievable!" I shriek, and kick my flip-flops so they go flying across the suite. I skip around the rooms and halls of our LeGrand Royal Palace Suite!

"It's literally insane!" says Sunny. "A five-star hotel." She walks to the closet in one of the rooms. "Dude! We have our own robes, slippers—oh my God, the bathrooms have TVs!"

Sunny cracks open the sliding glass door and steps out onto the narrow patio with the pool. "This is so sick. Check it out, Riv. We're *rich*!"

In my room, with my gigantic king-size bed, I crouch down and hide the shoebox with the ticket, tucking it safely under the bed. Then I join Sunny outside on the balcony overlooking Seattle.

It feels good to be outside again. I look out at the view of a thousand skyscraper buildings. You can't really see a lot of sky. But a shaft of sun makes its way to our little balcony space, and the warmth feels so good on my face. I lean against the railing and gaze out at the skyscrapers and the busy city down below.

I turn to Sunny. "Um, question?"

She looks at me, eyebrows up. She's happy. She says, "Yes?"

"Okay, don't get mad, but like, I'm just wondering, since we haven't even turned in the ticket yet—"

"Yeah?"

"How are we paying for all this?" I ask.

Sunny laughs and bumps into me with her shoulder. "Silly!" she says, smiling wide. "Vic put money down. He's paying for everything!"

"Oh," I say. Then I look at Sunny and I go, "But, I mean, why?"

Sunny laughs again. "He's our adviser," she says. "That's how it works. He going to get a percentage of our winnings for helping us."

I say, "Wait. What do you mean?"

"He gets like, say, twenty percent," Sunny says matter-of-factly. She kicks off her shoes, sits on the edge of the pool, and dangles her feet into the water.

I roll my jeans up and sit, dipping my feet in too, and I silently do the math in my head. *Twenty percent of $1.7 billion: that's $340 million!* I turn to face Sunny. I go, "Twenty percent? Really? That's a lot of money."

Sunny laughs and kicks her toes so they make a splash. Then she slides right into the water and pulls me in too, both of us fully dressed.

I sink to the bottom of the pool. And we look at each other underwater and smile wide. Then we both pop up for air, laughing and splashing. And Sunny says, "River, we just won 1.7 BILLION DOLLARS!!!! Trust me! Don't worry so much!"

## 130

He's back.

Vic DeAngelo arrives with a bang, or actually a loud, "Ladies!" that he hollers. He walks right in and across the suite and sits down on the big leather sofa.

As soon as he sits, his cell phone rings.

I'm staring at him, bright red in the cheeks and totally mortified, because all I'm wearing is a robe and Cricket's hat!

I just got out of the pool. My clothes are in a chlorine puddle in my private bedroom off the kitchen. And since we don't have our new clothes yet, and since my old clothes are soaking wet, Sunny and I sit down with Vic DeAngelo in our matching LeGrand white robes that go down to our knees, and these slippers with an embroidered loopy cursive *L* on the tops.

Vic clears his throat. He rubs his hands together. He says, "Big things, ladies!" Then he and Sunny share a look.

I glance at Sunny like, *What's going on?*

Vic DeAngelo takes a phone out of his front suit pocket and holds it out to me. "A brand-new phone for you," he says.

I'm like, "Seriously?" and I reach for it. It's the latest iPhone that I've been wanting so bad. The exact same one that Emi has.

And then Vic DeAngelo smiles again at Sunny—and again, I'm like, *What?*

Vic DeAngelo says, "River Ryland, you are blowing up!"

"Huh?" I manage, confused.

Vic says, "A streamlined branded account across all the socials!"

I stare back at him. I have no clue what he's talking about.

"River, just look!" Sunny says, sounding impatient. She leans in toward me and my new phone that I am holding in my hands. I look down and tap on the glass and my mouth drops open. I'm like, *What in the heck?!!!!!!!!!*

"Your new profile," Vic says proudly.

"@billiondollargirl_official," I read out loud. "But—this already has fifty-seven million followers! And the photo, wait. Where'd you even—"

My eyes are glued to the screen. This is crazy. I am staring at a selfie of me. I know where it's from. Emi made me an Instagram. I had like, seven followers. I thought we deleted it, but apparently not. I look back up at Vic. "How did you even find this?"

"You're going viral, kid!" Vic is thrilled. "Did you notice the blue checkmark? I had my team pull some favors. You're verified, baby!"

I look down again. I'm like, *This is crazy.* Underneath, the photo caption says, *@billiondollargirl_official: THANK YOU GUYS SO SO SO MUCH FOR 57 MILLION I LOVE YOU ALL!!!*

And I look up at Vic DeAngelo. "But I didn't even write that and—"

Vic cuts me off. "I've never seen anything like it. You're the new reigning queen. My phone has been ringing since your name was leaked and—"

Now I go, "What? How was my name leaked?"

Vic laughs. "I didn't waste any time. You're all over the news!" He says this like it's the best thing ever. "We're positioning you." He pauses to give me this creepy wink. "Your hashtag is trending."

"I have a hashtag?"

"Young, pretty, rags to riches—you check all the boxes. My team posted it five minutes after we spoke with Sunny. Within an hour, #BillionDollarGirl was trending overnight! And it's just going to get bigger after we clean you up."

"Clean me up?" I say, confused.

"I have my best stylist team coming in this afternoon from Hollywood. Wait until you see what they can do," he brags. "Total transformation. You'll look like a supermodel."

I can't speak.

I look to Sunny for help. But she is *loving* this.

Vic stands up. "Ladies," he says, "I need to get back down to the lobby and make some calls."

The three of us walk toward the elevator. "Timing is everything," Vic DeAngelo tells us. "That's why we're waiting to turn the ticket in. We want to get ahead of this. I already have top talent agents reaching out. We're leveraging the win, triple-A-list companies looking to diversify are eating you up. I'm gonna get some very big endorsement packages together. We already have brand and licensing deals lined up. Beauty tutorials, fashion—we're going to focus on content and make you lots of money!"

"But don't we already have a lot of money?" I ask, confused.

Vic bursts out laughing. "Kid," he says, "you can never have enough."

## 131

Vic hasn't left yet. We're still standing by the elevator in the suite. He stops to look down at his gold watch. Then he silently points to his earbuds. "*I've got to take this*," he mouths. "Jimmy!" He talks loudly. "I'm here with her now," he says, winking again.

I look to Sunny, but she's glued to her new phone. Vic gave her one too.

Vic walks away from us. A second later he's back. "Good news!" he announces, and Sunny looks up. "We have merch that will drop after the presser tomorrow morning. I'm already fielding calls on literary and film."

"I don't get it," I say to Sunny only. She has her head down again, scrolling. "Sunny!" I say sharply. She suddenly looks up.

"What?" she laughs. "Listen to Vic."

Vic presses the elevator button and the doors open. "You're a hot commodity, kid!" he tells me. He points to his ear, and I realize he's also still on a call the whole time he's been talking to me. "This is my guy at YouTube," he explains. "Your channel is verified. I've hired a team of digital creators to help push out some amazing content. Like and subscribe!" He takes his phone out and puts it on speaker. "Jimmy, tell our girl here what we're gonna do." And now a stranger's voice comes out of the phone and into my ears: "River, we're building your brand and clout," the man says. "You're an influencer now!"

"But I'm only thirteen—I haven't done anything yet."

Sunny laughs. "Riv, relax! Just go with it!"

Vic glances at his watch again. "American Eagle's calling me in ten," he says. "They're drooling at your engagement level and followership. We're talking brand takeover and an in-feed video endorsement ad. They're going to pay through the teeth to get a piece of you," Vic says.

## 132

"Hello, gorgeous!" Divia gushes, smiling at me as her team of assistants marches off the elevator and straight into the suite. Everyone is carrying packages, stacks and stacks of shoes in fancy boxes, and expensive-looking colorful glossy bags.

Vic is gone. It's just us girls now: me, Sunny, and Divia's all-gal style squad!

The team piles the towers of boxes and bags into Sunny's room and mine until there's no more space on my king-size bed. Dresses are laid out, shoes are lined up along the carpet.

Then, in the main room of the LeGrand's Royal Palace Suite, we all push the furniture out of the way. Divia walks over to the sound system and cranks up the volume. Our suite is transformed into a high-fashion runway show, starring me and Sunny!

I go first.

It's hard to pick! There must be twenty boxes' worth of brand-new shoes, jackets, coats, dresses, skirts, jeans, tops, and bags spread out all over my bed. I take my new iPhone and toss it onto the bed, because I mean, that many strangers following me is freaking me out.

It's not just the stuff Divia's team bought that's in here. Even more things keep coming up and are being carried into the suite! It's the strangest thing: companies who want to sponsor me are giving me stuff! How crazy is that? Like, when you have money, people give you things? When you don't have money . . . well, you know what I mean!

I slip on outfit number one, a simple summer dress. It's light pink, with bright red straps that cross in the back.

"Let's see!" Divia calls out, and I step out of my room and stride like a supermodel on a runway, and I can't stop laughing. I twirl and my cheeks turn red. To round out the full look, I still have Cricket's hat on, and my hair is down and wavy and totally wild. "Hooray!" cheers Divia, as I stride past her, giggling.

The whole team claps.

"So pretty!" I hear.

"I think this is a home run," one of the women says. "It's a pink dream!"

The bass of the music is thumping.

After outfit one, I take a seat on the leather sofa next to Divia and join in the fun.

Sunny is next.

"Sunny, Sunny!" we chant and clap. And here she comes!

Sunny works it. She's got that confidence. She practically glides down our makeshift runway in her Gucci silk skirt, bright coral top, and high strappy sandals, to rave applause.

After outfits one through fifteen are tried on, I pick outfit number one, the pink tank dress with the bright red straps, for our big press conference tomorrow morning.

Sunny picks her outfit too: a short leather skirt, and a top that's very plunge-y. It's blue.

And now we are getting professionally fitted.

I am standing before a wall of mirrors, wearing my press conference outfit. Divia looks at me as the seamstress kneels and hems my dress. "You look very classic," Divia says. "Very elegant!" She smiles.

"Thanks, Divia," I say, and stare at myself. I actually kind of like how I look. I love the way the pink dress and my trucker hat look, it's like, kind of sassy and tough. I like it a lot. My hair is still messy, and as the seamstress works her magic, I twirl a strand of my hair around my finger, and as I do, I'm hit with this distant scent of the bonfire from my "birthday" party on the cove with Cricket and Till—and suddenly, my chest kind of hurts. I wish I could tell them. I wish they were here. I keep Cricket's mermaid hat on my head. For some reason, I don't want to take it off. It's like, some part of me thinks if I keep everything just the way it is, just so, Sunny will stay okay, and all this good won't go away . . . which sounds totally crazy, I know. But it's just this feeling. I've always had it. Sunny needs me to keep things in control.

"I love your hat," I hear Divia say, and I look at her smiling at me in the mirror. "I've always been fond of mermaids," she says.

And I say, "Me too."

## 133

Once we have our new clothes, Vic's "handpicked" celebrity hair-stylist, Frédéric, bursts in. He's loud. And the first thing he does when I sit in the salon-style chair? He snatches my hat off my head and hands it to his assistant, who drops it in the trash!

I'm like, "Wait—"

"That's not a good look." He smirks. "You don't want to look like some rando tween." Yes, he actually says this to me! And you know what really makes me cringe? Vic DeAngelo is back, half watching, half working his phones. "You can't dress like a teenage boy," Vic says, looking up. "You're an influencer now!"

I hate this guy.

Frédéric is talking—something about "silicone" and "super-shiny" and "apply it properly." I have no clue, because I'm not really listening! I'm staring at Cricket's hat in the trash.

*I'm so mad!*

I think about jumping up and grabbing it, but these people seem to know better than me, so I sit and don't move.

I watch Frédéric strip Great Bear out, every swim to Turtle Rock, every fire on the beach, all the love. He makes a face and looks at me in the mirror and says, "Hon, have you ever used a brush?"

He actually says this to me.

Then he calls over a man with an apron and orders him to "get these kinks smooth." The guy with the apron silently slathers my hair with some type of serum. Whatever is in this stuff makes my eyes sting. I can't stand the fumes.

"We're going to let that soak in." Frédéric touches my shoulders and I flinch. "We're going to smooth it out and give you a nice, deep, rich golden buttery blond."

I go, "Wait, you're coloring my hair?"

Frédéric laughs, then says, "Trust me," and in a matter of minutes, my hair is slathered in more syrupy goo and covered with plastic wrap. Frédéric's entire team moves in: pulling and poking and "pampering" me. I'm pretty sure Vic DeAngelo is filming this.

Soon, I have an octopus of hands and fingers working every inch of me. One lady is threading my eyebrows, plucking them with a string, another is laser treating my lips, and soon I have crazy-long fake eyelashes. Nothing is not touched. My nails are done—lilac-pink, acrylic, with encrusted diamonds on the tips. My brows are lifted, sculpted, shaped. "Oh yes!" I hear. "Look how that opened up her pretty eyes."

It's like I'm not even here.

The gooey stuff on my head is rinsed.

Then Frédéric steps back in, admiring the work. He speaks to me in the mirror as he plays with my hair. "Don't take this the wrong way," he says. "You were a hot mess. This is better, one hundred percent!"

Ugh.

I sit perfectly still while Frédéric takes this ginormous brush and begins to blow-dry my hair from wavy to flat. My sun-kissed streaks, from two weeks of swimming to Turtle Rock, are now washed out, and my hair is now this totally fake golden yellow. "Ravishing!" says Frédéric, running his fingers through my hair. "This is a much more elevated look!" Then he takes sections of my hair and uses a hot flat iron to straighten it. I can smell my hair burning. It's like he's cooking out the last little bit I had left of Liv.

"No more icky frizz!" Frédéric says, raking my hair back with his hands.

I stare at myself in the mirror. I don't even recognize me! My brows have been waxed and shaped, and someone used a big brush of sparkly bronzer all over my face. My lips are glossy pink. My wild, twisty long hair is fried flat. I always wanted perfectly smooth hair like Emi's, but something doesn't feel right. I don't know how to describe it, but—I hate that someone decided how I was supposed to be. I just feel like—

This isn't me.

 **134**

At the elevator, Frédéric leans in and air-kisses my cheek. I kind of pull away before he goes, "Mwah!" Then Vic DeAngelo, Frédéric, and his entire celebrity team step into the elevator, and thank goodness, they leave.

Divia and I wave politely and wait for the doors of the elevator to close shut. The second they do, Divia turns to me and says, "What a knob-headed twit!"

And we both burst out laughing.

"I know it's not my place," Divia says, "but I did not like how that man spoke to you. I just want you to know, that was not okay with me. That was *not* cool."

"Thanks, Divia," I say.

## 135

Is there more?

Yes.

To be specific: oxygen infusion hyaluronic-acid facials. Even Divia joins in—Sunny insists—and Divia says, "If that's your wish."

After all that?

We feast on a midafternoon snack delivered to our suite personally by the chef—sashimi, sliced raw fish. "The freshest you can possibly have," he says. "I had this red snapper flown in this morning from Japan."

I grab a piece and pop it into my mouth and work hard not to make a face . . . *This fish doesn't taste like the salmon on Great Bear.* Still, I swallow it, then wash it down with water from Iceland in a plastic bottle.

# 136

Divia and the last of her team file out.

And now it's just Sunny and me. This place is huge. I don't really even know where Sunny is. She went off someplace with her phone about twenty minutes ago. I walk toward the kitchen. "Sunny?" I call out. Then I say it louder: "Sunny?"

No answer.

In the living room by the big leather couch, I look all around. The entire suite has been cleaned! The food in the kitchen has been put away. The half-full plastic bottles of water that were littered all over the place are gone. The partially eaten plates of sashimi are nowhere in sight. The dishwasher is on. The all-white counters on the kitchen island are wiped down. It smells like bleach, or like some type of polish. The floors are spotless. There were a lot of people in the suite today. It kind of got trashed and now—it's sparkling new again.

That's when I see her.

Not Sunny.

A maid.

She has dark hair pulled back tight into a ponytail. She has a uniform on: a light blue dress with a white collar, and a pressed white apron in the front. And she is standing next to one of those huge rolling housekeeping carts, loaded up with cleaning stuff: spray bottles to disinfect, stacks of folded white towels, and a black plastic garbage bag hanging from the handles, full of trash. For just a second we look at each other. She has tired eyes.

I don't walk toward her.

I just like, freeze. I manage this lame wave. Then suddenly an elevator off the kitchen opens that I didn't even know was there, and I watch the woman back into the elevator, pulling the cart. This elevator is not like the luxury high-speed one that we rode up in. It's ancient-looking and kind of dirty. The doors close quickly. And I have that pit-in-my-stomach feeling, you know? I mean, it doesn't feel right having someone clean up after me like that.

I look around.

It's so quiet now.

All the packaging that was strewn all over the place has been taken away. All Sunny's and my brand-new clothes have been folded and hung up. There are fresh towels. And fresh flowers! There's this fragrance in the air—I think it's piped in. "Sunny?" I call out for a third time.

"I'm in here," she finally says.

"Hi," I say, entering her room. She's sitting up on her giant bed, staring at her phone. She looks all glammed up. She's wearing a mash-up of a few of her new outfits: a sparkly hot-pink body-hugging top, the $1,100 leather skirt by Fenty, oversized gold hoop earrings, stacked jangly bracelets on both her wrists. Her long hair is down and around her shoulders. Frédéric darkened it, so it's back to the color it really is. Sunny honestly looks straight out of *Vogue*.

I climb into bed next to her.

I go, "How much fun was that?"

"That was awesome," she says without looking up.

I try to tell whether she's in a good mood or bad, but I can't read her face. I inch over closer and curl up next to her. But—

"Hey, don't mess up my hair," she says, pushing me away.

I sit up a little. I reach for the TV remote. I turn to Sunny, excited. "What do you want to watch? Like, we can watch *any* movie! We can have a sleepover party, just me and you," I tell her. Right when I say that, exactly right then—

I hear, "Hello!"

There's no doorbell. Like I said, the elevator just opens up into the suite. My heart begins to speed up. Even from Sunny's room, I know that voice.

I know who it is.

## 137

It's Jax.

"Babe?" he calls out.

"Coming!" Sunny says. She immediately springs up and begins moving very fast, buckling on her brand-new Louis Vuitton high-heel strappy sandals.

I get the worst uneasy feeling watching Sunny as she stands and leans in toward the mirror and applies sparkly lip gloss. She checks her hair and tucks a stray strand behind her ear. Then she walks out.

I'm following right behind her. I'm like, "Why is he here? What are you doing? You said it was just gonna be me and you! Sunny! Are you going out?"

She doesn't answer me.

She strides toward Jax.

He's waiting by the elevator in his jeans and a button-down shirt. "This place is money, babe," he says. They kiss, and then he goes, "Hold on, I need to piss," and Sunny points as he walks right past me and into the suite. Sunny calls out, "There's a bathroom just off the kitchen on the right."

"Found it!" Jax yells.

I'm standing out here by the elevator in my white terry-cloth bathrobe, watching Sunny look into the mirror on the wall, checking herself again. She relines her lips, then puckers them so they make a sound.

"Sunny, for real. Please tell me," I try again. "Where are you going? What time are you going to be back?"

She's not answering me. It's like I'm not even here. She presses the button for the elevator to come. Jax is back now. The doors slide open, and the two of them step on. Sunny looks at me watching her. She goes, "River, stop! We're just going out to celebrate. What do you want from me?"

The elevator doors begin to close, and I shout, "I want you to be a mom for once!"

Suddenly, Sunny jams her arm in between the doors, holding them to keep them from closing. The look on her face kind of makes me afraid.

I take a small step back.

"River," she snaps. "I can't believe you're doing this to me in front of Jax." Her face is red. "What did Jemma tell you? I know she thinks everything that happened, it was all my fault. I know she blames me."

My throat tightens. What is she even talking about? She's scaring me.

I try one more time. I go, "Sunny, please, can't you just stay?"

Sunny laughs. "I can't believe you're crying about this!"

"I'm not crying!" I yell back.

"River, chill. You're an influencer now. Go take some selfies. We're living the dream." And now she smiles at me. "Riv, I'm just going out for a little while." Then she mouths, "Don't wait up," and laughs as she drops her hand, and that's it. The elevator doors shut.

She's gone.

## 138

I sink to the floor.

My back against the wall.

I'm so *mad*.

I hate her. I hate her so much right now. I hate myself for trusting her. I don't think I've ever felt more alone. Tears stream down my face and neck. I can't hold it anymore.

## 139

I have no idea how long I've been crying, but I know the sun has set, and the blackout shades have automatically lowered down. I scrape myself up off the floor and walk across the suite in the dark. The whole place is pitch-black and silent. I feel around with my hands through the living room and the kitchen. Then I enter my dark room and flop face-first onto the enormous bed. I can't take it. Whenever I'm with Sunny—I'm always alone.

She always leaves.

What is wrong with her?

What's wrong with *me*?

I lie like this with my face pressed against the cool sheets, crying softly, until finally, I reach with my hand and feel around the bed for my stupid new phone.

*Hi, Emi!* I tap out the text. I know her number by heart. I have to squint, the screen is so bright. *It's River*, I type. Then I wait.

Emi is my last hope. A second later the phone vibrates in my hand, then—*OMG! emoji-heart, emoji-kiss emoji-hug. RIVERRRRR!* I read Emi's text. *My mom and I are freaking out! We saw you on the news on TV! You're all anyone is talking about! Where are you? We want to come and hang out!!!!!!!!!!!*

*Oh, um*, I type. And I'm about to tap in *the LeGrand*, when I see the three dots, like Emi's typing. I wait, I squint at the screen. Then, *ding*: *River!* I read. *This is Maxine, Emi's mom!* That's weird. She's never told me to call her that. *We are so happy for you! We'd love, love, love to see you, hon!*

I smile for a sec. I tap in: *Really? You'd drive to Seattle for me?*
I wait for the dots.

Then: *yes!!!!!! and tell your mom, I'd be more than happy to show her some houses by us in summit hills!*

I read it twice. *Houses?*

Emi's mom is a real estate agent.

And everything comes flashing back.

How bad I felt on the second-to-last day of school. The last time I saw Emi and her mom, and how her mom was all fake and waving to me while Emi told me she couldn't hang out with me anymore because of Sunny. Now she wants to show Sunny houses?!!! I hate it when people are mean to you, and then something good happens and they want to be your best friend. My fingers are wet from wiping the tears out of my eyes. I wipe them against the sheets and then manage to text, *Sorry, gotta go.*

Then I delete Emi's mom's text and throw the stupid phone across the bed. The bed is so big it doesn't even fall off. *I'm so mad at myself right now.* I stare up at the ceiling. It's completely dark. It's an eerie kind of silence. It's like separate from the world outside. I don't hear anything but the low whir of the air-conditioning blasting out cool air.

I push play on the sound machine—and a second later, the room is filled with the roar of ocean waves.

No. I click it off.

It's not like the real thing, and honestly, it just make me more sad. It was easier when I didn't know what I was missing. Now I know. And everything just hurts. *I miss Till, Cricket, Jemma, Ms. Birdy, Nash, Zeus, and Lulu—I miss them all.* I wish so bad that I could call them! They'd know what to do. But there's no phone service on Great Bear. No email. It's a satellite blackout spot. The only way to communicate is through letters that arrive by ferry.

*I miss them so much.*

I close my eyes. I breathe in deep. I pretend I'm in the lighthouse. I visualize the room: my single bed on one side, Cricket's on the other, the four windows all the way around, the breeze coming in, the owl babies talking. I can picture it all. I wish I was there. I feel so trapped. My eyes well up with tears again. *I have nobody.* Nobody can really help me—

Unless . . .

Out of nowhere, it hits me. I know what I can do!

## 140

I pop up to my feet, standing on top of the gigantic LeGrand king-size bed in the dark. "Shades up!" I command, and I say it strong with my fist in the air, and just like that, the shades rise. Light from the trillion skyscrapers lit up in the night comes beaming in. I jump off the giant bed and land with a thud, slip on the slippers, and then actually run! Me and my tear-streaked cheeks. I go skidding and sliding across the living room floor. It's dark. I stumble and slip and I'm laughing all of a sudden because I keep thrusting my fist up into the darkness and saying, "Shades up! Shades up!" and soon the entire suite is illuminated by the skyscrapers' glowy bright lights.

In the spa space, I go straight for the chair where Frédéric was. I have my plush LeGrand robe on, and all my fingers crossed on both my hands. *"Please be here,"* I whisper to myself. *"Please be here,"* I say, scanning the space. It's been cleaned up. The floor is swept, the chairs are rearranged. It's spotless. I peer into the wastebasket where Frédéric's assistant trashed my hat, and my heart just sinks.

It's empty.

There's nothing there.

Come on! Do you think I give up that easy? No way.

I look all around, the counters, the sinks. Nothing. But when I do one more round of looking and I see it, sitting on a ledge, I actually say, "YES!" *I love that maid,* I think to myself. *She must have saved it! She fished it out of the trash!*

I grab the hat and run, slipping and sliding across the living room, past the kitchen with all the snacks, straight back to my room. I toss Cricket's hat on the bed. Next, I open every drawer until I find my old jeans, dried and put away—also by the maid. "Oh my gosh, I really owe her big!" I whisper out loud. Then I take a running leap and bounce onto my bed. I grab Cricket's mermaid hat and plant it on my head. I tuck a few stray hairs behind my ears. It's not going to be easy. But it's so clear. I reach for the phone and put my plan into action.

# 141

It's not like I suddenly transform into a superhero. I'm nervous as heck. *"I can do this,"* I say, and I take these big, loud breaths. I've turned on all the lights in the suite. My hair is wet and down. I've taken a long, hot shower—with aromatherapy infusion—and wrapped myself in a towel. I smell like fancy soap. I do not comb my hair. My waves spring back. I step into a new pair of jeans with holes in the knees—I bite off the price tag with my teeth. "$1,340, for jeans that are already ripped?" I laugh, and slip a black hoodie on. Last, I plant Cricket's hat on my head and pull it down snug.

In the kitchen, I glance at the clock on the wall that is literally ticking seconds by, loud. "Ten p.m.," I whisper to myself. The press conference is at nine tomorrow morning. I do the math. I have eleven hours and an entire crazy plan to pull off.

## 142

Five minutes later, I'm pacing back and forth in front of the elevator doors. A buzzer rings. "Ms. River?" I hear. It's Divia. Her voice is coming through the intercom speakers. "Your visitors are here. Shall I send them up?"

"Yes, Divia!" I say. "Thank you so much!"

Three minutes later, the doors of the elevator slide open, and the second I see her, she embraces me in the biggest hug and I just start crying again. "It's okay," Ms. Martinez says. She places her hand on the back of my head and holds me to her close. "I'm so happy to see you," she says softly. "I'm so glad you're safe."

When I let go and step back, the front of my hoodie is damp from all my tears. I'm so embarrassed at how I acted that day in her office, because honestly, Ms. Martinez is the kindest person in the world. She and her husband drove here as soon as I called. She told me I could really count on her and she didn't lie. It was true. We talked, and she said, "I'm on my way!"

And now she's here.

They both are.

"River." Ms. Martinez smiles, then turns to her husband beside her. Oh, it's okay. I knew he would be coming too—we planned it that way. "This is my husband—"

"George," he says, extending his hand. My hand is wet with tears and snot, but I wipe it off on my jeans, and we shake. I'm kind of staring. First of all, Ms. Martinez's husband, George, kind of looks like a movie star. Google: "Randall Pearson, *This Is Us*." That's exactly who he looks like. He has the best smile. And he wears these cool black glasses. And his grip is strong and firm. He looks me in the eye. When I let go, I breathe in, and I smile at both of them. With George and Ms. Martinez here, I just feel safe. They drove all the way from Clarksville as soon as I called! I know I already told you that, but—they're so nice. On the phone, I cried so hard. I told Ms. Martinez *everything*. I told her how her phone number got smeared. And how I memorized it, and just did every combination I could think of until I got the right one.

The three of us are still standing just inside the suite. George smiles at me and says, "Maya has been thinking about you a lot."

I'm thinking, *Wait, who is Maya?*

Ms. Martinez quickly says, "When we aren't in school, River, please call me Maya, okay?"

"Maya," I say, and nod. It feels funny at first to call my principal by her first name. But tonight, she's more than that. The three of us walk past all the vases of flowers, and the art, and the spectacular views of the city. And it's funny, but George and Maya don't seem to really care that we're up here in this fancy place. They are entirely focused on me.

"Maya tells me you are *very* bright," begins George. "A math star, right?" He glances at Ms. Martinez—I mean, Maya—and then they both smile at me.

I shrug it off. I stop in front of the huge leather sofa and drop down and sit. I feel like I'm blushing. "I guess I'm pretty good at math," I say.

"Excellent," he says. George picks up a big, heavy chair and sets it down close to the sofa and the coffee table.

Ms. Martinez—or I mean, Maya—sits down right next to me. I keep sort of staring at her. And smiling, too. She looks so different than she does at school. Her hair is down. She isn't wearing glasses. And she's dressed in jeans and a simple blue sweater.

I suddenly realize I didn't offer them anything. I leap up. "I'm sorry, can I get you guys some water, or like, any snacks?"

"River," says Maya, "come sit." And I do. I sit back down next to her. She takes a deep breath, and her eyes connect with mine. "I want you to listen very carefully to my words," she says with the softest smile. "You don't have to give us anything. George and I are here for *you*."

I feel my throat get tight.

"We both want to be here," Maya says. She reaches and covers my hand with hers. Right away, my eyes fill up with more tears. I keep my hand right where it is and let the tears fall.

"I'm so glad I can be here for you," she says. "We both are." They smile at me and I really believe them. Maya goes on, "You are so strong," she tells me, and she looks right into my eyes. I look at George, then Maya, and I feel this warmth in my heart kind of spread. It feels like I'm finally safe. And I made it that way.

George reaches for his laptop and sets it on the table in front of us, angling the screen so that we can all see. Then he turns to face me, and his eyes are bright. "Ready?" he asks.

"Let's do it," I say.

## 143

George, Maya, and I spend the next couple of hours ironing out my plan. Things are going well! We order from the menu of Sushi Sora, and while we wait for the food to arrive, we go over everything meticulously, not just once, but three or four times. George is so smart and so nice.

When the food is delivered, we set it out on the table and sit down together, with plates and glasses of sparkling water. Maya is showing me the right way to hold chopsticks. "Okay, so the upper stick," she begins to explain. "There you go." She watches me as I pick up a pair. "Well done, you're doing it! Support it with your middle finger underneath. That's it!"

I am fiddling with the chopsticks, lifting a piece of sushi to my mouth, when I hear voices coming from over by the elevator and look up. As soon as I see them, I leap up and run into open arms.

"I'm so proud of you for asking for help," whispers Jemma. "I'm so glad to be here with you," she says. Then we hug the way she hugged me that day in the lodge, heart-to-heart, except now she knows I'm her niece. She holds on so tight. The biggest tears are streaming down my cheeks.

And look, if you think it's dumb that I'm crying and I can't seem to stop, whatever. I don't care! I've been through a lot.

Cricket's next. "I really missed you," she says, and now she's crying too. Oh, are you wondering how they got from Great Bear to the LeGrand so fast?

We flew them here!

It was Maya's idea. She figured it out and arranged it all. She has a friend at the Clarksville Sheriff's Department, and they dispatched their helicopter to Great Bear to pick up Jemma and Cricket and bring them here. Nash and Till stayed behind at the lodge with Ms. Birdy. The helicopter landed on the roof of the LeGrand! Divia met them up there on the helipad, then brought them to us. We all hug, the three of us. Then I make the introductions all around.

George.

Maya.

Jemma.

Cricket.

I have a *team*.

I feel so loved.

## 144

With the Seattle skyline lighting up the night, in the highest penthouse suite at the LeGrand, the five of us sit down to platefuls of sushi and I pour more sparkling water. Cricket says, "This is BONKERS!" and we all pretty much shake our heads and laugh.

"It sure is crazy," I say, and I'm suddenly starving. I show off my chopstick skills. This sushi is good. Or "bomb," as Cricket says. I turn to her and whisper, "Did you bring the stuff?"

"Oh yeah," Cricket says, beaming.

Then we share a knowing look the way best friends do. I glance around the table. Everyone is talking and just enjoying being together. And I watch and take it in. I can't stop smiling. Which of course is when I look up and see—

Sunny.

**145**

It's not what you think. Sunny's eyes are swollen, like she's been crying.

I rush over because, I mean—

It's Sunny. "Are you okay?" I ask her. I don't hug her, though. I'm a little scared, so I stand back and try to watch her face for clues.

I ask, "Did Jax hurt you?"

Everyone is silent.

Sunny shakes her head *no*.

I wait.

Her lower lip quivers.

She takes a big breath. "I was out with Jax, and I thought, what am I doing?" She pauses. She is fighting back tears. "I really messed up. You're such a good kid," she says, looking at me now. "I sometimes forget that you're only thirteen and—"

Suddenly, Sunny stops talking.

She stops because she looks over my shoulder and sees Jemma sitting at the table. For a second, I panic. My heart starts to race, but then—

Sunny surprises me.

Not with anything she says. It's what she does.

Sunny and Jemma, who look almost like twins, with their strong shoulders and identical three little bird tattoos and wildly wavy long dark hair, share a long, tearful hug, the first one since Sunny left Great Bear.

"I'm so sorry." Sunny is sobbing now.

"It wasn't your fault." Jemma repeats this over and over and hugs Sunny tight. Tears are streaming down both their cheeks. "I'm so sorry," Sunny whispers. "It wasn't your fault," Jemma says again.

Are you confused?

I am too!

It isn't until an hour later, when we flip a switch and ignite the gas fireplace, that we all sit together in the suite's living room. There's a really good vibe. We all ate and cleaned up the kitchen together. The lights are out, the room is dimly lit by the fire and the glow of the lights from the skyscrapers shining in the windows in the night.

I'm sitting on the sofa between Maya on my left and Jemma on my right. We sit close together. Jemma's hand is on mine. Maya is right next to me. George is sitting in the kitchen at the table, working quietly on his laptop. Cricket is in front of the fire, and Sunny is sitting on the shaggy rug, hugging her knees. And slowly, she tells the story.

Her story.

Why she left Great Bear.

Why she stayed away for so long. What happened that she's been blaming herself for all these years.

And here it is:

There was a terrible accident. It happened the year before I was born. Sunny took Nash out surfing. Sunny was fifteen, and Nash was only ten. They got swept up in the waves. By some miracle, the two of them managed to swim to shore. Nash was badly hurt: he got thrown on the rocks, and that's how he got his scar. The two of them were trapped overnight on the rocks. When the rescue came, before they reached Sunny and Nash, the boat capsized near the northernmost tip of Great Bear, way off the coast. It was so stormy. The rescuers were lost at sea. They were never found. It was Cal—Till's dad—and Jonas Ryland, my great-grandfather, the Viking.

And sitting here listening, and watching Sunny wipe away her tears, it's like an equation that I've been trying to solve for my entire life . . . I suddenly get it. I know why Sunny is the way she is. I always thought it was my fault. I always thought it was me.

## 146

It's way past midnight, and there are seven hours to go before we turn in the ticket at the lottery office tomorrow morning. Sunny calls Vic DeAngelo and tells him we will meet him at the LeGrand lobby first thing in the morning, and then we'll all head over to the lottery office together.

Maya and George get settled in the extra bedroom of our suite. It's big, with views of the city lights. Before we all go to sleep, we have one last meeting at the big island in the kitchen. We sit in a row on the tall stools that are pulled up to the white counter. George has his computer out. He is checking our list. We go over how we are getting to the press conference. Maya arranged a lift.

And last, George turns to Sunny and asks, "I know this goes without saying, but just to be sure, is the ticket in a safe place, and did you sign it?"

She goes, "Wait. What? Sign the ticket?" and she looks confused.

"It's the ticket that's the winner," George explains. "There are a lot of people who want to get their hands on that ticket. Whoever has it is the winner."

Sunny turns to me. "Get it," she says.

I spin around and make a dash for my room. "Don't worry," I call out. "I hid it really good!" In my room, I get down on my hands and knees and slither under the bed, and as soon as I look, my heart begins to pound. Then I look again. As if seeing the empty space between the carpet and the bed frame is not enough. I get flat on my belly, lie completely down, and use my hand to sweep the carpet under the bed. I don't really know why—what am I hoping for? There is some dust. There is a single old striped sock. There is no shoebox on this floor. The box is not here.

The box is gone.

## 147

Now it's three a.m. We all are sitting in the living room of the suite. I've got the worst knot in my stomach. For a moment we are all pretty silent. What am I thinking? What would you be thinking if you were in charge of keeping a shoebox worth 1.7 *billion* dollars safe and now it's vanished?

I can't even speak.

Maya breaks the silence. "Let's try to think," she says calmly. She's sitting next to me on the big leather couch. "Let's retrace your steps."

I look up at Sunny. I blurt out, "I think it was Jax!"

Sunny goes, "No," and shakes her head. "He's not the greatest guy, but he wouldn't do that."

"How are you sure?" I snap.

"I'm sure," she says, nodding.

And I begin to get louder. "But when he came up here, remember he walked right in and went to the bathroom? He had time. I mean—" I stop. My theory doesn't make sense because I've already searched the entire suite for the box. If he took the ticket, he'd have to do something with the box, right? He wasn't carrying any box when he left with Sunny.

So I just shut up.

It gets really quiet again.

Cricket goes, "Was anyone else in your room?"

I shake my head no.

And I actually am thinking, *I was so stupid to think my luck would change. Maybe good things aren't supposed to happen to me.*

I look around at everyone. Maya, Jemma, Sunny, George, and Cricket, who is lying on the floor. And I kind of realize, maybe this is the good thing. Maybe this is the prize. Having people who showed up for me. And then, at the exact same time, out of nowhere, it hits me: I know where the ticket is!!!!!

# 148

Now it's almost four a.m. Divia is here. Maya, George, Cricket, Jemma, Sunny, and I all sit and nervously watch Divia speak into her phone. "Hi, Tianna," she says. "This is Divia Gupta from the LeGrand, and I'm so very sorry to be waking you up. But—"

I am holding my breath. Literally, I can't breathe. "Yes, a shoebox," Divia says, and waits. "Uh-huh, that's right." She looks at me and gives me the slightest smile. "Okay, fantastic. Thank you, Tianna. That is enormously helpful." Divia takes a breath and lets it out. "Okay," she says, setting her phone down.

I sit up.

I watch Divia's eyes for a clue.

"The housekeeper, Tianna." Divia looks at me and goes on, "River, we are lucky you saw her. That you could describe her so well. Her name is Tianna Carter. And"—Divia waits, looking around at all of us—"Tianna *did* throw the box away. She thought it was trash and—"

"So it's gone?" I blurt out.

Now Divia shakes her head. "Well, that depends—"

"Depends on what?" Sunny asks.

Diva takes a deep breath, then lets it out. "There is a very small chance," she begins, "that the box and the ticket are still here at the LeGrand."

I go, "Where?"

"Well, I have an idea where it could be," Divia continues, looking right at me. "It's not going to be easy, or pretty."

I look around at my team: Jemma and Sunny, sitting together in front of the gaslit fire, Maya and George next to me on the big leather couch, Cricket and Divia standing up. Everyone is still here. Still with me. Still trying to help.

Sunny takes a heavy sigh. "It's your call, Riv. I get it if you don't want to do this anymore."

"We understand," Jemma says.

And I say, "What? No way," and rise to my feet. "I'm not quitting. I'm not giving up now!"

## 149

Ten minutes later, my all-girl team—Divia, Jemma, Sunny, Cricket, and Maya—piles into the service elevator off the kitchen, and I hit the button on the controls. The doors close.

"Good luck!" George calls out after us. He's going to stay at the base of operations and stall Vic when he arrives to take us to the press conference.

The service elevator is not fancy. It has a certain smell and it's small, kind of cramped. We pack in tight. Everyone is shoulder to shoulder, touching. "Good thing I love you all!" I say, and then we all kind of just crack up. The whole moment is ridiculous. A total long shot. There is almost zero chance we're going to find the box before the ticket expires at nine a.m. What does that mean? It's pretty simple. If we don't find the ticket, there is no winning 1.7 billion dollars.

After thirty seconds in the elevator, Jemma suddenly says, "Anyone notice we're not going anywhere?"

"Oh rats!" says Divia. "The service elevator has been known to be a little wonky."

I look over at Jemma, then Maya, then Cricket. I go, "Maybe this is just not supposed to happen."

Then Cricket's eyes get all wide and she says, "But maybe this is *exactly* how it happens!"

"Onward!" says Divia, as we pile out of the elevator and follow her to an emergency stairwell behind the laundry room. Divia uses a swipe card to open the door, then pushes. "After you," she says, holding the door. I go first, I lead the way, and my team follows behind.

All six of us descend the LeGrand emergency stairwell, down, down, down, in a single-file line.

As we get down one flight, I call out the floor number. "Thirty-four," I say.

Down, down, down,

"Thirty-three," Cricket joins in.

Down, down, down.

"Thirty-two," Maya calls out.

Down, down, down.

"Thirty-one," Jemma and Sunny sing.

Now times that by ten and finally, we are where we need to be. "Level Three-D," I read the door, and use my shoulder to push, and we emerge out of the fluorescent-lit empty stairwell into a cool cement basement that's dark. Divia hits bright overhead lights that sort of hum. The first thing I do is reach up and plug my nose. Then, "It smells like rotten eggs," I say, and laugh. We all do. All you can really do is laugh. The six of us are standing before three gigantic blue metal dumpsters overflowing with literally tons of LeGrand luxury-level trash, piled high in shiny black plastic bags. We are in the back of the LeGrand underground loading dock. Cricket stares up at the dumpsters. "Hey," she says with a laugh, "on the bright side, we got down here in time."

"That's true," Jemma says, smiling at me.

Divia nods. "In just a short while the staff will open the garage doors, and trucks will back in and haul this away to landfills."

"I guess we're pretty lucky," Sunny says.

I rub my hands together. "Okay, you guys ready?" I ask, and I'm smiling. We look so funny. I'm in my thousand-dollar ripped jeans and a black hoodie. Sunny is still in her going-out clothes, including her Fenty leather miniskirt, Divia's in her beautifully pressed light blue dress. Maya's in her sweater and jeans. Jemma and Cricket put on their best clothes to come into the city.

Divia passes out bright neon-yellow rubber gloves. We all are cracking up from the smell as we tug the gloves on.

Then, "Hands in!" I call out, and we all huddle up and put our gloved hands in a pile. One on top of the other.

## 150

*I*t's *not going to be easy* is right. These dumpsters are the industrial kind. They're very, *very* tall, three times as tall as I am, at least.

I tip my head up and stare at the hulking blue metal box, and try and figure out a way up. Then I have an idea. I mean, I've been climbing that dang rope for two weeks straight. "I'll go first," I offer, and step up to the first dumpster. I reach as high as I can and grab onto a metal rail and pull hard. Then I do that again, sort of like climbing a ladder, but there are no rungs. I pull myself all the way up, swing one leg over, and the first thing that happens is one of my thousand-dollar Balenciaga Triple S sneakers falls off. My bare foot lands in a soft, squishy, smelly, gooey mess. Then I fall completely over and in.

Don't worry!

I get up.

Our team is strong! Everyone goes to their respective dumpster and follows the route I mapped out, placing their hands on the rail and pulling up. Maya is first, up and into my dumpster: we're a team. Then Cricket and Divia, in the dumpster next to ours—and last, Sunny and Jemma climb up and into the third dumpster on the end.

Once everyone is up and on their feet, it takes five minutes at least for us to stop laughing our heads off. It's a combination of the fact that it's the middle of the night and that we only have a few hours to find one tiny slip of paper in all this trash. I think it's safe to say we've all kind of let go. I mean, the chances are not too good. And it's hard to explain how bad this garbage smells. Most of it is in huge black plastic bags. But a lot of them are busted open and there is garbage everywhere. After a while, I get a little bit used to the leaky juices and the stench.

"Ready?" I call out. I look at my team. I love them all for trying.

"Let's do this!" Maya answers, pushing up her sleeves.

"Ready, Cricket?" I ask.

"Roger that!" Cricket laughs.

"Divia?" I giggle.

"Absolutely!" says Divia. "Mind over matter!"

"Sunny? Jemma?" I turn and look at them standing in the heap of trash in the dumpster, together. They look happy. It's like no time has passed. "We're ready!" they sing in unison.

There's no clock to watch, but I can feel the seconds ticking by. "Let's do this!" I shout.

## 151

We work as a team. Each dumpster is like a small assembly line. Jemma and Sunny on the end, then Cricket and Divia, then me and Maya. After a while, Maya and I figure out a system. I clear a space for sorting (my job), and Maya drags the plastic bags over one by one. Then together we open them, dump them out, and sort through all the trash, all while being careful to look out for broken glass. Every so often, I catch a scent of the most foul-smelling garbage juice: meat, half-eaten dinners, fermenting in heavy plastic bags for days and oozing through leaks and onto my gloves, then finally, streaming down my arm.

Almost three hours in, it's looking pretty bleak. "I can't believe the stuff people throw away," I say as I reach for a brand-new-looking vacuum cleaner. I have found: three cracked iPhones, a whole bag filled with dirty towels, and an entire men's suit bunched up into a ball. And FYI, a lot of people don't recycle. That's not cool, okay? There are so many pieces of paper, crumpled up, thrown away, and hundreds of the clear plastic bottles of Icelandic water. Some are not even opened. I line them all up to recycle. At least I can do that. And I'm thinking about how weird this all is, how people just throw things out, when I hear Sunny scream, "FOUND IT!!!!!!!!!!!!!!" her voice hoarse with total elation. I look over. Sunny and Jemma are jumping up and down on top of their towering heap of squishy trash. They're hugging now. Sunny is clutching the shoebox in her right hand, holding it up for me to see. Sure enough, there it is. The one from her closet.

We all stop.

We all freeze.

We all stand. From the tops of the dumpsters we are in, we watch. My heart is pounding. I try to calm down. It's probably not there. Right? It's probably gone. I get ready to be disappointed. *It's okay*, I tell myself. Then I watch Sunny rip open the box and reach in and pull out the stack of photos and letters held together with the orange rubber band. We all are holding our breath, then—

"It's here!" she cries.

**152**

We take the stairs. We don't want to chance getting stuck in an elevator! We only have sixty minutes until this ticket expires and nobody wins! We sprint straight up all thirty-four floors. Well, every now and then, we pause to catch our breath and shout out, "Woo-hoo!" Then we burst through the back emergency door of the suite and run straight into the kitchen, screaming and smiling like crazy, covered in garbage juice.

George looks up from his computer. "Find it?"

And Maya says, "We sure did!" And then we all dance around the kitchen hugging, garbage juice and all.

## 153

The first thing we do? Sunny signs the back of the ticket! We all gather around her to watch. She takes the pen in her hand and signs the back of the single winning ticket in blue permanent ink. George picks it up and places it in his briefcase, then snaps the case shut. It's the kind with a lock. While we were gone, George worked some magic: somehow, he arranged to move the press conference to the LeGrand lobby to buy us time. Supposedly it wasn't that hard. The lottery office jumped at the chance for a bigger space, since we have the only winning ticket in the entire United States! "There's quite a bit of press," George explains. "Journalists are here from around the world."

"Seriously?" I ask.

"Yep!" he says.

Then, before we all even have a chance to wash up and change, the main fancy elevator doors open and in strides Vic DeAngelo. Talk about a buzzkill. All of us stop and look up at Vic. He's in his fancy suit with his crooked smile. "Where's our Billion Dollar Girl?" Vic asks when he steps into the kitchen. Then he walks straight up to me, eyeing me up and down. He shakes his head. "Listen, hon, we have a ton of interviews booked, you have a platform now, we're going to need you looking good. You *are* going to freshen up, I hope? Put on something nice?" He rolls his eyes and goes, "What happened to your hair?"

I almost tell Vic DeAngelo what I think. But I stop myself. Instead, I share a glance with Maya and take a breath. I turn to Vic and look him right in the eye, and I smile my very best smile, and say, "No problem, of course!" I back away, grab Cricket by the arm, and pull her toward my room. "I'll be ready in twenty minutes," I call out over my shoulder. Then we run.

# 154

There's no time for a shower, but I don't care. I've gone plenty of days without a shower. I bend at the sink and splash my face. I wipe off the gooey garbage slime with a clean white towel. I have less than thirty minutes to pull this off. Still in the bathroom, dressed in my undies and wrapped in my white fluffy LeGrand robe, I call out for Cricket and she enters, bringing her backpack in with her. I push the toilet seat cover down and sit.

The first order of business is Cricket getting to work on my hair. "Goddess warrior braids coming up!" she says, separating my long waves into strands and gently weaving them into a crown-braid pony. Then we open her bag. Inside, Cricket has brought exactly what I asked.

I slip my outfit on.

"Perfection," says Cricket.

I face the mirror and smile at myself. "It's like Cinderella but in reverse!" I laugh.

Cricket laughs too.

I look at her in the mirror and I go, "You know, meeting you on the ferry was one of the best things that's ever happened to me."

"Same," she says, smiling at me. Her eyes widen. "Are you nervous?"

"A little," I say. "But also, not really, because—" I pause, and now I turn to her. "It's like, for the first time in my life, we have a plan, and I can trust that plan."

# 155

Our big stealth move to avoid Vic is to have Sunny, Jemma, and Maya get him downstairs first. Genius, right? George is already meeting in the lobby with the lottery officials. He's turning the ticket in and getting everything all set. Cricket and I head down the emergency stairwell. I'm all glammed up.

Styled by . . . *me!* Makeup by the salt water in the bay. My pedicure compliments of running from the lodge to the lighthouse in bare feet, the calluses on my palms from gripping the rope. My hair is in full-on goddess warrior mode! I've got on my Great Bear hoodie and my old broken-in jeans, with rips made by wearing them, *not* by a machine.

When we reach the bottom of the stairwell and see the lobby-level door, I glance down at my tan toes, gripping Sunny's old sandals. The same ones she wore when she was my age. Then I take a breath and look up and over at Cricket like, *Are we really doing this? Oh my gosh!* The two of us stand and listen to the crowd on the other side of the door, which leads directly out into the LeGrand lobby.

My heart begins to pound.

Cricket grins. "Hey!" she says, looking directly into my eyes. "You saved my life on a rock, in the middle of the night, and you built a fire in a storm!" She laughs and puts her hands on my shoulders. "This is going to be cake!"

I smile at Cricket. She's just a ball of light. "Whoa," I say, noticing the cut above her eye. "Your gash is really healing up."

Cricket lifts her hand to her face and runs her fingers over the fresh new scar. "I know, right? I don't want it to fade. I want it to always remind me to be brave. You taught me that."

We share a smile that is like a thousand jumps off the lighthouse into the crystal clear water of the bay packed into one single glance. And that's it. I go, "Ready?"

Cricket gives me this huge grin. "You got this!" she says.

I take a big deep breath, and I lean into the heavy metal door and push.

**156**

When the door swings open and I walk out, I have to squint into the bright lights pointed at me. A zillion long-lens cameras click and flash. The lobby has been transformed into a press conference, with an actual podium with about one hundred microphones attached. The podium has huge flower arrangements on either side—I'm sure that's Divia's touch. There are hundreds of journalists squeezed into rows and rows of neatly arranged chairs, and LeGrand staff and guests are gathered all around the perimeter of the room. It's packed in here!

Everyone, and I mean *everyone*, is staring at me. I scan the sea of faces for Sunny and zero in on her, in the front row, sitting with Vic DeAngelo and his team. I take a breath and begin to walk toward them. I look right at Vic DeAngelo and give him a big *this is the real me, deal with it* kind of smile. Then I sit down beside Sunny. Oh, I should mention: Sunny is totally in on the plan. The first thing she does after I sit is turn to Vic and—"Vic," she says. "We're going to have to let you go."

"What?!!" he hisses back. He looks angry.

Sunny doesn't scare easily. "Vic, we paid for the hotel, and all the charges. And the clothes. And included a very nice fee for your time. It's all taken care of. We won't be needing your services anymore."

I'm not going to lie—this is quite enjoyable for me to witness. You should see his face! Vic DeAngelo is all like, "You're making a big mistake!" Then he lets out a string of "#$!%!," gets up, and storms out, his team trailing behind him, pushing their way through the crowd.

Now it's just me and Sunny sitting in the very front row. Oh, and

Divia is standing off to the side, smiling at me. She's in on this too.

The lottery official, a tall bald man in a gray suit, steps toward the podium and speaks. "Good afternoon," he says, and the room quiets. I glance over my shoulder and try to spot Jemma, Cricket, George, and Maya in the crowd, but there're too many people squeezed into this lobby. I can't find them in the mob of reporters scribbling on notepads and holding their phones up in the air. My heart is thumping. *Oh my gosh. This is really happening.*

The official leans into the bouquet of microphones. "Thank you all for coming," he says, smiling. "We're very excited. Our winners today beat one-in-three-hundred-and-seven-million odds to win the largest lottery grand prize in US history." He pauses to draw out the suspense. Then he leans in to speak again. "I'm pleased to present this check for 1.7 billion dollars to"—he takes a long breath, and my heart is racing—"Laurel 'Sunny' Ryland and her daughter, River." This is our cue! Together, Sunny and I quickly join the lottery official at the podium, where he hands us one of those giant checks—like, as big as a refrigerator door—and it's made out for *1.7 billion dollars.* Sunny and I stand in front of the crowd, gripping the oversized cardboard check, holding it up, as a hundred cameras click and flash. People are shouting my name, for me to look toward their lens. "River!" one man yells. "River, over here!" another calls out. We stand together, holding the check in front of us, smiling at the cameras pointed at us. And Sunny turns her head to me.

"You know where your name comes from?" she whispers, leaning closer. "Rivers connect the earth to the sea." She pauses. "You brought my family back to me," she says, looking into my eyes. "This is all you, Riv." She smiles and then turns to the lottery official. "My daughter will be accepting on our behalf," she tells him, and she hands me the giant check. Then Sunny follows the lottery official toward the side of the room.

Now, it's just me.

I set the giant check down, leaning it against the wall. I take a deep breath and exhale loudly and step up to the podium.

And I go for it.

## 157

I squint at the hundred flashes and cameras clicking. "Hi, I'm River," I say. Some dude shouts out, "Get closer to the mic!" Another yells, "Louder!" I lean in a little bit and speak directly into the microphones.

The next few minutes go just as Maya, George, and I planned. I share the story, my story of the bus, I describe the lady sitting beside me and how she offered me her food and her coat when I was all alone and scared. Then I stop for a sec and dig into my pocket and unfold the origami-style envelope. I hold the creased piece of paper up in the air. I say, "When I got off the bus, she gave this to me." Then I carefully smooth the paper out and look down.

" 'Dear girl,' " I read into the microphone. " 'I am giving you this lottery ticket. I don't know if you'll win, and it doesn't really matter if you do or don't. What I want you to remember is to hold on to hope.' " I pause for a second, and I look up from the paper at the cameras and the crowd. "I know, right?" I smile, nodding. "That's really what she wrote!"

There is soft laughter.

I go on: "I want to thank the woman who gave this to me and—" I suddenly stop midsentence. I stop because right this second, as I am looking out at the crowd, I catch a glimpse of—*oh my gosh*, standing in the way back, leaning against the lobby's check-in desk, is Nash, with his deep tan and his sparkly eyes and springy thick curls, and Till in his best crewneck sweater with hand-sewn patches on the elbows and an ear-to-ear smile. The second they make eye contact with me, I feel this good feeling in my heart. I wonder how in the world they got here, but they did! Then I see her. Supported by Nash on one side and Jemma on the other: Ms. Birdy. She's here! Now tears well up in my eyes. I look down the rest of the line: Cricket, Maya, and George. My people. They are all beaming at me. Nash flashes me a smile, and I just feel so sure. So happy. "I want to thank my family," I go on, and as I look toward them, everyone in the crowd turns to glance at the seven amazing humans standing in the very back row.

I wait for the crowd to settle down.

I have a surprise.

With my family here, and hundreds of cameras pointed at me, with journalists watching my every move, I clear my throat and say, "I have opted to take the full cash payment up front. That's eight hundred million, after taxes." I wait. More cameras click. More people are staring. Then I say the best part. I take my time. I smile, and I take a very deep breath and announce: "The money has already been spent. All of it." Now gasps and whispers ripple through the crowd. More cameras click. I feel so happy! I am standing tall. "My attorney, Mr. George Martinez, has put all the money into a family trust. The Maeve 'Birdy' Ryland Family Coastal Trust is an endowment fund set aside so that it will never run out. The money can be used only for the stewardship of Great Bear—protecting the waters, the lands and culture. Great Bear has been home to my ancestors for more than ten thousand years—it's one of our planet's few remaining treasures. My family has a small lodge that my great-grandpa built." I pause to catch Jemma's eyes in the back, and we smile at each other. "And listen," I go on, "it takes a long voyage to get to this place. You can only get there by boat, helicopter, or floatplane. Phones don't work. At night you can see more shooting stars than you have wishes for. The water is from the glaciers. We harvest our own food from the earth and sea. The trees give us life and literally help us breathe." I pause. "The Maeve 'Birdy' Ryland Family Coastal Trust has a single conservation mission: to keep Great Bear Island—one of the last remaining intact temperate rain forests on our planet—safe from clear-cutting lumber companies, oil pipelines, and the threat of mining. Great Bear's land and pristine waters, the salmon-spawning streams, the wetlands, the old-growth forest—all of it is going to stay wild, and protected, forever preserved for future generations."

I stop reading and glance up.

People look stunned. The lobby is now completely silent. "I want to say one more thing," I add. "Well, actually, two."

Now I don't need notes. When we practiced, Maya said, "Trust your heart. You'll know what to say." I look across the photographers and the arms thrust in the air holding up microphones, across all the journalists packed in seats, to my family: Jemma, Ms. Birdy, Nash, Till, Cricket, George, and Maya. I smile at them and I begin again: "So. A lot of people might think I'm crazy for spending all the money at once. But for me, living close to nature is the greatest gift of all. I wish you all could experience it." I pause, then go on, "I feel like everyone deserves that chance. We wake up with the sun and sleep under a ceiling of stars. Clean water is our luxury. The salmon, the birds, the insects, the wolves, the bears, the thousand-year-old cedars, we all depend on each other. It's the circle of life." I take a breath. "I'll be honest with you: winning the lottery was the farthest thing from what I ever thought would happen in my life." I wait and shake my head. "But now, looking back, it's like, every hard thing, every terrible mistake, has led me to where I am right now. So. I guess I just want to say, to anyone who is hearing or reading my words, I'm just telling you: Don't give up. Sometimes the best thing that can possibly happen comes disguised as the worst."

# Eleven months later

The first guests of our new season arrive today! I am standing on the dock overlooking the bay. I'm in my tall rubber boots, work jeans, and a button-down flannel. My hair is down, back to normal, wild, wavy, whipping all over the place in the wind. My head is tipped back and I'm squinting straight up at an endless blue sky. I can hear the faintest whir of a helicopter approaching! I look up toward the lodge, perched on the cliff overlooking our secret cove. "They're here!" I holler up. And within a few minutes, Jemma, Till, and Cricket (she just got in last night, back from college for the summer) are hustling down the steep stone steps to join me, Zeus, and Lulu on the dock. Together, we watch the chopper get closer and closer.

The helicopter is the only other way I spent the money besides the Maeve "Birdy" Ryland Family Coastal Trust. Nash picked it out himself. It's an H125, with big windows and transparent floors, so it has a view of the fjords and orcas, pods of sea lions, humpback whales, and uninhabited granite islands with crazy-big waterfalls. The helicopter has a range of 340 nautical miles, so now we can fly guests in for their stay. Since the press conference, thanks to coverage in the *New York Times*, the *Wall Street Journal*, and hundreds of news stories about Great Bear—requests for reservations started pouring in by mail. We are booked for seven summers straight! We practice ecotourism, try to have as low an impact as we can. We only have room for very few guests.

I stare up at the chopper approaching the bay. The navy-trained pilot expertly maneuvers through the steep green snow-capped peaks, hovers over the turquoise water, then sets down on the landing pad, a cedar-planked platform we built off the dock. If you guessed the pilot is Nash, you're right! I watch as he turns off the engine, waits for the rotor blades to stop, unclips his seat belt, turns all the switches off, pops his door open, jumps down, immediately opens the passenger door, and holds it up. Our very first guests of the season step out of the H125, down onto the dock. And with the chatter of chirping birds and the rush of water cascading off the cliff, and with a young baby black bear and her mama feasting on mussels on the opposite shoreline, we all reunite: Maya and George, their little boy, Demarcus—he's five and he's the cutest little guy. We all hug so tight. They are part of our family now. I love them so much. It's hard to explain how good it feels to have people I can really count on and trust.

There's one more person climbing out of the chopper's open door—

Sunny.

She doesn't live here with us. We're taking things slow. There's a lot of stuff she needs to deal with still. She's been at a special therapeutic residential center, getting help. She's learning how to take care of herself. Jemma is now my legal guardian. George helped us sort everything out. Honestly, I love it this way. I still get to see Sunny, but I'm safe.

Ms. Birdy died last winter at the age of ninety-seven, with all of us together again gathered beside her bed. I still feel her with me a lot. When I spot a Spirit bear—*mooksgm ol*—I feel like it's a sign, a signal that she's still here with us. Watching Ms. Birdy pass really made me think about how I want to live.

Every single second, the ocean pumps like a heart. The sun rises and sets. I have everything I could ever need. Fresh air, a bounty of food, the wide-open meadows, rivers running wild through the steep fjord-carved mountains.

My classroom is the forest, the bay, the streams, the white sandy beaches between the mountains and the sea. Did you know there are sixty-eight species of sea stars alone? There's a whole universe deep down underwater. My favorite things to do are swimming to Turtle Rock with Jemma and treasure hunting with Till along the coast. Sometimes I curl up with a good book in front of the fire. Oh! And I'm learning to surf.

As a family, we spend a lot of time sprucing things up and taking care of what we have. It's all about repair. Nash has been teaching me to use the timber frame chisel and slick to mend the railings on the cabins' porches, and together, we are rebuilding the engine of Till's dad's old dirt bike. I've already replaced the rings on the piston and installed a new kick-starter lever. We're going to surprise Till on his birthday. I have my own journal. I'm writing in it every day. I find it really soothing to paint and draw. When I go out on adventures, I take a tiny box of watercolors and the journal that I'm filling up. It's like I'm starting my own story, writing it my own way.

Each day I see the miracle that is the world: the grizzly bears that take the salmon that feed the ancient trees, eagles, wolves, white-sided dolphins that swim with me in the bay. I wake up with the sun, and I'm never, ever bored. Till and I are best friends, and we have so much fun. You can last a lifetime exploring this place! There are chores to do, and in the winter the water is bone-chilling cold. But there is wonder everywhere. And it never gets old. There is no place on earth I'd rather be.

This is my home.

I once heard Nash say, people are made of the place they are from. Then now, I'm made of ocean and cedar, of birds and bears. Of butterflies. Of wind and sun. I am River. I am someone.

# Afterword

This book is an exploration of who and what we value; of poverty and privilege; trauma and repair; the interdependence of all living beings; and our responsibilities to the air, the sea, the earth, and each other.

The real Great Bear Rainforest—the last remaining intact coastal temperate rain forest on Earth—has been home to the Kitasoo/ Xai'xais Nation (pronounced KIT-ah-soo/hay-hays) and other First Nations for thousands of years.

I have learned from the work of journalist Emilee Gilpin's "personal ethics of a storyteller" about the importance of being accountable to those whose stories, territories, lives, lands, and cultures we make reference to, whether in the realm of fiction or non-fiction, especially as a non-Indigenous storyteller.

Throughout the process of this book, I have been in conversation with Douglas Neasloss, Chief Councillor of the Kitasoo/Xai'xais Nation. Chief Neasloss has trusted my intention in telling River's story, sharing his cultural values, knowledge, and expertise in Indigenous-led conservation with me.

Chief Neasloss and the Kitasoo/Xai'xais Nation, through ventures like the Spirit Bear Lodge, have forged new approaches to building a sustainable economy through ecotourism and culturally based conservation. Today, people from all over the world travel to the northwest coast of Canada to witness and experience the pristine biodiversity of the Great Bear Rainforest and learn about the Indigenous Peoples and cultures that have stewarded their territories since time immemorial. I offer my utmost gratitude and respect to

Chief Neasloss and the Kitasoo/Xai'xais people working to continue to breathe life into their laws and values, and share them with outsiders, to ensure a healthy and living ecosystem for future generations.

The proper usage and spelling of the Sgüüx̱s words used in the book were authenticated by Krista Duncan from FirstVoices, a Kitasoo/Xai'xais language revitalization project. Krista is the great-granddaughter of Violet Neasloss, the last fluent Sgüüx̱s-speaking elder. Violet, a respected matriarch of her community, passed away in 2013 at the age of ninety-nine. To learn more about Kitasoo/Xai'xais language revitalization, stewardship, and culture, visit: klemtu.com.

One more note: If you are a young person experiencing abuse and neglect—please reach out to a safe, caring, and supportive adult (a teacher, principal, or counselor at school) who you can trust and ask for help.

River's Great Bear Lodge sits surrounded by steep carved coastal mountains, ancient forests, and glacial-fed rivers that feed the ocean on the Pacific Coast. Here there is a feeling of deep reverence for the lands and waters and all living beings. Wild salmon, a keystone species for the whole interconnected ecosystem, nourish the thousand-year-old spruce and cedar trees and all relations, human and nonhuman. Everything is connected, as Indigenous Peoples and cultures have been teaching for as long as anyone has been interested in listening.

All of this is true. All of this is within *you*.